S. E. A. R. C. H.

THE ARMAGEDDON PROJECT

By

Barry Lipsett

This book is a work of fiction. Places, events and situations in this story are purely fictional. Any resemblance to actual persons, living or dead, is coincidental.

Lipsett, Barry Shane, 1958-
S.E.A.R.C.H. : the Armageddon project / Barry Shane Lipsett.

ISBN 0-9732696-0-X

I. Title.
PS8573.I68S42 2003 C813'.6 C2003-910886-4

IMAGES BY NASA

Godspeed Publications
godspeedpublications@shaw.ca

AND MOSES CAME DOWN FROM THE MOUNTAIN.
HE FOUND HIS PEOPLE IN A STATE OF CHAOS.
WITH HIM HE CARRIED THE TEN COMMANDMENTS OF GOD.

"OBEY THESE TEN COMMANDMENTS OF GOD,
AND LET US SEARCH FOR THE PROMISED LAND."

SOME OF THEM DID.

One: The Escape

0035.0115.1645 LST

I stood there, hypnotized by the crystal on the Judge's desk. I could see the multi-colored light beams reflecting and bouncing off its many facets.

"Bella!" The Judge's voice had urgency to it. "I need you to listen to me. Verify your decisions in front of Caroline, my court recorder."

I looked over at Caroline, a strikingly good-looking woman. I nodded to her and said hello. The Judge focused his attention on her. "Caroline," he said, "you haven't said anything about my crystal. Do you like it?"

Caroline seemed uneasy. I caught a hint of nervousness in her voice. "It's the same crystal you've had on your desk since I came to work for you. It's always seemed to me to be a nice ornament. I've always liked it. It's quite beautiful."

"Do you see any lights emanating from it?"

"Is that what I should be seeing, your Honor?" Caroline stammered.

In a soothing voice, the Judge answered, "No Caroline. The lights are not something you should be seeing. Thank you."

The Judge turned his attention to me and fixed his eyes on mine. "I see what you see, Bella."

I took a step back. He had spoken no words. He had spoken with his mind.

The Judge motioned me to look back at the crystal. It was illuminated from the inside. Beams of colored light were still bouncing off its dozens of facets. The colors of the light were so breathtaking, it was difficult for me not to stare at it.

I looked over at Caroline. "Caroline, do you not see the lights?"

"Your honor!"

"It's alright, Caroline." The Judge took control again. "Bella's been under a lot of stress these past few years."

I looked over at Caroline. I felt nothing.

"Bella," the Judge continued, "you have chosen not to wait for your trial to conclude."

"That is correct, your Honor."

"You understand that there's virtually no chance the jury will find you guilty."

"Yes, your honor. I suspect that is why you have given me these options."

The Judge nodded in agreement. "You understand that very few of the people we have assigned to Tranquility have made the choice to come back."

"I understand, your Honor. I'm looking forward to finding out why. There is nothing left of the life I created for myself on Earth. I no longer have any feelings for this place. People are living and prospering on the Moon in a base I designed. Well, your Honor, I have to go."

"Bella Carrera," the Judge continued, "on this day, Year Thirty Five, January Fifteenth at Sixteen hundred hours and Fifty minutes, Lunar Standard Time, you are hereby assigned to Tranquility Base for a minimum of two years. The Space Exploration And Research Center Headquarters finds you innocent of all charges brought against you related to the conspiracy involving the destruction of Tranquility Base. If at the conclusion of your trial the jury finds you guilty, SEARCH will appeal on your behalf. You are to be transported to our Orbiting Headquarters immediately."

I went numb. "Thank you, your Honor."

After ten years of my life and every cent spent to defend myself, I was now going to live in the place I was accused of wanting to destroy. The irony of it was overwhelming. The Judge once again fixed his eyes on mine. He knew why this had happened to me.

As security came to escort me to the SEARCH airbase, the Judge said, "In the eyes of God, Bella. You will understand."

0035.0115.1700 LST

I had always wanted to travel into space, but the pressures of running a multibillion-dollar architectural organization required that certain sacrifices be made.

The pilot for the first leg of my journey was quite excited about carrying out his orders. "Sir, it's my pleasure to escort you to our Orbiter Command Center. My name is Commander Michelson. I will be piloting your transport. We have fifteen hours before lift-off. I've been asked to show you around the base and explain our operating procedures to you.

Do you have anything else you want to take along besides this shoulder bag?"

"No, Commander. This is it." In fact, I was thinking that it was probably too much.

I was impressed with Commander Michelson. He was five foot seven compared to my five foot ten, quite fit, and eight years my junior. I was thirty-seven, but felt much older due to the experiences of the past ten years.

"Mr. Carrera, if you'll just follow me to our car, we'll be on our way."

The trip to the base from SEARCH headquarters took an hour. Although I didn't have much to talk about, Commander Michelson managed to find out just about everything about me. Not that it was difficult to do. My trial has been the source of income for the majority of news- gathering agencies all over the world for quite awhile. I imagine that with my departure, they would now find someone else's life to destroy.

We arrived at the airbase at eighteen hundred hours LST and would be departing to the SEARCH Orbiting Headquarters at eight hundred hours LST.

Sounding so excited it was making me nervous, the Commander said, "Mr. Carrera…"

"Please just call me Bella, Commander."

Commander Michelson was thoughtful for a minute. "I can't, sir. It wouldn't be right." He continued, "I've made arrangements for us to get a few hours sleep before we begin the orientation." We were walking towards the main building. I could see it was fully integrated, with command posts, an air traffic control center, and what looked to be a hotel. "I've booked a room for you, sir. I live here on the base. I'll be back to pick you up at three hundred hours LST. The concierge will show you to your room. Feel free to order room service. You'll be receiving a wake-up call at two hundred hours LST." And with that, Commander Michelson was off.

♦♦♦

When I opened the door to my room, I expected to find a small suite with a bed, night- stand, T.V., and phone.

"Excuse me…" I called back to the concierge.

"Is there a problem, sir?" He seemed quite concerned.

"I believe this cannot be the room that the Commander had in mind. I'm only going to be here for a few hours and this suite looks like it was designed to be lived in by a family."

The concierge took my shoulder bag, walked into the master bedroom and placed it on the bed. "The Commander and the Hotel would like you to enjoy our hospitality. If there is anything you need, please don't hesitate to ask. If we don't hear from you, we've been instructed to give you a wake-up call for two hundred hours LST."

I was dazed. "I would like something to eat."

"Mr. Carrera, it would be best if you called room service for that. I hope you enjoy your stay here." The concierge glanced quickly around the suite and left.

It was a beautiful suite, about seven hundred square meters with a gourmet kitchen, a bathroom adjoining each of the three bedrooms, and a dining room with seating for eight.

The living room had a fireplace and seating for a dozen people on a variety of expensive sofas, love seats and chairs. The family room had a full theater screen and a full surround-sound system that could be accessed from any room in the suite. *Very nice,* I thought to myself.

♦♦♦

Because I'm not one who is able to sleep well on a full stomach, I thought it would be better to have room service send me breakfast at the same time as my wake-up call. I picked up the phone.

"Yes, Mr. Carrera. This is the front desk. How may we help you?"

I felt uncomfortable. "I would like to order room service."

"Right away, sir."

I listened to music on the phone for a minute.

"Yes, Mr. Carrera. This is room service. What would you like to order?"

"I would like to have breakfast sent up to me at the same time as my wake up call. That would be at two hundred hours LST. Do you have any recommendations?"

"Please hold the line for a minute, Mr. Carrera. I'll let you speak to the Chef." He was off the line before I could stop him. Now I was starting to feel embarrassed.

"Mr. Carrera, this is the Chef." I couldn't place the accent. "I would be honored, sir, if you would allow me to send up a small sampling of each of my favorite breakfast foods. Would you allow me to do that for you, sir?"

I wasn't expecting that at all. I must not have answered for a while.

"Sir, are you still on the line?"

"Yes, I am," I answered. "That would fine. I'm looking forward to sampling your dishes."

The Chef was happy. "Thank you, sir. I hope you enjoy what I prepare. Thank you." He hung up.

My mind was racing. I knew I was going to get only a few hours sleep. In order to relax, I jumped into the shower and then soaked in the Jacuzzi for a short while. It did not take long for me fall into a deep sleep.

0035.0116.0200 LST

When the phone rang, I picked it up.

"Mr. Carrera, your food is waiting for you outside your door. Would you like me to bring it in now?"

I was disorientated. "What time is it? Who is this?"

"This is your wake-up call, sir. I am the concierge. You're staying at the SEARCH airbase officer's hotel. I am outside your door with your breakfast. The time is two hundred hours and five minutes LST. You have until three hundred hours LST to eat and get your things together. That is when Commander Michelson will be here to pick you up."

That took a few seconds to sink in. "Yes. Just let me throw my robe on and I'll let you in. Thank you for your patience."

"Not a problem, sir."

I let the concierge in. "The Chef told me you allowed him to make a buffet for you. He's very grateful. Please enjoy your breakfast. We'll be in to clean up after you and Commander Michelson leave."

The concierge wheeled the buffet into the dining room and placed a dozen dishes on the table. "The Chef has made enough food for both you and Commander Michelson. He may wish to eat before you leave the hotel. I will let him know when he arrives. If there's nothing else you need, Mr. Carrera, I have other duties I must attend to."

I was very hungry and the food looked amazing. "I can't think of anything at the moment."

The concierge was at the door. "If you need anything, please pick up the phone and the front desk will assist you." And he left.

I had a feeling Commander Michelson would arrive sooner rather than later so I decided to have my morning shower and get dressed before I started to eat. As I showered, I thought about what was really happening.

Let's see, I thought to myself. *This is the last shower I'm going to be having on Earth, maybe forever. And this is the last breakfast I'll be eating on Earth, maybe forever. All because someone - and I know it is someone - believed that I had the intelligence, power, resources, and motive to destroy Tranquility Moon Base.*

I should not have started thinking about it, but I did. It drove me crazy that someone had the power to convince an entire planet that I was guilty of conspiring to destroy something I had designed as a place in which people could live. It made me feel and believe I was the most insignificant human to have ever been born. No one has admitted to knowing who masterminded my destruction, or why. Discovering the answers to those questions gave me a reason to get up every morning.

♦♦♦

The phone rang again and I picked it up.

"Mr. Carrera, this is room service. Commander Michelson is here and would like to know if you're ready."

My mind was still a bit cloudy. "Tell him I haven't had my breakfast yet, and he's welcome to join me."

"Thank you, Mr. Carrera. I will tell him."

There was a knock on the door. "Mr. Carrera, Commander Michelson is here."

"Come in, Commander. I'm in the dining room."

Commander Michelson walked into the dining room and saw the buffet laid out on the table. The only word that came out of his mouth was "Wow!"

"Would you like some coffee or juice to go with your breakfast, Commander?"

Commander Michelson looked at me. He could see that I wasn't in the best of moods. He changed his mood to be more compatible with mine. "I would very much like to join you for breakfast, Mr. Carrera. Thank you for asking."

"You're welcome, Commander. Please help yourself."

♦♦♦

Commander Michelson and I didn't say too much while we ate. He knew I was in a state of mind to which he could not relate. I felt obliged to keep the lines of communication open. "So, Commander, how are the Eggs Benedict?"

"Very tasty, Mr. Carrera. And what about your fresh fruit salad? It looks quite refreshing."

"It is, Commander. I strongly recommend it."

"Thank you, Mr. Carrera. I do believe I will indulge. The waffles look good."

"Yes, Commander. How about those waffles? I'll split them with you."

"Sounds good to me, Mr. Carrera."

We ate all of it, each of us recommending to the other what we should try. And at the end of our meal, we both felt satisfied.

"Commander, was there a particular dish that stood out in your mind as being outstanding?"

"Actually, Mr. Carrera, they all seem to go together quite well. No one dish seemed to be better than the rest. My compliments to the Chef."

"Thank you, Commander. I'll make sure he gets the message." I walked over to the phone and placed a call to the front desk.

"Yes, Mr. Carrera. This is the front desk. How may we help you?"

"Commander Michelson and I have finished our breakfast and will depart shortly. Please give the Chef our warmest regards and thank him for preparing such an outstanding breakfast."

"I will, Mr. Carrera. Thank you. I hope you enjoyed your stay with us."

"I did. Thank you." I hung up. It was now three hundred hours LST.

"So, Commander, what's the plan?"

"We need to get over to the transport facility. It's only a few minutes from here. When we get there, I've been asked to show you the few things you'll need to know when you arrive at Tranquility base. Are you ready to go?"

I looked around the suite one last time. "As ready as I'll ever be, Commander. Let's go."

We made our way down to the front of the hotel and left for the Orbiter Command Center.

0035.0116.0310 LST

"I noticed, Commander, that there isn't any air traffic today. I was hoping to see a few orbiters taking off and landing."

Commander Michelson nodded his head. "Please don't confuse this particular base with a civilian one, Mr. Carrera. The air traffic here is regulated to fit our needs. And what we need to do today is make sure you get to the Orbiting Headquarters."

Suddenly my mouth was dry. "Are you saying this is being done for my security?"

"Yes, sir."

Commandeer Michelson pulled up to the main entrance, parked the car and grabbed my shoulder bag from the back seat. We made our way into the building.

"We are scheduled for departure at eight hundred hours LST, Mr. Carrera. That gives us just less than five hours. If you'll follow me now, we'll get started."

"May I have my shoulder bag, Commander?"

Surprised, he turned and looked at me. "Of course, Mr. Carrera. I didn't realize I was carrying it." He handed me my bag.

"Thank you, Commander."

The Command Centre was a massive two kilometers long and three stories high. It took us at least fifteen minutes to make our way to the back of the building. When we exited, I was able to see two familiar-looking orbiters sitting on the tarmac. I recognized them from watching the SEARCH television network. If I had gone into aviation design, I probably would have designed an orbiter identical to these ones. I was always amazed at how impressive they looked while taking off. They had a lifting body design, with the fuel tanks, engines and air intakes carefully integrated into the body. The wings swept back from just behind the cockpit, and then flared out and down at the back. They could take as many as fifty passengers at a time to Orbiting Headquarters.

Despite my situation, I was excited. "Commander, which one of these orbiters are we taking up?"

We stopped walking. "Neither one, Mr. Carrera. I've been requested to ask that you choose between one of two other orbiters that I've designed. Both have been thoroughly air and safety tested, but neither one has been in orbit."

"They both use a new type of power plant that does not require oxygen or internal fuel tanks. These power plants have been used exclusively on the moon for more than five years now, so we know they are safe. But they are also more powerful than anything we've used before. It has taken us two years to adapt these power plants to work properly in Earth's atmosphere, and we have made mistakes." Commander Michelson gestured to his right. "Do you see anything over there, Mr. Carrera?"

I looked in the direction the Commander was pointing. "I see what appears to be a lot of burned up trees."

"Yes, you're right. Twenty-five hundred hectares of prime forest used to be over there. We have replanted, of course, but it will be at least fifty years before it returns to the way it was."

"May I ask what happened, Commander?"

"Of course. I have been asked to show you what happened. We have it all recorded."

My mind was still working on the orbiter thing. "I'm still a little curious about this request for me to choose a new orbiter. Are you telling me that I *must* choose?"

"Yes, Mr. Carrera. I am only following orders. If you wish to file a report and speak to someone about it, I'm sure arrangements can be made. But only after your arrival on Tranquility Base."

"I see." I felt powerless. "Okay, let's see what happened to the forest." I was furious.

♦♦♦

"This is our propulsion laboratory, Mr. Carrera."

We had walked past the two orbiters and into a two-story building. "As I said before, we have spent two years adapting what we now call our Space Drive power plant to Earth conditions. Everything we've done has been recorded. This building contains the computers that designed our new generation of orbiter and is also connected to the largest and most sophisticated air tunnel facility on the planet. The two orbiters I designed have been picked to go into production. One is designed to transport up to three hundred paying passengers to Orbiting Headquarters. The other one is designed to take two highly trained combat mission specialists into orbit with the capability of docking with the Orbiting Headquarters. The cockpits are the same on all the orbiters and are identical to the ones you will find on the moon transports. Any questions so far, Mr. Carrera?"

I looked around at all the glowing computer screens. I felt lost and overwhelmed.

"I'm not exactly sure what you were talking about when you described that second orbiter. It sounded to me like you were describing a military aircraft. Would that be accurate, Commander?"

The Commander took a few seconds to answer.

"Yes, Mr. Carrera. We have designed an orbiter that the United Earth Air Defense is going to use as their air superiority weapon. We will be going into production within the year. SEARCH will not, however, be using the orbiter for that purpose. We are a corporate entity and we believe it is in our best interests to provide our government with the best defensive systems we can. If we are ever attacked, we know that there will be a response. Does that answer your question, Mr. Carrera?"

I was now fully engaged. "Yes, Commander. Please continue."

"Thank you. Now it's time for you to see what this Space Drive is capable of doing. I will be describing to you how it how works as we watch these clips. Please feel free to ask questions as we go."

"I will, Commander."

Commander Michelson punched a few keys and a large section of the wall separated to reveal a rather impressive screen.

"If it gets too loud for you, Mr. Carrera, just let me know." I nodded.

The screen lit up and I saw a man standing beside what had to be the Space Drive.

"He's just there for scale, Mr. Carrera. The reactor section of the drive has a diameter of three meters. All the cylinders surrounding the reactor contain what it needs to ignite and operate. It uses lasers to initiate and control the reactor. The plasma it creates is what we use for thrust and in this test it has been directed out the back thruster nozzle. The plasma is contained and controlled by magnetic force. The Space Drive is designed to supply itself with what it needs to run for optimum performance. It generates enough electricity to keep this building running for a year."

I looked at the Commander. He was grinning.

"It takes five minutes to create and compress enough plasma for thrust to be produced. Internal temperatures run as high as ten thousand degrees C. If for some reason we lose control of the reaction and temperatures exceed our parameters, certain key components are designed to melt, which will cause its power supply to shut down. In that event, all remaining plasma is vented. We have checked to see that the safety components work. Mr. Carrera, that is how our forest was destroyed. We didn't take into consideration what would happen once the plasma hit the atmosphere, and neither did our friends on Tranquility Base."

♦ ♦ ♦

It didn't seem all that exciting at first. All there was to see was a great big reactor sitting on the tarmac. But after a few minutes, something around the thruster nozzle started to glow. It gradually built up to a respectable bright blue-white flame a few meters in length. Commander Michelson continued his narration.

"All we can see right now, Mr. Carrera, is the visible portion of the thrust. Please note that there isn't a cloud in the sky. What we didn't take into account was the invisible portion of the thrust. The material that makes up the core of the reactor is a completely man-made compound. It was created specifically for this."

Commander Michelson stopped talking. I could hear the sound of a rocket or orbiter powering up. The exhaust trail was getting noticeably longer and the cameras had to pivot in order to record it all.

"The cameras used to record this were ten kilometers away because we weren't sure if the Space Drive going to blow up. We used this test to make sure the safety features worked properly. The reactor will be going super critical. I'll keep the volume down."

The plasma from the nozzle now looked like a solid white beam of light. Even the reactor itself seemed to have taken on a few colors.

"The plasma trail is now five kilometers long, Mr. Carrera. As I said before, that's just the visible portion. Now, as the camera pivots toward the forest, notice the smoke that's starting to billow from inside. You will also see that some of the trees have caught fire."

"How far is the forest from this test?"

"Fifteen kilometers, Mr. Carrera. And there is no way for us to shut the reactor down at this point."

It took a few seconds to fully comprehend the impact of what the Commander was saying. The screen was now split horizontally using two cameras. One focused on the reactor, the other focused on the plasma and forest. The Commander was keeping the volume in check. A very high-pitched whistling sound could be heard through the roar of the reactor's fury.

"Mr. Carrera, I believe you will find the bottom screen more interesting."

I focused my attention on the bottom screen, which showed the burning forest. I noticed that the plasma trail was almost three-quarters of the way to the edge of the tree line. There was a massive forest fire under way.

"Keep watching, Sir."

I glanced at the Commander and then back to the burning forest. Just as I started to refocus on the forest fire, the forest blew up. My mind began to reel as I saw a huge mushroom cloud form on the horizon. I looked at the Commander. He had a pained expression on his face, like he had just seen it for the first time.

The cameras began to shake and the reactor was now white-hot. It looked like it was ready to explode. A few seconds later, the reactor shut down. Plasma began venting from all its open exhaust ports. The forest was gone. The mushroom cloud was growing larger as wind from the blast rushed back in to fill the vacuum created by the explosion.

"Mr. Carrera, we were expecting the reactor to blow up, not the forest. The explosion created a crater two kilometers wide. It has since filled with rainwater and created a new lake. It should be quite a nice place when all the trees grow back."

I was speechless. "What caused the explosion?"

"We believe that if we were to try to create the same thing again, Mr. Carrera, we would fail. In other words, and officially, it was a fluke accident. That's all I can offer you."

"I understand, Commander."

♦ ♦ ♦

We left the propulsion lab and walked across the tarmac towards the hangers that housed Michelson's two orbiters.

"Commander, have you given names to your two orbiters?"

Commander Michelson looked at me. "No. Do you think I should?"

"No, Commander, I don't think you should. It's just that every building I've ever designed has been named. I would expect that at some time in the near future your orbiters would be."

"I expect you're right, Mr. Carrera."

We were now entering the hangar. As we did, interior lights were activated. What I saw were two completely different orbiters. The commercialized orbiter looked extremely elegant and took up most of the hangar. It reminded me of the early supersonic transports I had seen in pictures.

"Given the power of the Space Drive," Commander Michelson explained, "I designed this shuttle to be as aesthetically pleasing as possible. I took design cues going back to the earliest supersonic airliners. I believe when people see this, they will want to fly in it." I nodded in agreement.

"There are six reactors powering this orbiter. They're attached under the wings. You can see the air intakes for each one."

As we began moving around the orbiter, Commander Michelson continued his orientation. "In order to use the reactors, we had to design a rather complex air flow system that would cool the plasma. While these orbiters are accelerating to escape velocity, the main purpose of the reactors is to move air. When mach ten is reached, we power up to full throttle. The orbiter then stops behaving like an aircraft and begins to behave like a rocket."

"Both orbiters are capable of a vertical take-off and landing, but the built-in maneuvering abilities of our combat version far exceed those of our commercial orbiter."

We continued walking around the commercial orbiter, as Commander Michelson explained the design features. When we stopped beside the combat orbiter, the Commander placed his hand on its landing gear. "This orbiter has been designed to be as effective in an Earth-bound dogfight as in a space dogfight. The reactors we use on these orbiters are much different from the one you saw a few minutes ago. These use a two-stage compression sequence and have two separate compression chambers."

"If you choose the commercial orbiter, Mr. Carrera, we will be able to leave without any preparation. The flight plan is predetermined and designed to be as comfortable as possible because it will be carrying passengers. The flight shouldn't last more than forty-five minutes. There is only enough core material to make one flight. It also has a reserve supply for emergencies, should a powered landing be necessary."

"If, on the other hand, you choose this one," he said, slapping the landing gear of the combat orbiter, "I'll need to prep you."

Commander Michelson had piqued my curiosity. "What exactly does that mean, Commander?"

"Not too much, Mr. Carrera. You'll need a flight suit and something for your stomach. And I've been asked to give you this." He handed me a vest.

I put it on. "What's this for?"

"I don't know, Mr. Carrera. I do know that everyone on Tranquility Base wears one."

It had quite a few pockets. The material was not familiar to me, but it was very comfortable. It felt warm. I pointed to the five horizontal bars on the right front on the vest and the five diagonal bars on the left-hand side.

"Do you know what these are for, Commander?"

He had a smile on his face. "I'm sorry, Mr. Carrera, I don't. Time to choose, Mr. Carrera."

I smiled back. "Let's take the hot rod."

Just for an instant, the Commander looked ecstatic.

♦♦♦

"Mr. Carrera, I have thought about a name for this orbiter."

"And what would that be, Commander?"

"I'd like to call it the Intruder."

"Have you suggested that name to anybody?"

"Not yet."

"Well, Commander, for the time that you and I are using the Intruder, that name works for me. Maybe the name will stick."

"Maybe it will, Mr. Carrera. Now if you follow me, we'll get you suited up and be on our way."

We made our way into one of the rooms located along the far side of the hangar. Commander Michelson and I stepped into the flight suits that were waiting for us. They fit snugly over our clothes and were equipped with small external oxygen supplies and built-in retractable helmets.

"Mr. Carrera, these suits were designed specifically for the Intruder. They are 'light' spacesuits. They will automatically compensate for excessive G forces and will protect us from the vacuum of space if the need arises. There is a one-hour supply of oxygen built into the suit. We will be hooked up to external tanks in the Intruder. The suit transmits our vital stats data to the SEARCH Medical Center and is programmed to alert us if anything out of the ordinary is being detected. Also, a small amount of space sickness medication will be injected into our oxygen supply, if needed. Any questions, Mr. Carrera?"

I was just anxious to go. "Do you have a flight plan, Commander?"

It appeared that Commander Michelson had expected a different question. He took his time to answer while adjusting both his suit and mine. "Is there a particular route you'd like to take, Mr. Carrera?"

I waited until I had the Commander's full attention. "The fastest, Commander."

He understood.

♦♦♦

"Alright, Mr. Carrera. The first thing we need to do is get you into the Intruder."

I agreed. We were now standing under the cockpit, which was six meters above us. Commander Michelson was instructing the Intruder's computer to respond to the name 'Intruder'. "I think you will like how this is done, Mr. Carrera. Intruder, please initiate loading procedure for Mr. Carrera and me." The canopy retracted back into the fuselage and two seats came up and over each side of the cockpit.

"Mr. Carrera, if you will have a seat, Intruder will take you into the cockpit, lock you in and hook you up. I'll be right behind you." It took only three minutes before we were both behind the flight control panels of Intruder.

"Mr. Carrera, please note our time of departure." It was eight hundred hours LST.

The canopy closed and our spacesuits deployed the helmets. I was breathing almost pure oxygen for the first time. I liked it.

"Mr. Carrera, by your hands on both sides, you will notice the flight control sticks. If you feel the need to grab onto them at anytime during our flight, please do so. I will control Intruder until we dock with the Orbiting Headquarters. By the way, Mr. Carrera, this is a first for all of us."

"Thanks for reminding me, Commander."

"You're welcome."

And with that, Commander Michelson proceeded to ignite the two reactors and clear his flight plan with the control tower. We began moving out of the hangar.

"Commander, where is the control tower?"

"If you look to your right, you will see it starting to emerge." The control tower was rising out of the ground. "The tower is thirty stories with the control center taking up the twentieth to twenty-eighth floors. The communications array makes up the rest. We keep it underground for security reasons."

I thought it looked like a tree.

"Control, this is the Intruder. Are we cleared for take-off?"

"Please hold, Intruder."

Commander Michelson looked at me and shrugged. "This is standard procedure, Mr. Carrera."

"Intruder, this is Control. Please hold for an incoming orbiter."

I looked at the Commander. "Where is it?"

"Control, this is Intruder. Will the orbiter be visible to us?"

"Intruder, this is Control. The orbiter should be visible directly in front of you. It will be landing in one minute."

"Thank you, Control."

We both saw it gliding down. It looked like it was going to fly right over us. It came within a few hundred meters and touched down.

"Intruder, this is Control. You are cleared for take-off at your discretion."

"Thank you, Control. Alright, Mr. Carrera, here we go."

As we started to move forward, I noticed there was no vibration coming from the Space Drives.

"Mr. Carrera, as I'm sure you are aware, we will not be going supersonic until we are over the Pacific." We lifted off vertically and began to accelerate. "If you look at the screen directly in front of you, Intruder will give you a simulated view of our flight plan."

I saw a small version of Intruder flying over the California terrain heading out over the Pacific. When Intruder hit the Pacific, it started to accelerate. There was a Mach counter on the bottom right of the screen and it was moving up rapidly. It hit Mach five.

"Commander, it appears that we are not flying at a very high altitude on this simulation. Is there a reason?"

The Commander didn't answer right away. Within a few seconds, I saw the Intruder start to climb rapidly. It was at mach five and was now flying like a rocket. The simulation ended.

"In answer to your question, Mr. Carrera, you did ask for the fastest way to Orbiting Headquarters. Hang on now. We're going supersonic."

I was pinned to my seat by the accelerating force and the G forces of the long arc we took to reach vertical. The ride was phenomenal.

"O.K., Mr. Carrera. We'll now be accelerating to Mach twenty-five and entering orbit." And with that, Commander Michelson took us to escape velocity. Within a few moments, the sky turned black.

♦ ♦ ♦

"Mr. Carrera, we will be orbiting three times before we see our Orbiting Headquarters. Please enjoy the scenery. Oh, by the way, the Intruder is designed to fly to the moon and back without the need for refueling."

"Is there a reason for divulging that information to me, Commander?"

"Just bragging a little, Mr. Carrera."

"Thank you, Commander."

As we orbited, I recognized most of the landmarks and geographical features from pictures and films I'd seen. I was taken aback by how beautiful planet Earth appeared.

Two: The Orbiting Headquarters

0035.0116.0920 LST

"How are we doing, Commander?"

"Just fine, Mr. Carrera. Intruder is locked on to the Orbiting Headquarters. We are just along for the ride. We'll be docked in forty-five minutes. We are testing the automated docking program. If there is a problem, I will take control of Intruder. How are you enjoying the ride so far?"

"I'm enjoying it just fine, Commander." I wasn't kidding.

I knew Orbiting Headquarters was big, but I definitely wasn't prepared for what I saw looming in front of me. The huge structure rotated around its central hub on frictionless magnetic bearings. The central hub, which contained all the command centers, loading docks, and launch facilities for both the Earth and Moon-bound traffic, was two thousand meters wide and sixteen kilometers long. All spacecraft were launched on a magnetic rail system, which accounted for ten kilometers of it. There were two ring systems rotating in opposition, each producing one G of force. The distance from the center of the hub to the outermost shell of the rings was sixteen kilometers. The first ring was one thousand meters from the entrance to hub, and the second ring was two thousand five hundred meters from the first. It was a perfectly balanced structure.

"Mr. Carrera, I don't mean to distract you, but if you look up and over to your right, you might see something of interest."

I looked to where the Commander had suggested and didn't see anything at first, as my eyes were adjusting to the light conditions. Then I saw a reflection. When I focused on it, I saw what the Commander was speaking about. It was colossal.

"What is that, Commander?"

Commander Michelson was smiling again. "That, Mr. Carrera, is the main component of the Mars Project. All the raw materials and fabrication come from Tranquility Base. We are in charge of outfitting it. That is why it's in Earth's orbit. It has only been visible from Earth for a few weeks now. Only one quarter of the construction has been completed. The target date for completion is ten years from now."

"How big is it?"

"It is exactly twice the size of Orbiting Headquarters. When it is complete, it will slowly make its way to Mars with two thousand SEARCH personnel. The estimated time of the trip is five years. It will then enter an orbit around Mars. It's designed so that all components needed to sustain a colony on the surface of Mars will come from the station itself. Mars will then have an Orbiting Headquarters and a base on Mars. Both Earth and Mars will use magnetic rail technology to send and receive supplies. Of course, there will be hundreds, maybe thousands, of supply modules orbiting Mars, waiting for the station to arrive. We haven't decided on the final location of the base."

My brain was becoming overloaded. "That's enough, Commander."

"Sorry, Mr. Carrera."

"No problem, Commander."

♦♦♦

As we approached Orbiting Headquarters, its size was starting to have an impact on me. Intruder was starting to feel very small.

"Commander, how well is autopilot working?"

"Very well, Mr. Carrera."

We were being guided through the entrance of the Orbiting Headquarters. As we began to move through the central hub I noticed something that looked vaguely familiar under construction.

"What is that, Commander?"

"That, Mr. Carrera, is going to be a full-scale working replica of the first International Space Station. We'll be using it as a laboratory and hope to also use it as a tourist attraction in the near future. It doesn't to take up too much space in here, does it?"

To actually see something that big just floating inside the hub made Orbiting Headquarters seem all that much bigger. "No, Commander, it doesn't."

We floated by the unfinished International Space Station and into the docking port. All of the autopilot programs worked flawlessly. We were the only spacecraft in port when we docked.

"Alright, Mr. Carrera, this is going to be your first experience with weightlessness. How's your stomach?"

"My stomach is just fine, Commander. How do we get out of this thing?"

"We will be exiting through that, Mr. Carrera," the Commander said, pointing straight ahead.

Coming towards Intruder was what looked like a loading ramp used at airports on Earth. "Where will it attach itself, Commander? There are no doors on Intruder."

"Just watch, Mr. Carrera. It will attach itself to the top of Intruder and form a seal around the canopy section. It will pressurize and we will float up and then down to the elevators. The elevators will slowly take us to the first outer ring section. When we arrive there, we will take off these suits, take a few minutes to get acquainted with our surroundings and then meet the people who will prepare you for your trip to Tranquility Base."

♦♦♦

Weightlessness wasn't a problem for me. As I floated up and down the loading ramp, I enjoyed some time to myself. Not that I didn't enjoy Commander Michelson's company. My mind was just a little overloaded.

The loading ramp had handrails, which we used to pull ourselves down to the elevator doors. The ramp was fully pressurized and its walls were covered with thick, soft padding. The elevator doors opened.

"Alright, Mr. Carrera. Pull yourself up using these handrails. Keep your back against the wall and press your feet down to the floor."

The elevator looked like it would hold around twelve people. I followed the Commander's instructions and the doors closed.

"Mr. Carrera, as we move towards the outer ring, we will slowly start to feel gravity. It will take about two minutes."

I felt like a kid on a midway ride. I gradually felt the gravity. When we reached the outer ring, I felt like I was inside an office building on Earth. The doors opened and we stepped out. There was no one waiting for us. We walked down the corridor. Commander Michelson seemed to know where he was going.

"Commander, I thought you said you've not been here before."

"I haven't, Mr. Carrera, but we have simulation rooms that we use to orient ourselves to unfamiliar surroundings. I know this station inside and out. You will be using similar programs on Tranquility Base."

We stopped walking and entered a room.

"Mr. Carrera, we can take our suits off here and if you like, you can have a shower."

As I stepped out of my suit, the thought of a shower sounded good. "I believe I would like that, Commander." I looked around for my shoulder bag. "I've forgotten my shoulder bag, Commander."

Commander Michelson looked embarrassed. "That was my fault. If you like, I'll have someone get it for you. It will be here when you're finished."

"That sounds good to me, Commander. Thank you."

Commander Michelson left and I took my time in the shower. When I came out, my shoulder bag was waiting for me.

0035.0116.1015 LST

My shoulder bag had a compartment for a fresh set of clothes and one for the pieces I wanted laundered. When I finished getting dressed, I looked at the vest a little more carefully. I found the material to be quite fascinating. There were two inside pockets and four pockets on the front. There were no buttons or zippers, but when I brought the two halves together, they sealed themselves together. This only happened when it was being worn. The vest opened when I pulled on the top part of the seal. I suspected personnel on Tranquility used the markings on the front of the vest as a means of identification.

0035.0116.1045 LST

I waited fifteen minutes for Commander Michelson before becoming impatient. I didn't have a clue how to call anybody to find out where he might be, so I decided I should try my luck at finding him myself. I grabbed my shoulder bag and headed towards the door. The door opened as I approached it. *At least I'm not locked in here,* I thought to myself.

The hallway was empty as I started to walk. There was a gentle upward curve to the floor. It felt strange when I started to think about it, I was actually walking on the ceiling.

I'm not the kind of person to open and close doors in an effort to find someone. Besides, I reasoned, this was a closed environment. Sooner or later I was bound to run into somebody. I started to wonder about the windows. I wanted to see the view. Then I started thinking about what a long walk it would be if I didn't find anyone. Fifty kilometers is a long way to walk.

I had been walking for about ten minutes when I noticed I was about to go through a door. As I approached, it opened and I walked into a space that was designed for people to relax in. There were windows, chairs and tables and four different sets of elevator doors. I sat down for a minute to look out the windows. We were slowly rotating into a full Earth view. *This is very strange*, I thought. There were maps and instructions on each of the elevator doors.

Two of the elevators went up to the tenth story of Orbiting Headquarters. The other two went to stations that held transports for traveling around the rings. I learned that Orbiting Headquarters was divided into thirty sections. Each section had its own set of ring transports and elevators. The maps gave a cross-section of both the rings and the central hub, and when I touched a section on the map, detailed directions appeared. *Very useful*, I thought. I didn't have the foggiest idea where I wanted to go. I went back to my chair and sat down. *Maybe someone will show up soon*, I thought. No one did.

0035.0116.1300 LST

I had been in the lounge for a couple of hours. I had seen Earth come in and out of view seven or eight times. I wasn't keeping track. I was becoming hungry and thirsty. Commander Michelson had said I would be meeting the people who would take me to Tranquility Base. I thought it best to go find them.

I walked back to the maps by the transport doors and began looking for possible routes to places I might find people. I found the Launch Command Center for Earth and Moon transports located in the Central Hub. When I tried to get the directions, I was informed that access was denied and that I should use an alternative route.

Fine, I thought. I started looking for anything that could be a facility to prepare for a launch. I found something called the Moon Launch Preparation Center. It was located on the tenth level, exactly half way around the ring from where I was. I was instructed to take one of the elevators to the tenth level, then board one of the ring transports that run the entire circumference of the rings (transports on levels one through nine ran in one kilometer segments), and tell the transport where I wanted to go. I was to then follow the instructions that would be waiting for me and make my way to the Prep Center.

One of the elevators opened. Impulsively, I checked to make sure I had everything, including my shoulder bag. *This is it,* I thought to myself. I got in the elevator and the doors closed. A female voice asked me, "What level, please?"

"Tenth," I responded. And twenty seconds later, the doors opened on the tenth level.

I stepped out of the elevator, not knowing if anybody would be there. No one was. There were instructions on the wall in front of me. They were illuminated from behind and inside the wall. Not like a screen, but built into the wall. *Very interesting effect,* I thought. Unobtrusive, yet it got your attention. I was instructed to board the first transport that was available. They ran opposite to the rotation of the rings so as not to subject the occupants to too much G force.

The room itself was designed specifically for transporting people around the ring. *Like a bus station,* I was thinking. There were fifty such rooms. And the transport only stopped if there were people to be picked up.

It took five minutes for my transport to arrive. I was quite sure it would be empty. It was. I stepped in and sat down. The same female voice I heard in the elevator asked… "What is you destination?"

"Moon Launch Preparation Center," I responded. Each transport was designed to hold sixty people sitting two abreast with an aisle between them. There were fifteen rows and no windows. The transports travelled an average speed of one hundred kilometers per hour and the seats were designed to cushion the body from the G force. As I started to move, I suspected I wouldn't be making any stops along the way. I was right. My trip took ten minutes.

I remembered there would be instructions waiting for me at my stop, but when I stepped out of the transport, I was more than a little shocked to see someone waiting there. When I heard the person say, "Welcome aboard, Commander Carrera", I passed out.

0035.0116.1445 LST

I heard a voice calling my name. It was a far-off sound, like one you'd hear when you're not fully awake

"Commander Carrera! Wake up!"

I opened my eyes and found myself looking into a pair of unfamiliar eyes.

"Where am I?"

"You are in sick bay. You passed out a little while ago. I am one of the Doctors up here. My name is Doctor Montgomery. Please call me Doctor."

I turned my head and looked around the room. It was small, containing only the bed on which I was laying, a chair and a picture of some far-away galaxy.

"How long have I been out, Doctor?" I sat up and swung my legs over the side of the bed.

"Not long, Commander. About an hour." He had a concerned look on his face. "Tell me Commander, do you pass out often?"

I was trying to figure out how I had suddenly become a Commander. "Well, Doctor, when I was running my Architectural business, there would be times when things would come at me all at once and I would lie down for awhile. But I've never passed out before."

"I see." The Doctor seemed more relaxed now. "That makes sense, then. I'll inform the Doctor on Tranquility Base that there may be times when you will become overloaded and may need to take a nap. How does that sound?"

"I'd really like to know how I became a Commander, Doctor, and of what I am in Command."

"I can't answer that for you, Commander. You will receive that information when you arrive on Tranquility Base. You are in perfect health. My orders are to escort you to your moon transport and see you safely on your way. Any objections?"

The fact that I would soon be on my way to the moon filled me with every emotion I've ever experienced, but I quickly brought myself under control.

"No objections, Doctor. Let's go."

"Your shoulder bag, Commander."

"Thanks, Doctor."

0035.0116.1500 LST

Doctor Montgomery and I didn't say too much on our way down to the moon transport. He asked me a few questions about my eating habits and the physical activities I enjoyed. He let me know that he would be sharing the information with his counterpart on Tranquility base. Apparently, the base was not a place where secrets were well kept. It was more like a small town where everybody knew everyone else's business.

Orbiting Headquarter personnel are well trained in the art of moving around in a weightless environment. I was glad to have the Doctor there to coach me. The central hub contained a series of tubes running along its entire length. I was amazed at how fast you could get around with just a few pushes of your arms. When an exit or portal was near, the walls of the tubes became transparent so you could see where you were going, or which transport to board.

I still hadn't eaten. "Is it possible for us to find something to eat, Doctor?"

"The transport is well stocked with food and liquid refreshments, Commander. If you can wait until you are on your way, that would be ideal."

I paused briefly before responding. "That is agreeable to me, Doctor."

"Thank you, Commander. Your transport is coming up on your left. As you know, we send a lot of supplies to the moon from here and we use remote-controlled transports for that purpose. When we send new personnel, we usually send them with a pilot, although the personnel transports have the same remote control capabilities. We have yet to lose one of our transports. We believe it would be in your best interests to take the personnel transport and let us use the remote control. You will be the only one on board and will be seated in the pilot's seat during launch and touchdown. I know it probably sounds quite odd to you, Commander, but you need to trust that we know what we're doing."

I did. "Why should I sit in the pilot's seat?"

"Thank you for asking, Commander. First, you'll get a feel for the controls and what it's like to pilot one of the transports. Secondly, it's quite a rush when you get launched from this station."

I could see the transport as soon as we hit the transparent part of the tube. There were three main thruster nozzles in the back and several smaller ones on its belly and front. I couldn't see any landing gear.

"Does this use the Space Drive, Doctor?"

"Yes, Commander. All of our transports do. This particular one uses one Drive. We have others that use more. This transport was designed to carry ten people. Officers actually. I'm sure you'll find it quite comfortable. Your trip should take about twenty-four hours. I will familiarize you with the interior. As you can see, this transport is not very big."

I noticed he used the word 'should'. I was starting to sweat. We turned into a short tube and entered the transport.

We floated into the area that contained the ten officers' seats.

"This is the area you will be in for most of your trip, Commander. As you can see, the seating has been arranged to give everyone free movement. The seats recline and are adjustable to ensure you sleep as comfortably as possible. You will notice a simple yet effective system to hold you in place when you are seated."

The seats were in a staggered configuration. I floated over to one of them and took a closer look. There was a system of belts, some for the legs, others for the body. They looked simple enough to use.

"Okay, Doctor. What's next?"

"Let's head into the cockpit, Commander."

As we floated towards the bulkhead, a door opened. We floated into the cockpit, which I recognized from being in the Intruder.

"Doctor, do I wear a spacesuit for this trip?"

"No, Commander. There are emergency suits on board. After we're finished here, I'll show you where the suits and your supplies are located."

I sat down in one of the pilot's seats and immediately the belts from an auto-restraint system wrapped around me. I looked over at the Doctor. "This feels quite familiar, Doctor. Is there anything I need to know?"

"Anything can happen, Commander. Be prepared for anything."

I looked out the window. I couldn't see to the end of the launch tube ten kilometers away. "I'll try, Doctor."

"You may not have time to try, Commander."

"Are you trying to scare me, Doctor?"

"Did that scare you, Commander?"

"Yes, it did."

"Then I'm not trying."

For a minute I was unable to speak. The Doctor was patient.

"How do I get myself out from these restraints, Doctor?"

"Tell the computer to disengage the restraints."

That seemed simple enough.

"Computer, disengage restraints."

The computer responded and I floated out of the pilot's seat.

"Let's finish the tour, Doctor." I was angry again.

"I hope you are not angry with me, Commander. This is the way we do things around here."

I stopped. "No, Doctor. My anger is usually directed at me. I'm not angry with you."

"Good. Let's check the suits and supplies."

We made our way into a room behind where we slept.

"Commander, in these cabinets you will find a large assortment of foods and liquids." The Doctor opened one of the cabinets. "All the foods and liquids are labeled. The solids are individually wrapped. All the liquids have a built-in straw. Please deposit the empty packaging into one of the disposal units for recycling." He proceeded to help himself to a snack. "Everything is quite tasty, Commander. Please help yourself."

"What are you eating, Doctor?"

"It's an energy bar. Fruits, nuts, a little chocolate."

"I'll have one of those."

The Doctor smiled and handed me a bar. I was very hungry. I took a bite. It tasted good. "Thanks Doctor. This is just what you ordered."

He thought about that for a minute and then started to laugh.

"Very good, Commander."

"Where are the suits, Doctor?"

He motioned me to float over to where he was.

"They are nothing fancy, Commander. They are designed to keep you alive in the event of a hull breach. He pulled down on a small red "t" shaped handle. "Just pull on this handle and they slide out." There were twelve suits on the floor.

"These suits work the same way as the one you wore on the Intruder. Just put your feet where you see the footprints and the suit will put itself on. Remember to keep your arms a few centimeters from your body so can you get them in. The suit has enough oxygen for about ninety minutes. Located throughout the ship are outlets to which you can attach an umbilical cord for an external supply. There is a twenty-four hour supply for twelve people. That should be enough time to successfully rescue a disabled transport anywhere between here and the moon. We have been fortunate in that we have not had to test the system. Does that ease your mind a bit, Commander?"

"Quite a bit, Doctor. Thank you."

"Good. We'll launch in five minutes. Let's go back to the cockpit."

I sat myself into the pilot's chair. The Doctor made sure everything was in order.

"God be with you, Commander."

"God be with you too, Doctor." Doctor Montgomery left the transport.

Launch Command came on the air. "We launch in three minutes, Commander. There is a countdown clock located on the bottom of the screen to your left. Enjoy your flight. Your transport will be in the control of Tranquility once you exit Headquarters. It's been good having you aboard."

I didn't know what to say. "Thank you" is what came out.

Three: Learning To Fly

0035.0116.1545 LST

I watched the count down clock. Three… Two… One…

I had my hands on the flight control sticks as we started to accelerate down the launch tube. It was a smooth, controlled and extremely powerful acceleration. I shot out into the blackness of space and felt the transport adjust its trajectory. As my eyes gradually adjusted, I was able to see stars. I quickly felt myself free from the force of acceleration.

Tranquility Base came on over the radio. "Commander Carrera, this is Tranquility Base. Do you read?"

"Loud and clear, Tranquility. Is there a problem?"

"Not at all, Commander. Just making contact. Everything looks perfect from here. If you need to contact us, just ask for Tranquility. The computer will connect us. Enjoy your flight, Commander. We'll see you in twenty-four hours. Tranquility out."

"Thank you, Tranquility… Computer, disengage the restraints."

For the first time in many years, I tasted freedom. It was something I thought I would never experience again. I knew it wouldn't last.

I floated back to the eating area and picked out a few packets of food and something to drink. As I ate, I started to think about the base. I knew Tranquility better than most of the people living there - the materials, how it was constructed and why it was designed the way it was. My design had been picked for a number of reasons. People seemed to feel at home there, and it was the only one designed to work in an Earth-like gravity. Tranquility Base has eighty percent Earth gravity.

I let my mind wander, and floated into the lounge/sleeping area. I picked out a chair, strapped myself in and adjusted the position until I was comfortable. I fell asleep the instant my eyes closed.

0035.0117.0145 LST

An alarm sounded, and my eyes opened instantly. The sound was deafening. In between blasts of sound, I heard a female voice. "Please take control of the transport." I released the straps and as I floated out of my seat, noticed that the transport was rotating around me. I directed myself towards the cockpit and the door opened. I pulled myself into the pilot's seats and the restraint system locked me in. I grabbed hold of the flight control sticks.

"Tranquility Base, this is Commander Carrera. I have a problem."

"Commander, this is Tranquility Base. We are aware of the problem. Please stand by."

The alarm was still blasting. "Computer, disengage the alarm." It stopped.

"Commander, this is Tranquility. We have discovered a virus in your flight control and guidance systems."

"What is this virus doing, Tranquility, and how was it introduced?" I knew how much damage a virus could do.

"Good questions, Commander. We suspect the virus was introduced during a routine system check. It could have been planted at several different levels. We'll be working overtime in order to find the source."

"Can you destroy it, Tranquility?"

"Not at this time, Commander. We don't know anything about it."

"What damage has it done so far, Tranquility?"

"It has paralyzed your auto flight control and destroyed your auto guidance system."

My hands started to ache from gripping the flight control sticks so hard. I released them.

"Do you have a plan, Tranquility?"

"We are reviewing our options, Commander. Our Commander will be taking control now. We'll get you home, Commander."

"Commander Carrera, this is your Commanding Officer. My name is Till. Commander Till. Please address me as Commander."

My Commanding Officer. That would take getting used to. "Yes, Commander. Commander Carrera here."

"May I call you Bella, Commander?"

"Yes, sir."

"Good. In case you were wondering, Bella, we didn't plan this, so we need to make some decisions. Your ship is in a slow roll heading out towards some unknown destination. If we don't rescue you, you could end up in a black hole somewhere. Or you might end up in an orbit similar to that of a comet, and come visit us every seventy-six years. It's hard to predict these things. But we do have a few options. As mentioned before, we could rescue you. We have a lot of leeway with that option. Or we could have our friends at Orbiting Headquarters rescue you. Or we could have you try and take control of your ship and fly it home. That would require that we download Max. Max is the program we use here to help us fly our transports. It's an extremely sophisticated piece of software designed for Maximum Human Interaction. We believe Max could restore flight control to you. It has its own guidance program and would help you fly your transport. We've not tried this before, so if it works, we'll all be quite smug. If it doesn't, we'll have to launch a boring rescue mission. You'll be flying past the moon and out of rescue range in six hours. Max will take fifteen minutes to download. I leave the decision to you, Bella. Call us back with your decision. You have fifteen minutes. Tranquility out."

Fifteen minutes. I had already made my decision. I wanted to fly this thing.

"Tranquility Base, this is Commander Carrera."

"Yes, Bella. This is Commander Till. What have you decided?"

"I want to fly this thing, Commander."

"Excellent, Bella. We'll start downloading Max right away. While that being done, let's go over how the control sticks work."

"Sounds good to me, Commander."

"Good. Let's start with the control stick on your right. Please take it in your hand."

"Got it, Commander."

"O.K. You won't feel the control sticks move very much. Using them together smoothly takes a lot of practice. Max needs you to actively use the controls as much as possible. The program will automatically correct your errors. We will not download Max's voice, but Max will be recording your every move and will use them as starting points for interacting with you when you arrive here. Understand?"

"Yes, Commander."

"Good. Now, the right-hand control is used to move the transport forward and backward. Push and pull the control in the direction you want to go. It is also used to turn the ship left and right. Put pressure on the stick to move the transport in the direction you want to face. You'll notice that the upper part of the control flexes when squeezed. This fires thrusters on the belly of your ship when you need to go up. Do you have all of that, Bella?"

It seemed simple enough. "Yes, sir."

"Good. Please take the left-hand control."

"Got it."

"Alright. The left hand controls the ship's rotation. Push forward to make the nose go down. Pull towards you to make the nose go up. Moving the stick to your left or right will cause the ship to rotate up to the left or right. Squeezing the upper part of the stick will fire the thrusters, causing the ship to go down."

"Using both of the controls together is like rubbing your stomach and patting your head at the same time. Max is almost downloaded. Please stand by, Bella."

Both control sticks were in my hands and I was anxious to get back on course. It took a few minutes for Commander Till to reconnect.

"Bella, this is Commander Till. Max has successfully downloaded and is waiting for your input. Do you have any questions?"

"Yes, Commander. I'd like to know if it's possible for me to see where I am in relation to the moon. There are several blue screens in front of me. I'd also like to be able to see how this ship is rolling in relation to a horizon so I can attempt to stop it."

There was silence for a minute. Then Commander Till came back on air.

"Yes, Bella, all of that is possible. May I ask how you know about these things?"

"Yes, Commander. Aircraft design fascinates me, but I chose architecture as my profession. I've learned a lot about aircraft over the years, but I never did learn how to fly."

"That explains it then. All right. Max is going to display your positions on the three screens directly in front of you. The top screen will show you where you are in relation to the moon. The one just below that will be your horizon. The bottom one will show the course you need to follow to get here. Your landing will be computer-controlled. The virus has not affected that program. We will stay on the air with you, Bella. Would you prefer to see us or just leave things the way they are?"

Three of the screens were activated, and I saw for the first time where I was and how much I was rolling. "Let's keep things as they are, Commander."

"Good, Bella. It's time for you to fly home. Time is not on your side."

All I saw out the windows were stars. I was slowly rotating. I needed to see the Moon, and I needed to stop the roll.

"Where's the Moon?" I asked myself out loud. I looked down and saw the Moon on one of my computer screens. I lost my focus for a few seconds. "Tranquility, this is Commander Carrera."

"This is Till, Bella. How are you doing?"

"I have an image of the Moon on one of my screens. Is Max responding to my voice commands?"

"I'll check that for you, Bella."

Commander Till responded quickly. "Yes, Bella. Max is responding to you. Would you prefer that Max didn't?"

"No, Commander. It'll be fine."

I put pressure on the left-hand control stick and kept my eyes on the horizon indicator. I felt the transport respond and watched as the ship stopped its roll and leveled out. I moved the right-hand control to my left and felt the transport start to turn. I was looking for the Moon. I glanced at the top screen. It showed a representation of where I was in relation to it. I was way off course. As I looked up, I saw the moon in my window. I was now traveling sideways, away from my destination. I worked the controls and managed to stop the sideways momentum. I then began to accelerate towards the Moon. I didn't notice if Max was helping with the ship controls. My eyes were fixed on the three screens that showed my location. Whenever I noticed I wasn't on the course that was plotted on the bottom screen, I made what I thought were the right adjustments.

The moon grew in size as the hours went by. As it started to fill the windows of the cockpit, a sense of panic began to overwhelm me. "Tranquility, this is Bella."

"Commander Till here, Bella. You're doing fine."

"Thank you, Commander. I was wondering when that auto-landing program would kick in? I'd hate to crack up such a fine ship."

"I'll check on that, Bella." He sounded like he was smiling. "Your landing program will commence in two minutes. You're on course and I don't believe you'll need to make any more adjustments. I'll see you in my office in approximately one hour. Thank you for flying Air Tranquility. Over and out." Commander Till went off the air.

"Commander Carrera, this is Transport Control. You are clear for landing. Your Transport will bring you in on auto. Landing procedure commences in two minutes and you will land in fifteen. Please remain seated and enjoy the ride."

Two minutes passed and I was traveling towards Tranquility base just a few kilometers over the surface of the Moon. My mind was blank and my body was numb. I looked at the surface as it went by, and found it to be both beautiful and foreboding at the same time.

"Thank you, Tranquility. I'll try."

Ten years after being accused, I was about to start a new life.

Four: Commander Wallace Till

0035.0117.1530 LST

The transport started to slow down as I passed over the outskirts of Tranquility base. I noticed that my computer screens were displaying information about the status of the transport. I passed over what looked like a control tower, and the transport came to a stop. The landing pad was below me and I started my decent. Three minutes later, I was hovering over a magnetic field a meter from the ground. The restraint system released me and as I stood up, I heard the outside hatch being opened. I walked out of the cockpit.

Standing in the doorway of the transport was Corporal Daily. I stared at him for a minute. He stared back. He was wearing a vest. It was closed. On the right-hand side was one horizontal bar, and on the left side were five diagonal ones.

"Welcome to Tranquility Base, Commander Carrera. I'm Corporal Daily. That was awesome flying. Commander Till is expecting you. I'll wait for you outside."

Everything was happening so quickly I felt completely out of control. It was an odd feeling just walking around the transport. I walked to the back room and retrieved my shoulder bag. I looked at the red handle and was glad I didn't have to use the spacesuits. I opened the cabinet that held the food and grabbed a couple of snacks and something to drink. As I made my way out of the transport, I thanked God.

♦♦♦

Corporal Daily was waiting just outside the transport door. We were about the same height, although he was thinner and younger than I. I asked him if it would be possible wash up before my meeting with Commander Till. He indicated that he had anticipated my request. "Absolutely, Commander." We were walking towards the entrance to the Base's transit system. "This will take us to Tranquility Central Command. Commander Tills' office is located there, along with the offices of all the senior Commanders. In your office, you will find what you need. You will, of course, be able to design the office to your liking."

While I knew the location of all the Command Centers, the living quarters, laboratories, sports facilities, etc., I felt it would be wise just to let myself be directed while in the company of others. At least for a while.

We stood on the platform for no more than two minutes, waiting for our two-seat car to pull up.

"How well is this transport system working, Corporal?"

"I've heard no complaints, Commander. In fact, a lot of people wonder how the system is able to dispense cars with the required number of seats so efficiently."

"I'm sure, Corporal, that if anyone was truly interested they would look up how it works in the library. It's not a complicated system. Many communities use similar systems on Earth."

"I'm sorry, Commander. You are right. Do you mind if I use that phrase next time someone asks?"

"Not at all, Corporal."

Five minutes went by and we stopped at the platform to Central Command. I let Corporal Daily lead me up to the top floor and into my office. "There are two offices on this floor, Commander, yours and Commander Till's. Would forty-five minutes be enough time for you to refresh yourself?"

"Yes, Corporal. That would be fine."

"Good. We'll set up your security system when we have a little more time. It only takes a few minutes. In the mean time, take this card. Whenever you approach a door that you are allowed to enter, the door will open. I'll be back for you in forty-five minutes."

"Thank you, Corporal." I took the card and stepped towards the door. It opened. I looked back and smiled at the Corporal.

"I'll see you in forty-five minutes." I slipped the card into one of my vest pockets.

0035.0117.1540 LST

I remembered this building. Before I stepped into the room, I closed my eyes and visualized what the interior would look like. When the image became clear, I focused my memory on what people would see when they looked out the windows. When that was clear, I opened my eyes and walked through the door. To my surprise, the office was completely empty. I had visualized it totally furnished. It also seemed larger than I had visualized. Computer simulations sometimes had that effect. I wandered over to the windows to see the view. It was perfect. The buildings and transit tubes were amazing in stark contrast to the light. In the distance stood the Earth Dome, glistening like a magnificent jewel, the one place where residents of Tranquility Base could escape to experience Earth. Everything was immaculate. I looked out the window for a few minutes. I felt proud and humbled by the sheer existence of the base. I closed my eyes and remembered how it was I got here. I needed to take a shower.

I walked around the office, which also included living quarters. I noticed a built-in washer and dryer. I dropped off my shoulder bag. Walking into the bathroom, I knew how I was going to redesign it.

As I stood under the steaming water of the shower, I tried to put things in a perspective. My mind was besieged with all the new senses and circumstances and it was working overtime in an attempt to put things in order. I stepped out of the shower and toweled myself dry. I put on a fresh set of clothes and my vest and sat down on one of the counter stools in the kitchen.

0035.0117.1625 LST

Corporal Daily arrived when he said he would, and we walked across the hall to Commander Till's office.

"Commander Till, this is Corporal Daily. Commander Carrera and I are outside your office." He appeared to be speaking into thin air.

A few seconds later he replied, "Alright, sir. Thank you."

I didn't hear anybody speak to him. "Were you speaking to Commander Till?"

"Yes, sir. He asked me to send you in."

"But I didn't hear anything."

Corporal Daily thought for a moment. "The vest we wear has many functions, sir. It won't take you long to learn how it works."

The door opened. "Please try and relax, sir. Commander Till is waiting for you."

"Thank you, Corporal."

I walked into Commander Till's office and saw him for the first time. His hair was silvery gray and he was in his mid-sixties. "Hello, Bella. It is good to finally meet you. In my opinion, the base you designed for us is a masterpiece. Everybody who lives here can't say enough about it. I'm so glad you decided to make this your home. Please follow me into my office. I have something I want to show you."

Commander Till was most gracious. I didn't have much of a chance to do anything but listen for our first encounter. We walked across to his office. It was quite substantial. Along one of the walls were a dozen different space suits. On his desk was a beautiful crystal with lights emanating from it. It looked familiar. It reminded me of the crystal in the Judge's chamber. It was difficult for me to take my eyes off it. I looked over at Commander Till. "Is this crystal what you wanted to show me, Commander?"

I could tell he was surprised by the way he looked at the crystal. "Holy…" He didn't finish the sentence.

"No, Bella." He walked over to his desk and picked up a book. "This is what I wanted to show you." He handed it to me. It was the book I had intended to publish for SEARCH. It was a technical manual for the base with all the data required to make the base secure if a terrorist attack was ever launched against Tranquility. I had made no hard copies of it. An extremely altered version of this very book was used to destroy me. The altered version made it appear that I had provided instructions on how to destroy Tranquility Base. I had been charged with selling this version to a known terrorist group, supposedly to help them destroy Tranquility. I knew that someone had broken into my computer files, downloaded a copy of the original book, altered it and then sold it. I had not been able to prove it.

"Bella, we know what your intentions were with regard to this book. We found the storage device you were using on your computer and recovered this data. We have just completed all the upgrades you suggested."

My office had been destroyed by fire a few weeks prior to my arrest. I had been certain nothing was salvageable.

Wallace continued, "We couldn't have introduced this as evidence in your defense, as it would have looked like it was manufactured. It took us two years to piece this all together."

I was unable to speak. I just held the book in my hands and looked at it. As I did, I felt the cleansing effect of innocence wash over me. And for the first time in ten years, I felt the spark of being alive.

"I am speechless, Commander. I would like to personally thank the person or persons responsible for doing this. Would that be possible?"

"Absolutely, Bella. In fact, the person who did this lives here on the base. Her name is Dominique Jardine. She designed all the system software that keeps the base habitable. She's also the most listened-to radio personality on the SEARCH radio network. She calls herself DJ. Have you heard of her?"

I felt like I should have. "No, I haven't Commander. I have not listened to the radio for quite a few years now. She must be good."

The way Commander Till was smiling at me reminded me of my grandfather. "Two billion listeners, Bella. She likes dance music. She's on six hours a day, six days a week. She is really looking forward to meeting you."

"Then we have something in common, Commander."

"Excellent, Bella. I'll arrange for a meeting. Also, I've been told that you would like to know what you'll be commanding."

"That's correct, Commander."

"The base, Bella. All of it."

Right at that moment, I felt the need to take a nap. "I think I need to lie down for awhile Commander. I'm feeling a little tired."

"I understand, Bella. I'll have Corporal Daily take you back to your quarters. I'll see you tomorrow."

"I'm able to make my own way back, Commander, if that's O.K. with you."

"That's fine, Bella. I'll escort you out."

"Thank you, Commander."

"You're welcome, Bella."

Commander Till escorted me to the door, and I walked across to my office. I entered and made my way into the bedroom. There was a bed and a set of drawers built into the wall. I fell into the bed with my clothes on and passed out.

Five: Commander Jacob Brodie

0035.0118.1115 LST

"Bella!" I knew I was lying in bed. My eyes were still closed. "Bella!!" The voice I heard belonged to a female. "Bella, it's time to get up!!"

I opened my eyes. There was light streaming into my room. I looked around for the owner of the voice. She was not in my room.

I rolled out of bed and into the washroom. When I saw myself in the mirror, I wondered how long I had been out. Judging by the growth of my beard, I guessed around fourteen hours. I remembered where I left my shoulder bag and retrieved my shaving kit along with a few other items. Just as I finished putting on a fresh set of clothes and my vest, I heard Commander Till's voice. "Bella, this is Commander Till. Good morning."

I hesitated. I didn't know where his voice was coming from. "Good morning, Commander. How are you today?"

"I'm fine. I see you've figured out how the communication system in your vest works."

That surprised me. "Not completely, Commander. Maybe we could get together and go over the finer details of it."

Commander Till chuckled. "Sounds good, Bella. Please come over and we'll go over a few things during breakfast."

I wasn't very hungry. "I'll be right over Commander."

♦♦♦

I remembered what Corporal Daily had done when we had arrived at Commander Till's door, and decided to do the same. "Commander Till, this is Bella. I'm at your door."

"Hello, Bella. Please come in."

The door opened and I made my way into Commander Till's office. The crystal was still there, but there were no lights this time. He was sitting at his desk and he motioned me to sit. "I know it takes time to get adjusted to new situations, Bella. But it's important that you learn how this base works and what we do as quickly as you can. I've assigned

Commander Brodie to you. He is the man responsible for keeping this base powered up. He also works with communications and has access to every part of the base. He is your right-hand man, so to speak, and he will show you everything you need to know."

I had one question. "I wasn't expecting to be named Commander of the base, Commander. What brought on the decision?"

"I can't tell you everything, Bella. We believe that it is in the best interests of the base that you be in command. You are qualified, based on your former life on Earth." Commander Till reached into his desk and pulled out an envelope. "This is for you, Bella."

He slid the envelope towards me and I took it. I opened it and pulled out a bank deposit receipt. "That's your pay for two year's service, in full and in advance. We know we can't give you back your life. It's deposited in your name earning interest in the SEARCH bank. It's in SEARCH's currency."

The amount of the deposit was equal to the amount of money I had spent to defend myself. I was rich again. "This is very generous, Commander. I don't know what to say. Thank you."

"You're welcome, Bella."

I sat for a few minutes wondering about my life. I had no clue how I would command this base.

Commander Till broke the silence. "I really don't know where to begin, Bella. I would imagine you would like to know a little about me and what I do. I think that would be a good place to start. Are you hungry?"

I found it difficult to talk. "At the moment, I'm not too hungry, Commander, but you're right. I'd like to know who you are and what you do. I imagine it would help me get a grip on my new job."

Commander Till stood up and walked over to the spacesuits hanging on the wall. "This is who I am, Bella. I have designed almost every suit used by SEARCH. They have gone through many changes and upgrades over the years. Much like myself."

I watched the Commander as he presented himself and the suits. They really were his life. I could tell by the way he looked at them. But I sensed there was something else. He seemed haunted. I felt the only way to find out why was to ask.

I got up and walked over to him. "I'm impressed, Commander. I recognize that these suits have been your life's work. You appear to be a little unnerved. Are you okay?"

He didn't respond immediately. "You're right, Bella. Many men have died in my suits because I was unable to foresee all the potential dangers. That is the motivation behind constantly improving them. Time has taken its toll."

Commander Till waited for me to respond. "I believe, Commander, that every good man would be able to say the same thing."

Commander Till looked up and into my eyes. "What? What did you say?"

I swallowed. "I said, Commander, that I've seen many people die — friends, family, strangers. And there were times when I felt it was my fault. I am an architect. There were times when I believed that if I had chosen to be a doctor, for example, my work might have saved those people. Does that make sense?"

Commander Till was still looking at me. "It makes perfect sense. Thank you, Bella."

I felt relieved. "You're welcome, Commander. I am curious about one other thing, Commander. I was wondering what your first name might be."

"Good question, Bella. It's Wallace. You may still call me Commander, Bella."

"No problem, Commander. Maybe we should go for breakfast now."

"Excellent suggestion. We have a small cafeteria on the first floor. That's where I'll introduce you to some of our food. We grow most of it here."

"I'm looking forward to it."

♦♦♦

The cafeteria could accommodate seventy-five people. The people who served us were volunteers who wanted to experience working for the SEARCH organization. Of course, they are all chosen carefully. Some of them would later become career personnel.

Commander Till briefed me on how the vest works, emphasizing the importance of wearing it at all times while awake. In addition to keeping everyone connected to the medical center, the communication center, and the computer, it was an intricate part of each spacesuit.

"Bella, if an emergency situation arises, communications will override the system to relay the situation. There are also loudspeakers in place. The entire base is under constant surveillance and wired for sound. You will always be on the air, except when you are in your quarters. It won't take long for you to get used to it. Security, communications, the radio station and a few other command centers have access and use the system. You have access to the entire system and can choose where you'd like to have it installed. With the exception of me, you have the highest level of computer access. That may not mean much right now, but I'm sure you will find it useful."

"It will take some time for me to absorb all this, Commander."

"I know, Bella. Commander Brodie will do all he can to help you. Relax. How's your steak?"

"You'd never know it wasn't real beef. It's very good, Commander."

"Good. Now, for dessert I'd like you to listen to something that was broadcast while you were sleeping."

"Very well, Commander."

Commander Till called the radio station. "DJ, this is Commander Till."

I didn't hear anything. Commander Till motioned me to stand by.

"I'm well today. I'd like you to play that broadcast you made yesterday regarding your new Commander." He smiled. "Thanks, DJ."

The speakers on my vest activated. I heard DJ. "As you know, reading the news is not one of my favorite things to do, but sometimes I just have to make an exception. With the permission of my newsperson, I have the following announcement. At ten hundred hours LST, our new Commander, Bella Carrera, was found innocent of all charges related to the conspiracy involving the destruction of our home. And if Commander Carrera is listening right now, I'd like to thank him for designing the most perfect place I've ever lived. Now back to some music… a little rock-and-roll to get the circulation going."

A wicked little drum and bass set filled the space around me. And then the broadcast ended.

"Wow!" I was staring at my empty plate.

"Did you enjoy your dessert, Bella?"

What I wanted to say was, "What do you think?" But instead I said, "I am most grateful, Commander. Thank you."

"You're innocent, Bella. No need to thank me. Now what do you suggest we do?"

I was very curious about the gravity that made the base feel so much like Earth. "Before I make any suggestions, Commander, I'd like to know if you've figured out what is causing the gravitational field on the base."

Commander Till wasn't too impressed. "We still believe that an ultra dense particle is responsible. We can't prove it. Our laser drills go down only so far. With all the holes we drilled, a pattern has emerged. It looks like a dome. So at this point we have concluded that the field is being generated by what the particle has created."

"So the theory remains the same."

"That's correct, Bella. Do you have another one?"

"No, Commander. It's just that there doesn't seem to be any way to prove it."

"Maybe we will some day, Bella." Commander Till sat for a minute. "I'd like you to suggest what we should do next."

"I think we should arrange a meeting with Commander Brodie."

"Excellent suggestion. Communications.... Commander Brodie, please. And relay through for Commander Carrera."

"Brodie here, Commander. Is there a problem?"

I could hear the conversation.

"No problem, Commander. I just finished breakfast with your new Commander, and he suggested that we get together sometime within the next hour."

"I'll need about that much time to finish what I'm doing, Commander. I can be at your office in one hour."

"That would be fine, Commander. See you in an hour."

I was nervous.

"He's the best in his field, Bella. I know you'll get along. He has one hundred and twenty-five people under his command. He's quite intense."

"We should make our way back to your office. And I'll prepare myself for Commander Brodie."

"Sounds good, Bella."

I looked at Commander Till for a few seconds. He seemed to have slipped into a very relaxed state. That made me even more nervous.

♦♦♦

We finished in the cafeteria and made our way into one of the elevators. Commander Till told the computer to take us to his office.

Like most people, I look around when I step into an elevator. I look at the walls, the ceiling, the floor, my shoes, and other people's shoes.

And even when I know the people in the elevator, I avoid looking at them directly if possible. I was in this 'looking-around' mode that I spotted 'D twelve-R fifty-four-Q ninety-eight' illuminated in the wall. It looked almost exactly like the sign I saw in the wall at Orbiting Headquarters. I placed my hand on it and tried to feel it. I noticed Commander Till looking at me.

"Have you found something, Bella?"

I pointed to the message.

"I don't see anything, Bella. What is it?"

I thought, *What do you mean, you don't see it*. But I said, "It's a message, Commander."

"What does it say, Bella?"

I swallowed. "It says D twelve-R fifty-four-Q ninety-eight."

Commander Till looked down at his feet and then reached into one of his vest pockets and pulled out a pen and paper. He handed them to me. "Write down the coordinates and put them in a place you'll remember. You'll not see it again. At least not in this elevator."

I did as Commander Till said, and handed back his pen and paper.

"What does it mean, Commander?"

As we stepped out of the elevator, he said, "I can't tell you. A few of us here see those messages, but we haven't yet figured out what they mean. Maybe you're the one who will."

"I'll work on it, Commander."

0035.0118.1445 LST

Wallace and I were relaxing in his living room when he informed me that Commander Brodie had arrived. I sat up in my chair. When Commander Brodie entered, I stood up, walked over to him and introduced myself.

"I'm pleased to meet you, Commander. I'm Commander Carrera."

"Good to meet you, too, Commander."

We both walked across the living room and sat down. Nobody said a word for a few minutes. We just sat and looked at each other. Then, at some point, we started to smile. Before long, we were laughing uncontrollably. Wallace took control. "Bella, this is Jacob. Jacob, this is Bella."

Wallace wanted Commander Brodie and me to be on a first name basis. Jacob looked over to me and we both nodded. "Please call me Jay, Bella."

"Pleased to meet you again, Jay."

"Likewise, Bella."

Wallace looked at both of us in a way that suggested he was about to say something that may adversely affect us. He nodded at Jay, then at me. "Jay…Bella, there is something I've been withholding until I was certain the Base would be in good hands. For the time being, this information is for the two of you only. Within the next year, we will no longer be able to say that the Moon belongs exclusively to the Space Exploration And Research Center Headquarters."

I looked at Jay. He was staring at Commander Till. His mouth was slightly open and he looked a little pale.

"Excuse me, Commander. Would you please elaborate a little? I heard what you said, but it seems to have affected Jay more than me."

Wallace nodded at me. He had seen Jay's reaction and was concerned. "Of course, Bella. Just give me a moment. I'll fill you in."

Wallace got up and moved toward his office door. Jay and I followed. As the door opened, I saw an intense white light pulsating from the crystal on Wallace's desk. It was unlike anything I had ever seen before. The crystal seemed to disappear when the light reached its peak intensity. I looked at Jay. Something inside me knew that he was causing the crystal to react.

Wallace asked, "Notice anything different about my office today, Jay?"

Jay sat down and looked around. "No, sir. Did you renovate?"

Wallace quickly got my attention, glanced at the crystal and shrugged. I knew by his response that Jay wasn't aware of the crystal's reaction. At that instant, the crystal's light show ended.

Wallace sat down at his desk "As both you and Jay know, SEARCH has very strict conditions that must be met in order for it to set up operations in a country. Two of the most important ones are that the country be a democracy and that it have a capitalist-type economy. Since its creation, SEARCH has rejected many offers. There have been a few instances where a country has totally changed its policies just to have us there. But now something different has emerged. Since we have turned the moon into an economic powerhouse, it has motivated those without a space program to group together and create their own. We will see the results of their work in the form of a complete satellite system scheduled to start launching within the year. The satellite system will include communications, geological surveying, mapping, mineral analysis and others for both the Earth and Moon."

"As a measure good faith, SEARCH has been invited to inspect all the hardware that is to be launched. In total, there will be nine hundred eighty-three new satellites circling the Moon and one thousand four hundred and seventy-six circling the Earth. We haven't found anything that looks like it might be a threat, but the implications can't be ignored. Needless to say, if our new friends believe they can make a go of it here, we will be involved in some very critical negotiations." Wallace looked at both of us to see our reaction and get some feedback.

I looked over at Jay. He looked back at me. It was clear he was at a loss for words. I asked, "Do we know who we are dealing with?"

Wallace continued. "We know that the technology required and the funds needed for such a large initial foray into space exploration could not have come from any one of the two hundred and forty nations and organizations involved. We have concluded, therefore, that the uniting of these nations and organizations was masterminded by a few very well-financed individuals who believe that our policies are unjust."

I interjected, "What you're saying Commander, is that SEARCH has made some very powerful enemies since its inception."

Wallace responded, "Unfortunately, that is the context of how we are dealing with it. The book you wrote is about how to make this base secure against a terrorist attack. As I said when you arrived, we took it seriously and implemented your suggestions."

"Are they intending to create their own base?"

"They have said they will if they believe they can make money by building one. We cannot stop them from trying."

I thought about what Commander Michelson said about the Intruder being able to fly to the moon and back. At that moment, I stopped believing he was just bragging a bit

Six: Cee

0035.0118.2300 LST

I had been in a deep sleep.

"We don't have much time Bella. Open your eyes!" The same voice had awakened me yesterday. I opened my eyes, expecting to find myself in my bed, in my apartment. I wasn't.

"My name is Cee."

I found myself confronted with what I can only describe as the most desirable-looking woman I could possibly imagine. She spoke in a soothing voice. "I understand you may be at a loss for words, Bella. To you, I am the most perfect- looking woman you have ever imagined. Please look around. When you're ready to begin, please let me know."

I've had dreams like this, I thought to myself. Where everything is so real that when you wake up, you can hardly believe what happened while you were sleeping. I got up and found myself in a lush, tropical oasis. The sky was clear and the air amazingly fresh. There were numerous pathways, and I started down one of them. Cee followed me. The plants and trees looked familiar, but then, I'd had dreams like this before.

"This is not a dream, Bella. This is a reality. And realities can be deadly."

I stopped and turned around. "What are you talking about?"

"You can see the light from the crystals, Bella. You know that not everyone does. In fact, very few do. You have been chosen. If you survive, you will be awarded a crystal. You don't have a choice about it."

I choked. "What do you me mean, I have been 'chosen'? What does that mean?"

"It means that you are in a position of great authority. Everything you do and every decision you make has an effect on the human race. What it means is that you are going to be helped and trained. There are those who have found it too difficult."

"Why me?"

"You believe. You obey the Ten Commandments because that was God's command, not because they are Man's laws."

"Are those are the reasons I have been chosen?"

"Not the only ones."

"What are the other ones?"

"That is what you will learn. I cannot tell you."

I felt fear at that moment. I wanted it to end and it did. When I turned around, I was at the door of my office. I saw Jay on the small door monitor waiting for me to answer. I checked the time. It was January nineteenth, eight hundred hours and thirty minutes LST. I let Jay in.

"Good morning, Bella. You don't look so good. Having nightmares?"

I needed a shower. "Kind of. How about I meet you in the cafeteria in twenty minutes?"

"I understand, Bella. I'll order some breakfast. I haven't eaten yet."

"Thanks, Jay. See you in twenty."

Seven: Max and the Race

0035.0119.0850 LST

I arrived at the cafeteria and found Jay eating his breakfast. He had ordered extra for me. "Thanks, Jay. I'm a little hungry."

"Good."

We sat and ate for a few minutes.

"So, Jay, what are the plans for the day?"

"As you know, Bella, it's my job to make sure you know everything I know about how the base works. Now, I could take you on a grand tour of the place, but I've decided that it would better to just dive right in and show you what we've found. Any objections?"

I hesitated. "What did you find, Jay?"

"Didn't you see it as you flew over the base?"

"What are you talking about?"

"The tower, Bella. Didn't you see it?"

"I saw a tower, but I thought it was the Space Traffic Control Center. It looks like an air traffic control tower."

"We didn't build that tower, Bella. We only discovered it when we landed, and just recently found a way of seeing it with our technology."

"But I saw it."

"You flew right over it and you're not a satellite."

"That's really strange, Jay. What is it?"

"Don't have a clue. Still working on it."

"Did you find anything else?"

"Yes." He didn't elaborate.

"Well, what?"

"I can't describe it. I'll have to show you."

Now I was totally intrigued. "When?"

"There's no big rush, Bella. There are a few things you need to do before we can go."

"Like what?"

"Do you know anything about Max?"

"I'm a little familiar with Max."

"So I've heard. But you don't know why Max was invented. Do you like to race?"

"You mean race cars?"

"Yes."

"I've never tried it. I was told Max was invented to help us fly Moon transports."

"That is something Max is used for. Let me explain. Max is a program to help you design and build what we call our racers. Every three months we hold a race and the winner is determined by several different calculations."

"I know of this race, Jay. I've seen it televised on the SEARCH network. I never had much interest in it."

Jay smiled and nodded his head. "Of course. Excuse me for not asking you what you may know of it."

"Not a problem, Jay. So what does the race have to do with me?"

Jay's smile grew larger. "You are now a participant, Bella! You have two months to train."

I leaned back in my chair. That possibility had not entered my mind. "This is a little sudden, isn't it Jay? You speak to me as if I have no choice about it."

Jay leaned forward. "You don't have a choice, Bella. The race is designed to keep Tranquility's senior officers and long-term inhabitants focused and trained. You are the senior officer, so you have no choice. We held our last race a month ago and DJ won. Including you, there will be thirty-two participants in the next race."

The competitiveness that I hadn't felt in years welled up inside me. "Okay, Jay. I'm in. Fill me in on the details."

"Excellent, Bella. Okay, first off, being the fastest doesn't necessarily mean you win. How much fuel you use and how much Max has to help are also factored in. Usually the one who completes the race with the least amount of help from Max is the winner. Commander Till has won the most times. The track is thirty-two hundred kilometers long, and two individuals race at the same time. That's it in a nutshell, Bella. Any questions?"

"Yes. Two months seems too short a time to design and build a racer."

"Of course, Bella. There will be one available for you to use. What you will focus on is training to run in the race. When Max contacts you, he will give you your time line."

"So I'm now officially in the race, Jay."

"It's a blast, Bella. I know you'll enjoy it once you get the hang of it. Commander Till has a new suit that he wants us try. He says it's his final edition."

"Is that your way of saying breakfast is over?"

"You're in command, Bella. Say the word."

"Let's do it."

We made our way up to Wallace's office. He was waiting for us.

♦♦♦

I caught Wallace off guard. "I'm going to win the race, Commander."

He looked me over and said, "I'm glad you're so enthusiastic about our little pastime Bella, but really, you don't stand a chance."

Jay was standing there, minding his own business.

"Of course I do, Commander. You're just scared to admit it."

That got him going. "Bella, when you where a kid, did you ever play with dry ice?"

"Yes."

"Then you know that when you place a certain size of it on a flat surface, it floats on the gas that is evaporating. And given perfect conditions, if you were to push it in order to propel it, it would continue on until it disappeared."

"Yes."

"That is the principle behind the racer. It floats on a cushion of gas. And the space drive is the only means of controlling it. It's not easy."

"I've heard you've won the most, Commander."

"That's true, Bella."

"That's what I intend to do."

Wallace looked into my eyes and smiled. "Excellent. God be with you. Now, I asked you both up here so you could be the first to use what I believe will be the final suit I design. Are you interested?"

Jay answered, "Yes, sir."

"Good."

We walked into Wallace's office and over to the wall where all his suits were hanging. When he instructed the computer to open his workshop, the wall slid towards us and over. We walked inside.

"This is my work space, Jay. I have everything I need here to design and build my suits. When they are finished, I load the information into the computer. The details of how to fabricate and build the suit are then sent down to our suit maintenance department."

I learned afterward that suit maintenance took care of all the suits. Whenever someone came back from an excursion, the suit would relay what it needed to the department. They picked up the suit and dropped off a replacement. All personnel had a fresh suit at their disposal.

I was excited. "What improvements have you made to the latest suit, Commander?"

"Good question, Bella. Because you've never worn or used one of these suits, it would be difficult to describe how much better these new ones are. Jay, on the other hand, has spent many hours in them. I believe he will notice the difference immediately."

We stopped in front of a suit that was waiting for someone to enter. The collar was fully extended and with the life support pack, it stood slightly less than one meter high. Jay climbed in and the suit started to rise up. When it reached Jay's neckline, the collar contracted. It took only a minute. The helmet didn't deploy.

Wallace sounded anxious "How does it feel, Jay?"

"Feels good, sir."

"Walk around a bit."

Jay walked around the workshop and into Wallace's office. "This is incredible, sir. It's effortless."

"Excellent. Now go over to my desk and pick it up."

Jay started to laugh. "Good one, sir."

"I'm not kidding, Jay. Go pick up my desk."

Jay stopped laughing. It was a big desk and weighed a couple of hundred kilos. "I'll try, sir."

He walked to the desk and looked for place to lift it. He moved the chair out from under the desk and squatted down underneath. Then he stood up, and balanced the desk over his head with one hand. "This is unbelievable, sir."

"Thanks, Jay. You can put it down now."

Jay lowered it gently to the floor. He stood there trying to comprehend what he had just done. "Nice suit, sir."

"Thank you, Jay."

I'd never seen anything like it. "How does it work Commander?"

"It might be better if I explained what I wanted to create first. These new suits are designed to prevent injury and death by what has been the one force I haven't been able to conquer up until now. Getting crushed by large, falling or moving objects."

I looked over at Jay. His head was bowed.

"These new suits are the equivalent of being inside a robotic tank. They can withstand several tons of force per square centimeter. They make a man capable of lifting or pushing an object several thousand times his body weight. All this is possible because of a new fabric that's been developed. It becomes rigid when a small electrical current passes through it. When coupled with the movable plate joints located at the hips, shoulders, elbows and knees, and then attached to the glove and shoe portions, which also use plate joint technology, it becomes a computer-controlled system that can literally walk itself back to safety."

I wanted one. "Commander, do you have one for me?"

"Yes, Bella."

0035.0126.1010 LST

I spent the next week designing and renovating my office and apartment. It was a good opportunity to learn how the base staff worked. I made some good impressions with them. I had the monitoring station installed so that I had full benefit of the view overlooking the base. Max made contact and gave me my time line.

♦♦♦

A familiar voice made contact with me using the communication system built into my vest. "Bella, this is DJ."

I was just on my way to my first race session. This was the first time she had called. "DJ, this is Bella."

She sounded as nervous as I felt. "Hi Bella. I'm taking a couple of days off and thought that if you weren't busy we could have coffee or something."

That sounded good to me but I did have plans. "Actually, I'm on my way to learn how to race. Max told me I should be done in three hours."

"Do you know who you're going to be racing with?"

"Not a clue."

"Me."

I lost my voice for a minute.

"Bella, are you still there?"

"Yes, DJ. How about we meet for dinner?"

"I don't date."

"I'm not suggesting a date. Just dinner."

"How about I meet you after you've had dinner. I'll pick you up at your place and I'll take you on a tour of the Earth Dome. I know for a fact that you haven't actually been inside, which I find very strange. It's so beautiful and peaceful."

"Okay, DJ. Pick me up at seventeen hundred."

"Okay. See you then."

As I made my way down to the 'garage', as it was fondly called, I wondered what she looked like.

♦♦♦

Commander Christopher Campbell was the man in charge of designing, building, and maintaining all the transportation used on the Moon. He greeted me as I stepped from the transit car. "Good to finally meet you, Commander. I've been asked to personally, shall we say, tutor you in the fine art of racer design and build."

We shook hands. "Thank you, Commander. Since we are both in Command, maybe we should use our first names. Please call me Bella."

Chris looked at me and said, "If you don't mind, Commander, I would prefer it if you let me address you as Commander. You may call me Chris."

"Maybe someday you will feel comfortable using my first name."

"Maybe, Commander."

I felt a little awkward. "Where do we begin, Chris?"

"The first thing we need to do, Commander, is familiarize you with the racer you will be using. It is the one in which Commander Till won his first race. We have been using it for this purpose ever since. At the time, it was the fastest racer ever designed. Of course, we have topped it since. There are a few features and design standards that all the racers have in common. The cockpit, which you will recognize, and the structures that hold the space drive in place, are the same for all."

"There are certain stress factors that must be built into your design. Certain parts of the course will subject you and your racer to a minimum of nine G's, so both you and your racer must be in good shape. The drive we use is much smaller than the ones you've seen, and not as dangerous. But it is still capable of bringing you within one Mach of escape velocity. The average speed around the course is thirty-two hundred kilometers per hour. The loop and some of the curves require certain speeds to navigate through safely. If Max calculates that you are going too fast or slow through the course, he will compensate. Have you ever watched bobsled competitions?"

"Yes."

"I think that whoever dreamed this up must have really enjoyed that sport."

"Why is that?"

"Because it's the closest sport I can think of to describe what this race is like."

"I'm looking forward to it."

"We all are."

"I want to see the racer I'll be using, Chris."

"Right this way, Commander."

The garage, which was one of the largest facilities on the base, was mainly underground. One of the larger facilities was the Earth Dome, with an area covering seventy-five hectares and reaching a height of one kilometer at its peak. The largest facility was the farm. It was the equivalent of two hundred thousand hectares. It provided enough food for the seventy-five hundred inhabitants of Tranquility, and was a major source of revenue in the form of food exports to Earth.

Chris and I spent two hours reviewing all the features of my racer. He instructed me on how to use Max to help design my own, and filled me in about the race simulator and the centrifuge. The last hour was spent on the racecourse, with Max in control.

"Alright, Commander. How does everything feel?"

I was in the racer with a racing suit on. "Feels good, Chris. You're sure I won't have to do any driving?"

"Yes, Commander. This first run is just to acquaint you with the course and systems. Max will be driving."

No matter what kind of transportation we were in, we always wore a suit, usually with the helmet deployed. The cockpits were capable of pressurization and life support, but these were used most often in cases of emergency. The helmets we used were designed to protect the occupants of the suits, therefore, the system would allow the helmet to be clear only upon request of the wearer and only if it was safe to do so. A system of sensors and micro-cameras located around the collar of the suit projected everything the wearer needed or wanted to see onto the face of the helmet. If someone called another to have a conversation while wearing the suit, the computer, if instructed, would project a small window with the image of the person called inside the display. During the race, because no one can react quickly enough to navigate at over fifty-six hundred kilometers an hour, the system interacted directly with the racer and projects an image, making it appear as though he were traveling much slower.

"Whenever you're ready, Chris."

"Just let Max know you're ready, Commander. That will activate all the systems and you will be on your way. I'll be here when you get back. I remember my first run, Commander...."

"And?"

"I didn't get sick."

"Have you won any races, Chris?"

"A handful, Commander."

"Good. Max, let's do it."

The racer rose a few centimeters and I felt a floating sensation. The cockpit closed and my helmet deployed. Everything I saw when my helmet was down was projected in such a way as to have me believe that it didn't deploy. I hadn't experienced anything as sophisticated on Earth.

"Chris, this Bella."

"Yes, Commander. Everything alright?"

"Yes. I was just wondering if the technology that drives the imaging system of the helmet is available on Earth."

"Certain versions of it, Commander. We haven't released all of it yet."

"Thanks, Chris. See you in an hour."

Just before I entered the airlock, I saw another message projected right in front of me:

H seventy six-S twelve-W fifty-four. "Computer, H seventy six-S twelve-W fifty four."

That was the fourth message I had seen. I had begun to store them in a personal section of my computer records.

Max communicated with me. "Commander..."

"Yes, Max."

"As you go through the run, you have the option of having me explain the course and the displays you see in front of you."

"I'd like you along for the ride, Max."

"Does that mean I'm to remain activated?"

"Yes, Max."

I didn't feel the platform rise to the surface. I was aware only that I had been moving, when the door to the airlock opened.

♦♦♦

There are thousands of kilometers of roads on the surface of the Moon. Several paving machines work twenty-four hours a day on the base. They are remotely controlled and guided by our network of guidance satellites. The racecourse and the centrifuge are located outside the base limits, where the gravity is moon normal.

Max began his initiation. "We are coming up to the beginning of the course, Commander. I will take you around once. The race is three laps. The fastest part of the race is the straightaway, which is eight hundred kilometers long. Speeds up to six thousand four hundred kilometers an hour can be attained. To you, it will only appear as one thousand six hundred kilometers an hour. The straightaway is not divided, and there have been times during aggressive racing where two racers have made contact and control of the racers lost. There are built-in safety features that will activate if I calculate that the driver cannot regain control of the racer. There have been times when that feature has caused certain drivers to ask that I be deactivated."

That made me laugh. "That's funny, Max."

"What is funny, Commander?"

That made me laugh even more. "Nothing Max. Please continue."

I felt a gentle push from the drive and was on my way to the starting line of the track. I assumed that because the racer rode on a cushion of gas, the ride would be smooth, but it wasn't. That was the trick to the whole race. The slightest bump could cause the racer to deviate in any number of ways, and it was the driver's job to keep it in line. As I approached the starting line, the heads-up display of my helmet activated.

Max continued. "As you can see, Commander, all the information you need is projected in front of you. The bottom right indicates your actual speed in kilometers per second. Escape velocity is two point three eight km/sec. That number will always be displayed under your actual speed. The bottom left is the amount of fuel you have used displayed in minutes."

"You will see a divided line projected on your display. It will look very much like the lines used on the highways of Earth, the difference being that it is your job to keep that line centered in the middle of your display. It is your focus. If you stray from the line, you will have to adjust accordingly. During this run, the line will remain in the center of your display at all times. Any questions?"

"Is that all the information that is displayed?"

"No. As you approach different turns and the loop, the minimum speed you need to be traveling will be projected above your actual speed. I have been programmed to take control if a driver is going to fast or slow."

"So I've been told, Max." We came to a stop. "How do we know when to start?"

"I count down from five and then say 'begin'."

"How about I count down from five and say 'begin' when I'm ready to go?"

"Whenever you are ready, Commander."

I sat for a few minutes and absorbed my surroundings. I placed my hands on the control sticks, counted down from five and said 'begin.'

The force of the acceleration took me by surprise and I watched the speed indicator go from zero to one point seven five km/sec in less than a minute. It took less than seven minutes to finish the straightaway. I decelerated and entered a sweeping S curve three hundred and twenty-kilometer long. The line never left the center of my display. I felt like I was speeding down an unpaved country road. The G forces pinned me to my seat.

I exited the S curve and came out on a short straightaway that went downhill through a tunnel and into the side of a three-hundred and forty degree, three-hundred kilometer long curve carved into the side of a crater. The racer hugged the side of the track at one km/sec. I leveled off for about ten seconds and went straight into the side of the crater. My display indicated the loop was next. It was carved inside one of the mountains that surrounded the crater. The racer decelerated to point seventy-five km/sec, and as I went through, I thought for sure I was going to pass out. I shot out of the loop onto surface track and immediately went through a vicious right-hand curve.

I accelerated and went racing through a four-hundred and eighty kilometer long S curve that put me on the six-hundred and forty kilometer long back stretch that twisted and turned in a way that would not allow full throttle acceleration. The final curve was a hairpin that was not banked. It required that I decelerate to a few kilometers an hour. The tracks then merged, and I found myself back at the start line exactly one hour after I left. I sat in the cockpit and the word 'jellyfish' popped into my mind.

"Commander Carrera." It was Max.

My mind was reeling. "Yes, Max."

"I'll be driving you back to the garage now."

I wasn't in any shape to make a decision. "Good, Max. Let's go." I knew that if I had been asked, I wouldn't have been able to stand up right at that moment.

It didn't take long to get back to the garage, but during the ride I kept wondering how it was possible for anyone to navigate the course.

Commander Campbell was waiting for me. "Welcome back, Commander. How was the ride?"

I remembered how Chris had felt. "I didn't get sick, Chris."

Chris blinked. "Thank you, Commander. Can I give you a hand?"

"That would be appreciated, Chris."

I managed to make it back to my office on my own.

Eight: DJ

0035.0126.1700 LST

"Hi, Bella. This is DJ."

Seventeen hundred. Right on time. I had arrived home an hour earlier and was just beginning to relax. I glanced at her image in the door monitor. "Please come in, DJ."

"Thank you, Bella."

This woman who stood before me had spent two years of her life piecing together the evidence that freed me. She was quite simply… stunning.

"I am at a loss for words, DJ. I am most grateful for the work you did. It quite literally saved my life."

"You're welcome, Bella. It was my pleasure." She looked embarrassed. "It was fun."

I understood that. I wanted to hug her but I didn't. Instead, I put my hands in my pockets. "So, how's the dome today?"

"I hear the weather's fine. Are you still up to it after your run?"

"I'm not as shaky as I thought I would be. I think the dome would settle me right down."

She smiled. "I think you're right. Shall we?"

I smiled back. "Let's do it."

She reached into one of her vest pockets and took out a small but exquisite crystal. Once again, the lights mesmerized me and then went out. DJ smiled again and put it back in her pocket. "In the eyes of God, Bella. You will understand."

I was looking at my feet. "I believe you." I then looked into her eyes. "We need to go to the dome."

"You're right. Do you know how to get there?"

"Yes."

"I will follow you."

It takes ten minutes to reach the dome from practically anywhere on the base. There are several different entry points. There was a specific part of the dome that DJ wanted to visit.

♦♦♦

"This is the rainforest, Bella. I find it the most fascinating. Whenever I visit, it seems there's always something new."

We were walking down one of the pathways, and as we did, a faint remembrance of my encounter with Cee invaded my thoughts. There really were some strange plants in this area.

"DJ, do you know where any of these plants came from?"

"I've never asked, Bella. I like computers and software." She stopped and looked around. She closed her eyes for a few seconds before opening them again and pointed to her left. "If you'd like to know more about the dome, then he's the man to see. Maybe he will talk to you."

"I don't see anyone, DJ."

"You will."

A few seconds later, a thin man with a long white beard and long white hair stepped out onto the path. "Who is he?"

"He tends the garden, so to speak. I've never heard him talk to anyone."

"He hasn't spoken to you?"

"No."

"What does he do?"

"He just looks into my eyes and smiles at me."

"That seems very odd, DJ."

She was smiling. "I think so."

"What's his name?"

"Samson."

I walked up to him. "Hello, Samson. I'm Commander Carrera."

Samson put his hands together and bowed a little.

"I understand that you don't talk much."

He nodded his head.

"Then how do you communicate when someone calls you?"

He pulled a small palm-sized device out of his vest and started moving his fingers across it. Out of my vest speakers I heard, "With this."

"Are you unable to speak?" I watched as he worked the device again.

"I choose not to. Is there something the Commander needs me to do?"

I thought about that for a few seconds. "No Samson. I'm pleased to have met you. We will probably see each other again in the near future."

"No doubt, Commander. Thank you."

Then he looked into my eyes and I saw infinity.

♦♦♦

"Bella!" It was DJ.

"Yes?"

"You okay?"

"Yes. Why?"

"You've been standing here staring into space for about a minute now."

"Really?"

"Really. What did he do?"

"He looked into my eyes."

"What did you see?"

"Infinity."

"Wow! So now what?"

"I'd like to see more of the dome."

"Let's do it."

We spent the rest of the day and several of the early evening hours exploring the rainforest. Many questions were unasked and many went unanswered.

♦♦♦

I discovered that DJ had similar experiences with the broadcast communities where she lived on Earth. Those experiences had compelled her to become a broadcaster. DJ and I had many things in common. She suggested I might try my hand behind the microphone. I made no commitment. I suggested we go for dinner and she didn't object. We said goodbye at the transit stop. Her living quarters were situated close to her work.

When I got home, it was close to midnight and I was to meet with Jay in the morning. When my head hit the pillow, the clock read twenty three hundred hours and fifty minutes.

Nine: Bad Plants

0035.0126.2350 LST

I lay restlessly in my bed, trying to fall asleep, but my mind wouldn't relax. I decided I would get up, activate my monitoring station and watch what went on at the base during the night.

I opened my eyes and was surprised to find myself in the same surroundings as when I first met Cee. It felt very different. A part of me knew I would not find Cee here. I got up and started to look around. Although I had seen this place before, it felt unfamiliar.

As I started down one of the pathways, I felt compelled to be cautious. As I walked, I examined all the plants. I recognized none of them. I walked up to a tree. The type of fruit growing on it reminded me of a peach, my favorite fruit. But there were no ripe ones.

I walked for a long time, trying to find something that looked familiar. Nothing did. I sat down a few meters off the path and rested my back against a boulder. I closed my eyes and heard only silence. I felt my heart pounding in my chest and started to take deep breaths to calm myself. As I did, something activated my sense of smell. It was very faint, but its very presence overrode everything else. I felt motivated to find the source of it.

I sat for a few more minutes and then got up to go hunting. The path I was on gradually became more difficult to navigate. The further I went, the more powerful the aroma became. At some point, the pathway disappeared. My hands, arms and body were being brutalized by thick plant growth as I struggled to go forward. I had to find the source of the aroma. I knew I was going in the right direction. I wanted a machete to make things easier.

I finally broke through the vegetation. In front of me was the source of the aroma, which by this time had completely taken control of me. It was a plant. It stood alone. There wasn't any other plant growth within a two to three meter radius surrounding it. That should have been warning enough, but I was totally consumed with the hunt. I moved toward the plant. It began to pulsate like a heartbeat. The pulsating became stronger as I moved closer. The trunk was coiled and twisted like a deformed spring. I walked around it. It was three meters tall and devoid of branches and leaves. One perfectly round, white, translucent fruit approximately one meter in diameter hung at the end of the trunk. This was the origin of the aroma.

As I walked towards it, it became slightly illuminated. I was standing an arm's length from the fruit. I just had to touch it. I reached out and placed my hand on its skin. It was warm to the touch and smooth like glass. I could not bring myself to remove my hand. Through my hand, I felt a substance from the fruit invade my body. It felt good. I became euphoric. I felt no pain. I put my other hand on the fruit and started to pull it off the plant. A long, slender, barbed, needle-like stem held it there. I kept pulling and the plant shuddered. The stem went down deep into the flesh of the fruit. As I pulled it off, I became ecstatic. My hunt had been successful.

I wondered what the fruit tasted like. I began to back away from the plant, imagining the taste. Just as I was about to turn and go back into the vegetation, it struck. Like lightning, the stem went through the fruit and through me just to the left of my heart. The stem snagged me with its barbs, and as the plant snapped back to its original shape, it took me with it.

I found myself hanging two and a half meters over the base of the plant with its stem skewered through me. After a few agonizing minutes, I started to slide down the stem and I was dropped. I landed on my back, the impact almost knocking me out. I still had the fruit in my hands.

I looked at where the stem had gone through me and I saw no blood, but I was starting to feel pain. Soon, great waves of pain began to course through my body. I felt myself needing to taste the fruit. I took a bite and the pain went away.

I woke up screaming.

Ten: Alien Encounter

0035.0127.0645 LST

It was still early when I got out of bed. I hadn't had a nightmare like that for quite a long time, and I wondered if it meant I was going to be ill. It would be two hours before Jay arrived, so I spent some extra time in the shower and made myself a good breakfast.

Jay arrived at nine hundred hours. "Good morning, Bella. You're looking well today."

I smiled. "I'm well, Jay. Still getting over the racer."

"Ah, the race. I recommend spending as much time as you can in the centrifuge. The simulator is good, but the centrifuge will better prepare you physically. Of course, there's nothing like practicing on the track."

"Are we limited as to the amount of time we can book the track?"

"First come, first served, Bella."

That sounded good to me. "So what are the plans for today?"

"We're going to my lab. Remember I said I'd be showing you what we found?"

"Yes."

"Well, today is the day. And what we found is located outside the base in moon normal gravity. You will understand when you see it. You'll need your suit."

"Where's yours?"

"In the transport. You can put yours on now. I'll put mine on when we get to the transport."

That made sense. I wasn't about to carry it.

Once again, I was feeling angry. Only this time I knew it was because I was out of control. The race weighed heavily on my mind. I'm not one who likes to lose.

I put my suit on and met Jay at the front door. "All I can think about, Jay, is not looking like a completely incompetent fool when it comes time to race. Do you know who I'm racing with?"

"I haven't even checked to see who I'm racing with."

"DJ."

Jay grimaced. "Ouch!"

"No kidding."

"Bella, I remember how I felt after my first race."

"And how was that?"

"Like I would never win."

That was exactly what was bugging me. "That's what I'm feeling, Jay. Thanks."

"No problem. Let's go."

Jay seemed anxious as we lifted off in the transport. "My lab is located on the dark side of the Moon, Bella. That's what I call the side that doesn't face the Earth. It will take fifteen minutes to get there. I would appreciate your refraining from asking questions until we arrive. Everything is quite self-explanatory."

"No problem, Jay. I've got a lot of things on my mind. I'll just watch you pilot this transport."

The ship was designed to transport Jay's power station prototypes wherever he needed to take them. Many of them took up the entire cargo area. We landed on a pad close to the labs surface building. It was a small building, about five hundred square meters. Most of the lab is underground.

As I stood up to leave the transport, I immediately noticed the difference in gravity. It surprised me. "Jay."

"Yes, Bella."

"I'd like to walk on the Moon."

Jay started to laugh. "Okay, Bella. Follow me."

We were on the landing pad, so when Jay stepped out of the transport and headed off onto the surface, I followed. The ground was soft and we sank a few centimeters into it, but because of the suits, no extra effort was needed to move through it. We walked about one hundred meters, stopped and turned around. There, bathed in the light from the lab, was the transport. The effect reminded me of a solar eclipse.

"Bella, I'm going to ask the computer to see if there's anything behind the lab. This will give you an idea of how the helmet works."

Slowly the light started changing. The transport and lab became less visible, illuminated only from the lights located on the back of the lab. Soon, a tower became visible. My mouth went dry. "What's that, Jay?"

"It's a tower very similar to one on the base, Bella. The dimensions are a little different, but these and the others have two things in common: each has nine sides, and the dimensions of each tower are based on the number 'three'."

"*Others*? How many others are there, Jay?"

"We've found seven hundred and forty-five."

"What????" I lost my mind for a few moments.

"Calm down, Bella."

"I can do that… give me a minute." That seemed like a lot. "You said 'so far'. How many more do you think there are?"

"Don't know. They are difficult to find. We aren't speculating on how many. Some are harder to locate than others."

I had to move. "Can we start walking back to your lab, Jay?" My helmet returned to normal.

"Let's go, Bella."

It seemed like a long walk back. We entered the airlock, stepped into Jay's lab and took off our suits.

"The lab is quite basic, Bella. Would you like a tour?"

The building we were in was designed as a lounge area, and had all the amenities. In the middle of it all were the elevators. "How big is it, Jay?"

"I have several levels, each one designated for different tasks. It's several thousand square meters. I don't know if you'd find it interesting."

"I'll pass on a tour, Jay. Let's go see what we've found here."

Jay took us down to the fourteenth level. "Only you, Commander Till and I, have access to this level Bella. This entire complex was designed to house and protect what we found. What we found is something extremely difficult to transport and we keep temperatures approaching absolute zero to prevent a reaction. If you'll follow me, I'll take you to the lab."

We went through a series of doors. Jay identified himself at each one.

"It seems like excessive security, Jay."

"Maybe so, but it was your book that indicated the need." That shut me up.

We passed the last security check and entered the lab. On the far wall was a window ten meters across and seven meters high. Both the left and right-hand walls were filled with computers. We walked towards the window and Jay instructed the computer to illuminate the room behind the window. A blue light filled the room. Jay asked the computer to bring out one of the objects.

"This glass is two meters thick, Bella. The lights we are using do not generate any heat. I call it the blue room."

♦♦♦

Doors surrounded the blue room, behind which were several thousand of the objects. Each object was three meters in diameter and had its own transport.

I tried to describe it. "It looks like a huge round piece of leaded glass sculpture, Jay."

"Yes it does, Bella, but it isn't. Each one of these objects weighs nine million kilos in moon normal gravity. The surface looks smooth, but it's not. When we found the first one, we lost a man who had run his hands over the surface. It ripped the fabric of his suit like it was made of tissue. We didn't get to him in time."

I swallowed.

Jay continued, "We have a series of tunnels that enable us to bring the objects down. We then place them in one of the rooms. All the objects we have found have been located on the dark side. We believe that is because whoever created them did not want us to know they were here."

"I have a record of what happened when we tried to transport the first one we found to the base. It was recorded by one of our satellites." We moved over to one of the monitors and Jay asked the computer to access the record. The screen lit up, and I had a bird's eye view of the transport moving slowly across the Moon surface. It was just starting to cross into sunlight. "Bella, I'm going to zoom in on the object." The object filled the screen. "Watch the center of the object, Bella."

After a few seconds, I started to see the interior of the object light up. It gradually became more intense and began to grow in size. The image pulled back to include the transport and the dozen men who were operating it, stopped. They all disembarked and surrounded the object.

A voice came on the air. "Command, do you see what this thing is doing?" There was a hint of anxiety in his voice.

A different voice responded. "We see it. Stand by."

The satellite image pulled back some more. The intensity of the light from the interior of the object was growing rapidly. The men were starting to back away.

"Command, we believe we are in danger. Please advise."

"Release the object from the transport and get out!!"

The men returned to the transport and disengaged the crew cockpit. As they did, an intensely focused beam not unlike a laser shot out from the object and into space. The men were now a kilometer away. The intensity of the light grew and I started to feel the same way I did when I first saw the Space Drive. I felt it was going to explode and feared that the men were not far enough away from it. Within seconds, my fears were viciously justified as the object disappeared with a blinding flash of light that filled the screen. I had to look away to protect my eyes. When I looked back at the screen, all I saw was a crater. Readings on the monitor showed that it was exactly three kilometers across and one point five kilometers deep. I was unable to speak.

Jay broke the silence. "We lost twelve good men, Bella. There was no heat generated in the explosion. The power crystal just disappeared. All the material that used to be where that crater is… just disappeared."

I backed away from the screen and looked over at the thing in the blue room. I blurted out, "Son of a bitch!!" Out of the corner of my eye I saw that Jay was about to say something. I put my hand up and he stopped. I took a few minutes to gather my thoughts and then asked, "What have you done, Jay?"

Jay hesitated. "What do you mean, what I have I done?"

He was on the defensive. "You've done something, Jay. Something with those objects we've found."

"How do you know?"

"I can't explain how I know. Chalk it up to experience."

"Well, I made one of them into a weapon."

"A weapon?"

"Well, I think it's a weapon. I haven't tried it yet."

"Okay. Why not?"

"Because I'm still trying to figure out why both the computer and the software I designed to fabricate the weapon stopped working the instant the work was done."

"What exactly do you mean by 'stopped working'?"

"I designed a machining device that used ultrasound to carve a specific design out of one of the objects."

"Go on."

Jay continued. "I believe the reason there was an explosion was that the energy that caused that beam of light was not being dispersed fast enough, and the energy being absorbed was not controlled."

"I have created a design for what I call the power crystals, that may allow for a faster dispersion of energy. I also designed a mechanism to control how much energy is absorbed. So far, I have not been able create more than one. I've tried rebuilding, redesigning and reprogramming. Something is not allowing more than one of them to exist."

I was shaking my head. "That's the strangest thing I've heard since I arrived here."

"It's true."

"I believe you." I had some questions. "May I see it?"

"Sure, Bella."

Jay requested that his creation be brought out. Slowly, a transport came into view and stopped in the middle of the room. It was beautiful. Except for a few extra cuts, it looked very much like a diamond balancing on its side. I was amazed at the precision that was needed to have something balance like that.

"You'll notice, Bella, that it has nine sides. I was able to find the exact spot where the beam comes out of the power crystals. They're all identical and absorb X-rays without an adverse reaction. I was able to take pictures of the interior structure. If you step over to this monitor, you'll be able to see what it looks like."

The monitor lit up and I saw a complex crystalline structure inside. There was a nine-sided outermost ring plainly visible. "Do you think that maybe these power crystals, as you call them, and the towers you've found are designed to work together?"

"I believe that's accurate."

"Maybe we should found out."

"How do you propose we do that?"

"Let's try the weapon."

"On what?"

"On one of the towers."

Jay stopped for a second. "What do you think will happen?"

"I don't know. We might disappear in a blinding flash of light if your weapon doesn't work. Or we might put a hole in one of the towers. Or maybe something else will happen. Have you got anything better to do today?"

"No."

"Then let's do it."

"It will take me a couple of hours to mount the weapon on the transport and check all the systems."

"Okay. Did you make a visual record of how you created that object?"

"Yes."

"How long did it take?"

"A few hours."

"I'll watch that while you prepare."

"Okay, Bella."

◆◆◆

It took Jay exactly two hours to prepare. In that time, I learned how the object was made. The record itself was quite boring, but it was fascinating to watch the ultrasonic device that Jay invented slowly carve the shape out of the impossibly dense material that made up the alien power crystal. It consisted of a ring four meters in diameter, which was surrounded by ultrasonic transmitters that were able to rotate three hundred and sixty degrees in the blink of an eye. I watched in fast forward as the ring moved over the crystal. The fact that something was preventing us from making more was just a little disturbing.

Jay came back in the room… "We're ready to go, Bella. I don't intend to disappear in a blinding flash of light. We'll be two kilometers away from the device."

"Think that's far enough away?"

"Are you questioning my expertise?"

I found myself on thin ice. "Sorry, Jay. I do find it a little disturbing that we only have the one."

"So do I."

"I place myself in your more than capable hands, Jay. I'm ready to go."

"Let's do it." We were about to leave the room.

"Bella, this is Commander Till."

"Yes, Commander. Bella here."

"I understand you're about to try out our weapon."

"That's correct, Commander."

"We've programmed one of our surveillance satellites to record the event."

"Do you have any thoughts as to why we can only make one, Commander?"

"God knows, Bella."

"Thank you, Commander."

♦♦♦

We put on our suits and walked onto the landing pad.

"Bella, the transport we will be using is a ground unit. The cockpit is capable of flight if we need to get back to the base in a hurry. Our target is located in a sunny spot an hour from here. Once we arrive, I will lock the weapon on target and arm it. I will control it from our perch. The one uncertainty we are dealing with is not whether or not I can stop the power crystal from exploding, but how long the beam will be active. Once there is enough energy built up in the power crystal and the beam is active, I will stop the flow of energy into it. I don't know what's going to happen after that."

"Are you a little excited, Jay?"

"Not a little, Bella. Here's the transport."

The transport was hooked into the satellite guidance system and stopped before us as if awaiting some secret command. Both doors opened and the cockpit slowly lowered. Jay and I climbed in.

"Bella, I won't be pressurizing. We have on-board life support, so use this connection to activate." He showed me the umbilical cord attached to my seat and I plugged it into my suit. "I'll try to explain how everything works during our trip out, so when you see it in operation you'll know what you're observing."

"Sounds good, Jay."

♦♦♦

We were moving at the unremarkable speed of twenty kilometers an hour on one of the more recently paved roads.

"The entire assembly we are transporting is designed for the weapon. It is mounted in a ring that is attached to a system that enables the weapon to pivot and rotate in any direction. One third of the power crystal is designed to absorb infrared energy. The interior is designed to contain the energy and compresses it. The other third is designed to focus and further compress the beam. I have designed a simple system that enables me to control the reaction by covering and uncovering the section of the power crystal that absorbs the energy. All the absorbed energy eventually dissipates."

"Bella, I know these power crystals were not designed so I could make weapons, but what's done is done. I believe they were designed to store and release energy like a battery. We have yet to discover what they were designed to power."

"Maybe we will learn more about them today."

"One way or another, we will learn something."

I couldn't argue with that. I made a call. "DJ, this is Bella."

"Yes, Bella. This is DJ. How are you today."

"I'm well, DJ. Are you on the air at the moment?"

"I will be soon."

"One of our surveillance satellites will be recording today. In the interest of base security, I ask that you not broadcast what you see. Actually, that's an order."

"Thanks, Bella. DJ out."

I was now starting to take command of the base. The part of me that was missing was starting to return. But, because people I didn't yet know surrounded me, I still felt alone. I remembered that feeling.

♦ ♦ ♦

The tower stood two hundred and forty-three meters tall in a flat plain that was surrounded by foothills. We dropped the power crystal half a kilometer away from the tower and parked the cockpit on the crest of a foothill two kilometers away from the assembly.

I was a little anxious. "Nervous, Jay?"

"A little, Bella."

"Maybe we should test fire it before we take a shot at the tower."

"Bella, there's nothing else to shoot at."

I surveyed our location. "You're right. Alright, so now what?"

"I'm going to bring the power crystal out of the transport and check to make sure all the systems are working properly."

"How are you going to aim it?"

"The mechanism has a system of cameras that will feed through to my heads-up display. When I've locked onto the place I'm going to shoot, I give the order to fire."

"Sounds good. Can you feed the same information through my display?

"Absolutely."

Jay spent a few minutes giving commands to the computer. The transport opened its cargo bay. It split down the middle and the casing that held the power crystal rose up and cleared the transport.

Jay linked up our displays and he zoomed in on the assembly. "Everything looks fine, Bella. The computer is saying that everything is working as designed. I'm going to expose the front two-thirds of the power crystal. Please say something if you see any indication that energy is being absorbed."

"Okay, Jay."

The housing for the power crystal was cylindrical in shape and designed to keep the crystal near absolute zero. The front two-thirds of the casing disappeared and the needle-sharp business end of the power crystal was exposed. It gleamed in the sunlight, but didn't appear to be absorbing any radiation.

"Looks good to me, Jay."

"Everything looks good, Bella. The power crystal is stable." We watched for a while longer just to make sure. "I'm activating the aiming and firing controls, Bella. You'll see what I'm seeing. Once I've got my target locked, I'll expose the remaining part of the power crystal."

My heads-up display activated and the image shifted to the tower as seen through the cameras around the central ring of the weapon. The tower was featureless, and I wondered if Jay could see something I couldn't. A small bull's eye appeared on the side of the tower.

"I'm locked on, Bella. As soon as the beam hits the tower, I'm going to turn off the aiming display. I want to see everything that happens."

"I think it would be best if my targeting display was turned off now. I think someone needs to watch the crystal power up."

"I think your right, Bella. I'll switch you back now."

I was back to having a full view of the area. I waited for Jay to give the order to fire. It took only a few seconds.

"Computer, initiate firing sequence."

The instant he gave the order, the remaining third of the crystal was exposed. I asked my computer for infrared detection, and almost immediately I could see that the power crystal was absorbing radiation. "It's going, Jay. And fast."

"Okay, Bella."

The interior of the power crystal lit up and became more intense as the seconds went by. Images of men trying to outrun the explosion I'd seen flashed through my memory. I again asked my computer to switch back to my normal display. The intensity of the light increased to the point where I wanted to shut it down.

"How's it looking, Bella?"

"It's starting to scare me, Jay."

"Anytime now, Bella."

Just as he spoke, the beam activated. I heard him say, "Bulls eye." The casing returned to cover the back third of the power crystal.

All the energy that had built up in the power crystal was focused into an intense beam. It hit the tower, and both the beam and the energies that had built up in the crystal were absorbed almost instantly. By the time Jay had switched back to watch the show, there was nothing to see.

"What happened? Where's the beam?"

"The tower absorbed it. Anything on the tower that indicates it was hit?"

"Let me check."

I waited a few moments.

"Nothing, Bella. I want to see what happened. I'm going to replay what you saw through my display."

"Okay, Jay." I waited for Jay to review the record.

"Jesus, Bella."

"What, Jay?"

"It works!"

"What about the tower, Jay? How do we get in?"

"We could try exposing the tower to a longer burst from the power crystal."

"I get the feeling that the tower will absorb anything we throw at it."

"You're probably right. But this is the perfect time to see how long we can generate a beam."

"What are you saying?"

"I'm saying that I don't know if the power crystal will explode if we keep feeding it what it needs to generate the beam."

"It sounds like you just said you're willing to sacrifice the power crystal."

"I am."

"The tower is inside the blast radius."

"Yes, it is."

"Let's do it."

We really didn't know what to expect. Jay gave the order to fire, and the power crystal started to absorb infrared radiation. It took exactly the same amount of time for the power crystal to start generating its beam.

♦♦♦

"The tower is absorbing it, Bella."

"I'm not too surprised, Jay. How's the stability of the power crystal?"

"It's balanced. The amount of energy going in is the same as what's going out."

"Is that because of the tower?"

"I don't know, Bella. But the power crystal is not in any danger of exploding."

"Any effect on the tower?"

"Not that I can see. Now what?" We left the beam active for five minutes and it didn't look like we were going to blast our way into it.

"Jay, will you switch my display so I can see the beam hitting the tower?"

"Do you have a feeling, Bella?"

"A feeling? No. I just want to see it." Jay switched my display. I expected to see the beam disappearing into the tower. "Jay, are you and I looking at the same thing?"

"Just a second, Bella. We are now."

"Do you see what I see?"

"Holy…"

The tower was starting to glow where the beam was striking it. We watched for a few minutes as small thread-like lines of energy moved up and around the circumference of the tower.

"What do you suppose is going to happen when the energy field completes its way around the tower, Bella?"

I was excited. "How am I supposed to know?"

"Calm down, Bella."

"I'm sorry. How's the power crystal?"

"It's fine. Should I disengage?"

"Not yet. I want to keep feeding the tower for a few more minutes."

We watched the tower. The energy field was continuing to move up and around it.

"I'm going to speculate about what's going to happen, Jay."

"I'm all ears, Bella."

"When the energy field completes its way around the tower, I think it will join the other lines of energy moving up the tower. When it reaches the top, I suspect it will shoot out the top of the tower until all the energy is gone."

"That's quite a theory, Bella."

"Just watch, Jay."

The energy field completed its journey around the tower. When both sides connected, more small, thread-like lines of energy began moving up the tower.

"There, Jay. See that?"

"I see it, but I don't believe it. How did you come up with that theory?"

"It's the way we design all buildings, Jay. Carrying loads are dispersed throughout the building. I just thought these towers might do the same with energy. I think we should shut down the power crystal now."

Jay shut down the power crystal and we watched as the energy slowly made its way to the top of the tower. The effect was quite psychedelic. "It's nearing the top, Bella."

"I see that, Jay."

"Do you see what's happening?"

The energy was starting to accumulate at the top, but it was also beginning to break up and accumulate in equal quantities in the central part of each of the nine sides of the tower.

Jay concluded. "It doesn't look like it's going dissipate out the top of the tower Bella."

"No, it doesn't. It looks like we're going to have nine separate beams."

We watched as the energy finished accumulating and as it did, nine beams of energy shot into space until there were no more left.

I immediately received a call. "Commander Carrera…"

"Commander Carrera, here. Who's this?"

"This is Commander Irvine, sir. Satellite Central Command."

"Yes, Commander. Is there a problem?"

He sounded upset. "Not if you consider losing a satellite a problem."

"What do mean, losing a satellite?"

"I mean, Commander Carrera, that when the tower shot off those beams into space, one of our satellites was in the way."

I tried to calm him down. "Was it an important satellite?"

"Not really."

"So what happened?"

Commander Irvine controlled his voice. "It disappeared, sir. Just vanished. It's gone."

"Was the beam larger than the satellite?"

"It was."

"I don't know what to say, Commander Irvine. We're dealing with unknowns here."

"I understand, sir. I just thought you should know."

"Thank you, Commander. I'll be in touch."

"Thank you, sir."

I waited a few moments and then relayed what happened to Commander Brodie. I asked the computer for a visual. "Jay…" A small window appeared in my display with Jay's image.

"Yes, Bella."

"One of those beams hit one of our satellites."

He looked concerned. "Really? What happened?"

"It disappeared. Vanished. It's gone."

He now looked amazed. "Wow."

"Wow? That's all you have to say?"

"Yes."

"We should head back now, Jay."

"Okay, Bella."

We climbed into the cockpit of the transport and drove silently toward the weapon assembly. Jay hooked us up to the assembly and we drove toward the tower. Because of the size of the transport and the width of the road, we had to drive around the tower to get back to the lab. The base of this tower was eighty-one meters at its widest point.

"Jay, stop the transport!"

"What… what's wrong?" The transport stopped.

I couldn't talk. I pointed to my left toward the tower.

Jay looked over his shoulder and saw it. The tower was open.

♦ ♦ ♦

We both knew instantly that the proximity of the power crystal had caused the tower to open. And although I didn't ask, I was sure Jay wondered why he hadn't thought of that before. "Bella, do you know how much time I've spent trying to figure out how to get into these things?"

"I know, Jay. So, I guess we should look inside."

"I agree." The cab lowered and we stepped onto the ring road surrounding the tower. Jay cautioned me. "Don't touch the tower with your suit. It only *looks* smooth."

The opening in the tower was twenty-seven meters across and twenty-seven meters high. As we stepped through, I noticed the thickness of the walls. The computer measured them at three microns. The interior was illuminated. "Where's the light source coming from, Jay?"

Jay looked around the tower. "The Sun, Bella."

The floor was smooth. The interior was empty and immaculate. We started walking towards the center. I looked up as far as I could see. I could not see to the top.

As we neared the center, we saw something. "What is it, Jay?"

"Looks like a depression of some sort."

Walking closer we saw a perfectly round depression two meters across and one meter deep. We stood for a minute examining the depression and Jay said… "I think that's where the power crystals go, Bella"

"That makes sense."

As I finished my sentence, we felt something move. "What was that?"

Jay was looking around. "We're moving, Bella. We're moving up." We were on a nine-sided platform twenty-seven meters across, moving up the tower. Jay blurted out, "We must have activated something."

"No kidding, Jay!"

We stopped nine meters from the top of the tower, which was sealed with a dome structure. The tower had tapered to twenty-seven meters across. The platform fit seamlessly.

"Now what, Bella?"

"We wait. I think this is a timed affair." Without warning, the dome opened. "Hang on, Jay."

A nine-sided six-meter section of the floor started to rise. We cleared the top of the tower by three meters. The view was unreal.

"Bella, this is Commander Till.

"Commander Till, this is Bella."

"What do you guys think you're doing?"

"I… I don't know Commander. Looks like we've figured out where the power crystals go."

"I want you guys back at the base."

"We'll be there as soon as we can, Commander."

"Careful, Bella."

"Thanks, Commander. Jay, Commander Till just called."

"And?"

"He wants us back at the base."

The platform started to descend. We were back on the ground in a few minutes.

Eleven: The Centrifuge

0035.0128.1115 LST

When we arrived at the base, Commander Till informed us that while we were in the Tower, we were completely cut off from Tranquility. He strongly suggested that Jay and I take a week off. I didn't argue. Before I turned in for the night, I arranged to use the centrifuge and made time to design my racer. I was looking forward to mastering the race.

As I drifted off to sleep, I was not expecting an encounter with Cee.

"Hello, Bella."

I opened my eyes and found myself in a familiar location. "Hello, Cee."

"You've had quite a day."

I stood up. "It was quite a day."

"Would you walk with me?"

"Are we going anywhere in particular?"

"No. Just a walk"

"Sure. Let's go."

We started down one of the pathways and walked for a few minutes. I felt the urge to take her hand or put my arm around her. She stopped walking and asked. "Do you smell that, Bella?"

I took a deep breath. It was the same aroma as the one in my nightmare. "Yes I do, Cee. I recognize it. It belongs to a plant that kills."

"It's very powerful, Bella. It still has the power to trap you if you arrive back here and are weak."

"And how would that happen?"

"I can't tell you. Walk with me." We walked for a few more minutes. "Do you recognize that tree, Bella?"

"Yes." It was the peach tree. The fruit was ripe.

"If you find yourself overpowered by the plant, pick the ripest fruit off this tree. It will restore your strength. It is like an antidote."

I found myself wanting to hunt down the source of the aroma. "I believe I need one already. Does it affect you?"

"No, Bella. This is just for you."

My mind was starting to become foggy. I walked toward the tree and looked for the ripest fruit. I saw a deep orange-red fruit with beads of moisture clinging to its skin. I reached up and pulled it from the tree. I inhaled deeply and smelled the sweetness of it. I took a bite. It was cool and the flesh was firm. Juice ran down the sides of my mouth and my tongue came alive. As I swallowed, I felt myself regaining control my body and my head started to clear. I finished the rest of it. It tasted good.

I heard Cee's voice behind me. "Remember this, Bella."

I turned to look for her and found myself in my bed. It was time to get up.

0035.0129.0630 LST

"Commander Carrera, this is Chris."

This was the third day of my time off. "Yes, Chris. How's our schedule?"

"Looks good, Commander. I'll be by to pick you up in fifteen minutes."

"Thanks, Chris."

I had scheduled this day for my first use of the centrifuge. Chris was the man in charge of the facility, so I asked him to show me how it worked. He arrived at my door right on time.

"Good morning, Commander."

"Morning, Chris. How are you this morning?"

"Fine, sir. I'm looking forward to showing you the centrifuge."

"I'm looking forward to seeing it, Chris. Shall we?"

We headed down to the transit stop and got into the car. As we did, Chris asked, "How much do you know about the centrifuge, Commander?"

"Not very much. I was tempted look it up on the computer, but I thought it might be more interesting going in blind."

"I see. Well, I'll start by telling you that it is located outside the base in moon normal gravity. Please stop me if I repeat things you already know."

"Will do, Chris."

"It is located eight kilometers beneath the surface and was created as a result of one of the power crystals being detonated. It is exactly three kilometers in diameter, an absolutely perfect sphere."

That shook me a little. "I didn't know that."

"We have created a system which allows you to actually fly inside the facility. It is designed so that you will be able to train yourself on all our transports. As far as the race is concerned, you will be able to recreate the twists, turns and the loop in order to train your mind and body. There are suits at the facility. The centrifuge is kept in a vacuum."

"Is there a training program?"

"All the data that has been collected regarding your physical condition, and any experience you've had while at the controls of our transports, have been downloaded into the training program of the centrifuge. So, the answer is yes, but no two programs are alike."

"Thanks, Chris. Anything else?"

"Not for now, Commander. We'll be arriving in a couple of minutes. Be careful when you get out of the car. We'll be in moon normal gravity."

"Thanks for the reminder, Chris."

"No problem."

We arrived at the transit stop. The transit line ended here. We exited the car and I was surprised by the lack of gravity. "Where to, Chris?"

"Follow me, Commander."

We walked through the exit doors and down a hallway. We ended up at another set of doors with a security guard standing by. He greeted us. "Hello, sirs. What can I do for you today?"

Chris introduced us. "We've booked the centrifuge. I'm Commander Campbell and this is Commander Carrera."

The guard looked at me. "Y-y-yes, sir. Please." He motioned us to go through the doors.

I smiled at him as we went through and said. "Relax."

♦ ♦ ♦

We entered the preparation center and were the only two people there. The prep center held the suits and contained a small lounge with an observation window overlooking the interior of the centrifuge. The simulation capsule was clearly visible, but the size of the interior was not.

Both Chris and I suited up. We entered the airlock and waited for the pressure to equalize. The simulation capsule was eight meters away. As we walked towards it, Chris had the computer activate the lights. The capsule was attached to a reciprocating control arm that was two and a half kilometers long. It was balanced on a tower that was one and a half kilometers in height. The capsule used its own power supply to maneuver around the centrifuge, and was surrounded by a series of rings that enabled it to rotate in any direction.

As we neared the capsule, the hatch opened and Chris said, "It will be just like flying, Commander. Let Max know which transports you want to learn how to fly. When you finish designing your racer, all its unique characteristics will be loaded into your training program, so you can use this facility to get used to it. Of course, nothing beats the track."

"Thanks, Chris." I climbed into the capsule and the auto restraints locked me in. I hooked up my life support to the capsule. "How long do I have, Chris?"

"The average session is about four hours, Commander. You have eight hours of air. You'll know when you've had enough. There are people manning this facility twenty-four hours a day, so if there are any problems, you'll be taken care of. I'll be going back to the Garage now, Commander, if that's okay with you."

I was excited. "Thanks again, Chris. That's fine with me. I'll see you later." The hatch closed.

Max greeted me. "Good morning, Commander."

"Hi, Max."

"What would you like to work on today?"

"The race, Max. The race."

"Do you have a racer?"

"Yes. The one I used on the track."

"And on what part of the race would you like to concentrate?"

"I need to train myself to use the control sticks for navigating the course, and I need to get use to the G forces of the loop and some of the turns."

"Done. The program you are about to run will require that you achieve a score of one hundred percent before you can advance. It may take some time."

I wanted to know how difficult it was going to be. "On a scale of one to ten, Max, how difficult will this be?"

"All the training programs I construct are designed to have you progress as quickly as possible."

For some reason, that answer totally satisfied me. "Let's get started, Max."

My heads-up display activated, and I saw what I had seen at the track. I heard Max's voice. "Five, four, three, two, one. Begin."

The control sticks did not operate the same way as the ones on the transports. I spent seven hours in the capsule. I was impressed that the centrifuge could make the ride as bumpy as the track. On my last run, I scored one hundred percent.

I slept very soundly that night. Achieving a perfect score on the last run of my training session made me feel like a kid again. It inspired me and I felt like I could accomplish anything I put my mind to. I spent the rest of my time off designing my racer.

Twelve: The Drop

0035.0204.0815 LST

Commander Brodie and I got back together the day after our break. We met in his seventh floor office, which was located in the same building as mine. Freshly brewed coffee was waiting for me along with a light breakfast snack. Most of his apartment consisted of living space with his office space being relatively small. He had spent the week figuring out how we were going to move the power crystals into the towers.

"So what have you come up with, Jay?"

"As you know, Bella, the biggest challenge for us is going to be the tower inside the perimeter of the base. So using that as our frame of reference, I concluded that if I came up with a way of delivering a power crystal to the tower at the base, it would work for all the towers we've found."

"That sounds like a good assumption, Jay. Of course, there is no way to test your theory, but we can test the equipment you'll need on another tower first."

"The one we tested the weapon on?"

"That would work for me, Jay. The logistics of delivering a power crystal to the base are going to be huge. The route you find for delivering the crystal must have the least impact on the base, if for some reason we lose control of it."

"That won't happen, Bella."

"I believe you, Jay, but the base is my responsibility."

"I understand where you're coming from, Bella."

"Good. So how long will it be before we can deliver the first crystal?"

"Give me two weeks?"

"I'll give you a week."

"I need ten days."

"Done. I'm going to fill Commander Till in on our plans. I'll be in touch if something comes up."

"Sounds good, Bella."

I called Wallace, "Commander Till, this is Bella."

"Yes, Bella. This is Commander Till. Did you enjoy your time off?"

"Actually, Commander, I did. Jay and I have some plans for the base I'd like to fill you in on. Do you have time today?"

"I'm free today, Bella. Anytime."

"Good. I'll be at your office in ten minutes."

I finished my coffee and breakfast with Jay and left for Commander Till's office. When I arrived at his door, it opened and Wallace greeted me. "Welcome back, Bella."

"I feel good, Commander. It has been a very long time since I've felt this way."

"A little euphoric, Bella?"

"That's it, Commander."

"I'll try not to bring you down."

"I don't know if you could, Commander."

"Just the same, Bella…"

"Thank you, Commander."

"So what are you and Jay up to?"

"We're planning to move the power crystals to where they belong, Commander."

Commander Till turned and walked to his office. I followed.

"Please have a seat, Bella. As you know, I gave you the base to command. But because I also live here, I'd like to know why you want to move the power crystals. Nobody here knows what the towers or the power crystals are designed to do. Many of us have theories. Some are good and some are terrifying. What makes you think we will not be in danger?"

"The ones who left them here have gone."

"Maybe they left so we would be the ones to destroy ourselves."

"Is that what you believe?"

"That is one of the theories."

"That had never crossed my mind."

"So now what do you think?"

"I think we have no choice. We have to do something. We know where the power crystals belong. We need answers. So, I think we should start with one tower and see what happens."

"I agree."

"What??"

"I agree, Bella. One tower. Let's see what happens."

"We chose the tower we tried our weapon on."

"Excellent choice. When's the show?"

"In ten days."

"Good. You should inform the base. A little excitement would be healthy."

"I'll leave that for DJ."

"I think you should do it. The base needs to know you are in Command."

"Alright, Commander. I'll make the announcement."

"Now?"

"I'll write it out."

"Good. Don't leave it too long."

"I'll work on it today and broadcast it sometime tomorrow."

"I'm looking forward to it."

"Thank you, Commander. I'll see myself out."

"Thank you, Bella."

I spent the rest of the day working on the announcement.

0035.0205.0700 LST

I'm up early - seven hundred hours - to prepare myself for my first mass communication with the base. I scheduled the announcement for ten hundred hours and had the computer activate my monitoring station so that as many people as possible would be visible. I made some breakfast and coffee. It had been a long time since I had done anything like this and I was a little nervous. At ten hundred hours I went on the air.

"Good morning, Tranquility. This is Commander Bella Carrera." I watched as people stopped their activities. "Some of you know who I am, but most of you don't. I am the new Commander of this base." I watched for some reaction. "Over the next several months, this base is going to be subjected to many changes, mostly from outside sources. As the man who will be held responsible for all that happens here, I believe you need to know what my priorities are. First and foremost, the safety and security of the base and the people who work here will always be my first concerns. But we also need to keep this base a profitable venture. That is something we should keep in mind." I stopped talking for a few seconds.

"Nine days from today, Commander Jacob Brodie and I will be installing one of the alien power crystals into one tower. This is something we need to do. It has been pointed out to me, however, that because we don't know exactly what we are getting into, we could be embarking on a path that could ultimately destroy us. There are many unknowns, but we don't believe there is any danger in installing one crystal. If Commander Brodie and I discover there is no immediate danger, we will continue installing additional power crystals."

"The tower on this base is our second target. That installation will require some special logistics, of which you all will be informed. If any of you feel these procedures will endanger you, you are free to head back to Earth."

"Personally, I don't think we will know what we are sitting on until a certain number of the power crystals have been installed. There is a possibility that we will figure it out before then." I stopped again and watched for some reaction. "The arrival of a potential competitor on the moon is strong motivation for us to figure this out. Their first satellite is scheduled to arrive in eleven months. We all have a lot of work to do, so I'm going to sign off now. Thank you for your time." I signed off.

Jay called immediately. "Bella, this is Jay."

"Yes, Jay. This is Bella."

"Bella, I'm speechless."

"What? What did I do?"

"Ummm… We were the only two that knew about the competition."

"Oops…"

"Don't worry about it. Excellent speech."

"Thank you. I'm curious, Jay."

"About what?"

"What's the absolute worst-case scenario regarding the power crystals?"

It took a few seconds for Jay to respond. "Are you sure you want to hear this?"

"Yes."

Jay replied, "A few believe the towers are designed to work together as a power source based on how and where they are located. But there is a theory that once we place a certain number of power crystals in the towers, the beams that each crystal generate would converge at the center of the Moon. This convergence would do two things. First, the center of the Moon would disappear. Secondly, the Moon would start to collapse from the inside, thereby affecting its integrity. Internal pressures would start to create moonquakes and stop the convergence of the beams. The moon would continue to collapse internally and pressures would start to build. Our computer simulation shows that the moon would eventually explode. The explosion would send to Earth, moon meteors large enough to wipe out all life on Earth. Of course, Bella, this is just a theory."

I thought for a few moments. "So, the worst thing you figure will happen is that we could start a chain reaction of events that could potentially wipe out all life that we know of in this solar system."

"Yes."

"That's quite a scenario. Do you know who thought that up?"

"No I don't, Bella. I believe it was someone living Earth-side."

"Scary fellow, Jay. See you in nine days."

"Thank you, Bella."

It took two days for all the inquiries regarding our competitors to stop. As more senior staff became aware, the news spread quickly. Many residents felt comfortable enough to call me directly. I learned a lot about the base.

0035.0207.0830 LST

I had no plans for the day and decided it would be a good day to practice for the race... "Max."

"Yes, Commander."

"Is the centrifuge available today?"

"Yes, Commander."

"What time?"

"Eleven hundred hours, Commander."

"Good. Please book me in."

"Done, Commander."

"Thank you, Max."

That gave me an hour to get ready. This was to be my second session. I spent the time pinpointing exactly what I wanted to work on.

♦ ♦ ♦

A guard at the door greeted me. "Good morning, Commander."

"Good morning," I responded.

I entered the lounge and put on my suit. The capsule was visible, and I focused on it for a minute. Then I left the lounge. As I approached the door to the capsule, it opened. I entered the capsule and hooked up my life support.

"Good morning, Commander," Max greeted me.

"Good morning, Max."

"What would you like to work on today?"

"Do you have records of when two racers collide on the straightaway?"

"Yes."

"I would like you to simulate a run through the whole course and include a racer trying to run me off using records of actual incidents."

"You know I can't simulate the exact course, Commander."

"Yes."

"No one has ever asked me to simulate a collision between two racers before."

"It will be fun, Max."

"Fun?"

"Sorry, Max."

"Done."

My heads-up display activated and in front of me I saw J fifty-six…L eighty-nine…D sixty-seven. I wasn't expecting a message.

"Computer, J fifty-six…L eighty-nine…D sixty-seven. How many is that?"

"Eighteen, Commander."

Max didn't waste any time… "Five…four…three…two…one… Begin."

I throttled up and felt the capsule accelerate. As I moved through the course, I realized I was using the information on my display without thinking about it. Like glancing at my speedometer and tachometer back on Earth. I felt my right and left-hand coordination improving.

I was coming up to the straightaway. "How am I doing, Max?"

"If you hadn't asked for a collision simulation, I would be moving you up a level."

"A perfect run?"

"Yes."

I was on the straightaway and heard a warning, "Collision…Collision."

"I can't see it! Where is it?"

My display changed and I saw a racer coming at me from slightly behind and to my left. My first instinct was to try and outrun it, but my right hand pulled back hard on the throttle and my left hand pulled to the left. The racer flew by me. I punched the throttle and my heads-up display returned as I started the course again.

"How was that, Max?" Silence. "Max?"

"Yes, Commander."

"Are you functioning?"

"Yes, Commander."

"That seemed like a long delay."

"I've had to construct a new set of parameters. You are now on level three. You may find this more difficult."

I didn't have time to think of a response. It *was* more difficult. Max included two collisions that caused me to lose control of my racer twice, but I eventually finished level three with a perfect score.

"Commander?"

"Yes, Max."

"I would suggest you try the track."

I felt like a kid who had just been given permission to take a cookie. "Okay, Max!"

Thirteen: Cee

0035.0207.2315 LST

I retired to my bedroom and fell into a deep sleep. A very loud voice caused me to awaken.

"Bella!!!!"

I opened my eyes and found myself in the oasis.

"Bella!!!!"

It was Cee's voice. I thought I was going to have a restful sleep.

"Bella!!!! I'm in trouble!!!!"

I got up. The air was hot and humid. I started down a path I thought would lead me to Cee. As I walked down the path, I noticed that the plants were different from those I had seen before.

"Bella!! Hurry!!!"

I started to run. She sounded scared. I'd been running down the path for about a minute when it came to an abrupt end and became a large open space filled with plant life and trees that soared hundreds of meters into the air. It reminded me of a rainforest. The air was very thick.

"Bella!!! Up here!!!"

I scanned the area for Cee's voice. I spotted a rock outcropping that rose up one hundred meters. I spotted Cee about fifty meters up. Her back was against the rock.

"Cee!!! Are you stuck?"

"Not exactly!!"

"What, then? What do you need?"

"It can't reach me up here, but it's hungry! I don't think he's caught your scent yet!"

"What?!! What are you talking about!!?"

"When you were a kid, Bella, did you study dinosaurs?"

"Of course!!"

"Was there any single one you found the most fascinating?"

I thought back. "I thought the Triceratops was kind of cool!!"

"Is that the only one?"

I began to sweat. "To be honest, Cee, I used to fantasize about what it would have been like to live in the same era as the T-Rex!!"

"Well now's your chance, Bella!!"

Just then a deafening roar filled the air. And out from the plants emerged a twelve-meter tall T-Rex that charged the rock and thrust his massive seven-ton body against the outcropping. I felt the ground shake and saw Cee fight to stay on the rock. The massive beast took off into the trees.

"Hey!!!" I yelled as loud as I could. I started to run towards the rock.

"Bella!! What are you doing!!?"

I didn't answer her. I kept running towards the rock. I picked up small rocks as I ran.

"Bella!!!"

"Where is he, Cee!!?"

"I don't know!! I can't see him!! What are you doing!!?"

"I'm going to distract him so you can get away!!"

"He's fast, Bella!!"

"When he starts after me, you get out of here!!"

"What about you!!?"

"Don't worry about me!! You're more important!!"

"No I'm not, Bella!!"

"Do as I say, Cee, and get out of here as fast as you can!!!"

My body was pumped full of adrenalin. I knew I had to try and get Cee out. My plan was to get the attention of the T-Rex and have him chase me through the plants and trees. I was hoping to out-maneuver him. His roar once again filled the air. I felt the ground shake as he charged towards the rock to which Cee was clinging. As he broke through the plants, I started to throw my arsenal of rocks. One of them hit him squarely in the eye. He stopped cold and roared again. I saw his eyelids move over his eyes several times. He then took several deep breaths and I knew he was sniffing for my scent. Everything then began to move in slow motion. He turned his head and pivoted on his left foot. I found myself looking straight into the eyes of one of the few creatures that continue to fascinate man. He was ten meters away and much bigger than I ever imagined. The atmosphere was stifling.

"Bella!!!!! Run!!!!!"

I looked up at Cee and then back at the T-Rex. I took off into the plants. I heard the T-Rex roar and felt the ground shake as he started to pursue me. I started to run and changed direction every few meters. I had no idea where I was going. All I wanted to do was keep moving. I heard him roar and felt the ground shake again. He wasn't far behind me and for all of my maneuvering, I wasn't making much progress, so I stopped. I decided to cut back and run back the way I came.

I thought T-Rex might keep running in the opposite direction, but I was wrong. He was waiting for me. His massive head came crashing through the trees and he snatched me up in his jaws. I felt my ribs crack under the pressure and I felt a tooth go through my left leg. I was still conscious as he snapped his head back and tossed me through the air like a rag doll. I landed in a tree and watched as a branch impaled my body. He ran towards me. He was coming to pluck me out of the tree and finish me off. As he came closer, I hoped that Cee had a chance to escape. I passed out.

♦♦♦

Much to my surprise, I regained consciousness. I opened my eyes and saw I was in a tree. My body was racked with pain. I ran my hands over it, checking for anything unusual. I found nothing.

I breathed a sigh of relief. As I did, I noticed a familiar aroma in the air. I lifted my head off the branch it was resting on, and looked at my body. I moved my arms to grip a branch and pulled myself up to a sitting position. My body hurt, but in spite of that, I felt the need to go hunting. I sat for a minute and tried to clear my mind.

A fragment of memory surfaced. I remembered that the aroma had emanated from something I should avoid, but I couldn't remember what. I started climbing down the tree, with the intention of finding out what was causing it. As I did, I noticed that the tree was loaded with my favorite fruit. I looked for the ripest one and picked it off the branch. I took a bite and felt instantly refreshed. My mind began to clear and the desire to go hunting disappeared. I then remembered why I should not pursue the aroma. It belonged to a bad plant. I then remembered everything that had happened with the T-Rex. I finished the fruit and resumed my climb down the tree. When I got to the bottom, I found myself standing in my bed.

I climbed down from my bed and looked around my room. I walked over to the window that overlooked Tranquility, and surveyed the base. A few seconds later, as I took in the view, I began to tremble uncontrollably. I was overwhelmed with fear.

Fourteen: The Drop... Part 2

0035.0214.0900 LST

"Bella, this is Jay."

"Hello, Jay. This is Bella."

"Good morning, Bella. Are you ready to transport and place our first power crystal today?"

"Absolutely. What is your plan?"

"It would be easier to show you, Bella. When will you be ready to go?"

"Anytime, Jay."

"Good. Would you meet me at my office in twenty minutes? I'll explain everything as we go."

"Sounds good, Jay. See you in twenty."

♦♦♦

I had been up for a few hours anticipating Jay's call. This was going to be an interesting day. I waited for Jay to answer his door. "Good to see you, Bella. What have you been doing these past few days?"

"Mostly designing my racer. How about you?"

"Planning and programming the computers for today, Bella. You know that."

"Yes I do."

"Is there something bothering you?"

"There are many unknowns, Jay. That's all I can tell you."

"I understand. Have you submitted any of your racer designs to Max?"

"Not yet. I'm going to do it by hand first. When I'm done, I'll ask Max to check it. That's how I do my work. I've never liked the idea of being dependent on a computer, although being here has forced me to realize that I am."

"Yes, we are. Our first stop is the Garage. By the way, I've been thinking about the conversation we had a few days ago."

"What about it?"

"You realize, of course, that if we believed there was any chance of our destroying the Moon by doing what we are about to do, we wouldn't do it."

"Of course. It was just a worse case scenario… right?"

"Right."

♦♦♦

Commander Campbell was waiting for us at the Garage. "Good morning, Commanders."

I said good morning and then Jay asked, "Is it ready, Chris?"

"Yes, Jay. If you and the Commander will follow me, I'll show you your new transport."

"New transport, Jay?"

"Yes, Bella. Chris and I have been working on a transport that will allow us to carry the power crystals anywhere on the Moon, with the exception of the base. Chris has spent the last few days testing and finishing it. Today will be its maiden voyage."

We were standing in front of a massive set of doors. Chris looked at me. "We've waited a long time for this, Commander. It's the most difficult transport I've put together. And the most powerful."

"I'm anxious to see it, Chris."

Chris had the computer open the doors and we stepped through. "Although we've designed transports that can lift a weight equivalent to one of the power crystals, it was the sheer density of the crystal that was the problem. As you can see, this large vessel is thirty-five meters long, including the cockpit. The cargo area measures thirty meters long, fifteen meters high and twenty-five meters wide. We are fortunate that the opening in the towers is large enough for us to fly into if there is a need. It was designed before we knew how large the tower openings were."

"The cargo bay is designed to dissipate the weight of the power crystal through its entire structure. We have taken into account the G forces associated with flight, which is the reason it cannot be used in anything but moon normal gravity. It uses eight space drives for control, which is a record for us. That also makes this transport extremely dangerous to operate. Although Max will be on board, this will also be a first for the software and it may need tweaking. Any questions, Commander?"

I was blown away. “No, Chris. Thank you.”

Jay was standing beside me and smiling. “Are you ready to go, Bella?”

“Let’s do it, Jay.”

“We’ll be able to access the surface from this hanger, Bella.”

“Let’s suit up.”

Jay had our suits stored by the hangar. We finished suiting up and Jay had the cockpit lowered so we could enter. Once again, the cockpit was as I had come to expect. We hooked up our life supports and powered up the drives. Chris stepped back into the Garage and the hanger doors closed.

Chris had a few parting words. “Hey, guys.”

“Yes, Chris,” I answered.

“Try not to crack it up first time out, okay?”

“Thanks for the vote of confidence, Chris,” Jay answered.

“My pleasure, Jay.”

High over our heads, a series of air locks began to open and the hanger started to depressurize. “Prepare for ascent, Bella.”

“Ready when you are, Jay.”

“Here we go.” The last air lock opened and we started a three hundred meter accent to the surface. As we rose, air locks closed behind us. “Bella, this is the last time this transport will be parked here. We have a special hanger at my lab that will keep it serviced. We have also been extending the transit line to my lab. It will be operational in a few days. Access to the line will be restricted.”

“Are you planning a sister transport to this one?”

“Is that your recommendation?”

“Yes.”

“Then we are. We’ll get started right away.”

“How are the controls?”

“Smooth as silk, Bella.”

We arrived at Jay’s lab ten minutes later. A container containing the power crystal was waiting for us on the landing pad.

“The container is designed to go through the opening in the towers and with as much grace as we could engineer, drop the power crystal into place. We will have five minutes to make the transfer before the towers system activates.”

“Will that be difficult?”

“Just stressful.”

"Oh well then… no problem."

"Sarcasm, Bella?"

"A little. I suppose if I tried to keep up with everything that goes on here, I'd lose my mind."

"Feeling out of control, Bella?"

"Totally."

Jay changed the tone of his voice. "Understood, Commander. How can I help?"

"Thanks, Jay. I'll let you know. So how are we going to do this?"

"I'm starting my descent. We will land with the cargo bay open with the container centered in the middle of the bay. The container will lift itself into its cradle and the ship will lock it down. Once we're loaded, I'm going to hover for a few minutes to make sure the structure is sound and all systems are functioning. Once that's done, we'll head off to the tower."

I felt the transport land.

"Loading has begun. You can watch on your computer screens, Bella."

"Thanks, Jay."

The container had begun to rise into the center of the transport. As it did, several large tubular structures located below and beside it moved and extended to support the container. As they locked on, the container started to retract the structures that had raised it up. The transport moved significantly as the weight of the container shifted to the cargo bay. More of the tubular structures moved in from above and locked onto the container. It was now surrounded and supported by a large number of structures. I could see how the weight was being dissipated and how the system would work in flight.

"How does it look, Jay?"

"Did you feel how much the transport moved, Bella?"

"Yes."

"It's really heavy. This is not a small ship."

"I know, Jay. Are you okay?"

"A little unnerved."

"Take your time."

Jay quickly focused himself. "I'm going to lift off now. We'll be hovering for a few minutes while the computer and I check all the systems." I saw Jay working the controls and felt the transport lift off the landing pad.

"How is it, Jay?"

"I'm programming the parameters for flight. Everything is working as planned and Max is online. Are you ready to go?"

"Waiting for you, Jay."

"Here we go."

It took only three minutes to reach the tower and land. We landed on the road ten meters from the tower. The cargo bay reversed its loading procedures and the container rested on the road. Jay flew the transport to a safe distance away. "The container has its own guidance system, Bella. I've programmed the location of the entrance to the tower and the distance to where the power crystal goes. It will take two minutes to reach the drop, forty-five seconds to unload, and one and a half minutes to get out of the tower. That gives us forty-five seconds to spare. I can control all of it from here."

"How many times have you tested the system?"

"I've cycled it through one thousand times. It didn't fail once."

"Is there a contingency plan?"

"Yes. If we need to, we can haul the container out, but the plan is for us to stay near the transport in case we lose control of the crystal. It will move us out of the area fast enough so we won't get caught in the blast area."

"That sounds like a good plan."

"Shall we get started?"

"Let's do it, Jay."

"You'll be able to see everything that's happening on your display, Bella."

"Excellent."

We stood outside the cockpit and watched as the container propelled itself down the road towards the tower. The entrance to the tower was not visible from where we stood, so when we lost sight of the container, the computer switched the display to appear as if we were sitting on top of it. We saw the entrance to the tower appear.

"Did you see that, Bella?"

"Yes."

"Did you notice how it opened?"

"No. It was too fast."

"I'll check it later."

The container turned into the tower and headed for the drop. It took two minutes for the container to reach its destination. Our display switched to the interior of the container. The power crystal was bathed in blue light. As the bottom of the container slowly opened, the crystal started to drop. The depression underneath the power crystal appeared and my hands started to feel sweaty. We were forty seconds into the procedure when Jay and I felt the power crystal drop.

Jay said, “Jesus.”

“What’s happening, Jay? Is everything working?”

“Everything’s working, Bella. We were five seconds early on the drop. Let’s keep our eyes on the power crystal.”

The display switched back to an external view of the crystal, as the container started back to the entrance. A few seconds passed and then the ground where we were standing began to vibrate. The cameras on the container were vibrating wildly, rendering them temporarily useless.

“What’s happening, Jay?”

Jay didn’t answer for a few seconds. “Remember that beam the power crystal generated? I believe the crystal is designed to fit in those depressions in a very specific way. My guess is that it’s trying to find its proper seating.” The vibration stopped as suddenly as it started. “I’m guessing it’s done, Bella.”

The container was now outside the tower with its cameras facing the wrong way. It was showing pictures of our transport on the road. Jay directed it to move back and show us an image of the interior of the tower. We could then see the power crystal seated in the center of the floor. “We should start to see something happen in fifty seconds, Bella.”

“Bella, this is Commander Till.”

“Yes, Commander. This is Bella.”

“What’s happening?”

“The power crystal has seated itself. We’ll know more in about forty seconds. Do you want a visual?”

“Sounds good. I’ve also got it on our satellite.”

“Jay?”

“Yes, Bella.”

“Give Commander Till our visual.”

“Done.”

“How does it look, Commander?”

“I’m speechless.”

“Five seconds, Bella.”

Jay timed it perfectly. As if on cue, the nine-sided, twenty-seven meter section of floor started moving up the tower. It took only a few seconds for us to lose sight of the power crystal, but we saw that it was being raised by something that went deep into the ground. It reminded me of a hydraulic lift.

"Let's shift to the satellite image, Jay."

"Right away, Bella." We were now seeing the tower from a birds-eye view, which felt a little strange since we were on the ground.

"How long before the power crystal reaches the top, Jay?"

"Ninety seconds, Bella."

"Bella, this is DJ."

"Yes, DJ. This is Bella."

"Hi, Bella. I'm watching. I was just wondering if this is something I should keep under wraps for now?"

"That would be a good idea, DJ. Thanks for asking."

"I haven't heard from you in quite a few days. Are you okay?"

"I'm fine, DJ. I'm just a little preoccupied. How about you?"

"A little later. Thanks, Bella."

♦ ♦ ♦

"Bella, this is Jay. Five seconds… stand by."

I focused on the top of the tower. The power crystal cleared the top right on time.

"Looks good, Bella. Four minutes."

I watched as the interior of the power crystal lit up. The satellite image was perfect. Jay had the transport power up for a quick getaway. I asked the computer to activate a window in my display that would allow me to see the images transmitted by the container. As the timer hit four minutes, an intense beam shot down the center of the tower. At the same instant, the opening to the tower closed. The beam illuminated the tower from the inside in an awesome display of power. The power crystal lowered back into the tower and the dome snapped shut. The beam stayed illuminated for ten minutes.

"Congratulations, Jay. You did it." He didn't respond. "Jay…!?"

Fifteen: The Drop... Part 3

0035.0219.1000 LST

It took Jay a few days to recover from his initial success with the power crystals. Today is the day we are dropping one in the tower at the Base. I had Samson evacuate the Earth Dome and all the facilities within a three-kilometer area of the tower. A forty-kilometer long road has been specially designed and built for the container holding the power crystal to the tower. It begins in moon normal gravity and it will take the container five hours to reach its destination.

I alerted the base to the fact that they may feel something like a moonquake as the power crystal is dropped and seated. I also managed to squeeze in a few laps around the racetrack. I believe some would say I had become obsessed with it. During my practice laps, I figured out why the racer I was using was so fast.

I felt anxious and called Jay. “Jay, this Bella.”

“Yes, Bella. This is Jay.”

“Are we ready for today?”

Jay was in good spirits. “Yes. I’m at my lab double-checking everything.”

“Good. I know we’ve finished the tunnel to your lab, so I’ll use it and meet you there.”

“Alright. When can I expect you?”

“How about twelve hundred hours?”

“See you then.”

“Thanks, Jay.”

The trip to Jay’s lab took forty-five minutes. For the first time since I had arrived, I listened to the radio station to pass the time. I really enjoyed it, even though DJ wasn’t broadcasting.

Jay was waiting for me at the transit stop. “Good afternoon, Bella. How was the ride?”

“A lot longer than flying, but it was pleasant.”

“It will gradually become faster. It’s designed to get here in twenty minutes.”

I took a few seconds to respond. “Are the people responsible for building this line being cautious?”

"That's quite accurate, Bella."

"Thank you, Jay. You seem in good spirits today."

"I am. And you seem unusually relaxed."

"I am. I've made tremendous progress with the race. I've figured out what made Commander Till's racer so fast."

"It took us awhile to figure that out. Do you still think you'll win?"

"That is my goal."

"It's mine, too. So, are you ready to go?"

"Yes. Is there anything I need to know before we go?"

"There are many unknowns, Bella. I'm a little nervous."

"Understood. Let's do it."

◆ ◆ ◆

Jay was meticulous in his preparations. We arrived at the road at thirteen hundred hours. The container lowered itself and we double-checked its systems.

"How does it look?"

"Everything is ready to go. What do you want to do for the next five hours?"

"How about showing me where some of the other towers are? We can keep track of the container using our tracking systems."

"That is a great idea."

"Thank you."

We lifted off and proceeded to locate the towers. Jay explained how his staff was choosing areas that might have a tower in them. All the towers located on flat plains had the familiar ring road built around them, but there were also numerous towers located on the tops of hills and mountains. Some of them would require the transport to be flown inside the tower in order to drop the container for the power crystals.

Jay sounded very much like a tour guide. "If you look at your screen, Bella, you will see the pattern we are using to locate the towers. Unfortunately, it doesn't seem to work very well, so it's clear we've missed something. Maybe you'll find it."

I studied the screen. There were lines emanating from each of the nine sides of the base tower. Each line was then loaded into the computer using a coordinate program, and a ship was dispatched to search the surface of the Moon for a tower. The coordinates looked very similar to the messages I had been seeing.

Jay continued. "We believe, Bella, that each tower is designed to feed power to another tower if it's in a position where there is no sunlight. We created a computer simulation that would mimic what would happen if different parts of the tower grid needed power at any given time. The big flaw with the program is that no towers exist where we think they should be. But it will give you an idea of what I'm talking about."

My computer screen lit up with a view of one of the towers. Beams of light shot out from this tower, and the scene quickly shifted to a light beam hitting another tower near the top. This tower was in darkness. After a few seconds, nine beams of light shot out from that tower and the computer then shifted to an above surface view. The nine beams hit nine other towers that were not in direct sunlight. More light beams shot out from those towers, hitting only towers that needed power. After a few minutes I was looking at a complex grid of towers turning light beams on and off, depending on which towers needed the energy. The simulation ended with my viewing the Moon from orbit and looking at thousands of points emanating light in every direction, surrounding the Moon.

"Very impressive, Jay."

"Thanks, but we are short a few towers."

"I'll take a closer look at the pattern. Maybe I'll see something you missed."

"I hope you do. We should head back now. The container is only fifteen minutes away."

"Time flies."

We landed the transport a few hundred meters from the tower. The container was moving onto the ring road. Jay lowered the cockpit and we got out.

♦♦♦

As the container approached the door, the tower opened. The container turned and began moving towards the center of the floor. Two minutes later, it stopped over the depression in the floor.

"This is it, Bella."

I had the computer put me on the air. "This is Commander Carrera. Stand by, Tranquility Base. We are about to make a drop." I shifted my view to the inside of the container and saw the power crystal bathed in blue light slowly lowering. "Time, Jay."

"Fifteen seconds."

The impact of the power crystal hitting its mark knocked us off our feet. I immediately checked with the base. "Tranquility, this is Commander Carrera. Damage report! Damage report!"

The ground began vibrating so violently that Jay and I were unable to get up.

"Commander, no damage has been reported. All systems functioning."

"Thank you." The ground continued to vibrate. "Jay, are you okay?"

"I'm fine. Man, what a drop."

A few seconds later, the vibrations stopped. We got up, relieved. I noticed we had lost the signal from our container. "What do you think happened to the container, Jay? I'm not receiving a signal. Are you?"

"Negative, Bella… The force of the drop must have knocked it out. We'll be able to check on it after we're done."

"I agree, Jay."

Jay's voice was full of excitement. "The power crystal should be moving up the tower. Switching to satellite view." The base looked awesome from space. Jay focused on the tower. "Here we go, Bella."

A few moments later, the tower opened and the power crystal cleared the top and was bathed in sunlight. The interior lit up and four minutes later, an intense beam shot down the center of the tower.

"Jay, how long before the power crystal retreats?"

"Should be just a few more seconds."

We waited. Five minutes went by. The crystal was still generating a beam. "It's not retreating, Jay!"

Jay did not know what to do. "Oh God. What should we do, Bella?"

"We need to get back inside the base, Jay. We'll access the situation from there. Let's go!"

Sixteen: Contact

0035.0305.1710 LST

It's been fourteen days since we installed the power crystal in the base tower and it's still generating a beam. We've felt nothing change on the base, but we're all wondering if anything will happen. With the exception of a few vital services and the radio station, most of the base has been shut down until we decide what to do.

Much to my surprise, all participants in the race have been spending a lot of time on the track. If we stay here, I suspect it will be a good event.

♦♦♦

"Commander Carrera, this is Commander Irvine."

"Yes, Commander. This is Commander Carrera. What's the latest?"

"Have you not been watching?"

"Watching what, Commander?"

"The tower, sir."

"Not today, Commander. Why?"

"The beam has stopped, sir."

"What??"

"The beam, sir. It has stopped."

"Give me a second, Commander. I'll switch on my monitor… got it." It had indeed stopped. As relieved as I was that the beam was no longer being generated, I felt as if something had just died.

"According to my calculations, it stopped exactly fourteen days to the second since it began."

"That's interesting."

"There's something else, sir."

"Please continue."

"I was observing the tower from high orbit when the beam stopped, and as it did, it opened."

I suspected the power crystal was burned out and the tower was open so that it could be replaced. "Where is the opening?"

"I'll transfer the image over to you, Commander."

What I saw was not the same opening. It was the same size but right beside where we went in with the power crystal. "Thank you, Commander. Is there anything else?"

"No, Commander. Thank you." I needed a few minutes to figure out what I was going to do next. I had a feeling I would be hearing from Jay very shortly. I was right.

"Bella, this is Jay."

"Good afternoon, Jay. I thought I would hear from you. I guess you know about the tower and the new opening."

"Yes."

"What do you suggest?"

"Let's go check it out."

"You sound excited."

"I'm intensely curious."

"Good one. Let's make plans."

"Excellent."

Jay and I were finalizing our plans when I received a message indicating that Commander Till wanted to speak with me.

"Yes, Commander. What can I do for you?"

"I suspect that you and Jay are going to make plans to investigate the opening in the tower."

"Your suspicions are correct."

"I would like to join you."

"Why, Commander?"

"If we are to abandon this base because of what we have started, then I would like to be a part of this final investigation. I have been here a long time, Bella."

"I know, Commander. I look forward to working with you. I'll be in touch with you shortly with our time line."

"Thank you, Bella. By the way, please call me Wallace."

I caught my breath. "Thank you, Wallace."

I switched back to Jay. "Jay, this is Bella."

"Hi, Bella. What did Commander Till want?"

"He'll be joining us on our investigation."

"I don't have a problem with that. When?"

"Tomorrow morning, nine hundred hours. We'll meet at my office."

"Sounds good, Bella. I'll have everything ready."

"Thanks, Jay. See you then."

0035.0306.0900 LST

"Good morning, Jay. Good morning, Wallace."

Jay looked at me like I must be crazy to call Commander Till by his first name.

Wallace saw his reaction. "It's okay, Jay. I asked Bella to address me by my first name. You, of course, may still address me as Commander."

"Yes, sir."

We were suited up and I addressed them both. "I'm going to ask DJ to evacuate the base if we are not back in seventy hours. Any objections?"

Jay and Wallace took a minute to think about it. Wallace responded, "I would evacuate all non-essential personnel. If there is trouble, a rescue attempt must be initiated. It would be better if it originated from here."

"You're right, Wallace. Thank you. I'll transfer Command over to DJ. I'll just be a minute." I walked over to my Command Center and called DJ… "DJ, this is Bella."

"Hi, Bella. This is DJ."

"Wallace, Jay and I are going out to investigate the tower. There is a risk involved. I am handing over Command of the base to you. Once we enter the tower, you will lose contact with us. If we are out of communication for more than seventy-two hours, your orders are to evacuate all non-essential personnel from the base. You will be in Command of any rescue attempts. Any questions?"

"This is rather sudden, Bella. Are you sure you want me to do this?"

"Wallace agrees with me. I'm not giving you a choice."

"Be careful, Bella."

"Thanks, DJ. Computer, connect me with all personnel."

"Done, Commander."

"Attention Tranquility. This is Commander Carrera. Commanders' Till, Brodie and I will be conducting an investigation of the tower located on this base. In our absence, DJ will have command of the base. If we have not returned within seventy-two hours, DJ will let you know what needs to be done. Commander Carrera out."

I walked back to Wallace and Jay. "Shall we?"

♦♦♦

We left my office and took the elevator down to sub-level seven. When we stepped out of the elevator, there was ground transportation waiting for us. There were four seats - two in front, two in back. Jay explained, "I've loaded this transport with everything we'll need for seventy-two hours. If need be, it can be pressurized."

"Looks good, Jay. Who wants the back seat?"

Wallace volunteered, "I'll take the back, Bella."

"Thanks, Wallace."

We climbed into the transport and drove toward the lunar surface access bay. Jay was driving. "Once we arrive on the surface, it will be an eight-minute drive to the tower."

As we entered the access bay, our suits became fully operational. The doors closed and the bay depressurized. It took only a minute to reach the surface. Jay was excited. "Here we go, guys."

I heard Wallace chuckle. I smiled. "Let's drive around the tower once before we go in, Jay. Maybe we'll see something."

"Okay, Bella."

We reached the tower and drove slowly around it. I didn't see anything but the opening. "You guys see anything?"

"Absolutely nothing," they responded. We stopped in front of the new opening.

"Any final thoughts before we go in?"

Jay said, "Not from me, Bella. I'm ready."

"How about you, Wallace?"

"I think we should drive in, Bella."

"You heard the man, Jay. Let's go in."

The same type of light we had encountered in the first tower we entered illuminated the interior. We drove to the center of the room. It was twenty-seven meters across, twenty-seven meters high and twenty-seven meters deep. We got out of the transport.

"Now what, Bella?"

"We wait."

We walked around the room looking for clues. We found none. As we started back to the center of the room toward the transport, our displays picked up a subtle shift in the lighting. Before any one of us could make a comment, the opening of the tower closed. We froze. The room started to descend. Slowly at first, then it started to increase in speed. When it stabilized, we resumed walking toward the transport.

I felt a twinge of fear. "You guys scared?"

Jay replied, "Terrified."

When Wallace didn't respond, I was concerned. "Say something, Wallace."

"This is the most exciting thing I've done in years." I cracked a smile and suggested we climb back into the transport.

Twenty minutes into the room's descent, our suit sensors indicated that the room had started to pressurize. We continued to descend for fifteen more minutes and then stopped. Five minutes later, the pressurization was complete and the tower opened again. We sat in the transport and waited for the computer's final analysis of the atmosphere.

Jay reported, "The atmosphere is perfect for human life, Commander."

"I'm going to open my suit. You guys wait until I say it's okay." My helmet retracted and I held my breath. I exhaled and took in a small amount of air. It was fine. "It's safe."

Jay adjusted the transport to face the opening. "What are your orders, Bella?"

The light flooding into the tower was very bright. We couldn't see out. "Let's see what's outside, Jay."

Jay started the transport and we moved slowly towards the opening. I noticed that his hands were gripping the control sticks a little more tightly than usual. As we drove through the opening, Jay stopped the transport. We sat there staring at our surroundings. I heard Wallace behind me say, "In the eyes of God."

Jay was having difficulty speaking. "This… This is impossible."

I was also barely able to speak. "What does this look like to you, Wallace?"

It took a few seconds for him to respond. "It looks like a scene from one of those Caribbean vacation spots."

Indeed it did. Lapping up on a white sandy beach in front of us was a blue ocean of water with crystal clear, blue sky overhead. To our left, in the distance, was a small village. To our immediate right was what looked like an administration building. Jay managed a few words. "Now what, Commander?"

"I don't know. Give me a few minutes to think." I looked around and felt my mind and body going numb. I surveyed the building and the roadways leading into the village. "This is what we're going to do. Jay, I want you to back up. We'll go back to the base and get it up and running. I believe the power crystal was powering up this complex. When we have the base back on track and running smoothly, we'll come back and take a closer look."

Wallace responded, "Thank you, Bella."

"No problem, Wallace."

Jay backed the transport to the middle of the room. When he stopped, the door of the tower closed and we immediately began to move back up to the surface.

Seventeen: The Race… #1

0035.0330.1045 LST

It's the day before the race and the Base is finally back online. It took longer than anticipated, and the process of dealing with my counterparts back on Earth was extremely frustrating. I assigned Wallace the task of investigating what our visitors left behind. He has chosen four others to help him. I discovered that the towers were aligned differently from the way Jay had originally thought, and we have found more towers, based on my findings.

DJ reported that while we were descending from the tower, another opening had appeared. She was confident we would make it back. There were no complaints aired regarding her appointment as Base Commander.

The race will take three days to complete. DJ and I were scheduled for the middle of the second day. I was already feeling the tension.

0035.0331.0545 LST

I arose early on the first day of race. My curiosity was getting the better of me. I had, of course, seen recorded footage of the races, but I had not experienced the mood of it before. I was completely caught up in it. The producers of the show had mastered the ability to have the audience completely mesmerized in both audio and visual formats. The estimated audience for the three-day event was close to half a billion people per day. Our advertising revenue for this three-day event was astronomical. When I thought about the number of people who were going to be watching me, my hands started to sweat.

Jay and Chris were the first to race. I am not a betting man, but if I were, I would have put my money on Jay. Not because he was better than Chris, I just wanted him to win.

I activated my monitors and made myself comfortable. The two racers were at the starting line and could not have looked more different. This was the first time I had seen their work. Jay's racer was designed to show off the power plant. All the supporting structures were cleverly hidden behind pieces of hardware. His cockpit seemed to hang in midair while attached to the rest of the machine. Chris's racer had flowing lines and looked more like a machine that would be equally at home on an Earth racecourse. He sat back with the power plant behind him. I knew they were evenly matched. No results would be posted until the day after the final pair had raced. The race started at precisely six hundred hours.

♦ ♦ ♦

Both racers accelerated down the straightaway and entered the first pair of sweeping S-turns at the same time. The cameras showed them as they entered the first tunnel that led into the three hundred and forty degree turn that lined the crater. The cameras zoomed in as they rounded the crater and it was easy to see they were both fighting to stay in the line. As they hit the straightaway leading into the massive loop, it appeared that Chris was ahead. The cameras switched to the interior of the loop and they finessed their machines around and through it. An overhead camera located at the exit of the loop showed them shooting out of the mountain into the right-hand turn. Both racers slowed almost to a stop in order to get around the final hairpin that led back into the straightaway.

I was working on something that would allow me to get through that turn faster. I believed it was the one place on the track where I could pull ahead.

As they headed down the straightaway and back into the S curves, Jay was ahead by one racer length. It was a good race. Although Jay finished a few hundredths of a second ahead of Chris, that didn't necessarily mean anything. We would have to wait until everyone had finished to see the final order.

I watched three more races that day. They all appeared to be close.

0035.0401.0745 LST

I woke up early. All thoughts I had about this day were gone. I had never before felt such clarity. There was absolutely no room in my mind for anything but the race. It scared me that I hadn't done any mental preparation for what I was feeling.

I spent a couple of hours cleaning up my space and fixing myself something to eat. As much as I wanted to relax, something was preventing me from doing so. After a short while, it became clear to me that when I was focused on doing things that were going to help me race, I felt a release of tension.

0035.0401.1100 LST

I found myself in the Garage several hours sooner than I thought. Chris was there and he greeted me. “Good morning, Commander. How are you today?”

“Good morning, Chris. I’m feeling good. How about you? How was your race?”

“To be honest, I didn’t do as well as I would have liked. There were times when I thought I was going to completely lose it, but we won’t know for a couple more days. Waiting for the results is the most stressful part of it for me.”

“Why do you think that is, Chris?”

“Because I want to win, Commander.”

“We all do, Chris.”

“I know, Commander. Can I give you a hand with something? You’re here quite early.”

“I’ll be fine. I’m going to check out my racer. I’ll be in my bay if anyone comes looking for me.”

“I’ll let them know, Commander.”

“Thanks, Chris.”

0035.0401.1400 LST

It was an hour before my scheduled race. I had just finished putting on my suit when there was a knock on the door of my bay. I opened the door and was surprised to see DJ. “Hello, DJ. Isn’t this bad luck or something?”

She started to laugh. “What are you talking about?”

“I mean visiting the competition before the event.”

She started laughing again. “Is it for you? I mean, I’m sorry if it is, but I meant no harm. I just wanted to say hello.”

I had spent my life competing for wins, and secrecy was an essential part of the process. I supposed this wasn’t the same. “No harm done, DJ. I just wasn’t expecting to see you. Are you ready to race?”

“Absolutely. Do you want to see my racer?”

That got my attention. “That would be great!”

0035.0401.1410 LST

DJ opened the door to her bay and we stepped in. What I saw in front of me stopped me in my tracks.

Even though I knew her racer wasn't activated, it seemed that it was already floating off the ground. And there was something else. The shape of it reminded me of the racer I was using, but this one looked so new and immaculate that it was difficult to believe it was based on the same design. I tried to find the words. "It's absolutely gorgeous, DJ. I'm so impressed."

"Do you really like it?"

I turned and looked at her. She looked delighted. "I really do, DJ. I would be hard pressed to design something more beautiful."

She blushed. "It's not just beautiful, you know. It's a winner." She walked over to her machine. "Look at this, Bella." She was standing beside the cockpit. I walked over to her. She placed her hand on top of the cockpit and pressed down. It gave with the force. "I don't feel the bumps." She started to giggle. "It makes the race less stressful."

I took that as a cue to get back to my bay. "You've given me a lot of incentive to complete my racer, DJ. Thank you. I hope you do well."

"I hope you do well, too, Commander. Thank you."

I left DJ's bay and walked back to mine.

0035.0401.1445 LST

I sat in my racer counting down the minutes before the autopilot activated to take me to the starting line. The intensity of my focus was astonishing even to me. When the autopilot engaged, a flood of adrenalin entered my blood stream and I felt my body react. I grabbed onto the control sticks and immediately felt a sense of oneness with the racer. The bay door opened and I moved out and towards an airlock. I glanced around to take a final look at the garage and saw DJ in her machine moving towards a different airlock. As I entered my airlock, I didn't know if I was going to win the race, but I felt as if nothing short of the Moon blowing up would cause me to lose control.

0035.0401.1459 LST

I glanced to my right and saw DJ in her cockpit. She appeared to be facing forward down the straightaway. At twenty seconds to the hour, my heads-up display activated and I heard Max give a fifteen-second warning. Five seconds before the race, Max began, "Five… four… three… two… one… begin."

My right hand pushed the control stick forward to full throttle and I felt myself pushed back into my seat. My left hand was working its controls to keep the racer going in a straight line. I could see my speedometer race to sixty-four hundred kilometers an hour, and before I had time to think, I needed to set up for the first set of S curves. I wanted to see if DJ was beside me, but something was preventing me from doing so.

I entered the curves faster than I had in any previous run, but the line never left the center of my display. I adjusted my speed as I went through the short tunnel and entered the crater, and held it steady at the minimum speed needed to navigate. As I hit the short straightaway that led into the loop, I accelerated to a fraction over the recommended speed limit.

As the G's started to rise, I felt my suit start to compensate. I was anxious for this part of the race to be over. My mind urged me to go faster, but a part of me knew it might cause me to pass out, so I held on. As I rounded the loop and shot out of the mountain into that vicious right-hand turn, I thought to myself, "Thank God… only two more times."

I sped through the back-end of the course toward the hairpin. I had recovered from the loop. The focus I had when I started the race had since returned. I slowed to almost a stop and rounded the curve that would take me back to the main straightaway. As I hit the straightaway, I punched the throttle and felt my body react to the rush of adrenalin that was pumping through my veins. It had been many years since I had felt so alive.

I was curious as to where DJ was on the course, so I asked Max. "Max."

"Yes, Commander."

"Where is DJ?"

"She's now entering the crater, Commander."

I blinked. "How many seconds is she ahead?"

"Eight point seven four six three seconds, Commander, and pulling ahead."

I was entering the tunnel. "Can I catch her?"

"I cannot answer that question, Commander."

I was rounding the crater and decided I would not try to catch her. "Can you estimate how many seconds ahead she will finish using the information you have?"

"Approximately twenty-five seconds, Commander."

I entered the loop. "I can live with that, Max."

"Thank you, Commander."

As I sped through my second lap and entered my third, I knew that I had kept the racer under my control. My body was starting to feel fatigued from the stress and constant pounding of the track. It took every ounce of energy for me not to push harder to get through the race. I now understood how easy it would be to lose total control during the course of the race.

DJ finished the race twenty-four point seven five six seconds ahead of me.

0035.0401.1800 LST

So I had done it. I had completed my first race. As Max took me back to the Garage and my bay, I started smiling. I couldn't stop. The fact that I couldn't stop smiling made me laugh, and the fact that I couldn't stop laughing made me laugh even harder. I laughed all the way back to my bay, not knowing or caring if anyone saw me. I laughed so hard and so long that my body started to ache. Tears began to form in my eyes, and that's when I stopped laughing.

As I sat recovering in my racer, I heard a voice. A deep voice. A voice that shook me to the bone. A voice that said, "Welcome to the Moon."

Eighteen: Noah

0035.0402.0010 LST

I drifted into a deep sleep. My mind and body were exhausted from the day's events. I felt myself floating a few centimeters off my bed. I liked the sensation. I had felt it before. Slowly, I felt my body drift down and make contact with my bed. When I felt settled, I opened my eyes.

I turned my head to the left and then to the right, and found myself in a familiar spot. It was the oasis. I got up. I was expecting a voice to call my name and waited about fifteen minutes. I heard nothing.

I walked down one of the pathways, not knowing where it would take me. I felt relaxed, even though I remembered having had traumatic experiences whenever I visited this place. I wondered if I would have an encounter with Cee.

As my mind wandered, I didn't notice that the path had ended. I found myself inside a small, primitive dwelling. I turned around to go back, but saw only a wall where the pathway had been. I wondered where I was. I looked around and saw a place to sleep and a fire pit, which I assumed was for cooking and for heat. I looked at my clothes and saw that I was dressed as I had been on the Moon. I felt very out of place.

Knowing that I had to walk through the door in front of me made me nervous, but I knew I had to do it. I poked my head out and looked around. It was predawn in a small, ancient town and no one was about. I stepped out and started walking down the street towards the outskirts. All my senses were on red alert.

I encountered not one soul on the road I walked, which led me out of the town. I was relieved that I didn't have to explain my presence to anyone.

I walked over the crest of a hill, wondering what was on the other side. In the distance, I saw a vast pasture with a house on it. I walked toward the house as the Sun began to rise. I enjoyed the warmth of it on my face and was able to observe some of the animals that lived on the land. Soon, I veered off the road and onto a path that led straight toward the house. I then heard a sound behind me, and froze. Long grasses lined both sides of the path and I was unable to see anything as I turned my head to look around. I cautiously moved forward. A few moments went by and then a loud roar filled the air. *Not again*, I said to myself.

It was over in an instant. Its front paws crushed down on my chest and I found myself nose-to-nose with a massive male lion. I was paralyzed with fear. The lion opened its jaws and roared, its deadly teeth only centimeters away. I screamed and gasped for breath. I grabbed its front legs and tried to move them off my chest. The lion looked at me and started to pant. His breath just about knocked me out.

I yelled at him, "Are you going to eat me or what?!!"

I heard a voice behind me. "He won't eat you, Bella. He's just protecting me."

I saw a staff prod the lion. "Off you go."

I rolled onto my side and struggled to catch my breath. My chest was racked with pain. "H-h-how did you know my name? Who are you?"

"My name is Noah. I was told to expect a visitor whose name would be Bella. That is you, is it not?"

I mind screamed, "Oh God!!!!!!"

"Bella? Are you okay? I have been expecting you."

I got up. I couldn't look at him. Looking at the ground, I said, "I wanted to see the Ark."

Noah nodded and said, "Everybody in this land has seen it, Bella. I do not mind showing it to you."

"Is it finished?"

"Yes. We leave in three days. I came back here to take a final look around."

"Three days?!!"

"Yes, Bella. Does that trouble you?"

"Can I come with you?"

"I have been told you would ask me that. I'm sorry, Bella. You cannot."

"But I will die in the flood!!"

"Maybe you will not. Do you still want to see the Ark?"

"Yes."

"Come along then."

And so Noah, the lion and I began a half-day trek to Noah's Ark. We walked through the forest where the trees had been felled to build it. Not far from the forest was a clearing where Noah had built his Ark. I stood and looked in awe and disbelief at what I saw before me.

I looked at Noah and said, "I know you and your family will survive, Noah."

Noah answered, "That is what I believe, Bella. My family and all the animals are inside preparing, as I must do. You have permission to look at the Ark for as long as you wish, but you may not enter it. I have been instructed to tell you that if you climb to the top of the mountain on the other side of the Ark, you will find what you need in order to survive the flood."

I walked with Noah toward the Ark and felt dwarfed by its immensity. *How in the world did this get built*? I kept asking myself.

I spent twenty-five minutes walking around to the other side of the Ark. Its ramp was down and Noah and the lion had started to climb aboard. I saw the mountain I had to climb and did not know how I was going to make it to the top in two days.

Before Noah and the lion had disappeared inside the Ark, Noah instructed me to wait for his return before I left. He came back a few moments later with a small vessel of water and some food. "This is all we can spare, Bella. God be with you."

"In the Eyes of God, Noah. I am honored to have met you."

"Thank you, Bella."

I turned and began walking towards the mountain.

♦♦♦

My walk slowly turned into a run. I secured my food and water so they would not interfere with my gait. As I ran, several different animals joined me and seemed to pace me as I ran towards the mountain. I enjoyed their company.

The sky remained clear as I continued my run into the night. The Moon was full and bright enough that I didn't have to stop. I saw that I was going to make it to the base of the mountain before sunrise. When I reached the base of the mountain, I looked for a place to rest and found a sheltered spot under an evergreen tree. Once settled, I ate some food and drank some water, and felt refreshed. My vest started to heat up as I drifted off into a dreamless sleep.

♦♦♦

I had not climbed such a big mountain before, but I was motivated by my belief that the only way back to Tranquility was to make it to the top in one and a half days. The climb started gradually enough, but as the day progressed, it became steeper. As I passed the point where vegetation became sparse, I notice that the Sun was making its way westward. I stopped and ate. The sky was clear. I finished both the food and water at that sitting, and I left the food pouch there. I kept the water vessel, thinking I might encounter a supply of water further up the mountain. I didn't know how far up the mountain I was, but looking out over the valley, the forest appeared far away.

I started climbing again, but it wasn't long before my progress started to slow. I began to lose focus. By the time the Sun had set, I was completely out of control and started to look for a place to rest.

♦♦♦

When I awoke, I could feel the heat from my vest surrounding my body. The Sun was shining on the other side of the mountain. As my eyes adjusted to the light, I saw that I was resting on a small ledge overlooking the valley. I could see the forest and the clearing where the Ark rested.

The ledge I was on was small. So small, actually, that if I had rolled over in the night, I would have fallen hundreds of meters straight down. I turned to see how I had ended up on the ledge. Apparently, I had managed to climb a rock face. I did not remember climbing onto the ledge and I had no idea how I had managed to do it.

I remembered watching men and women on television climb what seemed to be impossible vertical rock faces hundreds of meters high. That was where I was. The only way to the top was straight up. I didn't have time to dwell on the fact that I had never done this before. I recalled that those who did this sort of climbing stressed that finding a good handhold and a place to put your feet were two of the most important things about rock climbing.

I proceeded up the mountain. As the day wore on, I settled into a rhythm. My sense of time disappeared and I could not feel my body. At one point, I reached up to grab onto something and felt nothing. I started to panic. I hugged the rock and tried to think of what to do. My mind was in chaos when the thought formed that I might be just a few centimeters from the top.

I raised my hand up and bent my elbow. My hand hit a flat surface. I felt around and latched on to what felt like the top of a rock. I pulled as hard as I could to make sure it was secure, and then pulled myself up to the top of the mountain.

I lay there on my stomach for a few minutes, hardly believing I had made it. I felt the Sun on my back and stood up. My legs were wobbly and my arms, sapped of strength, hung by my side. I took a three hundred and sixty degree look around and saw that I was indeed on top of the mountain. I looked down at the forest, a carpet of green. My mind reeled in disbelieve, for I was at least a couple of thousand meters up.

On the horizon I saw what I recognized as a cold front with a black, curved cloud formation racing towards me. I was certain that I had never seen anything move that quickly across the sky. I saw lightning flash within the clouds, and while waiting for the sound of thunder, I counted the seconds so I could determine how far away the formation was. I didn't hear any. The clouds were moving quickly and I saw great volumes of water being released. I then remembered Noah and the reason he had built his Ark. I feared I would not find what I needed to survive the flood.

Clouds continued to race in and I began to hear thunder. The wind had begun to blow so hard I wondered if I would be blown off the mountain. The sky around me quickly became dark and rain began to fall all around me. I looked up towards the sky and was instantly blinded by a flash of lightning and deafened by a clap of thunder.

I held my hands over my eyes, trying to protect them. When I felt I could see again, I removed my hands and opened my eyes. I saw sunlight being reflected off a pane of glass, and I again shut my eyes to protect them. It was then I noticed that I felt warm and dry and that it was no longer raining. Slowly, I opened my eyes and realized that I was looking out of my bedroom window at Tranquility base.

I stood at the window and looked at my clock. I saw that it was early morning of the final day of racing. I decided to take the day off.

Tomorrow was the day we would learn who won the race.

Nineteen: And the Winner is…

0035.0404.1100 LST

I sat with my friends in the Commanders Lounge to await the results of the race. Showing on the video wall were spectacular wipeouts and collisions from previous races. The room was alive with anticipation. Jay, Wallace, DJ, Chris and I sat at one table, observing but not saying too much to each other.

I had done a lot of thinking during my day off. "Wallace…"

"Yes, Bella."

"There is something I need you to do as you explore what we've found."

"I'm listening, Bella."

I looked around the table and saw that I had everyone's attention. "If you conclude that it would be possible for everyone living on this base to inhabit the place we have found for an extended period of time, I want you come up with a plan to stock it with all the supplies we would need, and a plan that would evacuate the base as quickly as possible."

I watched Wallace. He swallowed and looked at DJ. DJ looked at me, her eyes wide open.

Wallace asked, "What's going on, Bella?"

"I have seen and heard many things over the past few weeks that lead me to believe it would be in the best interests of the base to have an evacuation plan. That is all I am willing to say at this time. This goes no further than this table." Everyone nodded.

Wallace continued, "This base goes deep underground, Bella."

"I know, Wallace. An ounce of prevention…"

"I understand, Bella."

That pretty much killed the mood at the table. We sat in silence. At ten minutes to the hour, an announcer came on the screen. "Well, I hope everyone enjoyed our little montage of scenes from years gone by. It amazes me to see how much the racers have changed and how much faster they have become. The results will be posted with the winner on top and everyone else in the order they finished." The scene changed to the interior of a hotel. "As you can see, there are a lot of people in Vegas waiting in anticipation, the favorite being Commander Wallace Till."

The whole room looked at Wallace. He stood up and addressed the room. "You all know that SEARCH does not approve of placing bets on this race. That is not why we race." The whole room spoke in unison, "Yes, sir!!"

"Good. Because I'm sure I didn't win this time." He sat down. He was smiling.

The room went silent for a minute except for the announcer in the background speaking of Wallace's many wins. And then a voice from somewhere in the room said, "Someone is going to lose a lot of money!" After a short delay, the whole room started to laugh. As the laughter died down, we heard the voice of the announcer, "And the results of this race are as follows."

The screen lit up with thirty-two names. Twenty-nine of them had little stars flashing beside them with a percentage beside the flashing star. The best percentage other than the winners' belonged to Wallace, at seventy-one percent.

My percentage was ninety-seven point five three eight.

The room went dead silent. Everybody in the room looked at me. The announcer was speaking. "For those of you who are new to this, the flashing star beside a name indicates a personal best in one area of the race. In this case, the flashing stars indicate that almost everyone racing has bested their fastest average lap time. Unfortunately, it has come at the expense of some other factors. Congratulations to Commander Bella Carrera… He is not the first one to win the race first time out, but he has set a new record for the best percentage for a first-time racer." The screen went blank.

Someone in the room started to chant, "Bell lla. Bell lla. Bell lla." Soon the whole room was doing it. Even my table. I stood up and raised my hands in victory and everyone started cheering. When the noise died down, I saw that the room wanted me to say something. All I said was, "Thank you."

Twenty: The Wallace Report

0035.0516.0930 LST

"Come in, Wallace." I was in my office and had just submitted to Max the final design for my racer. I expected to get the results in a few minutes.

"Good morning, Bella."

"Hi, Wallace. Can I get you some coffee?"

"That would be great. Thank you." Wallace sat down at my computer station and started setting up for his report. I returned with his coffee and sat across from him.

"So what's the good news, Wallace?"

"The bottom line, Bella, is we could, if we needed to, spend years down there."

"That's good. What's the bad news?"

Wallace sat and thought for a minute. "The bad news is… Will we have to?"

My fingers started to drum on my desk. "I don't know, Wallace."

Wallace nodded. "Are you waiting for something?"

I looked at the computer. "As a matter of fact, I submitted my final racer design to Max a few minutes ago. I'm waiting for the results. It's seems to be taking some time."

Wallace nodded his head. "Yes, sometimes it can take a while. I'll need the computer to show you everything. I've already loaded it in, so I'll start whenever you're ready."

"Let's wait a few more minutes."

I heard my monitoring station activate. I got up and walked into the other room. Wallace was right behind me. I hadn't ordered it to activate.

"That's odd. Computer, deactivate my monitoring station." Nothing happened. I called the computer again. "Computer, respond please." There was no response.

A voice I did not recognize called. "Commander Carrera."

"This is Carrera."

"Commander, this is Commander Clifton, Computer Central. I'm receiving reports of computer malfunctions from all over the base."

I looked over at Wallace. "I'm experiencing one right now with my monitoring station. Can you find the source?"

"I believe I have. Did you ask Max to review the design of your racer?"

"Yes."

"Well, it appears Max doesn't know how to evaluate the design. He's accessing other sources."

"Can he do that?"

"Yes."

Wallace was watching me as I spoke to Commander Clifton. He couldn't hear what Commander Clifton was saying.

"Is this a serious problem, Commander? The computer is not responding to my commands."

Clifton responded, "All systems have built-in reboot and recycle commands. The situation is not life threatening. We'll have to wait it out."

"Thank you for reporting in, Commander Clifton. Please take care of the situation. Carrera out."

Wallace was very curious. "What's going on, Bella?"

"Max is having a problem with my racer design."

"What kind of problem?"

"I don't know. He's started to access different computers and data banks to help him."

Wallace started to laugh.

"What's so funny?"

"What exactly did you design?"

"I'm not willing to show you just yet. We'll have to wait until Max is finished before you can start."

"Okay, Bella." We went back into my office and sat down.

Wallace was anxious to start. "How about if I tell you some of what concerns me about the alien space, Bella?"

"That sounds like a good idea."

"Well, the first thing is that it's really alien. What I mean by this is that when you're down there, you don't think about how incredible it is that some species was able to engineer and build the place. You think about what, who and why it was built."

"Have you come to any conclusions? Do you have any theories?"

"I have a theory, but it's not a pleasant one."

"We have time, Wallace. I can handle it."

"Okay, Bella."

Wallace sat for a minute to gather his thoughts. "Have you entertained any thoughts about why this moon was chosen by these aliens?"

"No. I've been trying to determine what it is they've left behind."

"And what have you concluded?"

"That they intended to live here."

"I agree. Where do you think they would live?"

"In that space we found."

"Is that the only place?"

"Yes."

"I don't believe it's the only place."

"I'm listening, Wallace."

"Based on what I found, I believe they intended to make the surface of the Moon habitable. I believe this Moon offers them a place that is close to the Sun for energy and that can be adapted to suit their needs."

"What about us, Wallace? I mean humans, here and on the Earth? Do you think that maybe we would mind?"

"I believe that is why they left. I think they began to develop and build here at a time when they thought we would annihilate ourselves as a species. At some point, they must have realized we were somehow going to survive."

"What are you saying?"

"I'm saying that the aliens must have believed the human race was finished and that when the time was right, they could take the Earth from us without any fuss because we, as a species, would no longer exist."

"So they left because they realized we weren't going to wipe ourselves out."

"I believe that is accurate."

I sat and thought about that for a few minutes. "Maybe they left and just haven't returned to conquer us."

"That's a possibility, but I doubt that it will happen. I'll show you once we get our computers back."

0035.0516.1045 LST

Max finally called. "Commander."

"Yes, Max."

"I've completed my analysis of your racer. I have no suggestions. It is perfect. I have sent an order to the fabrication plant. Everything you will need in order to build your racer will be in your garage bay within three days. If you need assistance, please ask me."

"Why did it take you so long, Max?"

"I had to create a master program specific to your racer. Yours is designed to perform differently from any other racer that has been designed on this base."

"What does that mean?"

"It doesn't mean anything, Commander. I drove your racer using my simulation program and it performed in a way that was unfamiliar to me. I found the solutions through other databases."

"I noticed that you said it was different. I designed it to be better."

"How you do in the race is still up to you, Commander. The program I created will prevent you from injuring yourself and destroying your machine."

"Thank you, Max."

I looked over at Wallace and he said, "I'm now very anxious to see your racer. Max hasn't taken that long before."

"I will show it to you, but we need to finish what we were doing first."

"No problem. Computer, please start the Wallace Report and activate the wall screen."

I snickered. "The Wallace Report?"

Wallace smiled and shrugged. The screen activated. Wallace and four of his crew entered the tower with an all-terrain moon vehicle behind them. All crewmembers had their cameras on. This was the edited version.

"Bella, I've divided my report into three sections: This first part covers the dome and water, the second covers the administration building, and the third covers the living quarters."

I watched as the tower door opened and light from the alien space filled its interior.

"The dome itself provides the light and is timed to mimic the sunrise and sunset on Earth. Although there is no replication of the Sun, during the night, stars fill the sky as though you were living in the Caribbean." Wallace and his team were walking towards the beach with the transport behind them.

"I brought a submersible with me to see how big that body of water is. As you can see, the sub is tiny, but it has all the instrumentation on board to do a complete survey. The water is fresh."

"How big is the dome?"

"It measures three kilometers at its highest point. From end to end, it measures twelve kilometers. That, of course, is from the surface of the water." The screen showed the submersible under the water. It was closing in on what appeared to be a wire mesh wall.

Wallace continued his narration. "What we are looking at now is what I believe to be a safety zone one kilometer from the beach. I believe it is there to prevent someone from going into deep water."

I watched as the sub rose up and over the barrier, skim along its top for a few hundred meters and then head into open water. The screen soon filled with a shot of a structure. It looked similar to what a cake sliced into nine pieces would look like if viewed from directly above, but with spaces between each piece. "What's that, Wallace?"

"I don't know. I suspect it's responsible for the gravity at this base. It's located in the deepest part of the water."

"And how deep would that be?"

"Twenty-four kilometers."

The screen changed to show a three-dimensional diagram. It showed a sphere with a diameter of twenty-seven kilometers. At the three-kilometer level, a ring encircled the top portion of the sphere. The next screen showed a cut-away of the ring with dome and the beach visible on the inside. The beach ran one third of the way around the inner ring. I studied the diagram for a few seconds.

Wallace said, "I believe that ring contains the infrastructure of the sphere."

"Could be, Wallace."

"There are currents in that body of water."

"What does that mean?"

"It means the water is being circulated."

"How?"

"I don't have an answer to that yet."

Wallace stopped the computer. "What do you think?"

I stared at Wallace for a minute. "I don't know what to think. Computer..."

"Yes, Commander..."

"I want you to load the information you have on the structure we found at the bottom of the sphere to see if a relationship exists between it and the model we are now using to find the towers."

"I have your information, Commander."

"Proceed."

"Based on the data, the answer is yes."

I glanced at Wallace. "Is it possible to display the results on screen?"

The screen changed. The model we were using appeared on screen. Beside it was a picture of the structure we found, but with nine bands intersected to form the shape of what an apple looks like when put through a slicer, but with the tops and bottoms joined. Both images matched and moved together. The towers on the surface were located above the bands of the structure we were seeing inside the Moon.

I continued, "How deep is the structure, Computer?"

"Eighty-one kilometers below the surface, Commander."

"What is it, Bella?"

"I believe the towers are designed to feed energy to that structure."

Wallace sat and thought for a few moments. "I would have to concur. Is that how they will create the gravity needed to keep an atmosphere surrounding the Moon?"

"That sounds like a good conclusion. How are they planning to create an atmosphere?"

"There are many techniques. There's a lot of water down there. Enough, if used properly, to create a breathable atmosphere. And there is no doubt in my mind that they know how to use it."

"How?"

"How what, Bella?"

"How did that water get there?"

"I have a theory."

"Let's hear it."

"I believe they towed it."

"What??"

"Like an iceberg, Bella. We know there are comets and small moons out there made up of large quantities of ice. I believe they managed to bring some of the ice to this moon, melt it and store the water."

"And we didn't see any of this happen?"

"Apparently not."

"Aren't we the fools?"

"Maybe. Should I continue?"

"I'll be fine."

"Good."

Wallace instructed the computer to start and I saw the team inside their vehicle moving towards the administration building. The vehicle stopped in front of an entrance. The crew climbed out and walked toward the building.

"As you will see, all the entrances open from the center outward, the way the tower entrances open. The hallways and rooms illuminate as we enter the building." As the crew walked toward the building, an opening appeared. As they entered the building, I saw a space similar to the inside of a typical human building. The crew was in a large foyer, twenty-seven meters high.

"The building material is similar to what we've encountered with the towers, but the surfaces are smooth. The dwellings are also built of the same material. This building is designed like an office tower. You'll see us come to a series of three elevators. There are nine levels in the building."

The crew walked down a hallway and I saw the three doorways lining one of the walls. Wallace stepped toward one and it opened. All five of them easily fit inside and the door closed. There were no buttons and they began to have a discussion about how to activate the mechanism, but there were no suggestions. They were silent for a minute and then they started to move. One of them asked what had happened and I saw the camera zoom in on Wallace.

One of the crew asked. "What did you do, Commander?"

He was a little pale and swallowed before he spoke, "I thought the words… Level two please… and we started to move."

The same crewmember asked, "Why did it respond to you, Commander?"

"Because I am in Command."

I looked at Wallace. "It responds to the thoughts of whoever is in Command?"

"Yes."

I turned back to the screen and watched as the door opened. The crew left the elevator and walked into a large, empty space. The windows activated and we were looking at a spectacular elevated view of the dome.

"All the floors are empty except the top floor, Bella."

"What's on the top floor?" Wallace pointed to the screen. The crew walked out of the elevator and into a totally dark space. I heard Wallace activate the lights on his suit. The rest of the crew followed his lead. A part of the floor became illuminated and then I saw what looked to be a Command Center. But not like one I'd seen before. "What is it, Wallace?"

"It appears to be a Command Center of some sort. I suspect it runs the dome, although I didn't find anything that I recognized as a computer."

"Do you think it might run on the same thought response mechanism?"

"If it does, it didn't respond to mine."

"Is that it?"

"That's all for now. It was much like exploring an unfinished building back on Earth."

"Do you think that means they're friendly?"

"It might. I'm not going to jump to any conclusions about them. What do you think, Bella?"

"I think they're trying to tell us something."

"What."

"I don't know." The screen changed to show the crew traveling down the road toward the village.

"The village has a total of six thousand five hundred and sixty-one dwellings. Some are designed for one, and others are designed for two or more. Each of the ones we checked out was different, so I'm assuming they're all unique. The population of the base could easily be accommodated. I believe we would need to set up communal cooking and hygiene areas, as we found nothing inside the dwellings that we could use for those things. Power supplies will also be needed. I believe the village could be made very livable."

"How about food supplies?"

"We could bring enough supplies to keep us well fed until our food growers got up to speed. Of course, we have plenty of water."

"It's good, Wallace. Let's get started."

"What do you mean?"

"I mean we should have all those things set up and ready as soon as we can."

Wallace hesitated. "Why? Is there something you know that you're not telling me? The base will find out what we are doing and start to wonder what is going on. The last thing we need is our people panicking."

"Then I will address the base before we start and we'll handle any concerns as they arise."

"Are you going to tell me?"

I looked at Wallace and saw the concern on his face. I wanted to tell him about Noah and what I had seen, but I couldn't. "No Wallace, I'm not going to tell you. What I'm asking you to do is in the best interests of the base. I hope you understand."

"I do, Bella, as much as I would like to say I don't."

"Thank you. The report was good. How long will it take you to set up our home away from home?"

Wallace smiled. "Two months."

"Excellent. Is there anything else we need to cover?"

"How about your new racer?"

I'd completely forgotten about that. "Of course!! Max, let's show Wallace my racer. Project a full size three-D image to the middle of my office."

"Yes, Commander."

Wallace swiveled his chair around to face the middle of my office. A few seconds later, the image of my racer filled the space. I wasn't able to see Wallace's face, but I saw his body react. Slowly, with his arms pushing his body out of his chair, he stood up and said, "Holy…"

The cockpit sat at the front of a long slender fuselage, which was suspended in mid-air. All the plumbing for the thrusters was in plain view with the space drive centered in the middle of the fuselage. Two swept back 'wings', which housed the flotation generators, extended out from the middle of the fuselage and two pods at the end of each wing supported the entire weight of the racer.

"Do you like it?"

"It's beautiful."

"Thank you."

"Are those wings? It looks like it's ready to take off."

"I designed them to look like wings. Inside each one are generators for the floatation devices. The gas is released at the end of each wing and under the fuselage. The fuselage is suspended where the wings connect to the body, effectively isolating the driver from the track. When the G forces cause the fuselage to come within a few centimeters of the track, extra floatation generators kick in. Would you like to see what it looks like going around the track?"

Wallace nodded his head.

"Max, run the track simulation." Wallace turned and focused on the wall screen.

My racer appeared on screen at the start of the course. "Begin, Max."

Wallace saw it right away as it shot down the straightaway. The wings absorbed all the inconsistencies of the track and kept the fuselage isolated. It looked alive, like a flying bird.

"I'm speechless, Bella."

Twenty-one: My Racer

0035.0520.1045 LST

I had no idea what to expect when I walked into my garage bay that morning. When Max informed me that all the parts for my racer were waiting for me to assemble, I had what you might call a small anxiety attack.

I made my way to the garage, walked into my bay and stood looking at more than one thousand parts neatly placed on the floor. There were also parts on benches, in boxes and hanging on the walls. I was mortified. Max had estimated it would take me three weeks to complete assembly.

"Max…"

"Yes, Commander."

"I have no idea where to begin."

"Understood, Commander. The first thing you need to do is make sure all the parts have been delivered. Use the inventory list I'm displaying and match the parts to the diagrams you see. When you finish one screen, ask me for the next. The last screen you see will introduce you to the tools you will use. Would you like some music while you work?"

That sounded like a good idea. "Thanks, Max. Pipe in the radio station."

"Yes, Commander."

0035.0520.2300. LST

"Commander…"

"Yes, Max."

"You've been working now for over twelve hours. Maybe you should take a break and come back tomorrow."

"I want to put something together before I leave today. I'm almost finished with the tools."

"Very well, Commander. What would you like to assemble?"

"What would be the easiest?"

"Preparing the floatation generators for installation."

"Great. Let's do that."

0035.0521.0015. LST

"I'm done, Max."

"Excellent, Commander. Should I start shutting down the bay?"

"Yes. I'll be back at eleven hundred hours."

"Very well, Commander."

I felt completely satisfied with what I had accomplished. I could hardly wait to finish my machine and drive it in the race.

Twenty-two: The Race… #2

0035.0701.0600 LST

I sat in my new racer waiting for Max to begin the race. Jay and I were the first to run. I wondered what his reaction to my racer would be. As Max began the countdown, my mind cleared and my body anticipated the start.

When the race began, I launched down the straightaway and began working my way through the series of twists and turns. As I hit the loop, I felt my racer absorb the G force. I felt confident and strong. I was pulling more G force for longer periods. I blasted through the loop into the sunlight and navigated through the next series of turns. My focus was on the hairpin.

I had spent hours practicing the execution of the hairpin. My racer was designed to take the turn at never-accomplished-before speeds. If I missed the turn, however, my race would be over.

"How are we doing, Max?"

"What do mean, Commander? You know I cannot tell you how well you are doing."

"I know, Max. Where's Jay?"

"He is two seconds behind you."

"That's good!"

"Anything else, Commander?"

"No, Max. Thank you."

I was using two different programs for the controls — one for the track and one for the hairpin. The program for the hairpin automatically switched back to normal once the maneuver was completed.

As I approached the turn, I switched programs. The braking thrusters activated and at the same time, the thrusters on my left pushed the back end of my racer around. Thrusters on my right kept me from swinging around, and a small amount of thrust from my accelerators kept me moving in the right direction. As we came around the curve, my racer was positioned correctly. The right-hand thrusters went full throttle to stop the sideways momentum. I went full throttle forward and the controls returned to normal.

"You're sure this is legal, Max?"

"Yes, Commander."

"How far ahead am I now?"

"Twelve seconds, Commander."

I was stunned... "Yes!!!"

Unfortunately, the excitement of getting through the turn had caused me to lose my focus. During the last two laps of the race, I lost control several times.

I finished thirty-one seconds ahead of Jay.

♦ ♦ ♦

Jay visited me in my bay after the race. "That is the most unreal machine I've ever seen!"

"I'm glad you like it. Do you know how you did?"

"When I found out how far ahead you were, I tried to catch you. Not so great. How about you?"

"When I found out how far ahead I was, I lost my focus. I have no idea how I did."

Twenty-three: And the Winner is…

0035.0704.1150 LST

In ten minutes we would find out who had won the race.

Wallace, Jay, DJ, Chris and I were sitting at my table watching the video screen. The room was quiet. The screen, unlike the first time I was here, was not showing a montage of wipeouts and crashes. Instead, it was focused on the hairpin turn. It demonstrated how the racers, as well as the angles of attack in navigating the turn, had changed over the years. It showed machines flying off the course at the hairpin. And, interspersed amongst these records, were clips of my racer taking the turn faster than had ever been done before.

It seemed to go on forever. I was starting to feel self-conscience, but still found it fascinating to watch.

0035.0704.1200 LST

The screen changed, and the announcer I had seen before appeared. He did not say who he was, and I had never asked. "This was a very close race. Congratulations to all. Of course, those of us who cover this event have seen some very eclectic racers over the years. But not one of us, in our wildest imaginations, ever thought we would see a creation such as Commander Carrera's racer. Not only is it beautiful to watch, but it works as well."

"You'll notice two stars flashing beside Commander Carrera's name. One of them indicates that he personally bested his fastest lap-time in competition. The other one indicates that he beat the fastest time to complete the race by twenty-three seconds." I froze in my seat. "And so without further delay, here are the results."

The screen changed and showed the results with the winner at the top. Again, I was first, with a result of seventy-three point four six seven percent. I was astounded. At the bottom was Wallace with sixty-seven point nine eight six percent. Jay came in second at seventy-three point four zero nine percent. Everybody in the room seemed to be in shock. It was very, very close.

I stood up. "I'm surprised. It would appear that we're all a little bit out of control. I'm looking forward to our next competition." I sat down.

People started to stand up. I saw some backslapping and handshaking. Several people came to my table and congratulated me.

Twenty-four: Tranquility II

0035.0825.0900 LST

"DJ, this is Bella."

"Yes, Bella. This is DJ."

"Good morning, DJ. I'm calling to tell you that you will be taking a few days off. Wallace has indicated that the Dome is now ready, so I'm going to spend some time down there getting familiar with it. I'd like you to do the same."

"That sounds like a good idea, Bella. When should I be ready to go?"

"How much time do you need? You'll be gone for a minimum of three days."

"Give me one day?"

"I'll give you two. Meet me at my office at nine hundred hours on the twenty-seventh."

"I'll be there."

"Thanks, DJ."

0035.0827.0900 LST

I opened my door and let DJ in. She was wearing her suit. "Good morning, DJ."

"Good morning, Bella. How are you this morning?"

"I'm fine. Yourself?"

"I'm well."

"Good. I'll just get my suit on and we'll be on our way. Please make yourself comfortable."

"I'll wait here."

"I won't be long."

DJ put down her pack and stood by the door. I collected my supplies and met DJ at the entrance.

"Ready, DJ?"

"As ready as I'll ever be."

"Let's do it."

♦♦♦

We made our way down to the garage, where Chris was waiting for us. "Good morning, Commander. Good morning, DJ."

We spoke in unison. "Good morning, Chris." He nodded in response.

I filled Chris in. "I've asked Jay to take care of the Base while we're away. I expect we'll be gone at least three days. When we get back, arrange to go down to the Dome. Let me know when you are going. Also, I may need you to take care of the Base, so be prepared."

I saw Chris' eyes open a little wider. He swallowed. "Yes, Commander."

"Where is our vehicle?"

"Right behind you, sir."

"What?" I turned around and saw our all-terrain vehicle. I didn't hear it pull up. I heard DJ chuckle. I turned and looked at her and saw her wink at Chris. Chris started to blush.

I cleared my throat. "Excellent, Chris. We'll see you when we get back."

"Thank you, Commander."

♦♦♦

DJ and I loaded our vehicle and climbed in. I took the controls and drove to the airlock. Our helmets deployed and we slowly ascended to the surface of our Moon.

DJ's face appeared in the small window of my display. "Thank you, Bella."

"For what?"

"This is exciting."

"I'm just doing what I believe is best for the base, DJ."

"I know, Bella." The window that was displaying her face disappeared from my display. The airlock opened. I drove to the road that led to one of the entrances of the tower and stopped. "Computer, open visual link with DJ." DJ appeared in the window display. "DJ, you know, when I was putting my racer together, I listened only to SRCH radio. You really are the best."

She smiled and said, "Thank you, Bella."

"You're welcome, DJ." I closed the window display.

I continued to drive towards the tower.

0035.0827.0955 LST

It didn't take as much time as I remembered to get down to the Dome. As we descended, I remembered my first encounter. I told DJ to prepare herself. We drove out of the tower and stopped. I wanted DJ to have a minute to take it in. I was still in awe. "What do you think?"

"It's staggering. I've studied images of this place on my computer, but didn't imagine its true size. The sky… it's so blue."

Wallace was waiting for us and I drove over to him. I asked him if I was right about the trip taking less time. "Yes, Bella, it took fifteen minutes. Our original descent took forty."

I nodded and looked around. DJ was doing the same. After a few moments, I turned my attention back to Wallace. "So where should we begin, Wallace?"

"We should start with our village and work our way back to the administration building."

"Sounds good. You ready, DJ?"

"Yes. Let's go."

♦♦♦

I decided that Wallace should drive, since he knew where everything was. DJ and I took off our suits and placed them in the transport. DJ took the front seat and I climbed into the back. We were about one kilometer away from the village.

Wallace began talking about what progress had been made. "Jay has come up with good solutions with regard to power and water, Bella."

"I'm looking forward to seeing what he's come up with."

"The road system within the village is quite extensive. We'll need a way to get around. Jay suggested a combination of personal transportation and mini buses."

"I'll have Chris submit a plan."

"That's a great idea. Do you have any questions, DJ?"

"Yes. Does the climate change?"

"Actually, it hasn't. The temperature on the beach is steady at twenty-seven degrees. Heat radiates from the sand. The village fluctuates between twenty and twenty-five. There isn't any wind to speak of, but we know that the air is being circulated. I don't think you'll be able to get a tan on the beach."

DJ and I both laughed. We were coming up to the village and I was able to see clusters of what would be our quarters. The whole settlement was built on a gradually ascending slope. It was clear that all homes had a view of the water. Its size was starting to make an impression on me. "I believe we need a name for this place. Any objections to 'Tranquility Two'?"

Wallace responded, "Not from me, Bella. How about you, DJ?"

I looked over at DJ. She looked lost in amazement. "Sounds good."

We had just driven past the entrance to the village when I asked Wallace to stop. "I think that all personnel with Command positions should have quarters in close proximity to each other. That will allow for better communication and make it easier for personnel to find us. We should be located right at the entrance, which means we should stop here and choose our quarters right now."

Wallace climbed out of the transport. "I'll be able to show you how our power and water is hooked up. Jay and his people have completed the installation for eighty percent of the quarters."

"Outstanding."

As DJ and I got out of the transport and began walking toward the first cluster, DJ said, "Bella."

"Yes, DJ."

"In regard to communications, do our vests work down here?"

"I don't know. Wallace?"

"Yes, DJ, the transmission and receiving capabilities of our vests work well down here. What we don't have is communication with the surface. We still need to figure something out. Any suggestions?"

"Not right at the moment."

"Maybe the answer will come to you."

"Maybe it will."

The roads and buildings were made with variations of the same materials we recognized in the power crystals and towers. As we walked around, I noticed there wasn't any evidence of vegetation. No lawns, shrubs or trees. Since there was no water source, I wasn't surprised.

♦♦♦

Wallace took us around the first cluster of homes. The way they were arranged reminded me of a townhouse complex. "We haven't found doors on any of these homes. I could speculate as to why, but I really don't have any idea. The way the entrances are designed, it would appear that they might not be needed."

We entered the first home and made a right turn down a short hallway to get into open space. The room we entered had a view of the water and was designed as a studio. There was a bed against the wall opposite the window.

Wallace led us into a small room that held a portable washroom. It contained a toilet, shower and sink. In one of the corners sat a cylindrical vessel, which held two hundred and fifty liters of water. Pressed up against the corner between the floor and the wall was a series of tubes. Some ran into other rooms.

"Jay and his crew are setting up several stations for water so we can keep our personal supply full. He suggested that we keep track of our consumption, so we'll have a record of how much each person uses."

"Every space will have its own power supply to heat, pump and purify water. Power will also be supplied to the cooking area and anywhere else it's required. The power units Jay designed will supply enough power to last each of us a minimum of five years."

"We are currently testing a recycling system that will break down all the waste we produce into harmless chemicals. Given our situation down here, it's imperative that we don't release anything toxic into our atmosphere and water. We'll have our results in a few days. If everything checks out, we'll begin installing immediately."

I was blown away. "This goes way beyond my expectations, Wallace. I'm beyond being impressed."

"Thank you, Bella. How are you, DJ?"

"It's unbelievable what you guys have done. I want to see more."

"Should we move on, Bella?"

"Let's check out a few more of these homes. Then you can show us how the water stations work and how the recycling stations will be integrated."

"My pleasure, Bella."

♦ ♦ ♦

We spent the entire day in our village, exploring and inspecting dozens of homes. I suggested that Samson be given the job of bringing some life to the village in the form of plants and trees. Both Wallace and DJ thought that was a great idea.

We watched the sky turn into a star-filled wonder. We picked our quarters and bedded down for the night. Wallace suggested we spend the next day exploring the beach. DJ and I agreed.

As I drifted off to sleep, I wondered how Jay was doing.

0035.0828.0900 LST

Wallace was right. He said I would have thoughts about who these aliens were, and that I would question why this place was designed and constructed. As I ate my breakfast, these thoughts and other questions filled my mind.

At ten hundred hours, I met DJ and Wallace outside. DJ climbed into the back of the vehicle. She was excited. "Come on guys. Let's go to the beach!"

Wallace and I loaded our stuff and climbed in. We headed out of the village to a spot where Wallace and his team were doing their research in the water and on the beach.

During our drive, DJ said, "I have a solution to our communication problem, Bella."

I glanced over at Wallace and then at DJ… "What have you come up with, DJ?"

"It's a simple solution. Clearly, we don't have the technology to broadcast up to the surface, so we should create a department whose purpose would be to create a series of relay stations that will broadcast messages to and from our respective positions. We know it takes only fifteen minutes for a one-way trip up or down. We could build a system around that."

Wallace blurted out, "That's brilliant!"

It was brilliant. "I agree. It will be your responsibility to set that up when we get back, DJ."

"Thank you, Bella."

As Wallace turned off the road and onto the beach, I said to him, "Remember what you said to me about how your mind filled up with thoughts and questions about the beings that built this place?"

Wallace turned his head and looked at me. "Yes."

"Are you still affected by it?"

"I've come to accept it. There are times when I find it quite distracting, but I recover quickly."

"That's good to know. I've had experiences of this kind before. It's good to know it will dissipate."

Three of Wallace's team members were working at the waters edge. We drove up to them and got out of the vehicle.

A team member by the name of Hirsche greeted us. "Good morning, Commanders."

Wallace responded, "Good morning, Hirsche. What are you guys up to today?"

"We've deployed four surveying subs at varying depths to see if we can find the source of the currents. The deepest will reach a depth of ten kilometers and will come within one meter of the wall." He pointed to a monitoring station. "You'll be able to see what they're broadcasting at that station."

"Thank you, Hirsche."

We walked over to the station and took a seat. The readouts on each of the screens relayed information such as sub speed and depth. Each of the subs had powerful flood lamps illuminating the areas in front and on the side. All the subs were close to the wall. No distinguishing features could be seen.

I stared at my screen for a few minutes. I was tracking the deep-water sub. The speed indicator showed that the sub was gradually increasing in speed. I checked the other subs, but didn't notice any variance in their speed.

"Hirsche."

"Yes, Commander."

"I need you over here."

"Yes, Sir."

Hirsche walked over. I pointed to the speed indicator. "Are these subs supposed to run at a consistent speed?"

"Yes, Sir."

"So what do make of this? This sub has been steadily increasing in speed. The others are not."

Wallace and DJ were now studying the situation.

"I'll review the sub's systems Commander and check for a possible malfunction."

Hirsche spent a few minutes checking the operation of the sub's systems. "The sub is working as it should, Commander. There must be some external force causing it to speed up."

"Can you speculate as to the cause?"

"Yes. We've theorized that there may be openings through which water may be circulating similar to a swimming pool with drains that allow the water to be pumped and circulated through filters and heating systems. There could be openings in which water is flowing or where water is forced out. The sub would have to be in close proximity for it to be affected either way."

Hirsche paused a few seconds. "The sub is being drawn in. The water flow over the surface of the sub is moving fractionally faster than the speed it should be going and will continue to speed up. There's a chance we'll lose the sub."

Wallace asked, "Do we want that?"

"It's not something we want, but if we want information about what is causing the sub to speed up, we'll need to be close to the source. The sub may not be powerful enough to counter the water flow. I can reverse the engine to give us a little more time and gather information. Should I proceed?"

I answered, "I leave it in your hands, Hirsche."

"Thank you, Commander."

All six of us were now fully engaged in what was transpiring. We didn't have to wait very long for things to start speeding up.

Hirsche continued his report. "The sub is beginning to rise Commander. I'm putting the engine in reverse. I'll be using the controls to stabilize the sub. All cameras and lights are activated."

"We're right behind you, Hirsche."

All eyes were fixed on the screen. The sub was rising quickly and its lights were shining off the wall. It hit nine kilometers and leveled out. *That figures,* I thought to myself. The sub continued to speed up.

"How are we doing, Hirsche?"

"I'm speculating a whirlpool effect, Commander. The computers are programmed to compensate. If there is a whirlpool, its power will determine how the sub reacts." The speed of the sub accelerated. "I have the engine in full reverse and it's not making any difference. I'm losing control of it. We should be seeing something very soon."

DJ saw it. "There it is."

We all stood up and watched. The sub was headed towards a three hundred meter wide opening in the side of the wall and it's lights began to reflect off the currents in the water. It than began to spin around, making it difficult to see what was happening. Its speed continued to increase and as it entered the opening, the signal stopped. The sub was gone.

"That's it, Commander Carrera. We'll be analyzing the data. Did you want a report?"

"I'm sure Commander Till will want one."

"Of course, Commander. Thank you."

0035.0829.0900 LST

DJ spent a couple of hours in the water while Wallace and I spent time creating a plan that would enable the staff of Tranquility to enjoy the space we were creating down here. We decided that a three to seven day stay would be a nice break for them.

Wallace and his team concluded that the first eight floors of the administration building would be ideal for our food-growing needs. We scheduled our day to see how things were progressing. DJ met Wallace and me by our transport and we headed off.

DJ asked, "What kind of plants are we growing, Wallace?"

"We have a variety of fruits, legumes and vegetables available to us. Growing conditions are optimized for each species with an average crop rotation of three months. Our processing and packaging will enable us to store a large percentage of our crops indefinitely."

"Sounds good."

As we approached the building, we saw a lot of activity around the entrances of the tower. Supplies were being unloaded. Wallace parked by the entrance to the building. We entered and walked toward the elevators. I asked Wallace how the building was responding to all the different people working in it.

"It's much more sophisticated than anything we have invented. We haven't had any problems with it. It doesn't take long for it to recognize an individual's thought patterns and respond."

DJ was curious. "What are you guys talking about?"

Wallace replied, "The building is able pick up an individual's thought patterns. We have developed similar technologies, but this is far beyond anything we've created. The complexity lies in that it seems to be able to distinguish an unlimited number of individuals. Over a short period of time, everybody who works in the building has been able to give instructions such as turning lights on and off successfully by just thinking about it. If there are a number of people working together, it works with the one in command. I can't imagine how they did that."

DJ swallowed. "Neither can I!"

There was an elevator waiting for us. As I stepped in, I felt something make contact.

I heard DJ's voice. "Bella, are you okay?" I looked at her and then at Wallace.

The door to the elevator closed and I said, "Apparently, we're going to the ninth floor."

I did not ask to go there, but I knew that was where we were going.

The doors opened and we stepped out. As we did, the entire floor lit up. Wallace was startled. It was the first time he had seen it like this.

The building, or whatever it was that had made contact with me, continued. "It's communicating with me!"

Wallace caught his breath. "What does it want?"

"It wants to show me."

"Show you what?"

"What I need to know. It believes me to be the highest in Command." I looked at DJ and Wallace. "I can't leave until it's finished. You don't have to stay."

I heard both of them respond, "We're staying."

I was grateful for that. "Thank you."

I glanced up at the twelve-meter high ceiling and saw the soft glow of lights. Directly in front of me was an overly large cubicle with three-meter high walls on two sides and a floor-to-ceiling window overlooking the interior of Tranquility Two. Each cubicle was nine meters wide and nine meters long. One meter from the floor, and tilted down at a forty-five degree angle was a three hundred millimeter long panel that ran all the way around the enclosure.

In total, twenty-seven cubicles stretched the entire length of the floor. I walked down to the first one. Wallace and DJ followed me. I entered the first unit and placed the palm of my hand a few centimeters from the surface of the panel. The panel directly underneath my hand lit up. Numerous symbols glowed different colors. I walked down the length of the cubicle, keeping my hand over the panel. The entire panel was responding to the proximity of my hand.

I turned and walked around the rest of cubicle. I noticed Wallace and DJ were copying my movements, but the panel wasn't responding to them. I moved to the next one and repeated what I had done before. It became clear to me that this was to make sure all the units were working.

I heard DJ's voice. "Do you know what these are for, Bella?"

I shook my head. "Not yet."

I repeated the procedure for all twenty-seven units. They appeared to be working, but their purpose was unknown to me.

♦♦♦

We were standing outside the last cubicle looking down a two hundred and forty-three meter long hallway.

Wallace looked at me. "Now what?"

I looked over my shoulder to my left. An opening had appeared in the wall. It was softly illuminated from the inside. "I don't know. Something has been activated."

I turned and walked through the opening. Wallace and DJ followed. The opening closed behind us and all sources of light were deactivated.

"Wait," I said.

My eyes focused on a small point of light. I felt myself moving towards it. A few seconds later, many more points of light appeared. I recognized them as stars.

I heard DJ's voice. "Unbelievable!"

I felt as though I were traveling through space. In the distance, I recognized the shape of our galaxy. We were moving towards it at remarkable speed. We entered our galaxy and flew past a variety of space objects: planets, suns, huge gas clouds, comets, and pulsars. It wasn't long before we entered our solar system. We flew by Saturn and Jupiter, and then into the asteroid belt. We navigated around them. Mars came up quickly and we found ourselves flying towards our Earth and Moon. We decelerated, orbited the Earth once and then flew back to the Moon. We came in low over the surface and passed over an image of Tranquility base.

DJ gasped, "How…?"

We pulled away from our Moon until we were able to see all of it. It floated in front of us and began to rotate. Several small green points of light shone from the surface, and I recognized them as the towers that had been activated. Thousands of red lights also shone from the surface. I believed they were towers that had yet to be found and activated.

We pulled away a little further and saw hundreds of our satellites orbiting our Moon. I was completely blown away. I then wanted this trip to end. Somehow it read my mind, and the room returned to the way it was when we had entered. The entrance appeared behind us and we left on very shaky legs.

I started walking back to the elevators. "Nobody say a word. That's an order." Wallace and DJ followed.

An elevator was waiting for us and we entered. We exited on the main floor and walked out of the building. As we did, we saw that the tower had activated. No one was able to come down or leave when the tower was on. It was clear that we were going to be here a few more days.

I turned to face Wallace and DJ… "I need to spend some time alone and gather my thoughts. I'll explain what I know tomorrow. Let's meet for breakfast at nine hundred hours."

Wallace looked a little wasted. "That's fine with me, Bella."

"Does that work for you, DJ?"

"Whatever you need, Bella."

"Good. I'm going to find some transportation back to my quarters. I'll see you tomorrow."

0035.0830.0900 LST

DJ, Wallace and I walked over to the kitchen that was set up for the staff and grabbed a table. I was anxious to tell them what I knew. "In simple terms, what we experienced yesterday was the equivalent of one of our monitoring stations. The cubicles are designed to record any problems or events that the occupant has experienced. If a problem is detected, a solution is provided. When a problem has been solved, it is noted. If an event has occurred or a problem needs to be addressed, that information is passed on to the one most qualified to resolve it. This is what they invented in order to manage themselves and their creations."

DJ was nodding her head. "But it works with you, too."

"I suspect that in time it may work with others."

Wallace agreed. "I think that's a good assumption. What about that room we went into?"

"It would appear to be a dedicated program that is designed to monitor the surface and the immediate space of the Moon. That would explain passing over Tranquility and the shot of all our satellites."

Wallace had the beginnings of a smile on his face. "You're not sure what else it was designed and programmed for."

"No, I'm not. I'm sure we'll find out."

"I'm sure we will. You scared?"

"Absolutely. You?"

"Totally. Should we try again for our food production factory?"

"Let's do it."

♦♦♦

We entered the building and walked into a waiting elevator. Wallace was confident we would end up on the right floor this time. And he was right.

We stepped out onto the second floor and took a few seconds to look around. Directly in front of us was a panel similar to the one I had seen on the Orbiting Headquarters.

Wallace explained, "Because of the complexity of the floor plans, each floor has a panel like this one. On them you will find directions to the crops you may want to inspect. The computer is linked to the communication systems of our vests. The floor plans are very much like a maze. If you happen to find yourself going around in circles, the computer will direct you back to the elevators."

Behind the computer panel were rows and rows of twelve-meter high floor-to-ceiling panels spaced two meters apart. A sea of green plant life covered everything. The lighting was optimized for fast growth.

"What are we growing on this floor, Wallace?"

"Several varieties of peas, green beans and corn. They grow very quickly."

The atmosphere was intoxicating. So fresh and pure.

DJ started to move excitedly towards one of the rows. "Permission to go exploring, Commander?"

"Absolutely, DJ. Wallace and I will see you later."

"Thank you." She took off down one of the rows.

"Where does she get all that energy, Wallace?"

"I don't know, Bella. She loves life."

"That may be it."

"Maybe."

"I'd like to try some of this food."

"How about at dinner?"

"That would be fine. I'm going to check out the other floors. If you have other things to do, I'll be fine on my own."

Wallace grinned. "As a matter of fact, I do have things to do. I'll see you and DJ at dinner."

"Thank you, Wallace."

♦♦♦

I started on the third floor. It was designed for growing foods like carrots and potatoes. The growers showed me how they were able to stack the trays where the vegetables were growing and still give each one the proper lighting and nutritional requirements.

Every floor was different. It was mind-boggling how well they were organized.

It was the eighth floor that really impressed me. This was where they had the fruit- bearing trees. Using the height of the ceilings to their advantage, the growers were able to create the equivalent of entire orchards on one floor. The trees themselves were pruned and manicured to perfection.

We had oranges, apples, cherries and lemons. It was truly amazing, and the aromas were unforgettable. Tranquility II was well on its way to becoming completely self sufficient.

0035.0830.1900 LST

I walked into the kitchen and met DJ and Wallace for dinner. Wallace had asked the cooks to prepare a buffet of all the foods that were grown and processed down here.

I was surprised to see that they had stacks of our simulated sirloin steak. I loaded up my plate and sat down.

"This is truly amazing, Wallace. I mean, I'm very impressed. Very, very impressed."

"Thank you, Bella. We're planning to build a small space where the inhabitants of this place will be able to pick and choose what they want to have in their quarters. Like a grocery store, but without the payment registers."

"Perfect." The food was great. "How did your exploration go, DJ?"

She sounded tired. "Fine. I'm going to give the growers a hand over the next couple days and learn a little more about the operation."

"Sounds fine."

"Do you know what this place is going to need?"

"No."

"A radio station."

I stopped eating, smiled and looked at her. "Are you volunteering to set that up?"

"No, but I'll make sure it happens."

"I leave it in your most capable hands."

She smiled back at me. "Thank you, Bella."

"You're welcome, DJ."

0035.0902.0745 LST

I don't know what it was that compelled me to get up, but whatever it was couldn't be ignored. I took a few minutes to splash some water on my face and get dressed. Walking outside to look around, I watched as the dome transformed from stars into the colors of a sunrise.

I walked down the road to look at the beach. I saw Hirsche and his team working.

We had accomplished a lot while we were down here. I felt it was time for us to leave. As I turned to walk back to my quarters, the tower caught my eye. I stood there and studied it for a couple of minutes. I wondered when it would finish and let us go back to the base. As I finished my thought, the tower stopped.

I turned and walked back to my quarters. I needed to get back to the base.

Twenty-five: Commander Jon Irvine

0035.0903.0745 LST

As Wallace, DJ and I climbed out of our transport into the garage, I heard Jay's voice. He sounded a little stressed.

"Calm down, Jay. Let's meet for lunch at twelve hundred hours in my office. We'll talk then."

"Okay, Bella. See you at twelve hundred hours."

Wallace was curious. "Something up, Bella?"

"Apparently. Something about the Unified Space Coalition and those satellites we're expecting."

"The Unified Space Coalition?"

"Yes."

"That must be what they're going to call themselves. What do they want?"

"I don't know yet. Jay and I are meeting for lunch in my office. Would you like to join us?"

"I would."

"Good."

DJ followed Wallace's lead. "Do you need me there, Bella?"

"No. If there's something you need to know, I'll fill you in."

"Okay. I'm going to take the day to get organized."

"That's fine, DJ. I'll expect you to be on the air tomorrow."

"I will."

"Good, I look forward to it."

"Really?"

"Really, DJ."

"That's good. I'm looking forward to it, too."

0035.0903.1200 LST

Jay arrived promptly at noon and Wallace arrived a few minutes later. I had prepared a platter full of sandwiches and some beverages. Both Jay and Wallace grabbed some to eat.

We sat down in my living room and ate for a few minutes. Then I asked Jay what had been going on. "So you've had an eventful few days, Jay?"

"Not that eventful. I just wasn't expecting a call from SEARCH headquarters. I find Commander Travis a little intimidating. He wanted to know why I wasn't able to contact you."

Travis is Chief Commander for the entire SEARCH organization Earth side. "Yes, Commander Travis can be a bit of a pain. He was the one I had to convince in order to start placing the power crystals in the towers. Very unpleasant. What did you tell him?"

"I told him the truth… that you and Commander Till would be unavailable until the tower finished recharging whatever it is that it recharges."

"And he accepted that?"

"Yes."

"Good. So now tell me why he called."

"He has been contacted by a man called General Isfantac, the leader and Commander of the Unified Space Coalition. General Isfantac wanted to know if we would be interested in using our tracking system to keep track of their satellites, with their satellites using different transmission frequencies. Commander Travis has graciously refused their offer, but has said that we need to make our own decision. Of course he suggests we give them the same answer."

"That's interesting. Did he say why he turned them down?"

"I didn't ask."

"I see. Not a problem, Jay. Let's call Jon up here and see if we can't figure this out."

♦♦♦

Wallace, Jay and I moved out of my living room and into my office. I called Jon and asked him to clear his day to meet with us. He arrived an hour later.

"So, Jon, I'm about to divulge some information to you that up until now has been known to only a handful of people. This information is not to be passed on to anyone. Is that clear?"

Jon looked at each of us and responded, "Perfectly."

"Good. As you know, we are expecting some company up here. The organization now goes by the name of The Unified Space Coalition and is led by a man by the name of General Isfantac. They are now in the process of readying over two thousand satellites for launch. Nine hundred and forty-three of them are scheduled to orbit our Moon. The rest are scheduled for Earth orbit."

I stopped and gave Jon a little time to absorb what he had just heard. He looked at me and swallowed. He indicated that I should continue.

"They have recently contacted us and asked if we would be interested in having their satellites linked to our satellite tracking control system using different transmission frequencies. Before I give them an answer, I need to know how our system works."

Jon looked around the office and then at each of us again. "That's a lot of satellites, Commander."

"I know, Jon."

"Our tracking system uses both active and passive systems. What the Unified Space Coalition is interested in is the active system. The active system is connected to an extremely powerful and complex computer guidance control system. It is designed to accurately track and control our constellation of seven hundred and ninety satellites."

"It is, of course, completely scalable to handle any number of orbiting objects. Any number of factors will cause our satellites to deviate from their intended orbits. Solar winds, micro meteor impacts, faulty hardware, software glitches and other events such as passing through meteor showers and magnetic storms can cause our satellites to either malfunction or require that orbital changes be executed."

"Our tracking system keeps our satellites in their proper orbits and automatically makes the required adjustments if an unforeseen event occurs. It will also take out of orbit any satellite that is not functioning properly and cannot be repaired. More often than not, it does that by crashing the object on the surface of the Moon."

"We have hundreds of receivers placed strategically over the entire surface of the Moon. Our satellites are never out of contact with the computer. The computer itself is self repairing and has access to several redundant systems."

Jon stopped. I looked at Wallace and Jay and then back at Jon. "So what are the implications of their request?"

"I would be extremely reluctant to allow any organization access to our tracking system, even though I'm sure they would argue that it would be mutually beneficial. Allowing their satellites to send a signal to our computers so that we could better track them does us no good unless we are able to control their satellites. They haven't supplied us with the schematics of their satellites, so we will not be able to control them."

"Our passive tracking system will enable us to track their satellites and keep our satellites out of harms way if one of theirs fails."

I motioned Jon to stop. "What are the chances of that?"

"We have a failure rate of less than ten percent, but we've been doing this for a long time. From what you have told me, this is a brand new entity. I suspect the large number of launches is to compensate for what I believe to be a much higher rate of failure."

"How high?"

"I can't give you any accurate numbers."

"Speculate."

"Between fifteen and twenty percent will fail, requiring the satellites to be taken out of orbit. It is possible they could control those events from their stations on Earth. I suggest we find out if they have that capability."

"I'll do that, Jon. Thank you."

Wallace had a question for Jon. "So, why do you think they asked us about the active tracking system?"

Jon responded, "Are we viewing this organization as a potential threat to us?"

Wallace answered, "Given the circumstances of its creation, we do not consider them to be our best friends, but rather, our competitors."

"I see. It is possible that if we allow them access to the tracking system, they could hack their way into not only the tracking computer, but our main computers as well. If that happens, they could shut down the base."

Jay sat up in his chair, a look of disbelief on his face. "Are you saying that Tranquility is that vulnerable to a computer attack?"

"No, Jay. I'm saying that we don't know what we're dealing with. We have systems in place that would alert us to the slightest improper or deviant signal."

"That's good to know."

I remembered my flight from Orbiting Headquarters to Tranquility. The origin of the virus that knocked out my transport was still a mystery. "I believe Jon's concern is valid. We can't take any chances of a computer attack. Is it possible that they could still gain access?"

"When it comes to computers, anything is possible. But the chances of an attack going undetected are slim. We are prepared to deal with an intrusion from our end."

"That's good, Jon. I want your team to be diligent."

"Yes, sir."

"Do we have anything in place that allows us to take a satellite out of orbit if it completely dies in orbit?"

"Yes. We have small remote-controlled recovery vehicles that we've launched to capture and bring back satellites that have failed for some unknown reason."

"I want those vehicles on standby. Just in case."

"Yes, sir. Commander?"

"Yes?"

"Why is there a General in charge of The Unified Space Coalition?"

"I don't know. I suspect we'll find out the answer to that question if all our precautions turn out to be needed."

Twenty-six: The Race…#3

0035.1001.0600 LST

I'm up early to watch the first day of racing. The distraction and focus that the race offered was something I greatly appreciated. The computer had picked Wallace and me to run in the last race of the three-day event. Wallace let me know that he had completely redesigned his machine and was looking forward to racing against me. I was also looking forward to it.

♦♦♦

Commander Travis and I had spent the previous three weeks making sure the Unified Space Coalition had systems in place in the event of a satellite failure in Moon orbit. We made it clear to General Isfantac that we would take any of their dead or failing satellites out of orbit if their systems failed to do so. He seemed a bit unnerved by our aggressiveness, but concluded that it would be in both of our best interests if we did that.

Their first satellite was scheduled to arrive on Year Thirty-five, November Fourteenth, Eleven hundred hours LST. They expected to complete their launch schedule on Year Thirty-six, May first, Eleven hundred hours LST.

As the first race commenced, I realized that in all the races that had been run since I arrived, not one collision had occurred on the straightaway. I wondered why that was, and spent the entire day wanting to see a one. None occurred.

0035.1002.0600 LST

I'm up to watch to first race of the second day and get ready for a day in the garage. Before I leave, I program my computer to monitor the day's races and record any wipeouts and collisions. As I worked on my racer, I anticipated seeing some good race action.

When I got back to my apartment later that night, I asked the computer to play back what I had asked it to record. There was nothing to see. I was disappointed.

0035.1003.0520 LST

It is the day I am to race and I am up very early. My mind is already at work going through my race. I know it is going to be a long and stressful day. All my energies are focused and I know I'll be going through periods of extreme excitement and total fatigue. No one has ever won three races in a row. That is my goal.

♦♦♦

At sixteen hundred hours, I'm down in my garage bay and suited up. Every system on my racer is in top condition. I had spent many hours fine-tuning the controls to get maximum performance out of my racer. I felt very confident.

♦♦♦

I climbed into my racer and placed my hands on the controls. It was fifteen minutes before the start of the race. I closed my eyes and waited for Max to take me to the starting line. I felt the floatation generators activate and my racer slowly elevated. I opened my eyes and watched as the door to my bay opened. I took a deep breath as Max guided me through the garage. I looked around and tried to catch a glimpse of Wallace and his new machine, but I didn't see him.

As I rode up the airlock to the surface, I felt my heart starting to pump faster. I saw that Wallace was already at the starting line. I wasn't able to see his racer from the angle I was approaching.

Max brought me to the starting line. "Five minutes, Commander."

"Thank you, Max. Max, can you project a three-dimensional image of Commander Till's racer onto my display?"

"Yes, Commander."

Max projected the image and it appeared in front of me. Its fuselage was long and narrow much like mine, but Wallace's cockpit was a third of the way down. His 'wings' were quite a bit smaller and not swept back. At the end of each wing were long slender cylinders that ran parallel to the fuselage. I suspected that was where the floatation generators resided.

"Thank you, Max. That's enough." The image disappeared.

"One minute, Commander."

I refocused myself and got ready for the start.

The ten-second warning went off and then I heard Max's voice. "Five… four… three… two… one… begin."

All the hours of practice and racing had conditioned my body to react faster than my thoughts could control it. I felt like I was just along for the ride.

As I approached the hairpin turn, my confidence level was high. I went around it easily. I pushed my racer out of the turn and into full throttle.

"How many seconds are we ahead, Max?"

Max took a few seconds to answer. "We are not ahead, Commander. Commander Till is right beside us."

"What??"

"Commander Till is running the same time as you."

Before I had time to recover from the shock, Max was warning that a collision was imminent unless I took action quickly. I was on the straightaway and Wallace was coming at me at an angle that would impact the back of my racer and send me spinning around. I reversed full thrust and saw Wallace shoot in front of me. I punched the throttle and aimed for his lane, forcing him to take mine.

He missed. I started to laugh. Wallace had opened the door. It was my turn next.

I spent the next lap thinking of a strategy for hitting Wallace. We were still neck and neck as we rounded the hairpin turn the second time around. I waited until he was just ahead of me on the straightaway. Then I accelerated and attempted to sideswipe him. He must have anticipated the move because I didn't even come close to hitting him.

By the third lap, Wallace and I seemed to have the same idea. We created a spectacular collision just before the finish line. Both of us completely lost control of our racers. Max needed to save us.

We were both disqualified.

Twenty-seven: And The Winner Is … #3

0035.1004.1150 LST

Wallace and I had a good laugh about our antics on the track. Everyone at the table was talking to us about it.

The infamous video wall was showcasing some of the more spectacular collisions that had happened over the life of the race. Some of them had to be seen more than once to be believed.

At twelve hundred hours, the announcer started his broadcast. "It appears that Commander Carrera has started a trend that will greatly influence the shape and style of future racers. We all look forward to seeing the shapes of things to come."

"Before the race started, there was much speculation on the part of this announcer and his many colleagues, as to whether this would be the race where we would have a three-time winner. Given the disqualifications of both Commanders Till and Carrera, that did not happen."

He paused for a few seconds. "Today's winner has run in many races. This is his first win. Congratulations to Commander Jon Irvine."

The screen went blank and then lit up with the results. It was another close race. Jon topped out with a result of eighty-nine point seven five one percent. The spread between him and the rest of the field was twelve and one-half percent.

I started clapping and yelling "Speech!!!… Speech!!!…" Soon the entire room was doing it. Jon finally stood up and gestured for us to quiet down. "This is not a feeling I've experienced before… I quite like it." The room got loud again. "Thank you." Jon sat down and everyone in the room starting talking. The atmosphere was different this time. No one was leaving.

I looked around the room. I felt empty. As much fun as it was jousting with Wallace, I didn't want to be disqualified again.

♦♦♦

After spending some time at Jon's table, I went back to my office. I realized while talking with Jon that I had only been training to avoid a collision.

"Max…"

"Yes, Commander."

"I want you to save my collision with Wallace to my training program."

"Done, Commander."

"Run it randomly when I'm practicing on the track."

"Done, Commander."

"Also, Max, I'd like you to program a series of events on the track where my objective is to hit the other driver."

"Done, Commander."

"Thank you, Max."

Twenty-eight: The Unified Space Coalition

0035.1114.1100 LST

"Commander Carrera, this is Jon."
"Carrera, here. Good morning, Jon."
"Good morning, Commander. It's here."
"I'll be right over."
I'd been waiting for that call all morning. I left my office and made my way over to Jon's station at the Satellite Control Center.

♦ ♦ ♦

Jon had been working closely with the engineers of the Coalition to make sure their systems would not interfere with ours. In the process, he had learned quite a lot about their systems.

"It arrived and established orbit at precisely eleven hundred hours, Commander."

That surprised me. "I suppose that's good news. What does it look like out there?"

"It's pretty basic. Two solar panels attached to a six-sided box. I'll bring the visual up on the screen to your left."

An image of the satellite appeared on screen. I saw two solar panels that seemed small compared to the size of the satellite. Several antennae jutted out from the main body. Light from the sun reflected off its sides and panels, "That's a good image for an object five hundred kilometers away."

Jon continued. "It's the first of several dozen. These are positioning satellites that emit and receive radio signals. We've allocated the frequencies they can use so they won't interfere with our systems."

"Their built-in computer systems analyze and process the signals to establish the positions of each satellite in the constellation. Each satellite is programmed to orbit at a specified distance from our satellites, the surface of the Moon and their own satellites. We have developed similar technologies."

I was studying the image as Jon talked. "Can they see our satellites?"

"They are using a high-frequency radar system similar to that of a bat. It can see our satellites and is designed as a defense mechanism. If it detects something is coming too close, it will reposition itself."

I was impressed. "It sounds like their system is designed to work with a minimum amount of input from ground sources."

Jon nodded. "That is accurate. That's the upside. The downside to the system is the amount of computer power each satellite needs to carry. It makes each satellite more complex and expensive and also means that if anything interferes with the ability of the computer to perform, potential problems will arise."

I nodded in response. "Do you foresee many problems?"

"As I've said before, there is always the potential for something to go wrong. Their technology appears sound, based on what I've studied. Any problems that do arise will be immediately seen. What is still unknown, though, is how the problems will be solved."

I agreed. "Keep me posted, Jon." The satellites were scheduled to arrive in small clusters starting tomorrow.

"Of course, Commander."

Twenty-nine: Completion

0036.0809.1625 LST

During the past nine months, sixty-seven of the Coalition satellites have lost their primary computer systems and rained down on us. Jon's prediction of satellite failure was accurate. Fortunately, each of their birds had a secondary unit designed to take them out of orbit and crash land in a remote spot. I feel lucky that none of the secondary systems has failed yet.

We are expecting the last of their satellites to arrive and establish orbit in a few minutes. As with any undertaking of a large magnitude, the Coalition has had to stop and solve problems as they occur, and so are a few months late in completion.

"On screen, Commander."

"What are we looking at, Jon?"

"These are the last three, Commander. They are part of the Coalition twenty-one-piece observatory. They will be establishing an orbit at one thousand kilometers."

Jon and I watched the satellites get closer. After a few minutes, we could see deceleration thrusters activate. A short while later, the orbiting thrusters kicked in.

"Looks like everything is okay, Commander. Orbits have been established."

"That's a relief. Thank you, Jon."

"You're welcome Commander."

I left Jon's station and made my way back to my office.

So that's it, I thought to myself. *The Coalition has completed its mission of satellite deployment*. I had an uneasy feeling in the pit of my stomach.

Thirty: The Decision

0036.1128.0945 LST

"Commander Carrera."

"Commander Carrera here."

"Good morning, Commander. Bill Travis calling."

Commander Travis and I had formed a close friendship over the last few months. "Good morning, Commander. I didn't recognize your voice. What can I do for you today?"

"There's something I'd like you to think about."

"And what would that be, Bill?"

"The fact that in just under two months, the two years you agreed to spend on Tranquility will be complete."

I did a double take. That had been on my mind. "I don't know what to think about it, Bill. I agreed to stay for two years. What would you have me think about?"

Commander Travis continued, "We've been engaged in quite a bit of discussion about it, Bella. The feeling down here on Earth and on Tranquility is that we would like it if you stayed on as Commander of Tranquility for as long as you want the position."

If Bill had been talking to me face to face, he would have seen that I had lost my ability to say anything intelligent. "What did you say?"

I heard Bill clear his throat. "I said you're welcome to stay on as Commander of Tranquility for as long as you like."

"That's what I thought you said." I wasn't prepared to continue the discussion. "I'm floored right at this moment, Bill. I'm going to need some time before I commit one way or the other."

"Understood, Bella. Try not to dwell on it too long. We'll need a decision before the end of the year."

"I'll have my decision for you by then. Thank you, Bill."

"I look forward to hearing from you. Commander Travis out."

♦ ♦ ♦

I felt like a fool. The invitation to stay on as Commander was not one that I had anticipated. There was no reason why I couldn't stay, but the thought of returning back to Earth and rebuilding my business was something I had been thinking about.

I had made very good friends here, and now, with the Unified Space Coalition present, I felt like I would be abandoning the base if I left.

I decided that I would be contacting Bill to inform him that I would be accepting the position.

Thirty-one: Samson

0037.1125.0900 LST

I sat staring at my notes, waiting for DJ to give me the on-air signal. Ever since the day I had agreed to stay on as Commander of Tranquility, I have been doing a weekly radio address. DJ had suggested it might be a good idea. She thought I should be the one to keep everyone informed as to what was going on, now that the Coalition had a presence here. After experimenting with the format and gathering feedback from listeners, I decided she was right.

I heard the end of the song and positioned my hand over the mike control. DJ finished her set and gave me the signal. My finger touched the 'mike on' key…

"Good morning, Tranquility. Commander Carrera here with your weekly update. We are fortunate not to have experienced any satellite failures this week. It was forecast that we might be plagued with a number of problems from both our satellites and the Coalitions satellites after that massive solar flare storm that ended yesterday. While on the subject of the Coalition, they have indicated an interest in finding a place to build their own base on our Moon. They are working on an artificial gravity generator that would allow them to build anywhere. Of course, this has peaked our curiosity. The Coalition is certain that they can create a profitable situation here. Negotiations are forthcoming. Personally, I wouldn't know where to begin, but I have been told my input will be needed. Having said that, I will be actively pursuing advise from all departments. Please let me know what areas we need to protect and what areas are available for development."

I couldn't believe the words coming out of mouth. The Coalition was the last thing we needed up here. We had been hinting to them about the alien structures to determine if they had detected anything, but as far as we knew, they hadn't. I glanced at DJ. The look on her face reflected what I was thinking.

"I know many of you are wondering what the Coalition has found that makes them feel so confident. I wish I knew. They haven't volunteered that information. When negotiations start, I expect the stress levels on this base and the rest of the organization to go up. It is important that we accept that this is really going to happen and take the appropriate action. I trust that everyone will cooperate. If you have any questions or concerns, please remember that my office is always open. This is Commander Carrera signing off."

DJ activated her mike and introduced a five-song set. I sat in my chair and watched her work the consol. She had a monitoring station installed to keep track of what was going on around the base, and incorporated what she saw into her show. She had mastered the skills needed behind 'the mike' to keep her audience coming back for more.

♦♦♦

I was about to get up and head back to my office when I received a call from Jon.

"Commander Carrera. Jon, here."

"Carrera here. Hello, Jon."

"Good morning, Commander. We have an unstable satellite in a decaying orbit."

"One of ours?"

"No, sir."

"Where's it headed?"

"Towards the northern polar region."

"Have you contacted the Coalition?"

"Yes, sir. It's one of their positioning satellites. They are aware of it and have confirmed the crash site."

"Good. Do we have a visual?"

"Yes, sir."

"Good. Feed it to the broadcast booth on DJ's station."

"Yes, sir."

One of the screens on DJ's monitoring station showed the satellite tumbling out of control. DJ turned to look at me, pointing to the satellite. Her voiced cracked as she said, "What's this?" She was using the internal communications system.

"It's one of the Coalitions' satellites. It's headed for the north pole."

She was perplexed. "What should I do?"

I tried to relax her. "Jon and I are just watching to make sure it will land where it's supposed to. No need to say or do anything."

"Okay."

"Would it be okay if I moved into your booth?"

"Sure."

I got up from my chair and moved towards her booth. As I did, the door opened. I walked inside and pulled up a chair. The door closed. I sat with DJ and watched the satellite.

♦♦♦

I watched as small rockets on the satellite ignited and made small adjustments in its course. I asked that one of the other screens display the decaying orbit of the satellite and its eventual crash landing site. A small flashing red light represented the satellite. DJ was keeping an eye on it. "Anything unusual, Bella?"

"Everything appears to be going fine. I'll feel better once it's on the Moon."

As I finished answering DJ, I noticed one the rockets had been burning for a long time. An instant later, the screen that been displaying the orbit went blank for a few seconds. When it flashed back on, I noticed that the landing area had changed. The screen went blank again. I glanced up at the satellite and saw the rockets burning again.

I made a call. "Commander Irvine, this is Commander Carrera!"

He answered immediately. "Yes, Commander. I see it! It's changing course very quickly!"

"Can we launch a retrieval vehicle?"

"I wouldn't know where to send it, Commander."

The screen plotting the orbit was flashing on and off. "We need to know where it's going, Jon!"

"I'm working on it, Commander…"

I waited a few seconds. Then I heard, "Oh no!!"

"What, Jon?"

"It's headed for the Earth Dome."

"What?!!"

"The Earth Dome, Commander! It's going crash right into it!"

I jumped to my feet. "Oh God! DJ, get off the air now!! That's an order!! Computer, evacuate the Earth Dome! Red alert! I repeat. Evacuate the Earth Dome! Red alert!"

I heard the sirens go off. I switched the monitors to display the interior of the Dome. The emergency exits were open and people were flooding through them. "Computer, how many people are left in the Dome?"

"Six Hundred fifty-nine."

"How much time before impact?"

"Three minutes."

"That's not enough time!!"

Everybody living on the base knew the dangers of this place. I knew how much time it would take for everyone to get out. We had practiced emergency evacuations on a regular basis in case such an event occurred. I had designed the Dome to survive impacts from small meteorites, but I wasn't sure what would happen if an object as large as this hit it.

I watched the satellite fire its rockets one more time and saw it turn. Its main thrusters were now facing the Dome. Something inside me knew that it would not only crash into the Dome, but also explode. I turned and looked at DJ… "I'm sorry, DJ."

"What, Bella?"

"They're not going to make it."

We watched as the satellite fell towards the Dome. And then, just before impact, it exploded like a grenade. The explosion caused thousands of pieces of the satellite to accelerate to an unstoppable velocity, tearing into the Earth Dome and destroying huge sections of it. The pressurized air inside exploded outward, causing even more damage. I hadn't designed the structure to withstand a catastrophe like what I was now witnessing.

I watched as cameras on the inside recorded loose objects being sucked up through the roof. People were scrambling toward the exits. For a few seconds, there was so much debris clogging the damaged parts, the vacuum sealed itself. The Dome had become fatally weakened and large sections of the structure began to shatter. Bodies became airborne and flew through the shattered Dome. What was left of the atmosphere was escaping through the roof.

The computer indicated that all emergency hatches were working properly and that damage was being contained.

"Computer, how many casualties?"

"Two hundred and fifty-seven casualties, Commander."

I looked at DJ. There were tears in her eyes. My mind scrambled to figure out what to do next. "Computer, any injuries reported?"

"Yes, Commander. Emergency medical units have been dispatched."

I collapsed in a chair and thought I might break down. DJ sat down beside me. Between sobs, she said, "It could have been worse, Bella."

I looked at her. "I suppose, DJ."

"You acted so quickly."

"Not fast enough."

♦♦♦

A few minutes later, I received a call. "Commander Carrera, this is Commander Travis."

"Carrera here. We've been attacked, Bill."

"Are you sure?"

"Yes. I'll send you the images." I asked the computer to send the visual report to the Commander.

"Are there any casualties?"

"Two hundred and fifty-seven, Bill."

"I'm sorry, Bella. You acted quickly. You did everything you could."

"Maybe, Bill. What are we going to do?"

"I don't know. General Isfantac has already contacted me. He insists that the Coalition is not a threat to us. He says we must believe him. He asked me to explain how they could possibly benefit from an attack on our base?"

"I have no idea, Bill."

"At this point, neither do I. What do you want to do, Bella?"

"I want to make sure the base is secure and that my people are taken care of."

"That sounds like the right thing to do. I'll get things in order down here and call you when I have more information."

"Thanks, Bill. I'll do the same. Carrera out." Not knowing if we were going to be attacked again, I wanted to evacuate as many people as I could. I focused my attention on DJ. "There's something I need you to do, DJ."

"Anything you need, Bella…"

"I want you to organize all non-resident personnel and take them down to Tranquility II. Make sure there's enough senior staff on hand to run the place. Report back to me when you're finished."

"Yes, Bella." She looked up into my eyes. "You knew this was going to happen, didn't you?"

I looked into her eyes. I remembered my meeting with Noah. "I knew that something disastrous could happen, DJ."

♦ ♦ ♦

"Commander Carrera, this is Doctor Alexander." Alexander is the senior Physician on Tranquility.

"Carrera here. Yes, Doctor."

"I need you down here in Central Sickbay."

"What's the problem, Doctor? Too many injuries?"

"No, Commander. Everything is under control. I understand we lost quite a few people. I'm sorry. No, I'm calling because of Samson."

"What's wrong with Samson? Why do you need me down there?"

"I need you down here, Commander. I'll see you shortly. Alexander out."

Clearly, the Doctor was not giving me a choice. I had to go and see him.

♦ ♦ ♦

I went as quickly as I could to sickbay and met Doctor Alexander at the door. "What's going on, Doctor?"

"Please follow me, Commander." I followed the Doctor through sickbay and saw many people waiting to be treated. Most of them looked frightened. The Doctor led me into an isolation room, where I saw Samson. He was laid out on a bed and appeared to be sleeping.

"Is he unconscious, Doctor?"

"Well, he's not in a coma. Please step over here and take a look at this."

I walked over to Samson's bedside. The Doctor lifted the sheet and exposed his left hand. I saw what the Doctor was talking about.

"Commander, have you ever seen anything like it?"

On the fourth finger of Samson's left hand was a ring. A crystal ring. I wondered why I hadn't seen it before. It was glowing and pulsing. Flashing points of color exploded within the ring. It was awesome. "What does it mean, Doctor?"

The Doctor didn't respond. Instead, he walked over to the light controls and turned them down until the ring was the only source of light. I saw shafts of light shooting out from the ring. I looked away for an instant and then realized that Samson's entire body had become luminescent! I could see it through the sheets. I swallowed and heard the

Doctor say, "We are the only ones who have seen this. You asked me before what it means, Commander. It means that God is working on him."

"I understand, Doctor. In the Eyes of God."

"I knew you would, Commander."

"May I see your crystal, Doctor?"

"Of course, Commander. Please follow me back to my office." The Doctor turned the lights back on and covered Samson's hand.

I followed the Doctor to his office. Sitting on his desk was a small, six-sided crystal that resembled a paperweight. Familiar multi-colored lights were dancing inside. They were the same as my display. "Why haven't I seen the ring before, Doctor? Everyone I've met who has one has either had it out in the open or has shown it to me."

"Is this the first time you've seen Samson's?"

"Yes it is, as a matter of fact."

"Well mine has been on my desk. I guess there was no reason for you to see it."

"Have you seen this display before?"

"Yes, Commander. The first time you came in. Are you going to be all right?"

I felt a little shaken. "I'll be fine, Doctor. Please let me know when Samson is back. And thank you, Doctor."

"In the Eyes of God, Commander."

0037.1201.1145 LST

Tranquility has now moved underground. We have concluded that any attack will be focused on what the enemy can see. If there is an attack, the damage will be confined to the surface structures of the base. I've cancelled the race until further notice.

We moved quickly to recover the bodies of our friends and lay them to rest. Wallace, Jay and Chris survived. The remains of the satellite have been recovered and are being studied by Jon and his team of experts. The nations of Earth that support SEARCH are on full alert and have placed the Coalition under microscopic observation.

"Commander Carrera. This is DJ."

"Carrera here. Hello, DJ."

"Hi, Bella. Tranquility II is fully operational."

"That's good news, DJ."

"Thank you. Anything new?"

"Actually, we've concluded that General Isfantac is telling the truth. We believe that his Coalition is not responsible for the attack."

"Then who is?"

"As you know, SEARCH has had many questions about the origin of the Coalition technology. The technology has enabled the creation of the Coalition. We suspect the ones who supplied the technology to the Coalition are responsible for the attack. It is clear they want something but we don't know what. We also don't know if we'll be attacked again. They have not made contact with either of us."

"Do we have any clues as to who they are?"

"Funny thing about that. General Isfantac has been their mouthpiece, yet he has never met any of people that supplied him with the technology. He says he doesn't care and doesn't want to meet them. I guess that was part of the deal. They've made him a very powerful man."

"I'm guessing he would now like to know."

"I'm guessing you'd be right. He has an entire planet ready to obliterate him and his Coalition."

"Do you think that may be the reason we were attacked?"

"What? To start a world war?"

"Yes."

"Maybe, DJ, but that's not going to happen. No retaliatory action will be taken at this time, but we are on high alert."

"So, what do you need me to do next?"

"I'll let you know, DJ. For now, you are free to spend your time as you wish."

"Thank you, Bella. DJ out."

0037.1208.0900 LST

SEARCH and our political Allies have been working on a plan to rid us of the danger posed by the Coalition satellites. Part one of the plan is to remove the satellites surrounding our Moon.

Jon and I were down in one of the Satellite Command Centers preparing to launch one of our retrieval vehicles. Everyone was watching and we were beaming the procedure back to Earth. I watched as Jon launched the vehicle. "Nervous?"

"A little, Commander. All eyes are on me, you know."

"I know, Jon. You probably feel a little like I did when I first arrived here almost three years ago."

Jon was totally focused on the job at hand. "You could be right about that."

The vehicle we sent up was designed to grab onto the satellite with its two articulating arms and bring it back to the lunar surface. It looked very much like a crab without legs. I watched as Jon guided the vehicle towards our target. It was the smallest in a group of satellites designed to relay information back to the positioning satellites to prevent orbital collisions.

"Commander, I'm ready to begin."

"Let's do it, Jon."

Jon speculated that if there were a defense mechanism on board the unit we were targeting, it would most likely be a program designed to have the satellite avoid a collision. Jon's offence would be to outmaneuver and outrun his target. He went straight at it.

"There it goes, Commander."

The satellite fired its rockets and moved sideways. "You're right, Jon."

"Yes. This should be interesting. I've programmed my computer to analyze all the moves. We should eventually be able to predict which way it's going to go. Of course, I just might get lucky and grab it before we figure it out."

As Jon approached the target again, he turned the vehicle so it appeared to be moving backwards. He then shot up and over the satellite. "What are you doing, Jon?"

"I'm hoping it will fly right into the arms." We watched as it went in a completely different direction.

"Try again, Jon."

"No problem, Commander. We'll figure this out." The satellite stopped. It appeared to waiting for Jon's next move. "Do you play chess, Commander?"

"No, Jon. Do you?"

"Yes."

"Then let the game begin, Jon."

♦♦♦

It took Jon's computer twenty minutes to begin displaying moves that would assist us with the attacks. At that point, Jon activated the program that allowed the computer to take over from him. "Only a matter of time now, Commander."

We watched as the retrieval vehicle responded to computer control. It never stopped moving, and was getting closer and closer to our target. In the meantime, I tried to determine how long it would take to bring down the more than seven hundred satellites we had in orbit.

"Commander, all the information we gather about this retrieval will be stored. With each successful mission, we'll build a database that should allow us to bring these satellites down at an increasingly faster rate. We'll try for two next time."

"Sounds good, Jon. Have you worked out how long it will take to bring them all down?"

"Not yet, Commander. I'll need more information before I give you an estimate."

"Of course, Jon."

We turned our attention back to the chase as the computer quite unexpectedly announced retrieval in less than fifteen seconds.

"Sooner than I thought, Commander."

I watched as the computer guided the retrieval vehicle to within grabbing distance of its arms. Before the satellite made its move, the computer instructed our vehicle to move to its left. The satellite fired its rocket and flew right into our vehicle's arms. The vehicle immediately clamped onto the satellite.

"Perfect, Commander. Our computer knew where the satellite was going."

"I'm impressed, Jon."

"Thank you, Commander. I expect the satellite to try and escape. We haven't disabled its ability to use its engines." We could see that happening as Jon was speaking. "By bringing the satellite down lower, its rockets will become ineffective against the gravitational pull of the Moon. If we're lucky, the satellite will use up its fuel supply."

"How about our vehicle's fuel supply?"

"We have plenty, Commander."

"Good, Jon. How long to get it down?"

"I estimate twenty minutes, Commander."

I watched as Jon took control of the vehicle. He started his descent. "How does it feel, Jon?"

"It's fighting a bit, but remember that these satellites were designed to maneuver, not to fly."

"I'll keep that in mind."

♦♦♦

"Commander Carrera. This is Travis."

"Carrera here. Hello, Bill."

"Hi, Bella. I've been watching the retrieval. It looks like we've figured something out."

"Jon's the best, Bill, but we're only five minutes into the descent. I still have my concerns."

"Understood, Bella. Just calling to say we're all impressed."

"Thanks, Bill. Anything else?"

"Are you planning a visit to Earth any time soon?"

That made me smile. "Who knows? Maybe when everything is back to normal."

"Thanks, Bella. Commander Travis out."

I focused my attention back on Jon. "How's it going, Jon?"

"It stopped fighting a few minutes ago. Looks good."

I had several satellites recording the process and a multitude of viewing angles from which to choose. I didn't take my eyes off the screen for longer than an eye blink when I thought I saw something flash across it. I focused back on the screen and saw that we no longer had a visual of the recovery vehicle with the satellite.

I heard Jon. "What the…?"

"What, Jon?"

"It's gone, Commander."

I wasn't sure if I heard correctly. "What did you say?"

"It's gone, Commander. The recovery vehicle and the satellite are gone." Jon was staring at me.

I looked at him. "We have to find it, Jon."

"Commander Carrera, this is Travis."

"Carrera here. Hello, Bill."

"Jesus, Bella. It's gone!"

"We noticed, Bill. Have you looked back at your recordings and found anything that might explain what happened? Did it blow up? We didn't see anything that would indicate an explosion."

"We haven't gone through all the recordings yet, but we did notice something. I'll send it to you. Travis out."

I waited a few seconds for the images to upload. Jon and I watched anxiously. Jon pointed at the screen. "There, Commander. Did you see it?"

"I saw it, Jon." It looked like a shooting star had collided with both crafts. They were vaporized instantly. "The question is, what was it?"

I called Bill. "Commander Travis, this is Bella"

"Travis here. Yes, Bella."

"We saw it, Bill. Any idea where it came from or what it was?"

"Not yet, Bella. We're reviewing all our recordings. When we find something, we'll let you know."

"You sound confident about finding something."

"We'll find it, Bella. We've been using our satellites to record. They offer quite a different perspective from yours."

"Thanks, Bill. Carrera out." I looked at Jon, who seemed almost paralyzed. "Are you okay, Jon?"

"I don't know, Commander. I've been watching the recording."

"And…?"

I heard him swallow and take a breath. "I ran it frame by frame just before impact."

I saw that Jon's forehead was damp. "You're scaring me, Jon. What did you see?" I waited but he didn't respond. I asked the computer to display what Jon had watched. The screen showed the recovery vehicle and satellite floating in space. In the top right corner of my display, I saw a small ball of energy moving slowly towards them. As it moved closer, it grew larger and the two spacecraft began to disintegrate. Moments later, the energy ball had reached the area of the two vehicles and totally engulfed them. There was a small explosion inside the ball and then it moved off the screen.

"Son-of-a-bitch!"

"Did you see it, Commander?" Jon's voice was shaky.

"I saw something. What do you think it was?"

He didn't answer me. He asked, "What do you think it was, Commander?"

"Jon, I'm ordering you to tell me what you think that was!"

Jon hesitated for an instant. "I believe that something took aim and fired a kind of energy pulse at those spacecraft."

"Thank you, Jon." It certainly looked like it. "If that was the case, then one or more of our systems may have seen where it came from. I want you find out where it came from. I'm going back to my office. Report back to me when you find what we are looking for."

"Yes, Commander."

♦♦♦

I didn't make it make to my office. I received an urgent call from Wallace. "Commander Carrera, this is Wallace."

"Carrera here. Hello, Wallace. What can I do for you?"

"You need to come down to sickbay, Bella. Someone needs to talk to you."

"Who would that be Wallace?"

"Samson, Bella…"

"Samson?"

"I'll explain when you get here. Hurry."

I rushed down to sickbay. When I got there, Wallace met me at the entrance to Samson's room. He took me aside before taking me to see Samson. "There are many things you do not yet know, Bella. Samson is not who he appears to be. I am the only one on this base who really knows who he is and why he is here. His real name is Dr. Samson Israel. Please listen carefully to what he says." Wallace seemed very concerned.

"Of course, Wallace. I'll listen."

"Good. Let's go in."

We entered Samson's room and I saw him sitting at a desk working at a computer. He turned his head to look at me as we walked in. "Hello, Commander."

"Hello, Dr. Israel. Wallace told me you'd like to speak with me."

"That is true, Commander. Please call me Samson."

"Yes, Samson. I'm very glad you made it out of the Earth Dome."

"Thank you, Commander."

"Wallace has told me you are not who you appear to be. Can you explain to me what he means by that?"

Samson weighed what he was going to say to me. "Have we recently been attacked, Commander?"

"Of course we have. The Earth Dome was destroyed."

"That's not what I mean, Commander. Have we just been attacked in the past hour or so?"

I glanced at Wallace, who had taken a seat beside Samson and was looking at him. I didn't know what to say. "Yes, I have reason to believe we have. How did you know?"

I saw Wallace clasp his hands together. Samson said, "As Wallace has told you, I am not who I appear to be, Commander."

"Who are you?"

"I am the one who invented what was designed to destroy every living creature on Earth, including the human race."

I felt myself getting very warm. "And what is it that you invented, Samson?"

Samson paused just for an instant. "Something called the Armageddon Project."

Thirty-two: The Armageddon Project

0037.1208.1145 LST

I pulled up a chair and joined Wallace and Samson at his desk. "So what exactly is the Armageddon Project, Samson?"

"Armageddon was the name given to a project designed to protect what we call the free world. The countries that support the Space Exploration And Research Center Headquarters commissioned it. SEARCH was never told of its existence."

A little history always helps put things in proper context. "But what is it, Samson?"

"Please, Commander. This is how I must present it."

"I'm sorry, Samson. Please continue."

"Thank you, Commander. The purpose of Project Armageddon was to act as a deterrent. We designed the system to activate only if all our defensive systems were compromised or destroyed. And believe me, Commander, those defenses were very extensive."

I thought carefully about my next question. "I believe you, Samson. Why are you here on Tranquility?"

Samson looked at Wallace, smiled and nodded his head. "We proved, beyond a shadow of a doubt, that the technology we created would work. When we reached that point, a decision was made to mothball the project."

"Why?"

"Because, Commander, it was designed to destroy everything. Every man, animal, and living thing. No God-fearing man or group would dare risk that."

"That sounds like an act of conscience, Samson. Maybe a little righteous."

"Yes, Commander. It was the right decision."

I still didn't know what the system was. "So what is the deterrent you created, Samson?"

Samson paused a few moments and said deliberately, "A system of satellites, Commander."

I looked at Wallace and then back at Samson. I already knew the answer to the question I was about to ask. "Are you saying that

SEARCH has allowed the system you designed to be deployed and activated?"

"Yes, Commander. I wouldn't blame SEARCH. Many people were involved. I believe the technology we created is now being used as a weapon against us. I believe, Commander, that we are in grave danger."

The way he said it sent a shiver up my spine. "What is the nature of the destructive force that was invented?"

"We invented a weapons system designed to work in high orbit. If activated, it was programmed to slowly arm itself. Its first priority program is to defend its own existence. The satellite creates a high-energy pulse that travels at the speed of light. The pulse itself is many times hotter than our sun."

I knew then that Samson was right. We were in grave danger. "I'd like to show you something, Samson."

"By all means, Commander."

"Computer, please send the energy pulse images to this computer terminal."

"Done, Commander."

We watched as the energy pulse crossed the screen and destroyed our recovery vehicle and the satellite. "Does that look familiar, Samson?"

I watched as Samson lowered his head and closed his eyes. I waited for his response, though his actions spoke volumes. He raised his head and opened his eyes. "That's it, Commander. It is running its defense program."

Hearing the words shocked me. "What do you suggest we do, Samson?"

"You must stop all attempts to take any more satellites out of orbit. The original plan for our defenses was a global network of Earth-based stations that would send a coded signal to the satellites every hour. This code would change everyday. Information would then be exchanged between the satellites and our computers on Earth. Some of the stations were to be highly visible. Others were to be hidden away in top-secret locations. We believed that if we were actually overpowered and defeated in a war that caused us to lose our land and homes, then those responsible would pay by having no world left to live in." Samson stopped and waited.

I nodded. "Please continue."

"We concluded that if we were attacked, the enemy would first go after anything resembling a communications link, and would attempt to disable our ability to communicate with our satellites. The disabling of the Earth stations would activate Armageddon, as it would stop receiving coded messages from those stations. If all the stations were found and disabled, Armageddon would power up and begin its mission of annihilation. I think the satellites have replaced the Earth-based stations and become part of the system. We must leave them be. We may not have much time, Commander. Clearly, Armageddon has been activated."

Samson stopped to take a breath. "If what I believe is true, Commander, I should be able to access the programs running the system. When designing the processors and software, I built in a gateway to access critical systems. If those that built the system used my design and the gateway remained undetected, I should be able to shut it down."

I thought about the defense mechanism. "Would Armageddon consider your attempts to communicate with it a breach of its defenses?"

"We won't know until we try, Commander."

"I agree. What do you need?"

"I need access to equipment that will allow me to communicate with the satellites."

"Whatever you need, Samson."

"Thank you, Commander."

♦♦♦

I left Wallace and Samson and headed back to my office.

"Commander Travis, Carrera here."

"Commander Travis here. Hi, Bella. I was just about to call you."

"Bill, have you ever heard of a man by the name of Dr. Samson Israel?"

"The name doesn't sound familiar, Bella. Who is he?"

"He is a man who worked on something called the Armageddon Project. He designed the computer hardware and software for it."

"Doesn't sound familiar, Bella."

"Regardless, Bill, we are in serious trouble. It is imperative that there be no action taken against any satellites in either Earth or Moon orbit until further notice."

"It's not entirely up to me, Bella. I'll get in touch with those in control and get back to you."

"Okay, Bill. Now why were you about to call me?"

"We've been trying to find the source of the energy pulse. We haven't been successful. The pulse seems to just materialize out of nowhere."

"Maybe what we're looking for was designed to be undetectable."

"That's a possibility I hadn't thought of."

"We'll keep looking, Bill. In the meantime, make some calls please."

"Right away, Bella. Travis out."

♦ ♦ ♦

"Commander Carrera, Wallace here."

"Carrera here. Hello, Wallace."

"Hello, Bella. I'm with Samson at Jon's Command Center. I think you should get down here. He's made contact." I checked the time. It had been less than an hour since I had left them. "I'll be right down, Wallace."

I knew the systems that Samson had designed were the ones now being used against us. Knowing that we might be able to disarm the weapon was encouraging. When I entered the room where Wallace and Samson were working, I noticed how quiet it was. Jon was sitting beside Samson, observing his every move. Wallace walked over and stood beside me. All I could hear was Samson as he worked at a keyboard. Every monitor in the room displayed a bewildering amount of information, none of which made any sense to me.

I leaned over and spoke to Wallace. "I feel useless here, Wallace. How long has he been in contact?"

"About twenty minutes, Bella. He said he's working on identifying himself. Once he has been cleared, he can move further into the system."

"Has there been any indication that his presence has triggered anything?"

"Not that we know of, Bella."

I nodded my head and continued to watch. Samson's hands were flying over the keyboard. Wallace and I stood there, waiting for something to happen.

Forty-five minutes after my arrival, Samson finally stopped. He stood up from his chair and turned to me. "Armageddon has recognized me as a non-threat, Commander. Up to this point, I haven't seen anything that indicates this gateway has been detected or compromised.

That is a good sign, but I must caution you that I have not attempted to access any systems that will affect the operation of the weapon."

That was good news. "What do you need, Samson?"

"I'm going to attempt to access the diagnostic systems. I need to know how all the systems are functioning before I attempt to disable them. I may be able determine the order in which the weapon powers up its systems."

That would be good to know. "We have not been able to locate the origin of the energy pulse, Samson. Was a component of the weapon that fired that pulse designed to be undetectable?"

Samson responded, "There were plans to incorporate stealth technology into the system, which would have made any attempt to destroy it from space or Earth very difficult. Given that we did not detect its presence until it fired, I believe it would be safe to assume that the main firing component of the system has been made undetectable to our scanning technology."

I took a few seconds to digest that information. "There must be a way of detecting something, Samson."

"I will know once I enter the diagnostic systems, Commander, but you may want to start looking for high concentrations of radiation. The system is not in a stationary orbit. It was designed to be in constant motion. You may be able to detect radiation trails and follow them back to their source. If you do, you will have found Armageddon."

I was taken aback. "Radiation? Are you saying the system is nuclear-powered?"

"It may sound crude, Commander. Remember, I spoke to you of total annihilation. The system is designed to last for one thousand years. If, by chance, humans were able to get close enough to the main component, the radiation would kill them within a few minutes. The system's final program instructs it to re-enter Earth's atmosphere and detonate at a predetermined location and altitude. Each detonation would be several thousand megatons. The resulting explosions were designed to take advantage of several factors including wind speed, Earth's rotation, and the amount of dust that could be generated. The result would be a planet completely enveloped in a deadly radioactive cloud that would block the sun completely. The planet would then be plunged into an ice age of undetermined length, and as the radioactive dust clouds slowly settled back to Earth, the radiations levels would insure that nothing survived."

I could barely speak. "How many are up there?"

Samson looked into my eyes. "The original plan called for several dozen, Commander." I couldn't believe I was standing in front of a man who could be part of such an atrocity.

As if reading my mind, Samson continued, "Now you know why the system was not deployed."

But it was now. "We have to stop this thing, Samson."

"I know, Commander."

♦ ♦ ♦

My instinct was telling me to start looking for the radiation trails, but I was unable to move. I stood beside Wallace and watched as Samson sat down in front of the computers and started working the keyboard. As I stood there, I saw one of the computer monitors flicker. I turned my head to look at Wallace. Before I was able to ask him if he had seen what I had seen, the entire monitoring system had shut down.

Samson stopped. "That's odd, Commander."

I felt a surge of adrenaline course through my body. My hands curled into fists. It felt like something bad was about to happen. And it did. The monitoring screens lit up and showed a man smoking what looked like a cigarette, sitting in a high-back chair behind a massive desk. He gazed around the room and then, to my surprise, looked right at me. He face contorted into a twisted grin.

He turned his head and looked directly at Samson. He spoke slowly, deliberately and in a deep voice, "Samson, you're alive." He paused to inhale some of his smoke. "Oh well, there was a ten percent chance that you would make it out of the Dome. Thank you for accessing Armageddon. It has made hacking into your computer system so much easier!" He stopped. His face once again contorted into a twisted grin.

Samson turned around in his chair and looked at me. He ignored the man on the screen and asked, "Do you know this man, Commander?"

I looked at the man on the screen. The man looked back me. He flicked some ashes into an ashtray and laughed. "No, Samson, I do not."

Samson filled me in. "There were only a handful of men who knew what I was working on. The man you see on the screen is one of them. His job was to ensure the technology we created for the weapon worked. He was my boss. He was in charge of the project. His name is Brath. Brath Frederick Fisco. I'm sorry that my actions have allowed him access to our computers."

"It's not your fault, Samson. We'll deal with it."
Samson turned back to face Fisco.

Thirty-Three: Brath Frederick Fisco

0037.1208.1545 LST

The first words out of Samson's mouth as he faced Fisco were, "Why, Brath?"

Fisco took a long drag off of his smoke and said, "Because it's what I wanted to do."

Samson paused before he spoke again. "You're using my program."

Fisco thought about that for few seconds. "Yes, well, I didn't have time to create something different. Besides, yours functions so perfectly. Interesting, the way you were able to incorporate a gateway to disable the program."

Samson spoke slowly. "We believed that if this weapon should fall into the wrong hands, we should take steps to assure there would be ways to stop it. The gateway is one of them."

Fisco grinned and nodded his head. "Yes. Too bad you survived the Dome explosion. But just so it's not a total loss, I'll tell you that if you succeed in destroying the weapon that's orbiting your Moon, the one that's orbiting the Earth will be instantly activated."

Samson stopped, turned around in his chair and looked at me with helplessness in his eyes. "Now what, Commander?"

♦♦♦

I looked away from Samson and turned my attention to the man sitting behind the desk. He had his eyes fixed on mine. "What do you want, Fisco?"

He took another long drag on his smoke. He sounded arrogant. "What makes you think I want anything, Carrera? I'm surprised you haven't asked if it was I that set you up."

I thought about that. "Was it you, Fisco? Was it?"

I could see anger in his eyes. He spoke slowly. "Yes, Carrera. It was I. Tell me Carrera, do you now know what it feels like to have lost everything? You spent your entire life building the most successful architectural business ever, and I took it away. I know that makes you angry, Carrera. Were there times you felt like taking your own life? I know there were."

I stood there, paralyzed.

"Aren't you afraid, Carrera? There were those who had the power to stop the deployment of Armageddon, and they did. I spent the better part of my life creating it, and it was taken from me. It was all I knew. And so now it is a reality. My creation. I've done what I've done because it was possible to do. It is what I wanted to do. I want to see the weapon I created do what I designed it to do. Destroy everything. Nothing more, nothing less."

"And how will you know, Fisco?" There was anger in my voice. "It's designed to last one thousand years. Do you believe you'll be alive to see the end result?"

Fisco grinned and laughed. "Of course not. There's a chance you'll be able to stop it, but I don't think you will. I have everything I need to live out the rest of my life in peace. Neither you nor anyone else will ever be able to find me, so I wouldn't expend too much energy on that endeavor if I were you." Fisco looked around the room again. "You bore me, Carrera. I'm going to sign off now. Good luck trying to stop Armageddon."

The screens went blank for a few seconds. When they came back on, they were the same as before Fisco had appeared. "I want you to continue what you were doing, Samson. But let me know before you start doing anything to the weapon's systems."

Samson nodded his head. "I need an assistant, Commander. Would you ask DJ?"

"Why DJ, Samson? Why not Jon?"

"Because, Commander, I have studied the system she created for Tranquility. It works on principles that are very similar to the ones that Armageddon uses. It won't take her long to figure them out."

"I'll ask her, Samson."

"Thank you, Commander."

Thirty-four: The Intruder

0037.1229.0900 LST

"I strongly advise against this course of action, Commander!" Samson was furious and was pacing around my office.

I remained at my desk. "I know, Samson, but the decision has been made. Our military believes it will be able to move quickly enough to destroy the weapons orbiting the Moon and the Earth."

Samson wasn't finished. "They do understand the meaning of hair trigger, do they not? Armageddon has been powered up. Its weapons system is one command away from being activated. If any of the Intruders or any of its launched missiles is detected, Armageddon will fully arm itself and begin its mission. Once it reaches that point, our chances of being able to shut it down will be close to zero."

"They are aware of that, Samson. We have to try. Almost all our personnel are now living underground in Tranquility II. I believe the precautions we have taken will prevent any life from being lost."

"That may be true, Commander. Are you prepared for the fact that we may also end up spending the rest of our lives down there?"

"I am aware of that, Samson. As we discussed, DJ and you will have permission to attempt a deactivation as the attack begins. You have said that you don't know how the weapon will respond, or how quickly it will activate. There are too many unknowns for us not to try, Samson. We have tried to factor in all possible scenarios."

"I understand the need for us to try, Commander. I do not agree with the method chosen. Armageddon is more sophisticated than you know."

"Duly noted, Samson."

♦♦♦

Samson went back to monitoring Armageddon. The attack was scheduled to take place on Year Thirty-eight, January Second, Ten hundred hours, LST. A squadron of one hundred Intruders are standing by inside the Orbiting Headquarters, each armed with fifty missiles that will home in on the radiation that Armageddon is emitting. Seventy-two separate and distinct radiation signatures have been detected circling our Moon. We must attempt to destroy those satellites.

We have not been able to detect in Earth's orbit any radiation of the type Armageddon emits, suggesting that Fisco might be telling the truth about Earth being safe unless we destroy the weapon surrounding the Moon. If we are successful, we believe will be able to use the same procedure against the satellites circling the Earth. If we fail, we'll all die underground and the Moon will become an uninhabitable wasteland.

Jon and his team found the systems to which Fisco's computers had gained access, purged them of all sensitive information, and isolated them from the other systems. All this was done so that Fisco would still be able to contact us. When he did, we believed we would be able to trace a signal back to his location.

0038.0102.0900 LST

Samson and DJ sat in front of their monitors, searching for anything that might indicate Armageddon had spotted our Intruders. While in stealth mode, the fighters do not communicate with each other or with any of the bases.

Samson turned to look at me. "Shall we begin, Commander?"

I checked the time. "Proceed, Samson."

"Thank you, Commander."

Samson and DJ started to work their keyboards. The diagnostic systems on board Armageddon allowed them access to any system they wanted to check. Their job was to disable the firing program before the Intruders launched their missiles. They had been practicing using a program Samson had developed. It enabled them to quickly bypass any blocks that Armageddon's defensive systems might use.

Fifteen minutes went by. "We're in, Commander. Let's hope the codes I'm using haven't been altered."

I swallowed. "Let's hope so, Samson."

I watched as Samson and DJ worked their way deeper into the program. Everything seemed to be going smoothly until a screen appeared before us. Samson froze. The screen flashed 'Password Required'.

DJ looked at Samson. "What should I do, Samson?"

Samson was stunned. "That is the last thing I expected. I don't know what to suggest, DJ. I don't have a password."

DJ looked at the screen and started inputting different words. After several attempts, the screen turned red and started flashing a countdown from ten. We sat in our chairs not knowing what to do or what to expect. I checked the time. In twenty minutes the missiles were to be launched.

When the countdown reached one, our screens went blank and I felt a knot form in my stomach. After a few seconds, the screens lit up again and we saw Fisco sitting at his desk. He took a good long look at each one of us. I wanted to jump through the screen and wrap my hands around his throat. He took a drag off his smoke and asked, "What are you up to, Carrera? Are you trying to disable Armageddon? Did my friend Samson tell you he could do it?"

Samson's body tensed up. DJ turned to look at me with a look of resignation in her eyes.

He continued, "Of course, there is always a chance you'll be able to. But not as long as I'm jamming your ability to send any signals to the computers." He started tapping a finger on his desk. He turned away from me and appeared to be studying something. "Now, what is it you were trying to prevent from happening here? You didn't go after the self-destruct program like I thought you might. It would appear you were trying to stop Armageddon from firing its main weapon, which, by the way, is now fully activated." He paused for a few seconds and then turned to face me. I watched as that twisted smile of his showed up on his face. "Could it be, Carrera, that you're expecting something? Something like an attack against Armageddon?"

An image of the Orbiting Headquarters filled the screen. The image zoomed in on the entrance to the Headquarters, and I saw a squadron of Intruders exit the facility — the same ones that were a few minutes away from launching their missiles.

Fisco returned to the screen. "As you can see, Carrera, I've been keeping an eye on things. If those fighters are planning to attack what they believe to be the power sources of the weapon, they are in for a rude awakening, Carrera. Those power sources are a decoy, Carrera. Unlike the original plans, I took extra care in shielding the power sources of Armageddon from outside detection. I'm afraid your plan may just mean you've sent all those men to their deaths."

The screens flashed, and we were now looking at the Moon from several different angles from very high orbits. Fisco's voice came over the speakers. "These are some of the views Armageddon has. Let's watch for a few minutes and see what happens."

My mouth was completely dry. I couldn't speak. Samson and DJ sat paralyzed in their chairs. I watched, as the clock slowly counted its way to ten hundred hours. When the clock read ten, all the screens displayed a series of explosions. I knew the missiles had found their targets. Unfortunately for us, they were the wrong targets.

Fisco's voice came over the speakers. "There you go, Commander. Your attack went off without a hitch." He paused a few moments. "Oh, I'm sorry. My mistake. There was one hitch." He paused again. "You blew up the wrong targets!" Fisco started to laugh. "Watch now, as Armageddon hunts down the sources of those missiles and annihilates them."

I didn't know what to do. The Intruders were in radio silence. There was no way to contact them. I watched the screen, and after a few minutes I saw numerous energy pulses being fired. I thought they would stop after a minute or so, but Armageddon continued firing for ten minutes. Hundreds of shots were fired. As the minutes passed, I saw that during each shot, the satellites named Armageddon lit up. By the time Armageddon had stopped firing, there were dozens of glowing structures in orbit.

Fisco's voice came over the speakers. "Show's over, Carrera. Armageddon reports one hundred hits. And given that's how many fighters I saw leaving your Orbiting Headquarters, I'd say my weapon is a success."

The screens went blank for an instant and then Fisco's image filled them. He looked ecstatic and spoke in a crazed way. "Now what are you going to do, Carrera. The next program on Armageddon's list is to take out anything in orbit that it doesn't recognize as part of its own system. This means that all your satellites are about to be vaporized." He started laughing again. I couldn't turn him off. Samson and DJ were devastated.

Fisco continued, "I can't tell you when Armageddon will attack, Carrera. You may have time to report back to your friends on Earth and tell them exactly what has happened here." He paused for a second to inhale some more of his smoke. "If I were you, I'd do that as quickly as I could. For all I know, Armageddon could start firing at any second. I'm going to sign off now, but before I do, you should know that you no longer have access to Armageddon. It is now operating as a completely independent entity with, for lack of a better expression, a 'mind of its own'. Good-bye, Carrera."

The monitor screens went blank. Samson, DJ and I waited for them to turn back on. Fifteen minutes went by and the screens stayed dark. I thought about how many men had just died trying to free us, and tears formed in my eyes. I heard DJ's voice, but could not comprehend what she was saying. Samson gripped the arms of his chair, his knuckles white from the pressure. I called Travis.

♦♦♦

"I know, Bella! Somehow, that son-of-a-bitch managed to intercept our broadcasting signals. We saw the whole thing."

"I'm at a loss, Bill. I don't know what to do. Any suggestions? We may not have very much time."

Bill turned and consulted with someone. "We have a communications system based on laser light that will enable us to keep in contact until Fisco's weapon decides to go after the base. It's called LENS, the Laser Enhanced Networking System. Ask your computer to activate it and we'll switch over. We don't need any of your satellites for this system."

I asked the computer to activate the LENS. After a few seconds, the computer indicated that I should proceed. "Can you hear me, Bill?"

"Loud and clear, Bella."

"Good. Now, what were you saying about Armageddon attacking the base?"

"Our experts believe that after Armageddon secures its orbital space, its next program is to start destroying anything that may indicate that humans are present, like the base, for example. It generates heat and radio signals. Armageddon will interpret these as human activity and destroy it. We don't know when the program will activate. We recommend you start shutting it down in order to preserve as much as the base as you can. Turn it off."

I looked at Samson. "What do you say, Samson. Are they right?"

"Yes, Commander. They are recommending the proper course of action."

I nodded back at Samson. "What you're saying, Bill, is that we need to retreat to Tranquility II. What will be your next course of action?"

"You probably saw what happened, Bella. The satellites are now visible. We will attempt to destroy them."

"And what about the ones orbiting Earth?"

"We are working on it, Bella. When the threat of Armageddon is removed from the orbit of the Moon, you may be able to help us destroy the threat orbiting Earth. But, first things first. It's important that you shut down the base."

"I'll get started right away, Bill. Thank you. Carrera out."

Thirty-five: The Ninth Floor

0038.0108.2200 LST

It is several kilometers beneath the surface, the deepest part of Tranquility. This room that I now occupy is the only one left that is pressurized and has a power supply. In it, I installed a monitoring station, an outlet for using the LENS, and a three-dimensional image creator that I can use to study the satellites named Armageddon. I activated the image creator.

Each satellite is a one hundred meters long, eight-sided cylinder with a diameter of twenty-five meters at its widest point with two solar panels on each side and a focusing lens protruding from the front.

Each solar panel is one hundred meters long, twenty-five meters wide with a one-millimeter thick surface that disappears, depending upon the angle from which it is viewed. Satellite dishes, antennae and numerous detection devices cover a faceted surface. The communication system is designed so that each satellite will be in constant communication with others of its kind.

From the front, the focusing lens of the satellite looks like a huge eye. It is almost as wide as the satellite and dark purple around the circumference, gradually turning into a deep red color. Towards the center of the eye, it becomes a bright orange. It floats in space, incased in its body. I know it is capable of deadly force. In the back, where dozens of thrusters reside, a sideways V shape is sculpted into the cylinder. The front to is sculpted, with a U shape, which is also turned on its side. The glowing, pulsating cylinder, with all the apparatuses attached to it, seems alive.

♦♦♦

I shifted my attention away from Armageddon and activated the monitoring station and the LENS.

Our satellites were still broadcasting, but they were no longer under our control. We had shut down communication between the satellites and their guidance computers so that Armageddon would have less with which to detect our presence. Without their computers to control them, it was inevitable that our satellites would begin to deviate from the orbits assigned to them. We were certain that Armageddon would find the broadcasting satellites easy targets. I hoped that a few of them might collide with and disable some of the enemy satellites.

LENS gave me the ability to command the computers back on Earth. They showed me images of what was going on in the orbit around the Moon. I would know when Armageddon started its attack.

0038.0109.0600 LST

Wallace, Jay and I are working on revolving, eight-hour shifts. I heard the sound of an airlock door open and turned to see Jay step into the room in his suit. He raised his hand in greeting. I responded by doing the same.

In order to get down to this room, we need our suits with their thruster controls activated. Without an elevator, we literally have to step through the doors and fall seven kilometers straight down. Our thrusters automatically keep us from falling too fast, bringing us to a soft landing in front of the airlock. It takes about two and half minutes to get down and one minute to get back up.

Jay walked over to the console. "Any action?" Jay was confident we would defeat Armageddon.

"Not yet, Jay. I've given Wallace and you access to Travis' computers. I'm using them to control a few of our satellites orbiting Earth. We can use them to monitor Armageddon's activities."

"Sounds good, Bella. You ready to go?"

"I guess so. See you back at T. II, if I'm up." I got up from the chair and let Jay take my seat.

"Thanks, Bella. Are we recording everything?"

I walked into the airlock. "Of course." My helmet activated and the door closed. I turned and waved good-bye. The airlock depressurized and the door to the elevator shaft opened. I stepped out and activated the thrusters. It took only about ten seconds to accelerate up to speed. Deceleration started fifteen seconds before I reached the shaft doors. I hovered for a few seconds before the thrusters pushed me through the door and I touched down onto the floor. I climbed into one of our commuter vehicles and headed towards the Garage, several kilometers away.

♦ ♦ ♦

Sections of the Garage are in close proximity to the Tower. As a way of making it easier to transport materials we need for Tranquility II, a tunnel, which used to be pressurized, links the Garage to the perimeter of the ring road that surrounds the Tower. A warehouse on the surface stores everything that comes and goes to Tranquility II.

I parked my vehicle on the platform used to bring our supplies up to the surface. With my thrusters activated, my suit placed me gently on the ring road in front of one of the entrances to the Tower.

I had become aware that the Tower was always available to us whenever we needed it. I wasn't sure if anyone else had noticed. I made a mental note to ask. Walking across the ring road, I looked up and saw the glow from the satellites named Armageddon drifting across the sky. Instinctively, I hurried into the shelter of the Tower. The entrance remained open for a few seconds and then closed.

As I descended to T. II, I thought about how much everything had changed. The base was now a dark and lifeless place, unfit for human habitation. No lights, no atmosphere and no people. An empty shell. In contrast, T. II was now a vibrant, living community of people working together to make the best of a bad situation. The hope that we would all be going back to our real home had had an intoxicating effect on many people. Knowing what I knew kept me, and those in Command, in a much different frame of mind.

It still took fifteen minutes to reach T II.

♦ ♦ ♦

Much to my surprise, DJ was waiting for me. "What's up, DJ?"

We walked toward my transport vehicle. "Nothing. What's happening topside?"

"Nothing yet." I climbed into the vehicle. DJ took the passenger seat. I started driving back to my quarters. I wanted to get out of my suit and take a shower. I looked at her. She looked very beautiful. "How did you know when I was going to arrive?"

She looked back at me. "You know I don't know, Bella."

I nodded. "I know, DJ. It's always a nice surprise."

She smiled. "Thank you, Bella."

As I drove towards our village, my eyes focused on how green everything had become. Samson and his crew were doing an amazing job. The ultraviolet radiation needed to grow the huge variety of trees and shrubs surrounding all our buildings had originally been provided by strategically placed UV lamps. But now, the dome was also radiating UV, and it had increased to the point where lamps were no longer needed.

I pulled into a space allocated for me in front of my quarters and got out of the vehicle. DJ lived in the same cluster. "I'm going to clean myself up DJ, I'll be available in about an hour. Meet me back here and fill me in."

"Sounds good, Bella. See you in an hour."

♦♦♦

I felt refreshed after my shower and changed into clean clothes. DJ arrived as I was finishing my dinner. We walked outside and sat on our shared porch. We had an unobstructed view of the dome and the beach, and in a strange way, it felt safe. The residents were keeping themselves busy. DJ seemed anxious to begin.

"So what's on your mind, DJ? I've only been gone a few hours."

"I know, Bella. Something is happening over in our agriplex. Some of the more senior growers have been taken up to the ninth floor."

I remembered our first encounter on that floor almost two and a half years ago. I hadn't been in the building since. "How about you, DJ? Have you been taken there yet?"

"Not yet, Bella."

I suspected in time she would be taken there. "They must have been a little surprised. What did they say about it?"

"They said that when they got off the elevators, they felt compelled to enter those cubicles we walked through. And when they did, something made contact with them."

I suspected it was the same thing that had made contact with me, and now knew that my prediction of more people being contacted was accurate. "And what did it want?"

"They said it was hard to explain. But the gist of it was that it was interested in knowing what we were doing and how we were using the building."

"And were the growers able to relay what we are doing?"

"Yes. They said it appears to like the idea that the building is being used to grow food. They said it wants to learn about how each floor is being used and about the different species that are being grown. They said it would like to help us."

I then knew that whatever it was that was reading our thoughts was designed to assist whoever inhabited this place. "Have you noticed, DJ, that the Tower seems to be available to us whenever we need it? I mean, it seems to be keeping this place powered up, but at the same time, not interfering with what we do."

DJ thought about that for a few seconds. "Now that you mention it, you're right."

"It's something I've just recently become acutely aware of, DJ. What else did the growers say?"

"They said it knows we are now inhabiting this place and will learn more about us. There may be people who end up on that floor without knowing why. It appears quite friendly."

I thought for a few moments. "DJ, there must be some kind of computer linked to the building, right? I mean, some kind of machine that's able to read our thoughts. We have to explain it somehow."

"That would certainly explain it."

"Do you think there will be side effects?"

"I can't answer that, Bella. You said before that whatever it is, it is designed to help whoever inhabits this place."

"That's exactly right, DJ. I think it's time I went back up to ninth floor. Would you care to join me?"

"Whenever you're ready, Bella."

"Let's do it."

♦♦♦

As DJ and I drove towards the building, I noticed Samson walking along the side of the road. I pulled over and called him. He walked over.

"Yes, Commander. What can I do for you?"

"I was just wondering if you'd like to join DJ and me. We're going to the agriplex to check things out."

Samson glanced at the building, focusing on it for a few seconds. When he looked back at me, he had a sly grin on his face. "I'd be happy to join you both. Thank you for asking me."

He climbed into the back seat and I started praising him for all the work he had been doing. "Thank you, Commander. I enjoy it."

We drove in silence for a few minutes, and then Samson asked, "Are we going to the ninth floor, Commander?"

I glanced over at DJ. She glanced back and smiled. "Yes, Samson. What have you heard about it?"

"Nothing, really. Just that there is some sort of control center up there. I have speculated that it's the reason ultraviolet light is being generated."

I had also thought about that. I was surprised to hear it from Samson. "That's what I believe, Samson. In fact, our minds may be causing it to happen. A few of our people have recently been taken there. You may also be taken there. I want you to see it. It may try to connect with you."

"That would be an interesting experience, Commander. What does it feel like?"

I hadn't thought about that before. "It is not an unpleasant feeling, Samson. At least it wasn't for me. I can't tell you what your experience will be like."

"That's a good answer, Commander. If it does make contact with me, I'll try to tell you how it feels."

I don't know why, but that made me smile. "Thank you, Samson."

♦♦♦

As we entered the elevator, contact was made. I named it 'T II.' It asked me which floor I needed. With my mind I said the ninth and we began to ascend.

When we exited on the ninth floor, Samson stood outside one of the cubicles and familiarized himself with his surroundings. I wondered if he was also checking to see if contact would be made. DJ and I waited, giving me the opportunity to re-orient myself. I felt no need to enter the cubicles, so when Samson was ready, we walked down to the end of the hall. When we arrived at the last cubicle, I saw the same entrance I had seen before. Without saying a word, we entered. As before, the entrance closed and we stood in complete darkness. I didn't know what to expect. We waited about twenty seconds, and then saw an image of our moon coming towards us.

Standing on my right, Samson inhaled deeply, as our moon became larger and larger. Memories of my initial trip, when I thought I might crash onto its surface, flashed through my mind. We slowly entered a very low orbit over the surface. We could see our roadways and buildings as we flew over them. We continued to orbit until we reached Tranquility, at which time we stopped. We were seeing images of our base after we had shut it down. We saw the remains of the Earth Dome and the damage its destruction had caused to other structures.

I heard Samson's steady breathing. "Are you okay, Samson?"

"I'm fine, Commander. What else will we see?"

"I don't know, Samson."

Slowly we started to ascend away from the surface into a higher orbit. We flew by some of our satellites and some of our enemy's satellites. I felt like I was in a spacecraft, as we turned and headed towards one of the glowing objects we called Armageddon. As we got closer, its immense size started to have an effect on me. What we were now viewing was much different from the scaled-down version we had studied. It continued to grow in size as the seconds passed.

I felt something grab onto my arm and squeeze with surprising force. The combination of surprise and pain caused me to cry out. I realized DJ had grabbed onto me. Her breathing was heavy and I suspected she was experiencing extreme fear. Next, I heard the sound of someone falling. From the light given off by Armageddon, I could see that Samson had fallen backwards and was now sitting on the floor. He couldn't take his eyes off the satellite.

We were all awestruck by the colossal size of the solar panels and moments later we found ourselves just centimeters from Armageddon's surface. Overwhelmed by its immensity and power, we made eye contact with each other and held on. It felt like we were flying just over the top of the satellite, which was as long as a football field. We could see the intense energy that was being produced inside the satellite, causing it to pulsate with bright light. Bolts of energy flashed through its outer layer. Every detail on the surface was visible. We flew around the antenna, receiving dishes, listening devices, heat seekers and the other exotic-looking hardware that covered the surface of Armageddon. Around the back of the satellite, we were confronted with dozens of huge thrusters and the twenty-five meter diameter of the enclosure. I stared at the thrusters and wondered what would happen to us if one of them suddenly ignited.

Much to my surprise, DJ began to exert an even more powerful grip on my already bruised arm. We inspected underneath the satellite and then ended up in front, looking right into Armageddon's eye. It felt like I was looking down the barrel of a loaded gun. Fear coursed through my body. As I stood there, overwhelmed by the sheer size and power of what hovered before me, it became clear that this creation was designed to do only one thing… destroy.

The image of Armageddon faded and the room became softly illuminated. I felt DJ's grip on my arm loosen. I glanced at Samson. He got up slowly from the sitting position he had assumed on the floor. I held my arm where DJ had assaulted it, and walked out of the room. DJ and Samson followed. We walked down the hallway without saying a word.

Thirty-six: The Attack

0038.0214.0400 LST

I opened my eyes and sat up in bed. I looked around the room for the familiar sight of my clock. I needed to know what time it was. I felt something was wrong. My entire body told me so.

I quickly gathered my thoughts. I had to get down to our control room. I ran a mental check of the schedule, which now included Chris, DJ, and Samson. Samson was on until six hundred hours LST, at which time Chris was scheduled to replace him. We gave ourselves an hour to get there from here. I would be arriving before Chris.

I cleaned myself up, grabbed something to eat and got into my suit. As I climbed into my vehicle, I dictated a message for Wallace, letting him know where I was. He would receive the message when he put on his vest. As I approached the Tower, which was in its power-up mode, it switched off and opened an entrance for me. I still wasn't used to having it do that. It seemed to take longer than usual to reach the surface. But I knew that was because I was in a rush.

I darted across the ring road, glancing up as I did. Armageddon was still orbiting. I didn't stop, as I jumped down to the loading platform. Over the past several weeks, confidence in my suit had grown to the point where I no longer thought about stopping before I jumped down the elevator shafts.As I drove down through the Garage and service tunnels, I was consumed with knowing why I was doing this. When I arrived at the shaft doors, I slammed on the brakes, quickly jumped in and glided down to the control room entrance. I waited impatiently for the airlock to pressurize. I knew there was a problem when Samson didn't greet me as I entered the room.

"Samson…" I was walking towards the monitoring station.

"Yes, Commander."

I was at the console. "What's going on?"

"Commander Travis called approximately forty-five minutes ago. We've been attacked again, Commander."

I let that sink in for a few seconds. "Our satellites? Is Armageddon going after our satellites?"

Samson spoke slowly and deliberately. "No, Commander. Brath caused one of his satellites orbiting Earth to intercept and destroy one of our orbiters that was on its way to Orbiting Headquarters. Over three hundred passengers and crew were lost."

I felt as if all the life had just been sucked out of me. I just stood there, staring into space.

I heard Samson call my name. "Bella! Commander! We should contact Travis."

Hearing my name brought me back. I was devastated. "Okay, Samson. Let's contact Travis."

♦♦♦

Travis was surprised to be talking to me so soon. He looked as bad as I felt. "We're paralyzed, Bella. The plans we had in response to Fisco's attack against Tranquility have now been canceled. We don't have anything in orbit we can use to knock out the satellites orbiting the Moon."

"We were in the final stages of completing our attack plans. Fisco said that anything that we attempt to put in orbit would be destroyed. We are now officially at war. The satellites named Armageddon orbiting Earth have become our priority. The satellites named Armageddon orbiting the Moon have now become your responsibility. We are now actively engaged in tracking the source of Fisco's transmissions."

I became very angry. "What were you thinking, Travis, allowing civilian orbiters to fly at all?"

Travis became defensive. I knew I was walking a fine line. "You and I both know those decisions are not mine to make. I understand your anger, Bella, but don't put the blame on me. We didn't want to cause worldwide panic based on speculation. Clearly, Fisco would have picked another target if that orbiter hadn't been available. He was going for high profile and he got it. We'll be taking immense heat for quite some time for not disclosing the situation. What Fisco has done to your base is widely known. Very few knew that the same system was deployed around Earth. Fisco has chosen to make it known. We know what's motivating him."

"So do I, Travis."

"And that is…?"

"He wants to see his weapon work. He's forcing us to act in ways that will cause Armageddon's systems to speed up activation. He is also creating an environment of fear, which is perhaps one of Armageddon's most devastating weapons. He wants us to not only lose control of our physical space, but also lose our minds in fear."

Travis responded, "That's what we believe."

I continued, "I believe Fisco desperately needs to see his weapon in action. This is what he lives for. We need to focus on destroying what surrounds us. Maybe those living aboard the Orbiting Headquarters can develop a weapon to be used against the satellites circling the Earth. I will put a team together and start developing a plan for our situation."

Travis was nodding his head. "There's already a plan in place, Bella. The plan that was to be used against the satellites orbiting our Moon has now been redirected to focus on the satellites orbiting Earth. That's believed to be the lesser of two evils. And before you fly off the handle, please understand that I didn't dream this up, and that I have no say in the matter."

I swallowed and listened to Travis.

"As you know, Armageddon is not yet visible to us, and we suspect that Fisco could, at any time, command those satellites to re-enter and detonate. The assumption is that he will. We have designated all our orbiting satellites as expendable, as we assume that Armageddon will go after them."

"When Armageddon begins to re-enter, thousands of intercept missiles and other weapons will be launched and activated. We know that Armageddon is programmed to detonate if it's not completely destroyed, and there are no guarantees that complete destruction will happen. A planet-wide decontamination plan is in place to handle whatever fallout occurs because of our failure. I know it sounds wrong, but it's better than having them detonate where Fisco has programmed them to detonate."

"What you need to do, Bella, is destroy the satellites surrounding our Moon. If Fisco was telling the truth about what will cause the satellites in Earth's orbit to activate, then it would be to our advantage to do so at this point."

My head was spinning. Before I had a chance to respond, I saw that Travis was receiving an incoming call. He motioned me to stay on. It was Fisco.

♦♦♦

Fisco seemed happy to see me. "Happy Valentines Day, Carrera."

That made no sense to me. "What??"

His face twisted up. "Oh, I'm sorry Carrera. Maybe a little history lesson is in order. Back in the days of Gangster rule in the United States, an event became known as the St. Valentine's Day Massacre. One gang completely wiped out its competition. That is about to happen in your orbit. In fact, it has just started."

One of my screens changed to show what was happening in orbit. The satellites named Armageddon had begun vaporizing our satellites. I looked directly into Fisco's eyes. My temper got the best of me. "I thought you said you didn't know when Armageddon was going to activate."

Fisco didn't blink as he stared back at me. He took a drag from his smoke. "I lied, Carrera." As he exhaled, he had one final thing to say. "If it flies, it dies, Carrera." He winked at me and cut off his transmission.

I heard the airlock activate, and turned to see Chris enter the room. He was surprised to see me. "What's going on, Commander?"

"Fisco has started a war, Chris. He destroyed a civilian orbiter on its way to the Orbiting Headquarters. We've been ordered to destroy everything in our orbit."

Chris stood in the middle of the room trying to make sense of what I had just told him.

I turned my attention back to Travis. "Everybody knows that what you are asking of me is going to take a little time."

Travis spoke clearly. "We don't have time, Bella. Put everybody on it. I wouldn't be surprised if many of your people have already thought of ways to retaliate. They'll jump at this chance."

Chris made his way to the consol. Samson got up from the chair and let him sit down. I saw him focus on the screen showing Armageddon blasting our satellites. He said, "I have a few ideas, Commander..."

Samson also spoke. "I've also put a few ideas together, Commander."

I looked at Travis. "We're on it, Travis. Samson and I are heading back to T. II after we brainstorm with Chris. Anything else?"

"Yes, Bella. God be with you."

"God be with you, Travis."

Thirty-seven: The Red Sea

0038.0214.1355 LST

I stood by the airlock, waiting for Samson and Chris to join me. They had come up with a plan to disable the satellites around our Moon, which would cause Armageddon to show itself in Earth's orbit.

DJ had arrived ten minutes earlier and was taking over for us. We filled her in as to our plans. She didn't allow herself to get too optimistic. At fourteen hundred hours LST, Chris and Samson walked to the airlock and we entered. There was a feeling of great anticipation. Samson had secretly invented countermeasures for Armageddon. Chris and I were extremely curious to see them.

For safety reasons, we staggered our ascent up the elevator shaft. Any collisions at high speeds would be disastrous. I climbed into my vehicle and waited for Chris and Samson.

♦♦♦

As Chris and I walked into Samson's bay, we were acutely aware that nobody had previously been allowed in his space before. Our suit lights illuminated the bay. Samson had installed a massive computer/research station. The bay was filled with rows of shelves, which were filled with containers.

Samson turned to me and a small window activated in my helmet display. I could see him speaking to me. "I had all the hardware manufactured and assembled before we left for T. II, Commander. I'll show you what I've created." We walked over to one of the shelves. Using an identification code, Samson opened one of the containers. Several dozen needle-sharp nose cones were protruding from the top of the container. Samson carefully reached into the container and pulled out one of the objects. It was one meter in length and shaped like a narrow cone. It was very difficult to focus on it because of the way light reflected off its multi-angled surface.

"This is a dart, Commander. I designed it to be invisible to the satellites in orbit. It has a navigation computer, thrusters similar to the ones we use on our suits, and an explosive charge in the tip. Each dart will be programmed to propel itself into one of the nozzles of the maneuvering rockets on each satellite. When the dart has found its target, the explosive charge will detonate and disable the satellite. Armageddon will then destroy the satellite."

"I have two hundred and fifty thousand of these devises. Loaded into my computer are the design specifications for all the satellites orbiting our Moon and the Earth. Several darts will be programmed to intercept the same target, so that if the satellites do detect the darts and evasive maneuvers are taken, at least one of the darts will find its target."

I was impressed. "What about the satellites named Armageddon, Samson? What have you come up with for them?"

"I'm glad you asked, Commander. Please walk with me." He took us to the back of the bay. Stacked against the wall were thousands of small, sealed containers.

"Inside each of these containers, Commander, are billions of nano-robots, which are being held in suspended animation. Exposing them to space radiation and the energy emitted by Armageddon will activate and power them. The light that Armageddon emits will act like a magnet, allowing them to stick to the surfaces of Armageddon. This same energy source will also power them. They are programmed to find and reach the main processing center of each satellite."

"I designed the robots to act upon Armageddon in the same way the deadliest of viruses acts upon our bodies. It will be a massive, invasive attack, causing Armageddon to become deathly ill. Armageddon, using its diagnostic programs, will attempt to fix the problems as they occur."

"The attack is designed to overwhelm and devastate Armageddon's diagnostic systems and its ability to fix itself. In doing so, I'm predicting that Armageddon will not notice that its processing center, where the self-destruct is located, is also being destroyed." Samson took a breath. "Would you like to see what they look like?"

I nodded my head. "Absolutely!"

Samson led us over to his computer/research station and sat down. He opened one of the compartments and pulled out three cables. He attached a cable to each of our suits and plugged them into his computer. "Our suits will power the computer, Commander. The images will appear on our helmet displays."

My display changed and an image of the robot filled my display. The nano-robot looked very much like a freakish type of ant made of crystal.

Samson explained, "You may notice that it looks similar to an ant, Commander. I did use the ant as my model, but as I explain how it works, that image may fade. You'll notice that it is divided into three sections. The largest section is in front. It contains a powerful heat pulse device. When the robot activates, it will appear to fly backwards as the heat pulse propels it towards Armageddon."

My display changed to display some computer-generated animation that showed how the robot was designed to fly.

"Once it lands on Armageddon's surface, it will use the heat pulse to create a tunnel. It is programmed to tunnel through Armageddon in order to reach the main processors. When it reaches the processors, the heat pulse will continue working to melt vital connections."

The animation continued, as Samson explained how the weapon worked. I saw numerous robots tunneling through Armageddon towards the processing units.

"Remember that billions of these robots are programmed to reach the central processors, each with its own heat pulse. The damage will be massive. Armageddon has nothing with which to defend itself against such an attack."

My display now showed billions of the robots converging on the processing center, and then it changed back to an image of one robot.

"The middle section is where the six legs of the robot are controlled and the last section is where the energy that runs the robot is absorbed, stored and released. Given that it is Armageddon's own energy emissions that are powering the robot, it will continue working until Armageddon is dead or it explodes." Samson seemed to pause for effect. "That's it, Commander."

My display went back to normal and I found myself staring at Samson. I was awed by his ability to create such destructive power. "I'm speechless, Samson."

"Thank you, Commander. Maybe Chris and I should start packing our darts for launch."

I found myself nodding my head again. Travis was in for a big surprise. "Of course, Samson. If you don't mind, I'd like to help you prepare for the launch."

They both responded. "Of course, Commander!"

♦♦♦

Samson had spent time studying the way Armageddon reacted to meteor showers. He noticed that it didn't react in a hostile fashion to either the space debris orbiting our Moon or to the small meteors that passed through its orbits. He created a program that would enable our launching system to put our darts in their orbits by tricking Armageddon's sensors.

While Chris went to get the transport for the darts, Samson and I prepared the shelving units for the transport. The units were designed to move onto the transport individually, which saved us time by not having to load and unload the containers. We both marveled at how easy it was to work in our suits.

After Chris arrived, it took us fifteen minutes to load the transport. He had also loaded twenty-five thousand launch modules onto the transport. Each module held ten darts. We climbed aboard and Chris took us through the service tunnels that led to the launch rails. The launch rails resided in Moon normal gravity, several kilometers away from the base. The loading bays were located two kilometers beneath the surface.

It would take one day for the launch modules to reach Earth orbit. We wanted the attacks to happen simultaneously. Our modules would orbit high above the orbits of Armageddon, and would launch the darts so they would arrive at their targets at the same time as the ones in Earth orbit.

♦♦♦

We entered the launch facilities and began loading the machines that would transfer the darts to the launch modules. The same machines would then begin to load the launch modules into the fifty launch rails. Each rail would launch ten containers at a time. The launch of all twenty-five thousand containers would take less than five minutes.

As we worked, Samson explained, "Armageddon is hunting for objects that have electrical signals, heat output and other indicators that would identify them as human- engineered systems. These containers will not be emitting anything that Armageddon can sense. As you can see, these modules are very small, about the same size as other objects Armageddon dismisses as non-threatening. The trajectory of the launch modules will be random until safely out of Armageddon's range.

Armageddon will compute them to be whatever I want them to be. The number of containers we are launching will insure our success, Commander."

"I believe you, Samson."

By the time we had finished, Samson had been up for almost twenty-four hours. We were all exhausted. We headed back to T. II to sleep for a few hours and to prepare Jay so he could coordinate the power needs of the launch.

♦♦♦

I took a long, hot shower before turning in. Physically exhausted, I climbed into my bed and set my alarm to awaken me in six hours. I shut my eyes, hoping that sleep would come easily, but my mind was racing with thoughts of our attack and questions of Armageddon's capabilities.

Believing that a glass of warm milk might calm me down, I got up and headed towards my kitchen. As I walked through my bedroom door, I found myself in the oasis, a place I hadn't been for quite some time. I was holding a two-meter-long walking staff in my hand. I looked down at my clothing. It resembled the type of clothing worn by the ancient nomads of the Sahara desert. When I touched my face, I felt a beard.

I saw only one pathway and knew I had to take it. I proceeded down the pathway, not knowing where it would lead me. I found the walking staff very useful as the path began to descend and become increasingly difficult to navigate. I soon found myself standing on a large boulder overlooking a massive congregation of people. I was near the shore of a body of water, which stretched beyond the horizon. I looked back over my shoulder, expecting to see the pathway, but it had disappeared. What I saw instead was a vast expanse of desert. At that instant, I felt heat.

I climbed down from the boulder and walked towards the people. I stood behind someone and tapped her shoulder. She turned around. It was Cee.

"Hello, Bella. It's been a long time."

She was the last person I had expected to see. It took me a few seconds to recover. "Where are we, Cee?"

"We are on the shores of the Red Sea, Bella. I have been traveling with these people."

I bowed my head. I tried to gather my thoughts. I looked at her. "How long have you been here?"

"A few days, Bella."

That meant we didn't have much time. "You know, then, that the Egyptians are on their way."

"Yes, Bella. The things you are about to see and experience might not be as you have read." She pointed to the shores of the Red Sea. I saw a funnel cloud rising up to the sky. "That cloud has been guiding us, Bella. At night, it glows."

Words failed me. Cee turned to look at me. She was as desirable as I remembered her to be. Out of the corner of my eye, I saw people moving. I turned my head and saw the crowd letting someone through. After a few seconds, two men stood before us. It was Moses and Aaron.

No words were spoken. Moses was holding a staff very similar to the one I was holding. And although the colors were different, our clothes were the same. I swallowed, as he looked into my eyes. In his eyes, I saw a man who had seen what no man before him had seen. I saw in his eyes, wisdom and compassion unlike anything I had experienced before. I had to look away. I bowed my head.

I felt Cee's hand brush my arm. I looked up. Moses had climbed up onto the boulder upon which I had been standing. He was looking intensely upon the horizon. He seemed to find what he was looking for and then climbed down from the boulder. Aaron handed him his staff. Moses looked at me as if to say 'thank you' and made his way back through the congregation.

I looked at Cee, and thought for a moment about what it was Moses was looking for. Then it hit me. *The Pharaoh's army.*

Many people wanted see what he had seen and clamored towards the boulder. I grabbed Cee's hand and we moved out of harms way. I watched as dozens of people climbed up the boulder and saw with their own eyes what Cee and I knew was coming. As the word spread, it was clear they were on the verge of panic. The people began to verbalize their fears. Moses knew what was coming.

I saw the cloud by the Red Sea disappear. Cee pointed over my shoulder and I turned to see a funnel cloud at least two kilometers in diameter, made of fire directly behind us. I felt the heat from it on my face. It made no sound. I looked back at the people. There was silence.

I grabbed Cee's hand and started running. I was looking for a place where I could see down to the shores of the Red Sea. I circumnavigated the edge of the crowd, looking for high ground and a clearing. I found my vantage point after five minutes. Cee was breathing deeply.

I saw Moses. He was standing on an outcropping with his arms outstretched, facing the sea. He was holding his staff in his right hand. A blast of hot wind almost knocked me off my feet. Moses' robes reacted from the same blast of wind, but his body remained firmly planted. A chill ran up the back of my spine. Something was happening. I saw the wind whip through the congregation.

I looked back at Moses. He remained motionless. The hot wind at my back gradually became stronger. I fought to remain where I stood. Suddenly, without warning, the Red Sea exploded upward and began to part in front of where Moses was standing. God had created a path through the Red Sea. The hot wind continued to blow around Moses, who remained motionless.

Cee stood with me, and we watched all through the night. Moses remained with his arms outstretched over the Red Sea until dawn broke. Only then did he climb down from the outcropping and walk onto the path that God had created through the Red Sea. The people followed him.

♦ ♦ ♦

I found myself walking through the Red Sea. The ground was bone dry and the waters towered over us. I walked to my left and right and touched the waters. They felt like glass and my hands did not become wet. I tried to push my hands into the water, but no matter how hard tried, I could not.

When Cee and I reached the middle of the Red Sea, I looked over my shoulder and saw that the cloud of fire had disappeared. I knew the Pharaoh's army would be pursuing us. I felt a powerful presence touch me and we as a group began to move faster. I turned around and saw the Pharaoh's army enter the pathway that God had created through the Red Sea. They were struggling to control their horses and chariots.I quickly found myself on the shores of the Red Sea. I saw Moses high above the shore with his arms outstretched over the Red Sea, holding his staff in his right hand. Cee and I scrambled further up the shore. I saw the Pharaoh's army racing through the pathway God had created through the Red Sea. And when the entire army was within the walls of water, the walls of water quickly collapsed. Within a few seconds, both the army and the pathway had completely disappeared.

When the waters had become calm, Moses lowered his arms.

Feeling the impact of what I had just seen and experienced, I leaned against my walking staff for support and squeezed Cee's hand. I bowed my head and closed my eyes. I thanked God for allowing me to see and experience what had happened at the Red Sea. Then I heard a voice say, "I love you."

When I opened my eyes, I was standing in my kitchen. My right hand was gripping the handle of my fridge. I checked the time. My alarm went off. I wasn't tired.

Thirty-eight: Counter Attack

0038.0215.1000 LST

"Commander Carrera."

I heard Samson's voice. I was still reeling from what I had experienced just a few hours before. "Yes, Samson. What is it?"

"We'll be launching in a few minutes." He was studying me. I was glad to be wearing my suit. "Jay is ready to power up."

"Thank you, Samson."

Samson, Chris, Jay and I had arrived two hours earlier with Jay's mobile power station. Chris assisted Jay in determining which systems were essential for our launch. I stayed by the transport, which was the size of a double-sized semi-trailer. Despite having appeared tiny inside the launch facilities, the trailer seemed large when we boarded. Samson double-checked each launch tube. When he had reached the thirtieth tube, only the lights from his suit were visible.

♦♦♦

None of the satellites in our Moon's orbit had survived the attack launched by the satellites named Armageddon. And, each of Armageddon's main assault satellites had become noticeably brighter.

Wallace was in the control room monitoring our location using the satellites in Earth's orbit. All the available Earth satellites were focused on our launch and programmed to detect any unusual behavior by Armageddon. I wondered if Travis would notice.

I saw Jay raise his hand with a thumbs-up sign. "Here we go, Bella."

"Throw the switch, Jay."

Jay lowered his arm and we had light. Each launch tube had its own set of indicator lights that showed us which tubes were ready to use. Our helmet displays allowed us to zoom in and magnify objects that were great distances away. One by one, all fifty tubes lit up.

"Looks good, Jay."

"Thanks, Bella. It'll take a few minutes before we know if they're loaded properly. We'll see a green flashing light on the ones that are, and a red flashing light on those that are not. I've got them wired to my station, Bella. I'll know immediately if there's a problem."

Each minute seemed to drag on. I felt restless and impatient. I was hoping that Armageddon wouldn't detect our activity and start blasting. I looked down at my right foot and noticed I was tapping it. The suit had become so tuned into the way I use my body that it was now invisible to me. I took control of my foot.

A few seconds later, the first green light came on. Jay's voice came over the helmet speaker system. "All systems go, Bella!!"

I saw Samson and Chris give Jay a thumbs-up sign. Then they turned to me and gave me one, too. Naturally, I returned it. "Alright, you guys. When all the lights are green, give me a ten-second countdown and launch those darts."

One by one the launch tubes loaded and we got green lights. As soon as the last one had turned, all three of them started counting down. When the countdown reached one, I heard Chris give the command. "Computer, commence launch sequence."

Immediately, we saw the launch indicator lights blink off. I wasn't prepared for the spectacle of it. Every time a module launched, a light signaled what was happening. We were launching twenty-five thousand modules in five minutes. The light show held my attention.

And then as quickly as it started, it stopped. Jay quickly powered down and disconnected his power sources from the launch facilities. We hurried back to our transport and rushed back to the control room.

♦ ♦ ♦

Wallace was waiting for us. "Nothing, Bella. Armageddon did not fire any shots and it showed no signs of detection. I haven't see anything either. Travis has been calling."

I asked the computer to play back from the time we started the launch. We had satellites focused directly on the spot where the containers left the launch tubes. We sat and watched for the five minutes we knew it took to launch. We saw nothing. The satellites focused on other non-visible wavelengths did not detect anything either.

I turned and looked at Jay, Chris and Samson. "Great job, you guys!"

Samson responded, "Thank you, Commander. We'll know more in approximately twenty-four hours. What would you like us to do until then?"

"If you can, try and get some rest. I'll meet you back here tomorrow at ten hundred hours LST. That is an order. I have a few things to do here so don't wait for me."

They acknowledged the order and left.

♦ ♦ ♦

Wallace and I contacted Travis. I asked him if he noticed how we were using their satellites.

"We noticed, Bella. That's why we've been trying to contact you. And given that Wallace wouldn't elaborate, we assumed that you and Samson have been busy."

I smiled and thought about that understatement. "We've just launched an attack against Armageddon's supporting satellites orbiting both the Earth and Moon, Travis. You have approximately twenty-four hours to ready your weapons and launch an attack to destroy the assault satellites orbiting the Earth."

Clearly, Travis was not expecting this. "You've done what??!!"

Wallace and I spent the next hour showing Travis what we'd done. When we were through, I asked him what he thought of the plan.

"I think you were wise to wait until the attack commenced before informing us. We'll be ready and waiting."

"Thank you, Travis. Let's hope it works."

"Thank you, Bella."

0038.0216.1200 LST

Wallace, Jay, Chris, Samson and I focused on a set of monitors. We divided them so that half of them displayed satellites in Earth's orbit and the other half displayed satellites in our Moon's orbit. In total, we were able to keep track of one hundred satellites at any given time. With the darts traveling at several thousand kilometers per second, the impact would be noticeable. We waited patiently.

♦ ♦ ♦

Samson saw the first one. It was orbiting the Earth. The impact from the dart had knocked the satellite completely off the screen. Travis made contact within seconds.

"We're watching, Bella. Everyone is standing by."

"This just might work, Travis."

Within minutes, we saw so many satellites knocked out of their orbits that it became difficult to track them. Several took multiple hits. I started feeling a little more confident.

Travis once again made contact. "Armageddon has started to attack the satellites in your orbit, Bella."

"Can you show us pictures?"

"Right away, Bella."

Several monitors showed Armageddon blasting away in our orbit. A sense of satisfaction washed over me. "What's going on in Earth's orbit, Travis?"

"There's been no response yet. Maybe it will take longer for Armageddon to activate. We're tracking several satellites that have entered Earth's atmosphere. They'll burn up before impacting the ground."

Before Travis could finish, he responded to a call from Fisco. He appeared to be extremely angry. When Travis put him on, he looked right at me. As he spoke, it was clear he was trying to control himself. "What do you think you are doing?" He took a long, hard, drag off his smoke and continued to stare at me.

Travis looked at me. "Would you care to answer the man, Bella?"

"Certainly, Travis. Fisco, we've launched an attack against Armageddon. We're taking your satellites out of orbit."

Fisco took a few seconds to respond. "All I see is Armageddon destroying its supporting satellites in your Moon's orbit, Carrera. The satellites you disable in Earth's orbit are programmed to re-enter Earth's atmosphere and burn up. What are you hoping to accomplish?"

I looked back at Travis. "Should I tell him?"

"I don't see why not, Bella…"

"We are attempting to have the satellites named Armageddon expose themselves in Earth's orbit so that we can annihilate them."

Fisco flicked some ash from his smoke into an ashtray. "I see." He took another drag. "Well, in order to do that, you'll have to destroy the satellites named Armageddon orbiting your Moon. I told you that already. The weapon orbiting Earth is not programmed to destroy its supporting satellites. As I said, they'll burn up as they re-enter."

I looked around the room. Samson looked dejected. I said to Travis. "I guess Fisco was telling the truth about that, Travis. Maybe we should alert our forces to the situation."

"I'll get right to it Bella."

I focused my attention back to Fisco. "We will win, Fisco."

"We'll see, Carrera. Maybe it is you who will be annihilated." He cut off his transmission.

Samson stood up. "I should start preparing our next attack, Commander. May I be dismissed?"

"Yes, Samson. Do you need assistance?"

"Not just yet. I'll be in the Garage."

"We'll meet there when we know how effective we've been."

"Thank you, Commander."

0038.0216.2045 LST

Wallace got up from his chair. "It's been twenty-five minutes since Armageddon last fired, Bella. What do you think we should do?"

I took my attention away from the monitors. The satellites named Armageddon had become intensely bright. "I think we should see if we're ready to start our next attack."

Travis and his crew had been tracking the number of satellites destroyed by Armageddon in our Moon's orbit. He was sure that Armageddon had destroyed all the satellites. They had also tracked close to nine hundred satellites re-entering Earths atmosphere. No supporting satellites had been detected orbiting the Earth.

DJ had joined us a few hours earlier as part of her regular shift. "We're going to go check on Samson, DJ. You're welcome to join us. You're the only one left who has a shift. There's no reason to continue monitoring at this point."

DJ looked at each of us and said, "If there is no reason for me to be here, then I'd be happy to join you guys."

Chris blurted out, "All right, DJ!"

DJ smiled and blushed.

♦♦♦

We found Samson at his computer/research station. He was reclined in his chair with his right arm swung over the armrest and his left leg resting on top of the work area. He was out cold.

He'd been busy. All the containers with the nano-robots had been loaded onto a transport and programmed for launch. I thought about placing my hand on his shoulder and shaking him awake, but Wallace suggested that I ask the computer to wake him. We watched as Samson slowly awoke. He took his leg down from the work area and swung his arm back over the armrest. He leaned forward and turned his chair around to face us. A small widow activated on my helmet display. I saw Samson's face. He looked tired. "Hello, Commander."

"Hello, Samson. You've been very busy."

"Yes, Commander. What is our status?"

"All supporting satellites in both our Moon's and Earth's orbit have been destroyed. The darts worked brilliantly."

"But the satellites named Armageddon orbiting Earth did not activate."

"Unfortunately not, Samson. But we knew that might happen. That's why you didn't program the darts to destroy the re-entry rockets on the satellites orbiting Earth."

"That is true, Commander. Still…"

"I understand, Samson. Are we ready to launch the nano-robots?"

"We're ready, Commander."

"Good. Let's do it."

♦♦♦

The six of us boarded the transport and headed towards the launch tube facilities. We were about half way there when I felt the transport shudder. "Stop the transport, Chris." The transport stopped. "Did any of you feel that?"

Everybody responded, "Yes."

I waited a minute. It happened again, a little stronger. "What's going on? What's causing the shaking? It feels like the aftershock of an earthquake."

There was silence for a few moments. Samson replied, "I believe, Commander, that the satellites named Armageddon have commenced the attach on Tranquility Base. What we are feeling is its destruction. We must hurry and launch this weapon."

I was alarmed to hear that. I wanted to go back to the control room and see for myself, but I also knew that Samson was right. We needed to get to the launch tubes. "Thank you, Samson. Chris, let's go. Full speed." The transport started immediately.

Thirty-nine: Annihilation

0038.0217.0145 LST

Sound doesn't travel in a vacuum, so I didn't know what was going on when I saw the bodies of Samson and Chris flying halfway across the launch tube facility. I heard Chris say, "What just happened? Are you okay, Samson?" I watched as the thruster packs on their suits brought them under control and back down onto the floor.

Samson responded, "I'm okay."

I looked back to where they had been and saw that launch tubes forty-three through fifty had exploded. The satellites named Armageddon had unleashed an attack and had scored multiple hits. I felt my suit activate and turn rock hard. Within microseconds, I was hit by pieces of shrapnel. Several more of the tubes exploded and my team was once again cast about. I issued an order to evacuate and return to the control room. Everyone acknowledged the order. The launch facility was on the verge of total destruction. The suits allowed us to move quickly and they protected us from flying debris.

We were unable to launch any of the nano-robots. They had all been destroyed.

♦♦♦

Before meeting everyone in the control room, Jay and I sealed the area. We were all happy to be alive and relatively unhurt. Wallace became the center of attention, and we all thanked him and complimented him on how well the suits had worked.

I activated the computer and LENS so I could see what was happening. The images that appeared on the screen were surreal. One by one, as they orbited around our Moon, the satellites named Armageddon took turns firing at the launch tubes and Tranquility base in a non-stop barrage. Tranquility was almost completely leveled. I was surprised that LENS had so far been unaffected, but suspected it was going to be only a matter of time before Armageddon would find it. I acted quickly and called Travis.

As I waited for Travis, I focused one of the satellites on the Tower. As I did, I saw the top open and the power crystal emerge and power up. As the interior of the power crystal began to activate, Armageddon began to assault the Tower. I stood transfixed, as the Tower absorbed everything Armageddon unleashed upon it. The shots did not affect the power crystal.

I wondered if we were going to be able to get back down to Tranquility II. I was unable to get a clear picture of the area surrounding the base of the Tower.

Travis responded to my call. “Armageddon found us, Travis.”

“I saw the satellites firing, Bella. We believe one of Armageddon’s systems was monitoring our satellites and saw that we had quite a few focused on the area during the first launch. It must have concluded that the area posed a threat to its existence and waited for the slightest indication there was human activity present. Were you able to launch?”

“Negative. We had just started the loading procedure. Everything was destroyed.”

“So we need a new plan.”

Samson interjected, “Commander, may I speak with Commander Travis?”

“Please, Samson…”

“Commander Travis, I can download the manufacturing processes for the nano-robots. I have them stored in my personal files. You could manufacture them as I did, and then launch them. We know that the satellites orbiting the Earth will not fully activate until ours are destroyed, so if you launch more than we need, enough should get through if Armageddon decides to take a few shots. The containers holding the robots won’t be considered a threat. They are programmed to release the robots quite a distance away from the target. You should be able to have them ready in less than a week. Should I proceed with the download?”

Travis was nodding his head. “Yes.”

“Computer, download personal file ‘nano-robot’ to Commander Travis.”

Less than fifteen seconds went by. “Got it, Samson. We’ll start immediately.”

“Thank you, Commander Travis.”

A more pressing thought entered my mind as Samson and Travis conversed. We had used up a great deal of out suits’ resources and we needed to get back to T II. "Travis, we need to get back to T II. We're all close to exhaustion and so are the resources of these suits."

"I understand, Bella. Get back as soon as you can."

"Will do, Travis. Computer, place this room on stand-by." I waited until the computer indicated the room was standing by. "Alright, you guys. First, we need to get back to T II. To do so, we may have to dig our way through some debris. I know it won't be a big problem with these suits, but we've been up almost two days and these suits have been working overtime. Secondly, once we are at the ring road, we'll have to cross it without getting blown away. Ready to go?"

Everyone nodded their heads.

♦ ♦ ♦

We were all surprised that the Garage appeared to be intact. Our hopes were that the trip through the tunnel connecting us to the Tower would also be uneventful. And it was, except for one detail. The tunnel ended in the wrong spot. When I saw that the tunnel had been destroyed, I ordered everyone to stop and de-activate their lights. We activated our night vision and climbed out of our transports. I wondered if the satellites named Armageddon had detected our lights.

Armageddon had taken out our warehouse, and with it, a large section of our tunnel. Now I understood why I wasn't able to focus on the base of the Tower.

We stood near the edge of a crater several hundred meters across. I could see part of the Tower across the way. I scanned the side of the Tower, looking for the opening. I didn't see it, so I asked my computer if it could detect an opening. It said there was one seven hundred meters up, based on a forty-five degree angle from our location. I motioned my crew to walk back into the tunnel so we could figure out a plan of action.

I said, "The Tower is open and waiting for us seven hundred meters from where we stand. Any suggestions as to how we get in?"

Wallace was quick with an answer. "We'll have to use the thrusters on our suits. The computer will control the flight into the opening."

"That sounds good, Wallace. Does everyone have enough propellant to make the jump?"

I waited as everyone checked their computers. Wallace, DJ and Samson reported that they would be fine. Chris and Jay's computers concluded that they would have enough to get up, but not enough to be guided safely inside.

"So what do we need to do?" I asked Wallace.

Wallace responded, "We'll have to go as a single unit, linked together. I've already asked my computer for the calculations. As soon as you give the command, we'll be off. We need to link arms at the elbows and the suits will lock us together."

"Thank you, Wallace." We walked to where we had been, and linked arms. I ordered the suits to lock and they did so at the elbows and shoulders. I also felt them become rigid at the waist.

After instructing the computer to get us in the opening as quickly and safely as possible, I gave the order to launch. The flight took ten seconds. We really felt it when Chris and Jay's thrusters lost power. Our thrusters compensated, and when we touched down on the floor, we were facing the opening. As the opening closed, a blast from one of satellites named Armageddon lit up the walls of the Tower. We watched, as the energy from the blast dispersed up to the top of the Tower. My throat went dry and I couldn't swallow. I heard DJ say, "That was close."

Samson responded, "The satellites named Armageddon must have detected the energy from our suits."

♦ ♦ ♦

It took fifteen minutes to arrive at T II. All we wanted to do was get out of our suits, grab some food, head to our quarters and sleep. When we stepped out of the Tower, it was daytime and it took us a few minutes to adjust to the light. As I turned towards my transport, DJ called my name. I turned to look at her. "Yes, DJ. What is it?"

She looked into my eyes. "I don't want to spend the rest of my life down here."

I looked around. I felt the same way. "Neither do I, DJ. Let's get some rest."

Forty: A Call To Arms

0038.0219.1000 LST

In spite of everything, I passed out cold from exhaustion and did not awaken for over twenty-four hours. When I stepped out of the shower, I was ravenous. After getting dressed, I prepared the food I had picked up on the way back from the Tower. As I ate, I ran a mental checklist of the things I needed to do before heading back to our control station. My plan was to stay here for two more days and then head back. I guessed that Travis would be in a good position to inform me of his progress with the nano-robots by then.

My first priority was to immerse myself in the activities of T II. I finished my meal and headed out to be with the residents. I would inform whoever was interested of our progress.

♦♦♦

After several hours of reconnecting with the residents of T II, I found myself at the door of our agriplex. Very few of those with whom I spoke wanted to know much of what was going on. Most said they were content to wait until it was safe to go back. When I mentioned that Tranquility was in need of rebuilding, all responded with sadness, but eagerly offered their services.

I stepped through the door and proceeded up to the second floor. I spoke with the people working there and thanked them for their outstanding work. I visited each floor.

As I entered the elevator on the eighth floor, I instructed it to take me back down to ground level, but it instead took me up to the ninth floor. When the doors opened, I tried to close them, but they wouldn't budge. I stepped out. I walked into the first cubicle and headed for the window and the unobstructed view. As I took in the sight of T II, I noticed that the proximity of my hands had activated the device that encircled the cubicle. Taking my eyes from the window, I placed my hands directly over the device. The entire apparatus lit up. As I watched the lights, T II made contact with me. The words that T II formed in my mind were "Is this outpost under attack?"

Before I had any chance of controlling what I was thinking, my mind replied, "Yes."

I froze. The conversation continued. T II asked, "Should we activate our defenses?"

I responded, "What are you talking about?"

T II answered, "This outpost has several defensive mechanisms designed to protect it from space objects or enemy spacecraft that may post a threat to life on the surface. What is the nature of the attack? I have concluded it to be artificial in nature."

It took me a few minutes to put an answer in my mind. "Enemy spacecraft in orbit."

"Are we taking prisoners?"

"What??!" Another uncontrolled reaction. "These are unmanned satellites."

"Understood. In order to activate our system, one more power unit needs to be installed to complete the array."

My mind went blank. "Please show me."

T II instructed me to walk down to the room at the end of the hall and enter it. As I did, the entrance closed and an image of our Moon floated in front of me and began to rotate. Thousands of points of light started flashing. Most were green, but many were white. "The green flashing points of light indicate which power units have been activated."

The Moon began to move higher. Near the south pole on the side of the Moon that doesn't face Earth (the dark side of the Moon, as Jay called it), there was a section containing several hundred flashing white lights, a few green ones and one flashing red light. For a brief instant, 'N fourteen-D ninety three- A eighty- seven' appeared right over top of the red flashing light. I added the letter and number combination to my file.

T II continued, "In order to activate the defense mechanism, a power unit needs to be installed in the unit flashing red. Are any of our spacecraft presently orbiting?"

"No. Do you have the ability to scan what is in orbit around the outpost?"

"Yes."

"Do you have the ability to show these objects in their precise orbits around the image of this outpost you have created?"

"Yes."

The image of the Moon moved to its former position. As it did, all the satellites named Armageddon became visible. I told T II, "All these objects need to be destroyed. Are the defense mechanisms capable of that?"

"Yes."

I asked, "When the power unit is installed, can you show me how the defense mechanism will destroy the enemy spacecraft?"

"Yes." I saw the Moon surrounded by a complex grid of light. The satellites named Armageddon continued orbiting. "Once power to destroy the objects in orbit is attained, an energy pulse will be released at your command." The light surrounding the Moon expanded outwards at an incredible speed. "Any object touched by the energy created by our power units will be eliminated."

I stared at the Moon in front of me for a few moments. The satellites named Armageddon were gone. "Is there any way of achieving the same result without installing the power unit?"

The answer T II gave was a definitive "No."

The Moon disappeared and a soft light illuminated the room. I turned and saw the entrance appear. I entered an elevator and descended to ground level.

I stepped out of the agriplex and commandeered a vehicle to drive back to my quarters. My mind was racing. I needed to talk to Wallace and Samson. "Computer, send a message to Samson and Wallace. Have them meet me in my quarters in thirty minutes. Please indicate when they've acknowledge the message."

A few minutes went by. I was almost back at my quarters. "Message received by both parties, Commander."

♦ ♦ ♦

The implications of what I learned while conversing with T II were profound. Wallace and Samson seemed to sense that the conversation we were about to have was of a serious nature. We were seated at my computer station.

"I've been given some new information about this place." I made eye contact with Wallace and Samson. "This first piece is about how T II defines itself. It calls itself an outpost." I reached over and activated my computer and let that sink in. The wall screen illuminated and displayed a picture of Tranquility base from orbit. Wallace and Samson sat back in their chairs and looked at each other. "As you know, after considerable debate, we decided many months ago that we should install what we now know to be energy suppliers, into as many Towers as we could find. When this decision was made, the consequences of our actions were not known, although many theories were offered. I now know one of the consequences and we need to make a decision."

Samson leaned forward. "Commander, what is it?"

I swallowed. "This outpost knows that it is under attack by enemy forces. It has built-in defense mechanisms that can be accessed. One of these defense mechanisms can wipe out the entire constellation of satellites in orbit with a single burst of energy. It will do so at my command."

This time, Wallace leaned forward. "If you're asking us if it would be okay if you accessed the defensive mechanism you just described, you have my vote."

I nodded and acknowledged his trust in me. I looked over at Samson and saw him gesture his approval. "Thank you. Now, what I wish I could do is hop into my transport, drive over to the agriplex, activate the defense mechanism, and destroy that which has imprisoned us, but I can't. There is something the outpost needs."

Both Wallace and Samson leaned back into their chairs. I could see them thinking. I waited.

Samson blinked. "Oh my God. We need to install more of those power crystals for it to work."

Wallace did a double take. "Of course."

I was impressed. "Actually, we need to install only one. We need to figure out how we can accomplish that. The satellites named Armageddon are not perfect, and I suspect the loss of their supporting satellites has crippled them a bit, even after making them more powerful in the process. I've seen them miss their targets hundreds of times. There has to be a way."

Samson was nodding his head. "That is correct, Commander. They are not perfect. It may take me a little time to find what we are looking for. Where does this power crystal need to be installed?"

"I'm glad you asked. Maybe that will help you find a solution to the problem." I turned my attention to my computer. "Computer, access Carrera file 'grid map' and display on screen."

What I expected to see was an image of the Moon rotating on its axis with a grid map superimposed over it to show the location of all the Towers we had found and activated. What appeared on the screen instead was almost exactly what I had seen on the ninth floor, with one major difference. Each flashing point of light - green, white and red – displayed one of the letter and number co-ordinates on top of it.

Wallace leaned forward. "You found the meaning of those letters and numbers."

I looked at him and shook my head. "I've never seen this before, Wallace. T II must have downloaded this while I was in that room. I recorded the combination you see over the red flashing light into my file when I saw it appear. That must be how access to this file was attained."

Samson sounded excited. "Is that red flashing point where we need to install a power crystal, Commander?"

"Yes."

"I believe I have a solution…"

"That was fast, Samson."

"Yes, Commander. Armageddon processes the flight path of objects it is tracking based on points of origin, flight speed and trajectory. The supporting satellites would have helped in the calculations. Armageddon fires shots based on where it concludes an object will be." Samson paused for a few seconds. "There is one calculation that may cause Armageddon to overload its targeting processors. If it works, it would create a situation whereby Armageddon would conclude the object is in a different location."

"That sounds good, Samson. What is it?"

"Escape velocity. If we flew faster than escape velocity without actually going into orbit, the satellites named Armageddon would not know where to fire. Every calculation made by its processors at any given time during the flight would conclude that the object is leaving the Moon, and the shots would be fired based on that conclusion. But because several thousand calculations are made every second, the processors would be canceling each previous firing command and redirecting. Flicking the on and off switch of a light drives people crazy. It paralyzes. It causes one to lose control. That is the effect this would have. It would be continually changing its mind, so to speak."

He'd done it again. Wallace was staring at Samson, unable to speak. I was almost in the same state. "Are you saying Armageddon would not be able to fire?"

"I'm not saying Armageddon will not be able to fire. Logic was involved in how it concluded that the area of the launch tubes posed a threat. Flying faster than escape velocity without actually escaping is not logical. Armageddon would see an object moving at escape velocity and have to conclude that it was leaving the Moon. That is a logical conclusion. We have to create a flight path that would have it appear, that at any given moment, the vehicle transporting the power crystal is leaving the Moon."

"Is that possible?"

Both Wallace and Samson nodded their heads.

"So are we going to do it?"

Wallace answered, "Yes. But I give my approval on the condition that we proceed only if Travis and our friends on Earth are unable to destroy the problem within an acceptable timeframe."

"And what would you say is an acceptable time frame?"

"Six days from today."

"And you, Samson?"

"I agree with Wallace, Commander. I'm telling you it is possible. There are many calculations to make. After all is said and done, one of us will be risking his life to make the delivery, and I suspect you will not be asking for volunteers."

Samson was right. I would be the one to make the delivery. I responded, "And I suspect that if I did ask for volunteers, you'd be the first to do so." Samson smiled and nodded his head.

I looked at Wallace and said, "We have two transports capable of delivering the power crystal. If I fail…"

Wallace placed his hands together and brought them up to his face. "In the Eyes of God…"

I heard a deep voice speak to me. It said, "They'll miss."

0038.0222.1145 LST

It was time to speak with Travis.

Samson pointed out before I left that he now believed we may have only one chance to make a successful delivery. He said that if we found the transport hangar intact, it would only be because Armageddon had not yet found it to be interesting enough to destroy. But, it would see our transport leave the area and begin making its calculations. He said Armageddon could very well start attacking the area and try to stop the transport. And he pointed out that an energy pulse traveling down the shaft into the hangar would have devastatingly destructive power and would probably destroy the second transport. I told him that we had better get it right the first time.

He likened the task of delivering the power crystal to the Tower to someone picking up a golf club for the first time and sinking a hole-in-one with his first swing on a par four. I told him that wasn't very reassuring. He said he might be exaggerating.

I entered T II's tower with Jay to make our ascent. We checked our suits and supplies one last time. We were both flush with adrenalin. In fifteen minutes we would be jumping from the Tower with our life support systems turned off. The only working piece of electrical equipment would be the computer that controlled our thrusters. We tripled the amount of propellant we normally carried. Our goal was to be in the tunnel in less than ten seconds.

♦ ♦ ♦

Jay had identified the Tower that required the power crystal as one that was on his schedule. He had already started working on a ring road for delivery. The original flight plans were already loaded into his computer, along with information about where the entrance would appear. He had given Samson all his data regarding the Tower.

Chris was working with Samson on a program that would satisfy the requirements needed to get a power crystal into the Tower, if that were necessary. According to Chris, one of the most difficult problems was creating a flight path that would enable his transport to carry its nine million kilogram cargo without self-destructing from the speed and G forces.

♦ ♦ ♦

Jay and I arrived at the top of the Tower. When the entrance opened, we ran towards the opening and jumped. Our thrusters kicked in as we left and we shot towards the tunnel entrance, which was seven hundred meters away. As we entered the tunnel, we rotated for maximum stopping thrust and were relieved to see that the satellites named Armageddon had fired no shots.

I felt the life support systems of my suit reactivate as my feet touched down and I inhaled deeply. It took seven seconds. A communications link between Jay and I activated. "You okay, Jay?" I looked at him and he gave me a thumbs-up signal. I returned the gesture.

We located a small transport and headed for the control room.

♦♦♦

When we arrived at the control room, I reactivated the computers and contacted Travis.

"Good to see you, Bella."

"Thanks, Travis. How are things Earth-side?"

"Well, with the air transportation industry basically out of business, our economic situation is becoming a large concern. We have massive unemployment problems. Airlines and vast numbers of businesses that depended on air delivery, including tourism, are going bankrupt. It's quite depressing. In less than two weeks, Fisco has turned our economic systems into chaos. A lot of people are angry and suffering."

"That's depressing news, Travis. How are our nano-robot plans progressing?"

"Yes, well, we're having a problem with them. We thought they would work. We followed Samson's manufacturing instructions to the letter, but there's a problem. Samson's robots were manufactured under Tranquility's gravitational influence, which is twenty percent less than the Earth's. That twenty percent is causing manufacturing difficulties in the way the crystalline molecules bond together. As a result, we have to re-think how we're going to mass-produce them in this environment."

"That doesn't sound good, Travis. How long before a solution is found?"

"We won't stop until we find the solution, Bella. Maybe ask Samson to work on it."

"Did you just say you don't know?"

"Yes."

"Well, what do you suggest we do then?"

"A few things have changed since the failure of the nano-robots. Since we as an organization no longer have any solutions to offer our most supportive governments, they have taken matters into their own hands. They are working on ways of regaining control. Do you have other launch tube facilities available on the base?"

"There's no way for us to know if we can use any of them, Travis. We've not been near them."

"I understand. A full power launch of an inert object aimed directly at Armageddon would be undetectable to its sensors. The impact would most likely destroy its ability to operate. We don't believe a launch of that kind, using our rockets, would be successful from here."

I didn't like the sound of that. Those inert objects would need a guidance system and a way to maneuver. The launch tube facilities he was speaking of were much closer to the surface than the ones Armageddon destroyed. Running at full power would surely be something Armageddon would detect. That would put several of us in immediate danger. I wondered if he was trying to tell me something. "You may be right, Travis. I'll check out our alternate launch facilities, and if I find they are operational, I will start working on something immediately."

"That sounds good, Bella. I'm sorry the news wasn't better."

"Yes, Travis. So am I. Fisco really has made a mess. I'll get back to you."

"Thanks, Bella. Travis out."

I looked at Jay. His eyes were open wide. The expression on his face was one of disbelief and despair. "We're on our own, Jay. We have a delivery to make."

Jay looked at me and nodded his head. "What are your orders?"

"We need to head out to your laboratory and check the condition of our power crystal transports."

"I'm ready, Bella."

"Good. Let's go."

♦♦♦

Before entering the tunnel to Jay's laboratory, we picked up a few extra flight lights from the Garage. These would be mounted on top of the transport and programmed to flash at staggered intervals. We believed they would make it even more difficult for Armageddon to calculate our precise trajectory.

We arrived at the laboratory to find it as Jay had left it. All systems were in a stand-by mode with the exception of the Blue room, which used its own power supply and was located ten kilometers below the surface. The original ten-kilometer deep shafts that were built to transport the power crystals to the Blue room had been enlarged and converted into a hangar that housed our two transports.

We entered the hangars to inspect our transports. Our suits provided the light. To Armageddon, the area on the surface would appear to be man-made, but it had not yet attacked. We opened a channel to our number one transport and had it power up the systems we needed to access. The cockpit doors opened and we entered.

Jay accessed the flight control computer and double-checked that the information about the tower we needed to access was intact. Once that was done, he instructed the computer to be ready to accept new flight instructions. I entered my computer over-ride codes. I instructed Max to accept the new flight protocols once they were loaded, and recalculate the safety parameters. Without the overrides, Max would not allow the transport to go beyond escape velocity.

Jay moved into the loading bay and doubled-checked that all the systems were functioning at one hundred percent. I moved to the top of the transport and installed the extra flight lights we had commandeered from the Garage.

When we were both satisfied with the transport, we prepared to transport one of the power crystals into the loading bay. As I worked with Jay, I wondered how Samson would take the news about his malfunctioning nano-robots.

Forty-one: The Delivery

0038.0224.0900 LST

I told Samson the news about the nano-robots when I returned from Jay's laboratory one and a half days ago. A blank look had come across his face, as if to say, "Why didn't I see that?" He apologized for his failure, and the spark of life that I had come to recognize as Samson, vanished. He quickly turned his attention to the flight program Chris and he had developed. As much as he wanted to display confidence in what they had created, his failure with the nano-robots prevented him from doing so.

We scheduled what would likely be our only chance of installing a crystal in the Tower for ten hundred hours LST tomorrow.

The fact that I wasn't able to practice the flight weighed heavily on my mind. An endless stream of possibilities and consequences, based on whether I was successful or not, made it difficult for me to focus. We would record the flight using Earth's satellites, as the flight path required that we fly over the side of the Moon visible from Earth in order to be in line with the side of the Tower that would open. Wallace, Samson, Jay and Chris would be in the control room. I had invited DJ, but she did not commit to being there.

0038.0225.0700 LST

I greeted everyone as they arrived at the base of T II's Tower. DJ had decided not to join us. We entered the Tower and went over our plans during the ascent. Samson would be leaving the control room shortly after arriving to install the flight path program in the transport computers. One hour later, I would head towards the hangar to prepare for the flight. Samson would evacuate the area and return to the control room by ten hundred hours LST.

♦ ♦ ♦

I looked at everyone in the control room. All were busy at their assigned stations, readying and aligning Earth's satellites for recording.

Samson watched for a few minutes. I walked over to him. "Are you ready, Samson?"

"Yes, Commander. Are you?"

"As ready as I'll ever be, Samson."

"Good. May I have your permission to go?"

"Yes, Samson. I'll see you in about one and a half hours."

"Yes, Commander. About one and a half hours."

Samson turned and entered the air lock. As he stepped into the shaft, he gave me a thumbs-up sign. I returned the gesture.

I walked back to the monitoring station. Jay was focusing his satellites on the route I would be taking. Wallace was keeping track of what Armageddon was doing, and Chris had taken control of one of Earth's more sophisticated satellites in an effort to detect the satellites named Armageddon orbiting Earth.

I sat in one of the chairs, closed my eyes and tried to focus. An image of Samson came into view. He was in his suit, sitting in the co-pilot seat in the cockpit of the transport, programming the computer. I could see the interior of the cockpit from different angles. I felt my body relax and my mind settle.

While Samson worked, he appeared to be having a conversation with Max. He moved into the pilots seat. I saw the restraint system activate and lock him into place. Knowing the system worked relaxed me even more. Samson then held onto the two control sticks. I saw the cockpit door close. I found myself looking directly into Samson's eyes. He said, "I will not let you down, Commander."

The sound of my own voice snapped me back to reality as I said, "Samson… No!!!" I sat upright and looked around the control room. Wallace, Jay and Chris were looking at me. We were silent for a minute. I got up out of my chair.

Wallace broke the silence. "What's wrong, Bella?"

"How long have I been out?"

Wallace checked the time. "About an hour."

"I just saw an image of Samson in the transport. I think he's going to…" I didn't have a chance to finish the sentence. The sound of Jay's voice made me stop.

"Jesus… Armageddon has started firing."

We looked at the monitors. They were focused on the Armageddon satellites, which were firing at a target around the dark side of the Moon. A target that could only be Jay's laboratory. Jay quickly took his seat and began looking for the transport. Within twenty seconds, we saw the ship with its flashing flight lights racing across the surface of the Moon. It would be traveling in a wide arc that became tighter as it got closer to its target. The G forces would be very close to the maximum that our bodies could withstand. We would see the ship for fifteen minutes, and then it would disappear from view.

I couldn't believe what was happening. The thought that Samson might take the transport was incomprehensible to me. I went over our conversations in my head.

After seven minutes, Armageddon was still firing at Jay's lab and had not taken one shot at the transport. One of our satellites caught the image of T II's open Tower. The power crystal reached skyward and activated. At that instant, Armageddon began to bombard it with fire.

Armageddon began shooting at the transport just as it was about to disappear from view, but was unable to get a precise fix on it. We lost sight of the transport after precisely fifteen minutes. We watched the southern orbits of the satellites. As they came into view, we saw that they were firing.

The trip to the tower was scheduled to take twenty minutes. As the timer clicked off twenty-five, we stopped watching.

Wallace turned to me. "What happened, Bella?"

"I don't know, Wallace. I've been going over our conversations. When we were here this morning, I asked him if he was ready. He said, "Yes." He asked me, "Are you, Commander?" I said, "As I'll ever be." Then he asked, "May I have your permission to go?" I said, "Yes."

"Do you think that's why he went?"

"I don't know, Wallace. I'm not going to assume anything at this point. I've not been in this kind of situation before. I'm very concerned about him and am wondering if he was successful."

"I understand, Bella. I'm at a loss, too."

The cockpit capsule was programmed to separate from the main transport and travel directly to the tunnel at Tranquility. It would be traveling faster than escape velocity as it hit the tunnel, and would begin to decelerate once inside. If Samson had been successful in delivering the power crystal, he would be there.

"Let's head back to the Garage and see if Samson is there."

We downloaded all our information. I put the room on stand-by and we left for the Garage.

♦ ♦ ♦

Samson's capsule was not there when we arrived. We continued to wait, longer than we probably should have.

"Chris, I want you to get our rescue ship ready for launch. Jay, I want you to help him. If Samson is still alive, he has approximately sixty-five hours of life support left. I'll need that ship ready in four hours."

Both of them replied, "Yes, Commander."

"You are not to leave this facility without me. Understood?"

Once again, they both replied, "Yes, Commander."

"Good. I'm going back to T II and I'm taking Wallace with me. We'll be back in four hours."

Wallace and I left the Garage and walked to the end of the tunnel. "I need to know if the power crystal is in place, Wallace. I need to be on the ninth floor."

"I understand, Bella."

♦ ♦ ♦

We stood at the end of the tunnel and powered down our suits to prepare for our seven-second flight. Our computers had locked onto the opening in the tower, which had appeared a few seconds after we arrived. I scanned the sky and saw several of the satellites named Armageddon flying high in orbit. The light they were emitting was now so bright, it would cause blindness without proper protection.

Wallace set his computer for a five-second countdown. I did the same and we took off together. In the seven seconds it took to get to the Tower, T II communicated with me. It wanted to know if I was ready to activate our defenses.

As I landed in the tower, I knew that Samson had been successful, but I didn't know what kind of shape he was in. When my suit had reactivated and the communication link between Wallace and I had been restored, I told him.

"Samson has placed the power crystal, Wallace. T II is waiting for me."

In the small window of my display, I saw Wallace nodding his head. "That is good news, Bella." He paused. As he spoke again, his voice was full of emotion. "He was my most trusted and closest friend."

I didn't believe what I was hearing. I felt scared. "What are you saying?"

I waited for a response. Wallace's voice was barely controlled. "I believe that he has died, Bella. Please do not ask me to explain why I believe that. You need to destroy those satellites."

"I know, Wallace. I will."

I refused to believe that Samson was dead. I felt anger welling up inside of me.

♦ ♦ ♦

We exited the Tower, walked directly over to the agriplex and went to the ninth floor. By the time we had entered the control room, T II and I had established a plan. The room darkened and an image of the Moon with half its surface bathed in sunlight floated before us and began to rotate. I requested that we be able to see exactly what was happening in real time. Seventy-two satellites appeared in orbit.

T II formed a question in my mind. "Shall we begin, Commander?"

I took a deep breath. "Begin."

We flew in close enough to the surface to see a Tower. It had a high concentration of sunlight on it. The tower opened and its power crystal pushed skyward. It took fifteen seconds to activate. When it did, energy pulses started to hit it. Armageddon had begun to fire upon it.

The image pulled away and we began to orbit the moon. As we flew over it, we saw all the Towers begin to open and expose their power crystals. The ones that had sunlight began to activate. As they did, Armageddon began firing on them.

As we crossed into areas without sunlight, we saw that those Towers were also open. Some of the power crystals were being raised higher than I imagined possible. Not one power crystal activated in areas without sunlight.

We moved into a higher orbit and crossed back into an area with sunlight. Many of the towers had raised their power crystals by one or two kilometers. One by one, the platforms containing activated power crystals began to glow. Just before we crossed into the unlit area, several of the nine-sided platforms began beaming the energy they were producing to a platform that exactly matched its angle. It happened very quickly. Within minutes, every Tower on the surface with a power crystal was connected to nine others. The ones in the sunlight began to feed their energy to the ones that were not. The power crystals that weren't bathed in sunlight absorbed the energy being fed to them, and activated. They then fed their energy to other towers.

Because of its location, the power crystal Samson had placed needed to be activated in order to feed energy to others. We were now crystal clear about how important that one tower was.

We flew into an orbit higher than Armageddon's. All seventy-two satellites were firing a non-stop barrage of energy pulses at the towers. Slowly the energy beams between the towers began to look more powerful and uniform in their intensity.

T II made contact. "In fifteen seconds, there will be enough energy stored to destroy the enemy spacecraft in orbit."

A command formed in my mind. "Fire when ready."

Fifteen seconds later it happened so fast, I didn't have time to blink. An energy pulse shot up from the surface and the satellites disappeared. The power crystals quickly retreated into their Towers.

Wallace gave off a nervous laugh. "Holy…" He didn't finish the sentence.

A question formed in my mind. "Has the threat been eliminated?"

T II responded, "All enemy spacecraft in orbit around this outpost have been destroyed."

"Thank you, T II."

T II continued, "Commander, similar spacecraft have started to appear in orbit around this space body." An image of Earth appeared before us. "They have begun firing upon it. Are these also considered a threat?"

We saw over one hundred satellites firing in orbit. "Yes, they are a threat."

"We can eliminate them."

"How?"

"I am capable of targeting individual objects for elimination. I require that you target the object."

"There are many important objects orbiting. Can you guarantee that the objects we target will be the only ones destroyed?"

"Yes."

"Good. Begin."

Once again, the towers began opening and the power crystals began activating, this time without Armageddon firing on them. Within minutes, the array had powered up.

"Ready, Commander."

Images of both Earth and our Moon appeared before me. I could see dozens of satellites firing and moving around in Earth's orbit. I focused on one. "Fire!"

Almost instantly, a ball of energy the size of a satellite shot out from one of the towers and traveled the distance between the Moon and the Earth. The energy that was released vaporized the satellite, causing the energy ball to disappear.

I focused on another one. "Fire!" The same result occurred. I felt Wallace's hand on my shoulder. "Please don't distract me, Wallace." He removed his hand.

I continued to focus and fire. One by one, the satellites began to disappear.

"Commander…"

It was T II. "Yes…"

"The spacecraft have now stopped firing at Earth. They have now started to fire on us."

I stopped. I hadn't noticed. "Show me."

T II displayed images of the satellites named Armageddon firing energy pulses from Earth orbit and hitting the energy grid. The energy pulses took two and a half seconds to reach the Moon.

T II said, "Several spacecraft have left their orbits clustered together in a formation and have ignited their main thrusters. They are moving towards us at high speed."

"Keep them under surveillance. They pose no immediate threat to us. Let's continue eliminating the ones left in Earth's orbit."

"Yes, Commander."

I continued eliminating satellites from Earth orbit. T II noted that the more satellites I took from orbit, the more satellites left to join the ones on their way here.

I had lost track of time. T II made contact and said, "There are no more enemy spacecraft in Earth orbit, Commander. There are now one hundred and fifteen enemy spacecraft heading towards us."

That was good news. I wondered if we could eliminate them all with one shot. "T II…"

"Yes, Commander."

"Can we eliminate those spacecraft in one shot?"

"I can cause a number of energy pulses equal to the number of enemy spacecraft heading towards us to fire simultaneously. Would that be satisfactory?"

"Absolutely. You may fire when ready."

"Please issue the command, Commander."

I cleared my mind. "Fire!

Wallace and I watched as one hundred and fifteen energy pulses left the towers simultaneously and found their targets. It took me a minute to absorb that we had eliminated Armageddon.

"T II… How many were there, and how long have we been here?"

"One hundred and forty four commander. You have been here three and a half hours."

"My friend and I need to go."

"Understood."

The images of the Moon and Earth disappeared, soft lighting came on and the entrance appeared. We had to get back to the Garage.

Forty-two: The Rescue

0038.0225.1545 LST

Wallace and I had started to ascend the Tower. Wallace wasn't himself. He sounded very solemn. "I'm sure Travis and the rest of our friends on Earth are probably just a little curious about what just happened here."

"I'm sure they are, but any explanation will have to wait. Did you notice how quickly those shots reached Earth? It takes light two and a half seconds to travel between here and the Earth. Those shots were traveling much faster than that."

"I hadn't thought about it."

"I wonder if the beings who built this place came here in ships that travel faster than light."

Wallace nodded. "That would probably be a safe assumption."

We reached the top of the Tower and walked to the opening. I looked up and saw Earth. There were no satellites in orbit. I looked at Wallace, who was also looking up.

I turned my attention back to rescuing Samson. I saw two figures standing at the entrance to the tunnel. I asked the computer to open a communications link. "Hello Chris and Jay. Armageddon has been eliminated. Is the rescue ship ready?"

Chris answered, "Ten-four, Commander."

"Good. Wallace and I will be right down. Please clear the entrance."

They both waved and moved out of the way. Wallace and I jumped and let our suits guide us into the tunnel.

♦♦♦

"Jay, I want you start powering up as much of the base as you can and give me a rundown of the damage. I need to know how much of the base is habitable."

"I'll get right on it, Bella."

"Chris, I need you to help Jay. Try to get some launch tubes ready for use. Wallace and I will go after Samson."

"Ten-four, Commander."

Chris had loaded the navigation program of the Tower's location into the rescue ship's computer. Wallace requested that he be allowed to pilot the ship. Before departing, we had to manually open air locks that would allow us to fly up to the Moon's surface. I was feeling a different kind of stress, now that we no longer had to worry about Armageddon. Everything had changed.

Of course Wallace was right about our friends wanting know what we had done and how we did it. The Moon was now home to the most powerful weapon in our solar system, designed to be controlled by one man - the one in command. I was that man.

It took ten minutes to reach the Tower from the base. Wallace and I didn't speak during that time. As we approached the tower, Wallace focused all the ship's lights around the surrounding area. We searched the surface for signs of the transport ship. After twenty minutes, we found no trace of it.

"Bella, could it be that Samson flew the ship right into the Tower?"

"That would certainly explain our inability to find it."

"I'm going to land the ship." Wallace landed on the ring road in front of the opening that appeared, and we got out of the ship. There was no light from the Sun to help us. I found myself holding my breath as we walked into the dark interior.

I asked the computer to activate the exterior lights of our ship and focus them so they would illuminate the interior of the Tower. With the help of our suits' lights and the ship's lights, we were able to see inside. The alien power crystal sat in the middle of the floor directly in front of us almost forty-one meters away. The space between the power crystal and us was spotless, with no trace of debris.

Scanning the interior, we saw the remains of the transport ship piled up against eight of the inside walls. The transport cockpit was undamaged but it's exterior was charred from rocket exhaust. A question formed in my mind. "What in God's name happened here?"

I heard Wallace's voice. "Samson! Are you here?" There was no answer. We couldn't see him. Wallace continued, "Computer, please direct us to Samson."

On our displays, a red image appeared in the debris that was piled up against a wall. We quickly ran over to it. It was Samson. We knelt down and checked and re-checked his suit, looking for any indication that it had been compromised. It was intact, but had powered down to minimum life support status.

"Wallace, is he alive?"

I waited as Wallace checked the built-in medic program. "Barely. We need to get him back to T II. There are no broken bones or internal injuries, but he doesn't appear to have any energy left in his body."

We grabbed Samson and took him back to the rescue ship. While Wallace stabilized him, I ran back into the tower and over to the cockpit. I had the computer open the hatch. Once inside, I plugged a storage cartridge into the computer and downloaded everything that had taken place from the instant Samson had entered the hangar. Once this was completed, I went back to the rescue ship, and Wallace flew us back to base.

♦♦♦

I took control of the ship, as we hovered next to the entrance of the Tower that would take Wallace and Samson back to T II. Upon our arrival, a retractable platform allowed Wallace and Samson to enter the Tower. After the platform had retracted back into the ship, the entrance to the Tower closed. I flew the ship back to its hangar.

I found Jay and Chris working in one of Jay's power substations near where I had parked the rescue ship. When I arrived, they stopped working and asked about Samson.

"We found him inside the Tower. He is alive, and Wallace has taken him down to T II. I can't tell you any more than that. His suit was down to minimum life support."

Jay sounded relieved. "That's good news, Bella. I'm sure he'll be fine."

"I hope so, Jay. Do you have enough information to give me a status report on our base?"

"Yes, Bella, but maybe you could first fill us in as to what happened with Armageddon?"

I looked at them both and wondered how they would take the news. "Absolutely. The built-in defenses of this outpost worked perfectly. All the satellites in orbit around our Moon were eliminated instantly and simultaneously. I was also able to destroy all the satellites orbiting Earth."

Jay and Chris looked at each other. Jay said, "We were in the tunnel and saw the energy beams emanating from the power crystal's platform. We didn't know what was happening."

I waited a few seconds. "The outpost responds to commands given by the one in charge. If it hadn't been me, it would have been someone else. We haven't spoken to anyone on Earth about this yet. I'm not sure what our future here will be. Is that enough information for you guys for now?"

They both acknowledged that it was. "Good. Do you have a status report for me?"

Jay continued, "Yes, Bella. Of course, there is nothing left of our surface structures. And because we shut down the base and depressurized before departing to T II, it would appear that damage to our underground structures was minimal. I estimate that after we begin powering up and re-pressurizing, we will have seventy-five percent usable space in the underground sections of the base."

That was better than I had expected. "Good news, Jay. Chris, how about the Garage and our remaining launch tubes?"

"I won't know how much damage was done to the Garage until we start re-pressurizing, Commander. With so much of it being close to the surface, it may have sustained structural damage that our diagnostic systems cannot detect at this time. Our remaining launch tubes are unscathed and can be put into operation quickly."

"Excellent, Chris. When we get back to T II, work with Jon to launch a new set of communication satellites. Once we have those on line, we can think about how we're going to rebuild. That is, if we're allowed to."

"Sounds good, Commander."

"Thank you, Chris. So, Jay, what is the first step in the re-pressurization process?"

"The first step is to begin the power-up. When that is complete, we'll have control of our decompression safety systems. We'll be able to pressurize the base one small section at a time. When we find a section that is uninhabitable, the system will seal it off until repairs can be completed."

"I'll need one week to complete the power-up stage. I have no way of knowing at this time if the power grids are intact."

"You have your week, Jay. I'd like you begin with the launch tubes."

"No problem, Bella. I'll have them done before we need to go back to T II."

"Thanks, Jay. I'm going to contact Travis. I'll be down in the control room."

Forty-three: Samson's Flight

0038.0226.0130 LST

I left Jay and Chris and made my way down to our control room. I put in a call to Travis and waited for him to respond.

"Bella..." He seemed at loss for words.

"Yes, Travis."

"What exactly just happened?"

"I thought you might want to know. That's why I called. Do you remember the debate we had in regard to installing the alien power crystals into the Towers?"

Travis looked away from me for a minute. "Yes."

"This place, Travis... it's an outpost. The beings who designed and built it incorporated a defense mechanism." I paused for a few seconds. "This defense capability was designed to destroy any space objects that would pose a threat to life on the surface of the Moon... and also destroy enemy spacecraft."

Travis's eyes became noticeably larger for an instant. "Did you say 'enemy spacecraft'?"

"Yes. The best way I can describe how it works is this: We use a program called Max when we pilot our ships. The computer, or whatever it is I'm wired into, is like Max. It works with its inhabitants to keep the place running smoothly and is programmed to make sure they are safe. Instead of voice commands, it responds to commands given by thought. The one who is in command has access to its controls. It seems to know who that person is without any input from us."

"I see."

"I'm aware that what I've done may be cause for concern. I expect there will be some discussion as to whether I'll be allowed to continue as commander of this base, given the destructive power I've demonstrated it to have. I've also indicated to some of my people that we may not be able to stay."

I paused for a few moments. "At this time we do not have the technology to extract the alien power crystals from the towers, so this place is armed and dangerous. Of course, we'd like to stay and rebuild the base, but we'll wait until everybody down there has approved."

Travis was nodding his head. He seemed a little dazed from all the information. "Personally, Bella, I do not have a problem with what you've done. Do you have any idea what other capabilities the outpost has?"

"I haven't asked. Should I?"

"I think you should."

I wasn't expecting his response. "I'll see what I can find out, Travis. We're working on re-establishing our communication satellite array. We should have it back up within a week. I must say I'm surprised by your response to what we're sitting on."

Travis thought for a moment. "We were all pretty scared when the Armageddon satellites disappeared from their orbits around our Moon. And we were terrified when they started disappearing from their orbits around our Earth. But when they were gone, everybody was so happy and relieved." He stopped speaking for a minute. "We were so happy that agreements were made that would ensure Tranquility's continued existence. I assume you'll be the one in charge of redesigning the base."

A wash of relief coursed thru me. "I was kind of hoping that would be alright."

"It's alright, Bella."

"I am relieved, Travis. Have you heard anything from Fisco?"

"Nothing, Bella."

"That surprises me. I thought he would have made contact by now."

"Maybe he's gone into shock. We're still looking for him. I'll let you know as soon as we have some information on him."

"Thanks, Travis. A few things require my immediate attention, so I'll sign off now. I'll be in contact shortly."

"I'll be looking forward to it, Bella. Thank you. Travis out."

♦♦♦

I reached into my suit and pulled out the cartridge containing Samson's flight information. I cleared the computer and inserted the cartridge. All twelve monitors lit up as the program activated. I could see the interior of the hangar from every angle. The monitor I focused on, however, was the one showing the interior of the cockpit.

I saw Samson enter the transport and sit in the co-pilot's seat. He inserted a cartridge into one of Max's receptacles.

"Max, I'm going to start downloading a new, modified flight program for you. Please let me know if you encounter any problems."

"Yes, Commander."

I saw Samson shift his position a little. He said, "If I'm the one who is to make this delivery, let Commander Carrera know before he starts his way down here."

Max replied, "Commander, I am not programmed to tell you if you are the one to pilot this transport. Also, Commander Carrera is currently not accessible to me."

"I know, Max. I was not speaking to you."

"But you are the only person here. To whom were you speaking?"

"Do you know what you are, Max?"

"I do."

"Explain."

"I am a software program designed to prevent loss of life."

"That is true. Do you know who created you?"

"Yes."

"Good. I was speaking with the one who creates me. Does that compute?"

"I understand, Commander."

"Good. As we leave the hangar, you will detect several bright objects orbiting. I want you to keep track of what they do while we fly to our destination."

"Yes, Commander."

As I watched Samson over the next several minutes, I experienced an eerie feeling of deja vu. I had seen that before in this room. I saw Samson moving into the pilot's chair and the restraint system activating. He placed his hands on the control sticks and I saw the cockpit door close. He said, "All systems go, Max?"

"All systems fully functional, Commander."

"Good, Max."

I saw Samson look around the cockpit. He then spoke the words I heard while I was resting… "I will not let you down, Commander."

♦ ♦ ♦

I was riveted to my seat. As I watched, Samson was thrown violently back into the pilot's seat of the transport. It only took a few seconds for the transport to reach the surface. I scanned the monitors and found the one that was focused on the satellites named Armageddon. They began firing almost instantly, but none of the shots came even remotely close to the ship.

Max reported, "Orbiting objects are releasing massive quantities of energy, Commander."

"Are we in any danger from them?"

"Not at the moment, Commander."

"Good. Keep monitoring them."

"Yes, Commander. I can no longer detect if they are releasing any energy."

"Are you saying we are out of range?"

"Yes, Commander."

"That's a good thing."

I found myself feeling very warm. Taking in all the different angles from the various on-board recorders, I watched for several minutes as the transport raced across the surface of the Moon. I knew Armageddon would begin firing again within a minute.

As if on cue, Max once again reported, "The orbiting objects have started releasing massive quantities of energy, Commander."

"Are we in danger?"

"No, Commander. The energy being released is focused on one area."

"Can you tell me where that is?"

"My calculations indicate that the energy released is being focused on Tranquility base."

Samson thought about this for few seconds. "Could it be that the energy being released is focused on the Tower?"

"I cannot be as accurate as that, Commander."

"That's okay."

I continued to watch, knowing that the flight was more than halfway over. The landscape constantly changed and Samson flew the transport with seeming ease. With just over five minutes left, the images on all the outside monitors shook violently. I leaned forward in my chair.

"What was that, Max?"

"Checking systems, Commander."

"Was it a blast from one of the orbiting objects?"

"Negative, Commander. Stand by."

It took only a few seconds, but it seemed an eternity. "Commander...." Just as Max began his report, the images shook violently again.

"Yes."

"We have a problem in the cargo bay. The initial acceleration and the G forces exerted on the supporting struts have caused a failure. Our cargo is no longer secure. If we continue to use this flight path, this ship will come apart."

"Altering trajectory, Max. I'm going to shift the transport to transfer the load. Let me know when the cargo area has stabilized. How long before we are scheduled to reach our target?"

"Four minutes, twenty seconds. Cargo area has not yet stabilized."

"Working on it. Will the cargo area survive our plan for delivery?"

"No, Commander. The deceleration will destroy the ship."

"Then we need another plan. We're going to fly this thing right into the Tower. The Tower is eighty-one meters across at its widest point, and seven hundred and twenty-nine meters high. You'll need to eject this cockpit as we clear the opening of the Tower and stop it from crashing into the interior of the Tower. Can you do that?"

"Not at these speeds, Commander. What about the cargo bay?"

"I don't care if it crashes. We just need to make sure it gets inside. At what speed are you able to eject me safely?"

"Less that half of what we are currently traveling."

"That will bring me down below escape velocity. How long before we reach the Tower?"

"Three minutes, five seconds."

"How much time do I need to decelerate safely?"

"One minute, fourteen seconds."

"Good. Tell me when to start."

My hands gripped the armrests of my chair. I felt my heart pounding in my chest.

"Cargo bay has stabilized, Commander."

"Do we have a lock on the entrance to the Tower?"

"Yes, Commander."

"Create an image for me."

One of the monitors changed, and an image of the Tower appeared. There was yellow outline where the entrance was to appear. This would be the image on Samson's helmet display. It grew larger by the second.

"Start deceleration, Commander."

I saw Samson pull back on the control stick. I remembered that Armageddon began firing near the end of Samson's flight.

"We'll be dropping below escape velocity in ten seconds. Those orbiting objects may start releasing some energy. How long before we enter the Tower?"

"Twenty-five seconds, Commander."

Ten seconds went by. "We're below escape velocity. What are the orbiting objects doing?"

Just as Samson finished his question, Armageddon began firing. "The objects have begun to release massive quantities of energy, Commander. We are not in any danger." The entrance to the Tower has not yet appeared. "Eight seconds to impact… Seven…"

I found myself yelling at the screens… "Come on… open!!!"

Max continued… "Five… four… three… two…"

Before Max could say 'one', the tower opened. I watched as the cargo bay smashed into the floor of the Tower. Seven monitors went blank. I saw Samson's body straining against the straps of the restraint system and flames on the remaining monitors.

Several seconds elapsed before the monitors began showing pictures again. The Sun illuminated the Tower's interior. The cockpit was sitting on the Tower floor. The cargo section of the transport was strewn all over its interior. Max was calling Samson, who was unconscious. I waited for him to move.

♦♦♦

Several minutes passed before Samson regained consciousness. When he did, he asked the computer to release the restraint system and open the cockpit. As he stepped out of the cockpit and onto the floor, he asked the computer to activate his suit recorder and transfer the images into the cockpit recorder. Another one of my monitors activated.

He walked around inspecting the cockpit. He thanked Max for doing a great job. He then turned his attention to finding his cargo. As he surveyed what remained of the cargo bay, he said, "Wow, that was close."

The cameras on the cockpit were active and displaying a mountain of debris, dwarfing Samson's image. It became clear that he was having a difficult time discerning one object from another.

The container for the power crystal was designed to withstand a much more severe impact than it had sustained in the crash, and I was surprised that I couldn't see it. Samson was looking for it. "Computer, please direct me to the container that houses the power crystal."

I continued to watch as Samson began walking towards one of the walls where a huge pile of the transport rested. When he arrived at the scene, he began to toss pieces of the ship aside, digging for the container. It took him five minutes to find it lying on its side. "Computer, run a diagnostic on this container. Is it fully functional?"

He waited a few seconds. "No. This container has sustained damage. Its drive mechanism has been destroyed."

"I see. Can you open it?"

"Yes."

"Please open it."

The container opened, and as it did, the three-meter-wide, nine million kilogram power crystal rolled out. Samson jumped out of the way. "Computer, do you have the specifications of this power crystal?"

"Yes."

"Using this suit, is it possible for me to roll this object into that depression in the floor?"

"I do not know, Commander."

"Well there's only one way to find out..."

Samson began searching the pile of debris. He picked out two pieces of metal sheet and walked to the power crystal. He placed one sheet up against the surface of the crystal and carefully shaped it into the same shape as the power crystal. He then did the same thing with the second piece. When he was satisfied with his work, he placed them both against the power crystal, one on top the other, put both his hands on the metal sheets, planted his feet, and pushed. The power crystal didn't move. His plan was to slide the top sheet over the bottom one.

He turned around and put his arms behind him. He told the computer to lock the position of his arms in place. He then took hold of the two pieces of sheet metal and pressed them up against the surface of the power crystal near the floor. The first piece of sheet metal stuck to the surface of the crystal. He held onto the second piece and bent his knees to lower his body. Using his legs, he pushed up against the power crystal. It moved, and the second piece of sheet metal slid over the one stuck to the power crystal. When the crystal had rolled enough so that he was no longer able to use the first piece of metal to slide the second piece over, he stopped. He continued by grabbing the first piece of sheet metal and placing it back in its original position, and repeated the procedure. He continued to work with the power crystal in this way for several minutes. As he worked, his breathing became heavy and labored. He reached the lip of the depression and gave it one last push. It fell in. I knew he was spent.

The instant the power crystal fell into the depression and landed, Samson was knocked off of his feet. He got up quickly but just as he did, the floor started to vibrate violently. Samson lost his balance and crashed to the floor, dangerously close to the power crystal. Barely able to speak, he ordered the computer to activate his thruster pack and hover until the vibration stopped.

I had a birds-eye view of the interior and could see how the vibrations were causing what was left of the transport to move towards the interior walls, with the exception of the wall that contained the entrance. When pieces of the transport made contact with the walls, the metal began to shred. It took three minutes for the power crystal to seat itself and begin to rise up the tower.

Samson landed by the pile of debris where we found him. "Computer, turn my life support to minimum." He sat down on the floor.

I pulled the cartridge from the computer and sat for a few minutes to gather my thoughts. I inserted another cartridge into the computer and asked it to download what had just taken place in this room. When the download was complete, I put the room on stand-by and headed back to T II.

0038.0226.0315 LST

As I stepped out of the Tower, DJ was there to greet me. "You look exhausted, Commander."

"It's been a long day, DJ. Have you seen Samson? Is he going to be okay?"

"He'll be fine, Commander. He wants to see you."

"That's good, DJ. He did an amazing job."

"That's what I've heard." She paused for a few moments. "Thank you for getting us out of here." Before I had a chance to respond, she leaned forward and kissed my cheek.

I smiled and placed my hand over the spot where she her lips had touched me. "You're welcome, DJ. Will you please drive us to see Samson?"

She was blushing. "Of course, Commander!"

♦ ♦ ♦

DJ dropped me off at Samson's quarters, and I called him to make sure he could see me. He responded immediately and I walked in. I found him casually dressed, reclining in his chair facing the window that offered the best view of T II. "In the Eyes of God, Samson. How are you?"

"Hello, Commander. Thank you for asking. I'm quite sore. The doctor says he's never seen anything quite like it. He thinks I've managed to sprain my entire body. It doesn't hurt when I blink."

"Ouch."

"Yes, Commander… ouch."

I walked over to his chair and gave him the cartridge containing the flight information. "I reviewed the flight recorder. You did an incredible job in delivering the power crystal. I understand what happened. What you did goes beyond description. No one else need see this. It's yours to keep. You may want to look at it when you're feeling better."

Samson gripped the cartridge in his hand. "Thank you, Commander. I will want to study it."

"I have something else for you." I reached into my suit and pulled out the cartridge that contained the recording of me watching Samson's flight. "This is a recording of my reactions while watching you on your delivery." I placed it in Samson's hand. "Please recover quickly."

Samson looked into my eyes. "In the Eyes of God, Commander. As fast as I can. Thank you."

"We've been given permission to rebuild Tranquility. Will you stay on to help me redesign and build a new Earth Dome?"

Samson blinked. "I'd be honored, Commander."

"Thank you, Samson. I'm going back to my quarters now to catch up on some sleep."

"I'll see you soon, Commander."

Forty-four: A New Beginning

0038.0301.1045 LST

"Computer, is Commander Till currently in T II?"

"Yes, Commander."

"Please connect me."

"Commander Till is standing by."

"Wallace..."

"Yes, Bella. Wallace here."

"I need to speak with you. Will you meet me at the cafeteria in ten minutes?"

"That will be fine, Bella. I'll see you in ten minutes."

"Thanks, Wallace."

I climbed into my vehicle and drove to the cafeteria. I had just finished a session with T II on the ninth floor and needed to clear my head. It was breakfast time and I could see the eatery was busy. I pulled into my parking spot and went inside.

Everyone was in a great mood. I spent a few minutes conversing with my friends and then grabbed a plate and tray. After loading up with some food and a glass of water, I found my table and waited for Wallace. When he arrived, I waved him over. He put his hand up and motioned that he was going to get some food. While I waited, I started eating.

Wallace came over and placed his tray on the table. He sat down. "I've come to know that when you behave in this way, something has traumatized you. Would you care to discuss it?"

I looked up at him. "Yes, Wallace, I would. Just under a week ago, during a conversation I was having with Travis after we eliminated the Armageddon threat, he asked me what else this complex was capable of doing. I told him that I hadn't thought to ask, but that I would."

"And..."

"And so I spent the morning with T II asking what else it was capable of."

"And what did it say?"

"It explained its purpose to me. It formed the explanations in my mind and used imagery to show me the results. In simple terms, it has the power to transform our Moon into a miniature version of the Earth with a rotation."

Wallace's eyes became a little larger. "I've speculated about that."

"Yes, so have I, Wallace. I want you to see it. It also said that while it was designed to do that, the components needed to run the program were not presently installed."

"I see."

"I then asked how the increased gravity needed to contain an atmosphere would affect the orbit of the Moon in relation to the Earth."

"And..."

"It said that in order for the Moon and Earth to co-exist, the Moon would slowly be moved into a larger orbit. Using its ability to vary the strength of the gravity it produces, it would use the Earth and Sun's gravity to gradually speed up the Moon's velocity, causing it to move into a faster and higher orbit that would continue to have the Earth and Moon co-exist."

Wallace absorbed what I had told him. "One would think a procedure like that would have devastating consequences on our Earth. The tidal action of the oceans would wreak havoc on the coastlines. Not to mention possible Earthquakes and severe weather changes."

"Maybe that's why the program hasn't been installed."

Wallace thought for a moment. "Assuming the aliens who designed and built this place are friendly and mean us no harm, the only reason to build this place and actually activate that program would be if there were no life on Earth to harm."

"If Fisco's plans had been successful..."

"Yes, Fisco. Maybe they knew that eventually something would happen to wipe out all life on Earth, allowing them to finish what they started here. Did you happen to ask T II why it was built? Does it know something?"

My head was spinning. "I didn't think to ask why, Wallace."

"I think you should."

"I will. Would you care to join me?"

"Yes."

"Good. Let's finish our breakfast and then get some answers."

♦♦♦

Wallace and I spent the next few hours on the ninth floor. I showed him the imagery of the Moon transforming into a miniature Earth. We asked if T II knew something about the fate of our species. No matter how many different ways we asked why T II was built, the answer remained the same. That surprised us. T II answered that it was built simply as a place for our alien friends to live if something devastating happened to their home.

0038.0305.0900 LST

"So that's it, Travis. They've prepared this Moon for habitation. I suspect that this is not the only one they've prepared." I watched Travis, as he tried to assimilate all the information. "I would like to thank you. Your request enabled me to actively take control of T II for the first time. Up until recently, it has been T II that has initiated contact."

Travis nodded his head. "You're welcome, Bella. I will pass all of this on."

"Good, Travis. I'm planning a memorial site where the Earth Dome used to be. I'd also like to hold a service for all those that needlessly died, and have all of those who were affected by the attack both on Earth and here be a part of it. Can you arrange that?"

"Yes, Bella. I'll do that. When would you like to hold the memorial?"

"Six days from today would be good."

"I'll get right on it, Bella."

"Thanks, Travis." I sat pondering in my chair for a few minutes.

"Is there anything else, Bella?"

"Yes, Travis. I'm wondering how much the Earth's population knows about what is up here. Has SEARCH or any of our supporting governments released any information about what it was that stopped Fisco?"

"As far as I know, Bella, all they know is that we've been experimenting with some new defensive technologies."

"Well, that's not exactly a lie, is it? During the service, I'd like permission to reveal to everyone what we have discovered up here. I believe we owe everyone the truth about that."

"I'll make sure you have everyone's permission to do so, Bella."

"Thank you again, Travis. Call me if there are any problems."
"Will do, Bella. Travis out."

0038.0311.1145 LST

We were packed into the main hall of the Garage. Several hundred thousand people were also watching and listening Earth-side. The service began at nine hundred hours. Music was playing and those who wanted to say something about friends and loved ones who had died during the attack were given an opportunity to do so. There were many misty eyes in the room. There came a point during the service when all was quiet and silence filled the room. I knew it was time for me to conclude the service. I made my way to the podium at the front of the hall.

♦♦♦

"Thank you all for creating such a beautiful memorial for all our friends. I am going to conclude this service by informing everybody about what has been happening here." I paused to look at and acknowledge Tranquility. "We, as an organization whose purpose is the exploration of our Earth and universe, have made a discovery. Our Moon has been prepared for habitation by a race of alien beings. The technologies they have created to accomplish this are so far ahead of what we are capable of at this time, it boggles our minds."

"It was our ability to somewhat control a portion of their technology that enabled us to destroy the threat that was created by Brath Frederick Fisco. Are these aliens a threat to us? We believe that the ones who transformed our Moon are not a threat, at least not directly. I believe the best way I can describe what they've done, is this: As God commanded Noah to do so many thousands of years ago they have built an Ark. I am aware that Noah's Ark did not have the built-in defense mechanisms that our Moon now has, but the Ark was designed to keep its inhabitants alive and protected in a specific environment over an extended period. What these aliens have created is not so different."

"So what is in store for us? I do not know. We have longed to explore other solar systems and galaxies, hoping to find intelligent, friendly beings. Maybe these beings were searching for the same. Maybe not. But we no longer need to wonder if there is intelligent alien life on other worlds. We know for sure there is. We should ask ourselves this question: For what threat were these beings preparing themselves? A space object threatening their home world? A war with a hostile race of aliens, who they believe may win and destroy their planet? Whatever the reasons, we are now involved, whether we like it or not. And we need to prepare ourselves. During the next several years, we will be engaged in redesigning and rebuilding Tranquility base. All the information regarding what we have discovered has been entered into our computer banks. I encourage all of you to study it. Once again, I would like to thank you all for attending and creating this memorial service."

I looked up from the podium and made eye contact with some of my friends. They nodded their heads as if to say, "That was good."

Forty-five: The Crystal Cave

0038.0924.1050 LST

The chaos grew slowly. As people started to realize that we were not entirely in control of what we considered our universe, they became outraged. Many grouped together to voice their opinions. Most thought our base should be taken over by the governments and populated with military. Some blamed SEARCH for the existence of the aliens.

We decided it would be a good idea to allow those who wanted to see for themselves what we had discovered the opportunity to do so. They would pay for the trip and accommodations, and we would develop and build facilities to take care of them. That was what turned everything around. The chaos slowly subsided, and bookings began to pour in.

♦ ♦ ♦

The surface of Tranquility Base was only a few weeks away from being rebuilt. All the materials from the destroyed buildings and transportation systems had been removed and would be recycled. The building sites were cleaned up and prepped for construction. Reconstruction would begin once the blueprints for the new base had been finalized and approved.

Samson and I were engaged in a conversation about some of the requests for the new Earth Dome. We were in my new underground quarters of Tranquility base. Samson had his finger on one of the requests. "What do you think about this one, Commander?" His finger was on one that inquired about the possibility of creating a diving pool with aquatic life.

"I like it. Not being a diver, I never would have dreamed of doing something like that."

"I like it too, Commander. It would be a great challenge. And maybe a really good tourist attraction if we do it right." He paused a few seconds. "I could teach you how to dive."

"I would like that, Samson. I can see the ads now. 'The Solar System's most exotic diving experience… The Sea of Tranquility'!"

Samson laughed. "I like it, Commander." He started playing with the crystal ring on his finger. He saw me watching him. "Are you wondering about this crystal, Commander?"

I shrugged. "A little. Yours seems unique."

"They are all unique, Commander. I believe you will have one soon."

I swallowed. "How?"

"I cannot tell you, Commander. We who have received them know who will also receive one. But we cannot tell you how you will or when you will. All I can tell you about this crystal is that I was once married. I loved and was loved by her. She passed away and is no longer with me. This crystal is a constant reminder to me that God is."

"How was it presented to you?"

"I cannot speak of that, Commander. And if you were look for someone who could speak of it, you would not find him. If you happen to meet someone with a crystal who speaks of how he or she acquired it, you will know that it is not the same as what you will be receiving."

"I see. It sounds very mysterious, Samson."

"It is, Commander. It is."

0038.0924.2200 LST

Samson's words had a powerful effect on me. I spent the rest of the day wondering about crystals. My mind was filled with questions. What will it look like? When will I receive one? How will it be given to me? Where will it come from?

I walked through my living quarters to my bedroom, satisfied with the progress we were making on the base. As I passed through the bedroom doorway, I expected the lights to activate as they normally did, but they did not. I heard the door shut behind me and I was plunged into complete darkness.

"Computer, open the door for this room." There was no response. I tried again… "Computer, activate the lights for this room." Once again there was no response. I thought it very odd that such a systems failure would occur.

In the darkness, I turned to face the entrance of my room. With my right hand, I reached out for the control panel to manually open the door. I felt nothing. Thinking I may have stepped further into the room than I had originally thought, I took a cautious step forward. With my hand stretched out in front of me, I again searched for the control panel. I moved my arm left and right. Still, I felt nothing.

My heart began to pound in my chest. I was disoriented. I started to walk forward, believing that I would eventually run into something. And I did. As I moved forward, I hit my shin on something very hard and bit my lip as the pain shot through my body. Losing my balance, I held my hand out to cushion my fall and fell against a wall made of something cold, rough and uneven, like stone on a rock face.

As I regained my balance, my eyes still had not adjusted to the blackness that surrounded me. I knew, however, that I was no longer in my bedroom. I took a deep breath. The air was cool and moist. I lowered myself to a seated position and found that the floor was also made of rock. I tried to calm myself down and began to wonder where I had been transported.

♦ ♦ ♦

Several minutes passed. My heart was still beating hard and the blackness made it impossible for me to focus. I looked skyward, hoping to see starlight, but I saw nothing. I lowered my head and closed my eyes, which had a soothing effect for a few seconds. Something inside forced me to open them again.

♦ ♦ ♦

Several more minutes passed. Out of the corner of my right eye, I saw a faint light. I turned my head towards it and stood up. I was consumed with the need to see the source of this light. Taking short steps, I slowly walked forward. My shin still ached from my earlier encounter with stone. As I moved closer, the light source became more intense. I began to see familiar looking outlines and colors emanating from it. I realized that the source of light was my energy being amplified by a crystal. My body relaxed.

When my eyes became acclimatized to the light, I stopped to look around. Above and around me I could see faint outlines of rocks. Light was being reflected off smooth rock faces. I looked down and saw the rock floor. I concluded that I was in a large cavern, and I walked with more confidence toward the crystal.

As I moved closer, the crystal continued to get brighter. It had five distinct, six-sided structures. They rose from a central base that was solidly attached to a small rock outcropping, which jutted from the stone wall. The crystal was deep blue in color. Beams of multi-colored lights bounced off the facets and were mesmerizing to watch. I wondered if this was my crystal. I put my hands on it, thinking it might magically dislodge from the stone. When it didn't, I tried to forcibly remove it. My efforts were not rewarded. I removed my hands from the crystal, turned my back to it and started searching for an exit from the cavern.

The light from the crystal made it difficult for me to find a way out. I was intent on finding an opening, and proceeded to check out all the possibilities. I worked my way around the cavern in a clockwise direction away from the crystal. I was three quarters of the way around when I noticed a faint light radiating from the blackness of what looked like a shadow. I made my way towards it.

The opening was not very big. It was high enough for me, but to squeeze through it, I had to turn sideways. Once I was through the two-meter-long opening, I remembered my climb up the mountain after meeting Noah. I stood still until I could see exactly where I was and how I was positioned. My eyes adjusted and I realized I was standing on a ledge. To reach the floor of the cavern, I would have to climb all the way down. The light I was seeking was being emitted from another, much larger and different-colored crystal situated on the other side of the cavern.

To my left and not far from the new crystal, more light was radiating from an opening in the cavern. A surge of adrenalin coursed through my veins as I started my climb down to the surface of this new space. As I walked across the floor of the cavern, I realized I had underestimated this crystal's size. It was a single, hexagonal crystal structure, at least a meter high and half a meter wide. It was flawless. The color was that of Earth's red sky early in the morning, with beams of multi-colored lights flashing brilliantly inside. I didn't try to move it. I just stood, watched and admired the crystal until my curiosity about what was in the next cavern overpowered my desire to stay.

I walked over to the opening I had seen. I crouched down to see into it. The light source was not visible. It was a tunnel several meters long. I would have to squat down to walk through it. As I came closer to exiting the tunnel, I found myself squinting because of the bright light. It was too uncomfortable to stay inside the tunnel and wait for my eyes to adjust, so I kept moving forward. I stood up as I exited. My eyes stung so I clamped them shut.

Slowly, I opened my eyes, giving them time to adjust. I was in a dome-shaped cavern. Thousands of crystals of various sizes and colors were scattered on the floor, embedded in the walls, and jutting down from the ceiling. The crystals closest to me were radiating the brightest light.

I walked around the cavern to see as many of the crystals as I could. I found it amusing to see them become brighter as I moved closer to them. I felt like I was conducting a symphony of lights. As I navigated my way around, I realized that I had lost track of the opening to the tunnel. The few times I had checked its location as a focal point, it had appeared as a dark opening in the cavern wall. After a few more minutes exploring, I found myself wanting to find it again.

As before, I sectioned off each part of the cavern and started a systematic search for an opening. It wasn't long before I found a substantial fracture in one of the walls that was large enough to walk through comfortably. It wondered where it would take me. Light from the cavern reflected off the sides of the fracture, enabling me to see for many meters. But soon the light began to fade.

When I reached the point where I could no longer see, I stopped to decide whether I should go forward or turn back. I decided it would be safe to move forward a few meters at a time. I thought that a crystal might again activate. I kept one hand against a wall for support. As I moved forward, the wall surface became smoother and the air noticeably warmer. After walking a few more meters, my hand touched something familiar. It took a few moments for me to recognize the control panel that would allow me to manually open my bedroom door. The instant I did so, the bedroom lights went on.

When my eyes finished adjusting to the light levels, I looked around and checked the time. It was September twenty-fifth, six hundred hours, Lunar Standard Time. Eight hours from the time I had found myself in the crystal cave.

0038.0925.0700 LST

I spent time in my shower, thinking about where I had been and what it meant. As I dried myself off, the idea that I should tell Samson about it entered my mind. After I had cooked and eaten my breakfast, I called

Samson. The computer replied, "Samson is not on the base, Commander. He has left for T II."

"When did he leave?"

"Fifty-five minutes ago, Commander."

I wondered why he had gone there. I assumed he had made plans with Wallace. "Computer…"

"Yes, Commander."

"Did he indicate when he may be back or why he went?"

"No, Commander."

"Computer, I'm going down to T II. If I am needed here, please inform the appropriate people. If anyone asks, I should be back no later then Eighteen Hundred hours."

"Understood, Commander."

♦♦♦

As I stepped out of the Tower and into T II, Wallace was there to greet me. He was in good spirits. "Good morning, Bella."

"Good morning, Wallace. How is T II today?"

"It's in good shape. And you?"

"I'm fine, Wallace. Have you seen Samson today?"

"I have, as a matter of fact. He's waiting for you by your quarters. Would you like a ride over there?"

I was taken aback. "He's waiting for me? But, I… But we didn't make plans to meet."

Wallace shrugged. "What can I say, Bella? I'll drive."

"Okay." I climbed into the transport.

As we neared my quarters, Wallace said, "DJ's with Samson, waiting for you."

I turned and looked at Wallace. "What's going on, Wallace? Why would DJ be waiting for me with Samson? My being down here was a decision I made just this morning. How would they know I was to be here?"

Wallace looked over at me. "In the Eyes of God, Bella. He works in mysterious ways."

I didn't say another word until I arrived at my quarters. Samson and DJ were waiting for me by the front entrance. "What are you guys doing here?"

DJ looked up at Samson, who shrugged. DJ looked at me. "We thought you might come down here and that you would enjoy some company."

That made no sense to me whatsoever. "I don't understand."

Samson motioned that we should go inside. I hesitantly agreed and went inside. I walked through the kitchen area and into the living space with the view of T II, and stopped dead in my tracks. I blinked.

Standing in the corner of the room beside the window was a gigantic piece of pure, snowy white-colored rock, one and a half meters high. It encased a single, massive, six-sided crystal structure that stood two and a half meters high and one meter across. Surrounding the base, were six, smaller, six-sided crystal structures, half a meter long and a few centimeters wide. They appeared to have grown right through the brilliantly white stone that encased the massive single crystal structure.

I touched it to see if it was real. It was marble and cool to the touch. It was extraordinary, sculpted in a way that enhanced the beauty of the flawless crystal. The crystal lit up, and thousands of multi-colored light beams bounced and ricocheted off its many facets. The white marble reflected the colors of the light beams. I wondered how the crystal had come to be inside the marble. I also wondered how it had come to be in my quarters. I wondered if I was still in the crystal cave, or if this was an extension of that experience. I began to feel dizzy.

I remembered that my friends were with me. I turned around to find them standing in the room, staring at the crystal. DJ's eyes were wide open.

Samson said, "It's beyond any words I have, Commander. Can you explain how this crystal came into your possession?"

I remembered the conversation we had about crystals. "No, I can't. I have no idea."

"It's awesome, Commander," said DJ, whose eyes had returned to normal.

"Thank you, DJ."

Wallace walked toward the crystal and examined it for a few moments. "It must be the perfect crystal for you, Bella."

"Thank you, Wallace. Is this why you guys were waiting for me? Did you know this was here?"

Samson looked at DJ and Wallace, and then at me. "We did not know why we were compelled to meet you here, Commander. We did not know when you would receive a crystal. We did not enter your quarters without your consent." He paused a moment. His voice was full of amazement. "This is, without a doubt, the largest crystal I've ever seen. It certainly isn't very portable. I wonder why."

Wallace volunteered an answer, with a hint of excitement in his voice. "I'm guessing we'll find out in time."

I stood there, looking at my friends and seeing my crystal through the corner of my eye. My reality had once again been altered forever, and I felt like I was dreaming. I walked over to the couch and sat down, needing time to absorb the events of the past few hours. My friends seemed to understand what I needed, and politely excused themselves.

As the morning passed, so did the shock of finding my crystal in T II and in my quarters. By lunchtime, I felt as if it had always been there. I stood up from my couch and walked over to the window. I enjoyed the view. T II entered my mind and asked for my presence on the ninth floor. I left my quarters and hurried over there.

About the Author

An entrepreneur, master salesman and consultant, Barry Lipsett has spent the better part of his life searching for products and services people need. His need to continually expand his horizons and skills is what started him on the path of writing.

Starting small, his first fictional writings were for radio advertising spots. He then expanded into short stories, the majority of which were of no consequence and filed away. But there were a few that refused to be filed and this is one of them.

He creates his work by describing actual events that have happened in the course of his life and then changes all names, times and places in which these events occurred.